W9-CMF-109

FALLEN
HEARTS

FALLEN
HEARTS

V. C. ANDREWS

POSEIDON PRESS

NEW YORK LONDON TORONTO SYDNEY TOKYO

POSEIDON PRESS
SIMON & SCHUSTER BUILDING
ROCKEFELLER CENTER
1230 AVENUE OF THE AMERICAS
NEW YORK, NEW YORK 10020

POSEIDON PRESS IS A REGISTERED TRADEMARK
OF SIMON & SCHUSTER INC.

POSEIDON PRESS COLOPHON IS A TRADEMARK
OF SIMON & SCHUSTER INC.
MANUFACTURED IN THE UNITED STATES OF AMERICA

Quality Printing and Binding By:
ARCATA GRAPHICS/KINGSPORT
Press and Roller Streets
Kingsport, TN 37662 U.S.A.

Dear Pa,

Despite all the sadness and hardships of the past, I am ready to forgive and to ask forgiveness, Pa. It has been almost two years since Tom's death—two years during which not a day has gone by I haven't missed Tom, and Grandpa, too. But now my time for mourning is over and my time for happiness and love and life is beginning. For I have wonderful news. I'm getting married. To Logan Stonewall, who you may remember was my childhood sweetheart. I've been living here in Winnerow, fulfilling my dream of being a teacher just like Miss Marianne Deale, who inspired me so to read and learn and dream and always to believe I could be whatever I wanted to be. It seems all my childhood dreams are finally coming true—all, that is, except my relationship with you. I want you and Drake and Stacie to come to my wedding, Pa. Pa, I would like you to walk down the aisle with me as my father and give me away to my husband. I am so happy, Pa, I want to put away all the bitterness of the past. I want to forgive you, and I want you to forgive me. Maybe now, at this long late date, we can act like a family should. Fanny will be my best lady. I hope you will, at last, be my father.

Love,
Heaven

❧ ONE ❧
Promises of Spring

I SAT ON THE LONG FRONT PORCH OF THE CABIN, READING AND rereading my letter to Pa. It was a warm May morning, spring already ripened into hot summer. It seemed my Willies world had awakened along with me—from the cold dark winter of death and mourning, gradually warming with the promise of spring, finally bursting into warm, burgeoning summer. The sparrows and robins were singing, flitting from branch to branch, gently shaking the leaves. Sunlight wove its way through the woods, threading strands of gold from birch to hickory to maple, turning the leaves transparent where the light bathed them. The world looked glorious and alive.

I took a deep breath, inhaling the sweet, fresh perfume of blossoming flowers and rich green leaves. Above me, the sky was deep cerulean blue and the little candy cotton puffs of clouds stretched and curled in delicious shapes, like babies stretching in sleep.

Logan had been there from the day I returned to Winnerow. He had been there through the terrible days after Tom's death, while Pa was in the hospital. He had been there after Pa had returned with Stacie and little Drake to his own home in Georgia. He had been there when Grandpa died, leaving me alone in the cabin of my childhood, now rebuilt and refurbished into a cozy home. He had been there on the first day I began teaching my dear students at the Winnerow Grammar School. I laughed to myself now, recalling that first day, getting ready to test my competence, to see if I really could be the teacher I'd always dreamed of being.

I had come out of the cabin, just as I had this morning, intending, as I did most every day, to take a moment's pause to sit in Granny's old rocker and look out through the Willies before starting my journey down to the school. Only on this first morning, when I opened the door, there was Logan standing by the steps, a wide, happy smile on his face, his dark sapphire eyes brightening in the morning sun.

"Good morning, Miss Casteel." He performed a grand bow. "I have been sent here to escort you to your classroom. It's a fringe benefit of the Winnerow School System."

"Oh, Logan!" I cried. "You got up so early to walk up here."

"It wasn't so early. I get up this early to open the drugstore. It's three times the size it was when we were high school students," he said proudly, "and demands a lot more work. Miss Casteel," he added, holding out his hand. I walked down the steps to take it and we started down the mountain path, just the way we had when we were high school sweethearts.

It seemed so much like the old days—when Logan and I trailed behind Tom and Keith and Our Jane, with Fanny taunting us, trying to provoke and tease Logan away from me with her lewd and lascivious behavior, finally giving up and running off in a sulk when she saw that he wouldn't divert his attention from me. I could almost hear my brothers' and sisters' voices ahead. Despite how hard our lives were then, the memories brought tears to my eyes.

"Hey, hey," Logan said, seeing my eyes begin to fill with tears, "this is a happy day. I want a big smile and I want to hear your laughter echo through the Willies, just the way it used to."

"Oh, Logan, thank you. Thank you for being here, for caring."

He stopped and turned me toward him; his eyes were serious and full of love.

"No, Heaven. It's I who should thank you for being as beautiful and as lovely as I remember you. It's as if"—he looked around, searching for the words—"as if time stood still for us and everything that we thought happened since was only a dream. Now we are waking up and once again you are here, I am here with you, and I have your hand in mine. I'll never let it go again," he vowed.

A tingle traveled through my fingers laced through his, a tingle of happiness that reached my heart and set it pounding the way it had that first day we kissed, when I was only twelve years old. I wanted him to kiss me again, I wanted to be that same innocent girl again, but I wasn't. And he wasn't, either. Why, only a few months ago rumors were flying that he intended to marry Maisie Setterton. But Maisie seemed to have disappeared from the picture of Logan's life as soon as I returned.

We walked silently along the wooded path. Red cardinals and brown speckled sparrows followed along, flitting through the shadows of the forest, moving so quickly and gracefully we barely saw a branch shake.

"I know," Logan finally said, "that both our lives took strangely different directions since the days when I walked you home from school, and all the promises we made to each other then might seem more like foolish dreams. But I would like to think that our love for each other was so strong that it has outlasted all the tragedy and all the hardship since."

We stopped to face each other again. I knew he could read all the doubt in my eyes.

"Logan. I'd like to believe that, too. I'm tired of dreams that die, dreams that were really too airy and weak to last or grow stronger as we grew older. I want to believe in someone again."

"Oh, Heaven, believe in me," he pleaded, taking my hand into both of his now. "I won't disappoint you. Ever."

"I can try," I whispered and he smiled. Then he kissed me, a kiss meant to seal a promise, but all my life I had seen promises broken. Logan sensed my hesitation, my fear. He embraced me.

"I'm going to make you believe in me, Heaven. I'm going to be all you could want in a man." He pressed his face to my hair. I felt his breath on my neck, his heart beating madly against mine. In this forest on the old trail, I felt myself wanting desperately to hope again; I felt myself softening. The Heaven Leigh Casteel who had been wounded badly as a child, tormented and seduced as a young girl, heartbroken as a young woman, turned hungrily toward the promise of happiness.

"In time I think I will believe in you, Logan."

"Oh, Heaven, dear Heaven, you've truly come home." Logan kissed me again and again.

Why was it then, that as he kissed me with all the love and passion in him, I thought of Troy, my forbidden fiancé, my dark, dead love? Why was it Troy's lips I felt pressing against my own? Why was it Troy's taste I craved? Troy's arms I felt pressing me against him? But then Logan kissed both my eyes, and I opened them, to his young, fresh, loving face, a face that had never known the depths of anguish and despair my sad, doomed Troy had succumbed to. I knew in my heart that Logan would bring me the kind of life I and my mother before me had been deprived of—a life of calm, respect, and honor.

Logan and I courted throughout the school year, and one day he knocked on my cabin door and said, "Have I got a surprise for you, Heaven." He looked like a mischievous little boy with a frog in his pocket.

"Are you going to blindfold me?" I played along with his sweet game.

He came up behind me and put his gentle hands over my eyes. "Keep them shut, Heaven!" Then he took my hand and I stumbled along behind him on the way to his car, feeling secure being led by his boyish enthusiasm. I felt the fresh breeze on my face as we sped away, I knew not where. Then the car stopped and Logan opened my door and reached for my arm. "Come out now, we're almost there," he said as he led me from the car, onto what felt like a sidewalk.

When he opened the door to the drugstore, I immediately caught the familiar scent of perfume and toiletries mixed with cold remedies and prescription medicinal smells, but I didn't let on that I knew where I was. I didn't want to dampen his great good humor. He sat me on a stool and busied himself somewhere behind the counter. It seemed like a half hour before his cheery voice returned and almost shouted, "You can open your eyes now, Heaven!"

Before me was a rainbow castle—built of ice cream, cherries whipped cream, and all things sweet and delicious. "Logan," I declared, "it's beautiful. But if I eat that, I'll be three hundred pounds in an hour. Then will you still love me?"

"Heaven"—his voice grew low and raspy—"my love for you is greater than youth and beauty. But this sundae isn't for eating— wanted to build you the most beautiful, sweetest castle you had ever seen. I know I can't compete with the riches of the Tattertons and the grand mansion Farthinggale. But that mansion is made of cold gray stone, and my love for you is as warm as the first day of spring. My love will build a castle around you, a castle no stone mansion can compete with. Heaven"—he got down on his knees in front of the astonished stares of all the customers in the drugstore—"Heaven, will you be my wife?"

I looked deep into his eyes and saw the love and sweetness there. I knew he would do everything he could to make me so very happy. What was the passion I longed for—the passion that had been stolen from me with Troy's death—when compared to a lifetime of gentle love, caring, and undying commitment? "Yes," I said, the tears already welling in my eye. "Yes, Logan, yes, I will be your wife."

Suddenly applause broke out around us, as all the customers beamed their happy smiles on us, the newly engaged. Logan turned beet red and dropped my hand, just as I was about to embrace him.

"Here, Heaven," he said, popping a cherry into my mouth, trying to cover his embarrassment at the public spectacle we were making. Then he pecked me on the cheek. "I love you forever," he whispered.

So a love born years ago, like a slowly blossoming flower, finally opened completely. I felt brighter and fresher than I ever had before. I had come full circle, erasing the pain of the past, as I traveled the paths now that I had traveled as a child, only now I was clearing my own path, rather than treading one that had been marked for me. Now I could make my own fate, as the forest makes its natural trails built on the most solid ground, the firmest earth. It was as if I'd suddenly reached one of those magical clearings in the forest, and I knew enough to build my home there.

Now my childhood sweetheart was to be my lifelong sweetheart. Dreams did indeed come true and I knew that things we often think are too good and too precious to be part of the real world really could be part of the real world. I was filled with hope and happiness again. I was a young girl again, willing to believe, to be vulnerable, to open myself to someone and risk my fragile heart. In this clearing, where the sun was strong and nurturing, Logan and I would be like the sturdy saplings, growing stronger and stronger until we became mighty oak trees that could withstand any bitter storm of winter.

I spent the next few weeks planning the wedding. This wedding would be far more than merely another marriage of a Winnerow man and a woman. Even though I had remained in the hills, living in Grandpa's cabin, I still drove an expensive automobile, wore fine clothing, and carried myself as a cultured and sophisticated woman. I may have put aside a wealthy existence as the heir to the Tatterton Toy empire, but the townspeople still saw me as a scum-of-the-hills Casteel. They might have approved of the way I was teaching their children, but they still didn't like me sitting in the front pews of their church.

When Logan and I attended church together, that Sunday, after our engagement picture had adorned the bride's section of *The Winnerow Reporter,* all eyes followed us as we made our way to the very front pew—Logan's family's place in church—a place I had never dared sit before. "Welcome, Heaven," Mrs. Stonewall said, a little nervously, as she handed me the missal. Logan's father simply nodded his head, but when we rose to sing, I sang out proud and strong until my voice, a voice of the hills despite its patina of culture, reverberated throughout the church. And when the service was over, after I had greeted the Reverend Wise with a smile that told him I would prove all his prophecies wrong, Logan's mother said to me, "Why, Heaven, I never knew you had such a dignified singing voice. I hope you'll join our ladies' choir." I knew then and there that Loretta Stonewall had finally decided to accept me. I also knew then and there that I would make all the others do the same, that I would make them open their eyes and look at all the hill folk and see us for the honest, struggling human beings we were.

That was why I planned the kind of wedding I did. Logan tried his best to understand my motivations, and even stood up to his parents' objections. I was ever so grateful. He was even pleased and amused by the way I planned to force the people of Winnerow to commingle with the hill people. I was determined to have the finest affair Winnerow had ever seen and when I walked down that aisle, the townspeople wouldn't see poor white trash that had come into money, but someone just as good and as refined as they thought they were. I remembered when I had come back to Winnerow years ago and walked down that church looking like a fashion plate, bedecked with rich jewels. Despite my fine raiment, the townspeople had looked down their noses at me. The hill people were supposed to take the back benches and those deemed worthiest of God were in the first rows.

My wedding would be different. I invited a number of hill families. I invited all the children in my class. I wanted my sister Fanny to be my maid of honor. I hadn't seen Fanny much in the two years since I'd returned to Winnerow, because Fanny did not seem able to put away her jealousy and resentment of me, even though I tried, as I always had, to help her in every way I could. Logan kept me up to date on Fanny's affairs and activities. Apparently, she was often the subject of conversation among the young men and women of Winnerow, and often he would overhear some of this conversation in his drugstore. Since her divorce from "Old man Mallory," the gossip was about her flirtatious involvement with a much younger man, Randall Wilcox, the lawyer's son. Randall was only eighteen years old, a first-year college student, and Fanny was a divorced woman of twenty-two.

The week after our engagement was announced, I drove up to the house Fanny had bought with old Mallory's money—a house high on a hill, painted a gaudy pink with red trim on the windows. I hadn't spoken to Fanny in over a year, since she accused me of stealing everything that was hers, when in reality it was she who had tried to pilfer everything that was mine, especially Logan.

"Well, what a surprise this is," she proclaimed in an overly dramatic fashion when she opened the door. "Miss Heaven herself come ta visit her po' white trash sista."

"I'm not here to fight with you, Fanny. I'm too happy for you to make me angry about anything."

"Oh?"

She sat down on her couch quickly, her interest seized.

"Logan and I are going to be married in June."

"Is that so?" Fanny drawled, her entire posture collapsing in disappointment.

Why couldn't she be happy for me for once? Why couldn't we be real sisters and care for each other?

"You knew we had been seeing each other again."

"How would I know anythin'? Yer hardly eva here and we hardly eva talk ta one anotha."

"You know what goes on in Winnerow, Fanny. Anyway, I would like you to be my maid of honor."

"Really?" Her eyes lit up on that. Then I saw the old spiteful fire return to Fanny's eye. "I just can't say yet, Heavin darlin'. I got a full schedule of ma own. What date exactly is your weddin' gonna be?"

I told her.

"Well"—Fanny pretended to think about it—"I had plans for that weekend, you know ma new man likes ta take me lots of places—ta college dances and such. But maybe I can change ma plans. Is it gonna be a faincy weddin'?"

"The fanciest."

"And are ya gonna buy yer lovin' sista a really fancy expensive dress? And will ya take me to the city to pick it out?"

"Yes."

She thought for a moment.

"Kin I bring Randall Wilcox?" she asked. "Ya probably know he's been courtin' me. I jus' know he'd look so gorgeous in a tuxedo. The men are wearing tuxedos, aren't they?"

"Yes, Fanny. If you'd like that, I'll have an invitation hand delivered to his house."

"Sure, I'd like it. Why not?" she asked.

And so it was done.

My invitation to Pa was the last one I mailed. I started down the mountain trail a little earlier than usual that morning so I could go to the post office before going to school for my final day of class. I think I was as excited as I was the first day I had gone down the trail to begin school myself. When I got to my classroom, my students looked up at me with faces filled with expectation. Even the usually sad and tired faces of the Willies children were fresh and bright this morning. I knew they had something special planned.

Patricia Coons raised her hand.

"I have something for you, Miss Casteel," she announced shyly.
"Oh?"

She got up slowly and came forward, proud to have been chosen as
the class representative. She shuffled her feet and bit one of her already
chewed-down nails.

"We wanted to give you this before you got all your other wedding
gifts," she said. "All of us here chillen," she added as she handed me
the package, wrapped in fine blue paper with a pink ribbon. "We even
bought the paper in your fiancé Logan, I mean Mr. Stonewall's store,"
she said and I laughed.

"Thank you. Everyone."

I opened the package. Inside in a rich oak frame was a beautifully
done needlepoint of my cabin in the Willies, and underneath it read,
"Home Sweet Home, from your class."

For a moment I couldn't speak, but I knew all the little faces with
their bright, happy eyes were on me.

"Thank you, children," I said. "No matter what gifts I get after
this, none will be as precious or as important to me."

And none was.

The time between the last day of school and my wedding day
seemed like ages. Minutes were more like hours and hours more like
days because I wanted it to come so much. Even all the plans and
preparations didn't make the time fly by, as I hoped it would. Still, the
anticipation built my excitement and Logan was with me as much as
possible. Replies to our invitations came flooding in. I hadn't spoken
to Tony Tatterton since the day I left Farthinggale Manor, the day I
learned of Troy's death. Partly, I couldn't forgive him for what had
happened to Troy, partly I was so frightened of the truth I had
learned, the truth that had sent Troy to his death. I knew I would no
longer be able to hear his voice without hearing the familiar timbre of
my own in it. What I had learned about Tony and my mother, even
two years later, still sent shudders down my spine. To have lived for so
long with the lie that Pa was my blood and kin, Pa who had rejected
me at every turn and whose love I had needed most, only to find out
that when Pa looked at me, he saw my mother's former lover, her own
stepfather, my father and grandfather, Tony Tatterton.

This knowledge frightened me to the marrow, not only for its taw-
driness and wrongness, but for what it told me of my heritage. I didn't
dare tell Logan. His innocence might be shattered by such despicable
ways of the wealthy who controlled the world. But there was something more. That last day on the beach with Tony, after he told me of

Troy's hideous death, a look had come into his eyes, a look that trans-
gressed any mourning, a look of such pure desire that I knew I must
stay away from him. This is why I didn't take his phone calls, why his
letters piled up on my desk unanswered, why it was Pa, rather than
Tony, who I wanted to be my father at the wedding. For in spite of
everything, and even though I now knew he wasn't my real father, I
still craved Pa's love; I already had too much of Tony's.

But since I didn't want Logan to know the shameful truth of my
heritage, I dutifully sent Tony an invitation to the wedding. And
Tony, sly fox that he was, wrote not to me but to Logan, explaining
that Grandmother Jillian was so ill he couldn't possibly leave her to
attend the wedding, but insisting that we come to Farthinggale Manor,
where he would host for us the finest wedding reception Massachu-
setts had ever seen. Logan was so excited by his invitation that I
reluctantly agreed to spend four days at Farthy before we headed for
our honeymoon in Virginia Beach. We would return to Winnerow to
live in the cabin until we could build our own fine house on the outskirts of Winnerow.

But not all our plans were to fall so neatly into place. On the morning of my wedding there was a knock on the cabin door. I had been up
nearly all night, too nervous and too excited to sleep. Still in my
nightgown, I went to the front door to greet a special-delivery postman.

"Good morning," he chirped. "Special delivery. Please sign here."

"Good morning."

It was a good morning, and not only because it was my wedding
day. There wasn't a cloud in the sea-blue summer sky. Today was my
day, and God had smiled down and made this day beautiful for me,
chasing away all the shadows and leaving me only sunlight. I was so
full of joy and fulfillment, I felt like hugging the postman.

"Thank you," he said when I handed the clipboard back to him.
Then he smiled and tipped his hat. "And good luck to you. I know it's
your wedding day."

"Thank you." I watched him go back to his jeep, and waved as he
turned around and headed down the mountain road. Then I closed the
door and hurried to the kitchen table to open the special-delivery mail.
Surely it was a well-wisher. Perhaps it had come from Tony, who had
decided at the last minute he would attend both receptions.

I tore open the envelope and unfolded the slim paper within. What I
read brought my heart down to earth like a balloon that had sprung a
leak. I sat down slowly, my pitter-patter heart becoming a thumping,
heavy lead drum in my chest. The laughter that had been on my lips

evaporated and tears filled my eyes, blurring the words on the page before me.

> Dear Heaven,
>   Unfortunately, business activities involving the circus will make it impossible for me to attend your wedding. Stacie and I wish you and Logan the best of luck.
>
> Yours,
Pa

One of my tears fell on the letter and began a quick journey over the paper, distorting Pa's words. I crumpled the letter in my fist and sat back, the tears now flowing freely over my cheeks and to the corners of my mouth, where I could taste their salty wetness.

I was crying for so many reasons, but most of all I was crying because I had hoped that my wedding would be the event to bring me and Pa together in a way we had never been. Even though it was Logan who talked me into inviting him, inviting him was a secret ambition of my heart. I had dreamt of him standing beside me, sleek and handsome in his tuxedo, holding my hand and saying the words *I do*, after the reverend asked, "Who gives away this bride?"

My wedding was going to be the crowning point of forgiveness—his forgiveness of me for causing the death of his angel, Leigh, when I was born, and my forgiveness of him for selling us. I was willing to accept Tom's belief that Pa sold us because he couldn't take care of us and he thought that it would be the best thing for us.

But now none of this was to be.

I caught my breath and wiped the tears from my face. There was nothing more to do about it, I thought. I had to concentrate on Logan and our wedding. There was no time for self-pity or rage. Besides, Pa had given me away long ago. At my wedding I would give myself.

About an hour before the wedding my sister Fanny arrived with Randall Wilcox to take me to the church. Randall was a polite, shy young man with sweet-potato red hair and milk-fair skin. His forehead was splattered with tiny freckles, but he had bright blue eyes that shone like tinted crystal. I had thought that maybe he looked older than he was, but he had an innocent and fresh appearance and followed Fanny about like a puppy.

"Why, Heaven Leigh Casteel, don'cha look virginal, this mornin'," she exclaimed and threaded her arm through Randall's so she could press herself to him possessively. She had her jet-black hair crimped and blown out, making her look loose and wild like a street prostitute

I had suggested she have her hair pinned up, anticipating she would do something just like this. "Don't she, Randall?"

He looked from me to her quickly, not expecting to have to testify in support of Fanny's sarcasm.

"You look lovely," Randall said softly, diplomatically.

"Thank you, Randall." Fanny smirked. I looked at myself in the mirror, adjusted some strands of hair, and snapped on my wrist corsage.

"I'm ready," I said.

"Sure ya are," Fanny said. "Ya always was ready for this day," she added sadly. For a moment I felt sorry for her, despite her blatant jealousy. Fanny always longed for attention, always longed to be loved, but always went about it the wrong way and probably always would.

"Fanny, the dress looks very nice on you," I said. We had driven to the city and chosen a light blue crinoline for Fanny to wear as the maid of honor. But Fanny had made alterations. She had lowered the neckline until the top of her bosom was exposed. She had tightened the sides so that it seemed painted on.

"Really? My figure has improved, hasn't it?" she said, running her hands up and over her hips, all the way to her breasts, looking lasciviously at Randall all the time. He blushed. "Even after I went through the birthin', I neva lost my figure like so many women do." She turned to me. "Randall knows our little secret about Darcy. Watch out, honey, that a whole brood of little Stonewalls don't soon ruin your figure."

"I'm not planning to have children right away, Fanny," I announced.

"Oh? Maybe Logan Stonewall's got other ideas. Maisie Setterton says he always talked 'bout havin' a big family. Ya told me that, didn't ya, Randall?" I knew Fanny brought up Maisie Setterton just to make me jealous.

"Well, I didn't exactly . . ." He looked so flustered.

"It's all right, Randall," I interjected quickly. "Fanny isn't saying it to be mean, are you, Fanny?"

"Why, no," she whined. "I'm just tellin' ya what Maisie said."

"See?" Randall started to laugh. Fanny saw she was the object of the humor.

"Well, she did say it," she insisted. "If ya didn't tell me, someone else did." Her smile turned to a smirk. "Anyway, I still can't believe you're going ta let Waysie marry ya."

"I have my reasons." I smiled to myself. Sure I did. And Fanny knew them. For Reverend Wise had bought Fanny from Pa, taken her into his home, made her pregnant, and claimed her baby for himself and his wife. I had tried to help Fanny buy back her child, but to no avail, and Fanny had still never forgiven me for my failure to do so. We shared the dark secret of her little girl's heritage and I wanted to look into Reverend Wise's eyes when Logan and I pronounced our vows. I wanted to blot out the words he had said to me when I went to him intending to demand Fanny's child. We argued and I told him, "You don't know me."

His eyelids parted to mere slots so his eyes glittered into the shade of his lids and he said, "You are wrong, Heaven Leigh Casteel. I do know you very well. You are the most dangerous kind of female the world can ever know. A great many will love you for your beautiful face, for your seductive body; but you will fail them all, because you will believe they all fail you first. You are an idealist of the most devastatingly tragic kind—the romantic idealist. Born to destroy and to self-destruct."

I wanted him to see a different Heaven Leigh Casteel, I wanted him to swallow his own predictions, his own religious arrogance, and his sinful hypocrisy.

"You may have ya reasons," Fanny smirked, "but I'll tell ya, that Waysie is sure gonna blow his stack when he pronounces you and Logan man and wife. I can't wait to see it. I surely can't."

"Shall we go?" I said.

The ceremony was all that I had dreamt it would be and more. Just about everyone we invited turned out. Four of my male students served as ushers in the church. I had specifically instructed them to escort people to the pews randomly on a first-come, first-serve basis, thus playing havoc with the unwritten segregation of the congregation. Hill and valley people sat up front with town people, some of whom were forced to sit toward the rear with other hill and valley people.

All of the hill and valley people were smiling at me, their faces filled with happiness and elation. Most of the town people looked dignified, wearing looks of approval. After all, I was marrying Logan Stonewall and completing what was, in their eyes, a complete transition from backwoods mountain girl to a proper town girl. I would be moving out of the cabin and into a home in Winnerow. I could see it in their faces —they thought that in time I would forget the hill people. I had won their respect, but not their understanding. They thought I had done all that I had done just to become one of them.

Logan's father stood beside him where Tom, my dear departed

brother, should have been standing to be best man. My heart skipped a beat and my eyes teared when I thought about his tragic death in the grasp of a furious beast. Except for Fanny, who strutted before me, tossing her hair about, turning her shoulders suggestively, and making eyes at every available male in the congregation, none of my family were here. Grandpa was dead and gone. Luke and his new wife were off working in his new circus. Tom was gone. Keith and Jane were in college, neither really as close to me as I would have liked. My real grandmother was back in Farthy, lost in her past, babbling gibberish to herself. Tony was at the helm of the Tatterton Toy Corporation, probably mourning this day, when I would belong to another man, never to him.

Reverend Wise, tall and impressive as ever behind his podium, lifted his eyes from the Bible and glared out at me. His slick, black, custom-made suit fitted him as beautifully as usual and made him appear as slim as he had when I first saw him.

For a moment he frightened me, as he always had, but when I locked my gaze on Logan, all the sad memories were lifted away. It was like a cloudy day that had suddenly turned bright. This was my wedding, my time, my moment in the sun, and Logan, more handsome than I ever thought he could be, stood waiting to take my hand into his, my life into his.

How wonderful a wedding of two people who were sincerely in love with each other could be, I thought. It was sacred; it was precious, and it did lift my heart and make me feel as though I were walking on air. I remembered the nights when I would look up at the stars and wish for a time when Logan and I would be like a prince and a princess. He had come into my life so dramatically, just like a story-book knight in shining armor, there to do my bidding, to devote his life to me, and I thought surely we were meant to be husband and wife.

My heart fluttered beneath my breast. Beneath my veil, my face flushed.

Reverend Wise stared out at me in silence. Then he raised his eyes toward the ceiling of the church and began.

"Let us pray. Let us give thanks. For the Lord has been generous. He has given us a chance to fill our hearts with joy. A wedding is a new beginning, a beginning of a new life and a chance to serve God in new ways. This could not be more true than it is for Logan Stonewall and Heaven Leigh Casteel."

He turned to Logan. "Logan Stonewall," he intoned, "do you take this woman, Heaven Leigh Casteel, to be your lawful wedded wife, to have and to hold, for better or for worse, in sickness and in health, for richer or for poorer, till death do you part?"

Logan turned to me, his face and eyes adoring. "I do with all my heart," he declared.

"Heaven Leigh Casteel"—Reverend Wise turned to me—"do you take this man, Logan Grant Stonewall, to be your lawful wedded husband, to have and to hold, for better or for worse, in sickness and in health, for richer or for poorer, till death do you part?"

I looked into Logan's eyes and whispered, "I do."

"Who has the rings?" Reverend Wise asked.

Fanny sashayed forward. "Why, Reverend, ah do," she smirked as she lifted her hands, palm up—each held a ring. Then she bent forward, displaying her full cleavage for the Reverend's eyes, checking to make sure he was looking and handed Logan and me our rings.

Logan smiled at me, the gentlest of smiles, as he slipped the diamond-encrusted wedding band on my wedding finger. "With this ring I thee wed," he said.

I then did the same.

"By the powers invested in me by God and our Savior Jesus Christ," Reverend Wise intoned, "I now pronounce you man and wife. What God has brought together, let no man tear asunder. You may now kiss your bride, Logan."

Logan kissed me with more passion than he ever had before. Then we walked arm in arm back up the aisle. When we reached the door, Reverend Wise called out, "Ladies and gentlemen, come greet Mr. and Mrs. Logan Stonewall."

Everyone was around us at once, especially the townspeople. It was as though the service, the pronouncement of the words, the wearing of the rings confirmed me as one of them.

Outside the church the Longchamps had started playing a lilting waltz. After everyone had greeted us in the receiving line, Logan and I were expected to dance first. I saw the hill folk hanging back, insecure and uncertain. I felt their nervousness as they filed through that proper ceremonial reception line. I kissed Logan on the cheek and said, "Hang on, honey." Then I went up to the violinist, one of the greatest hill fiddlers ever, and I said, "Play me some country foot-stompin' music," As he began to play, I could hear all around me the sound of the hill folk clappin' and tappin'. I took my husband around the waist, the memories of my hill days flooding back to me, and I broke out into the Willies' swing.

The town folk stood back as one by one the hill folks came forward to cut in on our dance. Logan was spun away by a pretty student of mine as my old neighbor Race McGee twirled me away. Then the hill folk began to pull the town folk into the dance. Never had I been so happy. Everyone was laughing, clapping, whirling around. At last the Willies and Winnerow were one.

Suddenly I saw Fanny in her skin-tight blue dress slink across the dance floor and tap Logan's partner on the shoulder. "Make way for the sista-in-lore, for the best lady!" Fanny shouted for all to hear. She threw her arms around Logan's neck and pressed her bosom into his chest, placed her hands on his buttocks and began whirling my astonished Logan across the dance floor. When the music stopped, she announced, "I guess it's time to kiss the husband, this time," and with that I saw her tongue slither out between her lips and thrust itself into Logan's mouth.

Finally Logan yanked himself away from her grasp, but Fanny's laugh rang out above the music, tolling its alarm to warn me. I listened, and I heard. But this was my day and I wasn't going to let Fanny, or anyone or anything, spoil it.

❦ TWO ❧
In My Father's House

LOGAN AND I WALKED OFF THE PLANE RAMP AND INTO THE BOSTON airport giggling like schoolchildren. We were both so filled with excitement that the flight attendants immediately remarked that we looked like newlyweds.

"Oh?" Logan said, teasing. "And how should newlyweds look?"

"Full of hope and laughter, their love for each other so obvious even the most insensitive person would look at them and smile to himself," the stewardess recited as if from her own lifelong dream.

"That's us," Logan replied. We had been like that throughout the plane trip, hugging, kissing, giggling, and sighing at each other. Every time the flight attendants walked by, they smiled or laughed.

Now we hurried down the long airport corridor, hand in hand, eager to get on with our visit, Tony's wedding reception for us, and our honeymoon. As we came around a corner in the corridor, I spotted Tony standing by the gate. He was dressed in one of his dark blue, double-breasted silk suits, a folded *Wall Street Journal* in his hand. He lifted it to signal me as we appeared. "There's Tony." I waved back. "I expected he would simply have Miles, the chauffeur, here to greet us."

"That would have been no way to treat newlyweds," Logan quipped.

"You're right," I said, but I paused and tightened my fingers around Logan's hand, knowing all that he would never know. Perhaps it was because I had been away from Tony so long, or perhaps it was the heart's way of reminding the mind that our true selves were revealed more in our eyes than in our words; whatever the reason, I felt the magnetism of Tony's eyes, drawing me back, as I had feared they would.

Strands of gray hair had increased around Tony's temples, but that only added to his dignified demeanor. As we drew closer, his sharp, penetrating gaze transformed into a look of shock.

"Leigh?" he almost whispered. Then immediately he regained his composure. "Heaven!" He stepped forward to greet us. "Heaven, welcome home. You changed your hair to the same color as your mother's. Blond . . ." His voice drifted off, as if kidnapped by the past.

"Oh, yes, I forgot, Tony," I said quickly.

"I told her she looks better with her natural brunette," Logan quickly interjected as he stretched out a hand toward the surprised Tony.

"Tony, this is my husband, Logan." I introduced them as they shook hands. I could see Tony already sizing up Logan, taking his measure, scrutinizing his face for traces of his weaknesses and vulnerabilities to see where and how Tony might manipulate him to his will.

"Welcome, Logan," Tony said at last. Then he turned his eyes on me, and I could feel his stare almost drinking me in. "I am so happy to see you back here again, Heaven. I've missed you terribly . . ." He paused and his voice grew misty. "It's uncanny how much you look like her now. I wonder . . ." Then he seemed to grasp hold of himself and quickly turned back to Logan. "And I'm happy to have you here as well, son."

"Thank you, sir."

"Oh, please, call me Tony." His blue eyes lightened. "I have enough people calling me sir around here. Did you have a good flight?"

"Wonderful. But, of course, going anywhere, being anywhere with Heaven makes it wonderful," Logan said. He put his arm around my shoulders and hugged me for emphasis. Tony nodded with a look of amusement.

"That's good. Behaving as a pair of newlyweds should. I'm glad you've begun your honeymoon at Farthy. The car's just outside. Don't worry about your baggage. I have a man looking after it. Let's get to Farthy, where you can relax and we can get to know one another quickly," he told Logan.

He turned to me again, his blue eyes now calm and unreadable. He had gotten hold of himself in his usual inimitable manner and was once again the man in complete control.

"How is Jillian?" I asked softly.

"You'll see for yourself," he said. "Let's not let anything put a damper on the joy of your arrival. I have a wonderful reception planned and the weather promises to be perfect," he said as we continued on through the airport. "My servants have been working like little beavers to sharpen up the grounds. Farthy never looked as proud or as majestic, but she rarely had as good a reason to look so."

"Can't wait to see all of it," Logan said. Tony threw a self-satisfied smile back at me as we emerged from the airport. His long black limousine was at the curbside. Miles stood beside it, holding the car door open for us.

"Miles." I rushed to hug him.

"Good to see you again, Miss Heaven. Everyone's really happy about your visit."

"Thank you, Miles. This is my husband, Logan Stonewall."

"Pleased to meet you, sir."

"Thank you," Logan said and we all got into the rear of the black limousine. "This is the way to travel," Logan said, stretching out his legs and leaning back against the rich leather seat. Then he leaned forward quickly. "Is this a bar?"

"Yes. Would you like a drink?" Tony offered.

"I think I would," Logan replied, which surprised me. He didn't drink alcoholic beverages very often. Tony pulled out the liquor cabinet and Logan asked for a highball.

"Heaven?"

"No, thank you, Tony. Right now it would put me to sleep," I said. Tony made Logan his drink as we raced down the crowded highway.

Tony looked at me. His smile was small and tight . . . amused. I felt my heartbeat quicken. The scenery outside flashed by quickly, but everything—sounds, shapes, colors—was vibrant, electric.

"Is Curtis still the butler and Rye Whiskey still the cook?" I asked Tony.

"Of course. Farthy wouldn't be Farthy without them."

"Rye Whiskey?" Logan laughed.

"His real name is Rye Williams, but everyone calls him Rye Whiskey."

"Not everyone," Tony said. "I still maintain some semblance of dignity when it comes to my servants."

I turned to look out the window. I wanted to come upon Farthing-gale Manor just the way I had that first time. I wanted to feel the same excitement, the same sense of newness. I remembered being impressed with a home that had a name, and now I thought I rightly should have been, for Farthy was like a living thing to me; it had its own personality, it housed its memories and its past just like some dowager queen, sitting back, still reigning supreme. Despite my reluctance to admit it, I was coming home, returning to a part of myself I had hoped I had overcome by marrying Logan.

We were heading north, away from the city. Soon the roadside was bordered by large, gracious shade trees and sprawling green lawns. It was a bright summer day and the foliage was in full glory. It was a day in which to hope, a day in which to begin a new life.

"You know," Logan said as we drove on, "I never realized it before, but New England looks a lot like the Willies, only without the mountains and the shacks. These homes are far from the shacks, huh, Heaven?"

"Yes," I said. "But the Willies wouldn't be the Willies without them," I added softly.

"We're going to live in Winnerow," Logan explained quickly. "We're staying at the cabin for the time being, but we plan to build something substantial relatively soon."

"Is that right?" Tony asked, turning toward Logan and narrowing his steady gaze. I could practically hear his thoughts. He was reconsidering his original opinion of Logan, sensing something unexpected. "Well, you're about to see something very substantial here," he added. "Farthy was built by my great-great-great-grandfather, and every first son who takes it over improves it."

"Really?" Logan said, his eyes widening. He turned to look at me, the excitement so vivid in his face that for a moment he reminded me of a little boy about to be presented with a fabulous new toy.

"It's just coming up," Tony announced. Logan leaned forward to watch for the break in the trees. Miles made the turn onto the long, narrow private drive marked by high, wrought-iron gates that arched overhead and spelled out with ornate embellishments FARTHINGGALE MANOR.

"I rode past this gate once," Logan said wistfully, "trying to get up enough nerve to go in to see Heaven."

"Oh? Looks like your patience and persistence paid off," Tony said and winked at me. I pressed my face to the window and watched the balsam, fir, and pine trees whiz by as we approached the circular drive. The great gray stone house loomed before us. The red roof rose high into the sky, a magnificent silhouette against the cobalt blue. It amazed me how it could still take my breath away. When I looked at Logan, I saw he was impressed.

"It does look like a castle," he said.

"And the princess is coming home," Tony added, putting his hand over mine and smiling.

Miles pulled the limo up to the wide steps in front of the hand-carved, arched entrance door.

"And so the tour begins," Tony announced. I could feel Logan's enthusiasm and excitement as he gulped down the remainder of his drink and hurried to get out of the car. I emerged far more slowly, suddenly feeling a little terrified. I looked quickly at the great hedges that formed the English maze. At the other end of those passages lay Troy's little cottage. Despite the bright sunshine and the clear blue sky, it looked to me as if a mist lingered about those hedges, securing their mystery.

Logan didn't know where the maze led, but he knew how much I had once cared for Troy. He even knew about our short and tragic engagement. He had learned all when he had taken care of me when I went into a fever delirium and he nursed me back to health at the cabin. It was Troy I called for, Troy I even thought I saw when I opened my fevered eyes and gazed upon Logan's concerned face. I remembered how hurt he was.

"Why can't you trust me?" he had asked when he thought me asleep, his voice tender, his hands gentle as he smoothed back the damp fringe of hair from my forehead. "I saw you with that Cal Dennison and I wanted to shove him through the wall. I saw you once with that Troy you keep calling for, and I hated him. I've been a fool, Heaven, a damned fool, and now I've lost you."

But he hadn't lost me after all, and now I felt guilty even gazing at the maze and thinking of Troy and the love that was lost when he took his life. I couldn't help the way those memories tore at my heart and brought tears to my eyes. I hid my face from Logan, knowing how unfair it was for me to think about another man I had loved, even if I thought about him only for a few seconds.

"Incredible," Logan said, his hands on his lips. His head bobbed as he surveyed the grounds before him.

"We'll go inside; you'll freshen up, and then I'll show you about . . . or would you rather do it, Heaven?" Tony asked me quickly.

"What? No, no, that's all right. I suppose I should go to see Jillian," I said, looking at the dark, high, and wide windows behind which my maternal grandmother had imprisoned herself.

"Of course," Tony said and led us to the front doors that Curtis opened perfectly on cue. He stood back smiling and I went forward quickly to greet him.

"Welcome home, miss," he said and I blushed. When I looked at Tony, I saw an expression of satisfaction. I half suspected he had told Curtis to say that. I introduced Logan, who gave him a quick, perfunctory greeting and moved farther into the house.

Once inside, Logan turned in slow circles, looking more like one of the hill people being brought down from the mountains for the first time. It made me remember, nostalgically, my own first awe-inspiring sight of Farthy. How long ago it seemed. How quickly I'd grown used to its riches.

I peered into the enormous living room and stared at the grand piano that Troy used to play whenever he came to the great house. For a moment I thought I could once again hear the lilt of Chopin, the kind of romantic melody that could charm and thrill me. I imagined Troy seated there, his long, slender fingers rippling over the keyboard. I trembled in the archway.

"Heaven?"

"What?" I turned slowly to look at both Logan and Tony.

"Talk about being in a daze," Logan said.

"I'm sorry, what did you say?"

"I was telling Logan that I had your old rooms prepared; I thought you'd be most comfortable there," Tony said.

"Oh, of course. Thank you, Tony. We'll go right up."

"Your bags have arrived and are being taken up now," he added. We started for the marble stairway.

"I've never seen so many murals in one room," Logan said, looking into the music room. "It's like a museum." Tony laughed. "My wife used to be an illustrator for children's books. That was before she went mad . . ." Tony fumbled around the word, obviously wishing to take it back. He cleared his throat. "I'm afraid I let her get a bit carried away in there."

Logan strained to look over the domed ceiling with its painted sky, its flying birds, a man riding a magic carpet, and a mystical castle half-hidden by clouds.

"Kids would love it in here," Logan said.

"I agree," Tony said quickly. "I hope someday there will be some to enjoy it." Once again he narrowed his gaze at me. "Why don't you lovebirds go upstairs and freshen up now? I'm sure you'd like to be alone before dinner."

But Logan continued his study of the ceiling, as if he handn't heard Tony.

"Logan," I said, "I would like to take a shower." I started up the stairs. "Logan?"

"What? Oh, yeah, sure."

Logan hurried up after me and we went to my old rooms. "Jeez, what a suite," he said when we passed through the wide double doors. The servants had brought up our bags and one of the maids was already hanging up our clothing in the bedroom closets.

Bright afternoon sunlight poured through the pale ivory sheets to make the sitting room look even warmer than usual. The green, violets, and blues in the delicate ivory silk wall covering were more vibrant than ever. It was as if the room had come to life, using all its charm and beauty to woo me back. Logan had seen only a small part of it, but he was already charmed, drunk, intoxicated by Farthy's majestic size and beauty. He dropped himself into one of the two small sofas and stretched out his arms.

"You did live like a princess," he said. "I can't believe you gave all this up to live in a cabin in the Willies."

"Well, I did," I said. "And you should be very happy that I did. Otherwise, we might not have ever found each other again." Then I softened my voice. "I am so happy to be your bride, Mr. Stonewall."

Impetuously I leaned over and kissed him.

"Heaven, darling," he said, "I don't know what I would have done without you. . . . If you hadn't . . ." He held me by the shoulders. "I would have lost you forever." We started to kiss again when I realized the maid was standing in the bedroom doorway.

"Will there be anything else, Mrs. Stonewall?" she asked. She was new, a woman probably in her early forties, a little too stiff and proper for my taste, but probably an excellent servant, I thought.

"No, I think not. Your name is?"

"Donna."

"Thank you, Donna. How long have you been at Farthy?"

"Just a week, ma'am."

"Hired just for us," Logan said. I looked at him, wondering if that weren't true.

"That will be all, Donna. Thank you." I watched her leave while Logan went into the bedroom and whistled.

"Talk about bedrooms for a princess," he said again. He was standing by the king-size four-poster bed with an arching canopy of heavy lace.

"And a bed meant for royalty," I teased, taking his hand and drawing him beside me.

He bounced on the mattress. "Great." He got up instantly and went to the large dressing and bathroom area and then wandered in and out of the walk-in closets while I began to get undressed for my shower. "I don't think there's a better honeymoon suite in any hotel in the country," he said.

"Well, I'm not sure, Mr. Stonewall. We'll have to test that out, won't we?" I felt flushed all over. Here was my own husband. I was eager for our marriage to be consummated. Although I was not coming to him a virgin, I was a virgin with him and I longed to know him as my first lover—had longed for that for over ten years. And now here we were, and he seemed nervous, uncertain of how to turn his boyish love for me into the mature passion of a man for a woman. I waited for him to take me in his arms, to prove with his body the love I saw shining through his eyes.

"I sure hope the one in Virginia Beach will be just as fancy!" Logan said. He turned and looked at me, now standing clad only in bra and panties in front of him.

"Are you going to shower and change?" he asked.

"I thought I'd lie down and rest a bit. Don't you feel a bit tired, sweetheart?" I made my eyes go soft and dreamy, willing him to desire me.

"No, I'm too excited to rest. I think I'll just go down and talk to Tony," he said.

"If that's what you want to do," I said, trying to hide the disappointment in my voice.

He kissed me quickly and left. This wasn't the way I had planned our afternoon. I was longing for him to take me in his arms and to drive away all the ghosts of my love for Troy that haunted this house. I needed to be with him here, only him, my true pure shining springtime love. I needed Logan to prove to me that passion could be found, forever in the arms of my husband. Why did my husband seem more interested in exploring than experiencing the boundless love we felt for each other? I sat down before the vanity and looked at myself in the mirror. Suddenly I had to laugh.

"I can't believe you, Heaven Leigh Stonewall. You're actually jealous of a house. And that's silly, isn't it?" My image in the mirror didn't respond.

After I showered and dressed, I went down the corridor to Jillian's suite of rooms. It had been well over two years since I had left her that day, framed before her arching bay windows, the sunlight pouring through her hair. I had come to despise her and had actually intended never to see her again.

Martha Goodman greeted me in the sitting room. She had been seated in the high-back French Provincial chair just to the right of the door to Jillian's bedroom, knitting. The moment she saw me enter, she smiled and rose to greet me.

"Why, Heaven. It's so good to see you again," she said, extending her hand. "Congratulations on your marriage. Mr Tatterton told me of your impending arrival."

"Thank you, Martha. How is .   my grandmother?" I inquired.

"Does she realize I have returned? Does she know I was married?" I asked with some interest.

"Oh, I'm afraid not. Mr. Tatterton did not prepare you for this visit?" she asked. I shook my head. "She's different, Heaven, quite different."

"How so?" I asked.

"It's best you see for yourself," she said, almost in a whisper. "Mrs. Tatterton is at her vanity table, preparing for guests," she added, tilting her round face to the right and nodding sadly.

"Guests?"

"People she says she has invited to watch an old movie in her private little theater."

"I see." I looked toward the bedroom door. "I'd better get this over with," I said and knocked gently on it. After a moment I heard Jillian's voice. She sounded softer, younger, happier.

"Yes?"

I looked at Martha Goodman, who closed her eyes gently and nodded before returning to her chair, and then I entered.

Jillian sat at her marble-top vanity table, dressed in one of her loose-fitting ivory floats trimmed with peach lace. She looked like a circus clown. Her hair was dyed a bright yellow and stuck up in thin, stiff strands. Her face looked like cracked porcelain, her cheeks blotched with bright red rouge. Eyeliner was slashed across her lids, the line drooping at the crinkly corners of her eyes. Her lipstick was thick, vibrant, caked at the corners of her mouth.

But when I looked past her, to her mirror, I saw to my horror a blank a oval of bare wall. The glass in the mirror that had once hung over the vanity table had been removed. Jillian sat before the empty frame staring into a memory of herself.

I looked to her bed and saw dress after dress laid over the quilt. Dozens of pairs of shoes were on the floor beside the bed. Dresser drawers were left open with undergarments and stockings dangling over the sides. All her jewelry boxes were open. Glittering necklaces, bejeweled earrings, diamond and emerald bracelets were scattered over the top of the dresser. The room looked as though it had been ransacked by a madwoman. I didn't know what to do. Jillian had deteriorated far more than even I could have imagined.

Then Jillian spotted me and smiled widely, a demonic smile that made her clownish appearance even more frightening and pathetic.

"Leigh," she said, with forced cheerfulness. "Thank goodness you're here. I'm going absolutely mad trying to decide what to wear today. You know who's coming, don't you?" she added in a loud whisper. She looked about the room as though there were other people within who could hear. "Everybody who's anyone. And they're all coming to see my theater."

"Hello, Grandmother," I said, ignoring her mad ramblings. I thought that if I didn't go along with it, I might snap her out of it. Instead, she sat back and glared at me as though she had heard other words.

"What do you mean, you don't want to attend? I purposely invite influential people to Farthinggale so they and their sons will meet you. You should be interested in boys your own age. It's not healthy for you to . . . to be around only Tony."

"Grandmother, I'm not Leigh," I said. "It's Heaven; it's your granddaughter," I added, stepping farther into the room. "I have gotten married, Grandmother. His name is Logan, Logan Stonewall, and we've come back to Farthy because Tony's making us a gala reception."

She shook her head, obviously not hearing a word I was saying.

"I told you, time and time again, Leigh, not to come to my bedroom half dressed. You're not a child anymore. You can't parade about like that, especially in front of Tony. You should have more self-respect, be more discreet. A lady, a real lady, doesn't do this sort of thing. Now, go finish dressing."

"Jillian." I thought if I used her Christian name, she might acknowledge me. I knew how much she hated being thought of as a grandmother. "Leigh's gone; Leigh's dead," I said softly. "I'm Heaven."

She blinked heavily and pulled herself into a stiffer sitting position.

"This is the last time I will put up with this," she croaked. "You are turning everybody against me. But everybody knows the truth, Leigh, the truth about your vile seductive behavior. Jealous? Me?" she huffed. "Jealous of my own daughter? Ridiculous." She turned and looked into the imaginary mirror and smiled a serene self-confident smile. "You will never be able to compete with my beauty, Leigh, a mature woman's beauty. You're still a child."

She studied herself in the imaginary mirror and then began brushing her hair again. "Yes, I know what you do, Leigh," she continued. "Tony's complained about it and I've seen you do it, so don't try to deny it. Your body's developing. I'm not going to deny that. After all, you're my daughter. You will be beautiful, vibrantly beautiful, and if you listen and work hard on your coiffure and your makeup, take care of yourself the way I do, why, you'll be as beautiful as I am someday." Suddenly she stopped brushing her hair and pounded her brush on the vanity. "What do you expect Tony to do? Of course he'll look at you, but that doesn't mean what you think it means. I've seen you brush your body up against his seductively, oh, yes, I have."

"Jillian . . ." I couldn't believe she was still blaming my mother for all that had happened. "You're mad, old woman, quite mad! My mother never did any of that! It was you! You who caused it all. My mother was pure and innocent! I know she was!" I was shaking with rage. I wouldn't believe my own mother had provoked Tony. Wouldn't, couldn't believe that! "It was your jealousy that killed my mother. Even your madness cannot change that."

She stopped speaking and straightened up sharply. "Why are you looking at me like that? You never knew I had been following you, did you? You never knew I was there, just outside his door, in the shadows, watching. But I was . . . I was. I couldn't bring myself to go in and put an end to it, but I was there. I was there," she whispered.

I stared at her. Could what she was saying be true? Could my mother have seduced Tony? I refused to believe. And yet . . . yet . . . I had seduced Troy. I knew the passion that ran in my blood; was it my mother's passion I had inherited? Perhaps that was what the Reverend Wise had seen in me when he predicted I would destroy all that I love and all who love me.

I rushed out to Martha Goodman, who sat calmly in the high-back chair, knitting.

"You've got to stop her!" I exclaimed. "She's going mad in there, making herself up over and over with layers and layers of rouge and lipstick."

"Oh, she'll get tired soon," Martha said smiling softly. "I'll talk her into her medication, convincing her its a vitamin that will help keep her young forever, and then I'll scrub her face clean and clean up the mess and she'll take a long nap. Don't worry."

"But doesn't Tony understand how bad she's gotten? Haven't there been doctors?"

"Of course there have, my dear. The doctors recommend she be institutionalized, but Mr. Tatterton won't hear of it. There's no harm. Actually, she's happy most of the time."

"She doesn't remember me, then, does she?" I turned back toward her bedroom.

"Not now, no. She talks about your mother a great deal," Martha said and looked down at her knitting, and I understood that she had overheard much ugly truth in my grandmother's mad babbling.

I left Jillian's suite quickly, actually fleeing from the images she had resurrected. When I returned to our suite, I searched for and found my mother's fat photo album. I studied her school pictures again, hoping to reaffirm my own belief that she was beautiful but innocent, wild but pure. If only for a moment, one moment, I could truly look into those blue eyes, I thought, I would know the truth. But did I want to know it?

"Don't tell me you're still cloistered in these rooms." Logan startled me as he strode into the room. I hadn't realized how long I had been sitting there, thinking about the past. I closed the photo album quickly.

"No," I mumbled. "I spent some time with my grandmother." Then I turned to my husband and put a bright smile on my face. "So, what has Tony shown you?"

"All of it," Logan said, shaking his head with admiration. "All of this paradise called Farthinggale Manor. I can't believe there's an indoor pool! That maze, the lake, those stables, acres and acres of beautiful land, and a private beach."

"Tony gave you the grand tour."

"I'll say. Of course, he's very proud of it, proud of what it is, proud of what he has made of it, and proud of what it can continue to be," Logan added. "He's a fascinating man, shrewd, very clever about business and about politics. I never realized what Tatterton Toys really is until he explained it just now."

"Is that so?" I sat back, a half smile on my face. Logan was acting like a bedazzled little boy.

He smiled and I threw my arms around him and kissed him. It was a long, passionate kiss. His embrace tightened and I felt the tingling that made me press my body closer to his.

"Every time I kiss you," I murmured into his ear, "I remember our first kiss. Remember?"

"Yes. I do remember," he whispered, but I had been the forward one. He had walked me home and stood there on the trail. I was so thrilled with the way he had fought for me that day that I couldn't wait for him to get up enough nerve to take me into his arms.

"You said, 'Logan, would it be all right and not too much like Fanny if I kissed you just once for being so exactly what I want?' And then you kissed me, but so passionately. . . ."

I turned away from him.

"What's wrong?"

"Nothing," I said. Then I gave him my most seductive smile.

"We have some time before dinner," I cooed flirtatiously.

"To start the honeymoon," he added, smiling widely, licentiously.

"Oh, Logan, I   "

He took me into his arms and kissed me. Then he began to undress me. I closed my eyes and let the sensuality of his touch erase all my thoughts. I let myself go completely to the will of our bodies together.

As Logan and I moved beside each other his kisses and caresses pulled me down into a sea of tenderness. And when he entered my body, the light of his love chased away all the shadows of my dark forbidden love. This was how it would be now, Logan and Heaven, Logan touching me, Logan kissing me, Logan caressing me, Logan making love to me with such tenderness. Not the wild forbidden passion I had known with Troy, not the sort of all-consuming love that made the world disappear and left you clinging only to love like a life raft in a turbulent sea, but the safe, gentle, lapping waves of love that were comfortable, soothing, like a warm pond in summer, like my life with Logan was meant to be.

Afterward, Logan fell asleep curled in my arms. In the dim haze of twilight I looked around me. Here I was, again at Farthy, having just made love to my husband. Years ago, within these walls, had my mother pressed her young body just as eagerly against her mother's husband to begin my maddening existence?

I closed my eyes. I understood how it was that ghosts lived on. They lived on in us, haunted us by making us thirst for the same things. My mother lived on in my desires. But my desires were pure, wholesome, for now I desired only my husband and would never desire anyone else. I nestled against Logan's warm, peaceful, sleeping body.

❧ THREE ❧
Offerings

WHEN I AWOKE THE NEXT MORNING LOGAN WAS GONE. THE SUN through the window sheers awakened me, and I turned to my new husband for morning hugs and kisses, only to be greeted by an empty pillow. "Logan?" I called. I quickly leapt from the bed and ran to the bathroom, tapping gently on the door. "Logan?" No sound greeted me, no rushing shower, no sweet morning songs from a happy husband at his morning ablutions. When I was a little girl, I always dreamed of the happy morning scene of my husband shaving, while I sat on the tub watching his masculine rituals. And already that morning had been stolen from me—and on the first morning of my honeymoon! And I thought I knew who had stolen it—the one who seemed to want always to steal my love and keep it for himself alone—Tony.

I remembered at dinner last night, Tony had insisted on showing Logan around the Tatterton Toy Factory today. "Oh, and you must come along as well, Heaven. After all, someday it will all be yours and Logan's," he added with a wink to Logan. I wasn't going to let Tony lure me into his old plan of bringing me into his business again. "No," I had insisted, "Logan and I were planning to have breakfast in bed tomorrow and spend a leisurely day strolling the grounds of Farthy, weren't we darling?" But Logan was already caught in Tony's web, intrigued by the promise of Tony's attention, hypnotized by the way Tony already treated him as a member of the family and heir.

I dressed in a bright floral-print voile dress that was part of my trousseau and started downstairs, figuring Logan might be breakfasting with Tony. Just as I rounded the head of the stairs, I heard the shrill, girlish voice of Jillian:

"Do I look especially beautiful today? This is such a special day. Tell me, am I the most beautiful of all? Am I? Am I?"

"You are, dear, the most beautiful of all," I heard Martha Goodman assure her.

I felt, with the disappearance of my husband, and the strange sounds emanating from Jillian's room, that the twisted world of Farthy was reaching out to trap me in its gnarled arms again. Almost against my will I was drawn to Jillian's suite. Oh, where was Logan, and why had I agreed to come here before our honeymoon? I should have known that nothing would have improved, that things would only have gotten worse.

"Martha?" I called. Martha Goodman appeared in the doorway. "Martha, what's going on?" I asked.

"Oh, nothing too unusual, Heaven," she replied, as if Jillian's voice always trembled the halls. "Mr. Tatterton was here late last night and he got Miss Jillian very excited about the reception. I didn't think she would remember him visiting her and telling her, but she's been preparing herself since daybreak."

"Then she realizes I am here and that I have gotten married," I said quickly.

"Oh, no." Martha shook her head sadly. "I'm afraid not."

"Well . . . how did Tony explain the reception?"

"He explained it," Martha replied. She smiled and shook her head again. "But Jillian heard different words."

"What do you mean?"

"I'm afraid she thinks it's her own wedding reception."

"What?" I crossed my arms about my chest, hugging myself as if I were a child that I, myself, was protecting from the terrible truth of Jillian's madness and jealousy. "I don't understand. Her own?"

"Meaning the reception that was given for her the day she married Tony and came to live at Farthinggale Manor," Martha said.

"Oh . . . oh, I see."

"Don't worry. It will be all right. Most everyone who has been invited knows how she is now," Martha assured me.

"Of course. If there's anything I can do to help, let me know," I mumbled and ran downstairs, looking for Logan, longing for his reassuring arms, longing to know my life was with him, more than ever.

The breakfast table was already being cleared by the servants. I went into the kitchen looking for Logan. Surely he wouldn't have left without even saying good-bye on our honeymoon morning. But in the kitchen I found only my old friend, Rye Whiskey.

"Miss Heaven!" he exclaimed. The stout black chef was happy to see me, but I could also see fear in his eyes when I stepped through the door. He went right to a salt shaker and tossed some grains over his shoulder. I didn't laugh. Rye was a superstitious man, inheriting a legacy of omens and rituals from his slave ancestors.

"Glad to see you, Miss Heaven," he said, "but for a moment there I thought I seen another ghost."

He had always told me how much I looked like my mother. Now, with my hair her color, he, too, was amazed by how much I looked like her.

"Don't tell me you're still seeing ghosts around Farthy, Rye," I teased. He didn't crack a smile. "Have you seen my husband, Rye, or Tony? Surely they haven't turned into ghosts overnight."

"Well, Miss Heaven, now, they left an hour ago, all puffed up with excitement because Master Tony was showing Mr. Logan his factory. That husband of yore's shore does know how to bring Master Tony alive, don't he, Heaven?"

"I'm afraid he does," I said quietly, thinking to myself I was more afraid than anyone could guess. But I didn't want Rye Whiskey to see my distress, so I went back to his favorite subject. "And just what ghosts have you been seeing lately? Tony's great-great grandfather or great-great grandmother?"

"Don't talk about the dead and gone, Miss Heaven. If you dig up their troubled past, you'll disturb their sleep and they'll haunt ya. I got enough hauntin' me these days," he added.

I had no doubt that Rye knew where the ghosts and skeletons were in Farthy, but like all old and dedicated family servants, he kept the secrets to himself. He was as discreet as an ancestral portrait—seeing and hearing all, but telling nothing.

"You don't look so bad for it, Rye," I said. Except for a little weight he had gained, and the further retreat of his graying hairline, he didn't look much different than he had the day I left. He was already in his late fifties, but he looked no older than a man in his mid-forties.

"Well, thank you, Miss Heaven. 'Course," he said with a twinkle in his eye, "I keep myself embalmed."

"Still taking a nip here and there, are you, Rye?"

"Just to prevent snake bite, Miss Heaven. And you know what?"

"I haven't been bitten yet," I recited along with him and we laughed.

"Going to be one big party tomorrow for you and your husband, and I'm glad of it. Farthy needs some happiness, needs people and music once again. I'm glad you're here, Miss Heaven. Really am."

"Thank you, Rye." We talked a little more about the preparations, and then I left him.

Eating alone at the table with Curtis standing nearby to serve my every need brought back memories. Even when Jillian was well, I had eaten breakfast by myself. And here I was, now a married woman, so different from the frightened, vulnerable girl who first came to Farthy, who was afraid of Curtis, who didn't even know how to eat in front of a servant. Oh, I had learned the ways of the wealthy, but the frightened girl lived on inside me, still intimidated by Farthy and its power.

But it was a magnificent summer day with not a cloud in the turquoise sky and I intended to enjoy it. After breakfast I went outside. There was just enough breeze coming in from the ocean to keep it from becoming too hot. I inhaled the briny scent of the sea and stepped into the sunlight.

The grounds around the manor were already abuzz with activity. The gardeners were putting the final touches on the lush green lawns and trimming the hedges into magnificent topiary designs of lions and zebras, fantastical storybook animals. A giant red tent, bigger than any circus tent Pa would ever own, was being erected on the back lawn. A bandstand fit for the Boston Symphony stood out in front of the deep turquoise swimming pool. Truckloads of white wrought-iron tables and benches were being brought in to be placed under the tent. I saw that Tony, not satisfied with the colorful beds of yellow, red, and white roses, blood-red poppies, elegant blue delphiniums, and a host of other exotic floral beds, had ordered oval and horseshoe floral arrangements to be hung from every available post and hook. The word *Congratulations* had been spelled out with red roses strung through an ivory lattice to be placed just above the stage.

I wandered away from the house and the noise of men shouting orders to one another as they unloaded things from the trucks. I walked, not thinking about where I was going, and found myself drawn to the beaches. Troy had been haunting me since I'd arrived at Farthy. Perhaps he would until I said good-bye one last time to my old lover who had drowned in this very sea. For a moment the realization that this was where he had perished took my breath away. The gray crashing waves looked more forbidding than ever. "Good-bye, Troy," I whispered to the waves that would never answer me back. "Good-bye forever, Troy, forever and ever." I sat down on the sand, gazing at the boundless horizon, where my past and present dissolved into each other as the sky dissolved into the sea.

Suddenly I heard my name and turned to see Logan striding across the warm sand, barefoot, with his trousers rolled up—he looked like one of the Kennedys, so confident and handsome.

"What are you doing, Heaven? I've been searching for you for the past half hour," he called.

"But Logan, I was looking for you. Where were you this morning?"

"I was too excited to sleep and I didn't want to wake you. Isn't this wonderful? All this excitement, all this energy. When I went downstairs, Tony was already up and we decided to visit the factory right then and there so I could be back to spend the day with you. Oh, Heaven, it was so great! And the factory . . . the main Tatterton Toy Store . . . it's marvelous . . . the way Tony has managed to create a system that maintains the unique style of each Tatterton toy. He has so many good ideas. I want you to hear them; I want you to think about them."

"Hear them? Think about them? What do you mean, Logan?"

"Let's go inside," he said. He was so excited he could barely stand still. He led me directly to Tony's office and flung open the door.

"Tony's a tyrant about his office," I warned him quickly. "He doesn't like anyone in here unless he is present to invite them in," I said. But Logan didn't move.

"It's all right. He told me to use his office."

"He did?" I was flabbergasted. "What is this all about Logan?" I asked. I was even more surprised when he whirled around Tony's high-back, black leather chair and sat down in it as if it were his own.

"What are you doing?" I queried.

He sat back and put his feet up on Tony's antique oak desk, smiling as if he suddenly saw himself to be a big-time business executive.

"It's all right. Really. Sit down."

I shook my head in confused amazement and sat on the soft, charcoal leather settee.

"Now, hear out all I have to say before you speak," he instructed, putting his legs back on the floor and leaning forward on the desk, "and promise to keep an open mind. Do you promise?"

I knew I was about to hear something I wouldn't like—some scheme of Tony's to control our lives. But I didn't want to burst the bright bubble of Logan's excitement. "And hope to die." I laughed.

He took a deep breath and then spoke. "Tony has made me an offer and I think we should take it," he said quickly.

"An offer? What kind of an offer?" I asked suspiciously.

"You heard him at dinner last night . . . all his plans for the company. Well, he can't do it all himself."

"He has very competent people working for him," I said. My heart was starting to pound. I could anticipate what was to come.

"Yes, but he's very family-oriented. Like he says . . . what's the point in having all this if you haven't a family to share it with?" Logan said, holding his arms out to an imaginary brood.

"What does this have to do with you? You're a pharmacist, working in your family's store." I saw he was stung by the cold tone in my voice, but I couldn't help how I sounded, nor could I help how I felt. It was in this office that Tony confessed to me he was my father; it was because of what was said in this office that Troy had become my forbidden love. It seemed to me that Tony was reaching out again, interfering, changing things, trying to control my life.

"I know what I am. The point is . . . is it enough? Will you really ever be satisfied, after knowing all this wealth and luxury, living in Winnerow for the rest of your life with me working in my parents' store, the only future being my inheriting the business? Granted, it's all right, if Winnerow is the only thing we hope to achieve, but . . ."

"Winnerow was enough for us before we came here, Logan. I don't understand this change of heart. What is it that Tony is offering you exactly?" I asked.

Logan sat back, a self-satisfied smile on his face, a face that had suddenly become unfamiliar to me, unlike the face I had known for so very many years, a face filled with ambition. He straightened his shoulders and looked about the office as though it had been his for years.

"A vice-presidency in charge of marketing," he announced. "I made some suggestions and he was very impressed. They just started to come to me, Heaven," he said, leaning forward again. "It was natural. I thought about different kinds of outlets, merchandising, advertising . . . it all spilled off my tongue with ease," he added, his face animated, his eyes wide. I stared at him a moment.

"You mean you would give up being a pharmacist?" I asked softly.

"Oh, Heaven, what am I giving up? Think about it. Think about what we could have; what we could be."

"I know what we have and I know what we can be," I said. I felt tears begin to well up in my eyes, but I fought back my urge to cry. "What would your parents say? They'll be heartbroken."

"Are you kidding?" He started to laugh. "When they see what I am gaining! They're not stupid. They'll work the store until my father wants to retire and then they'll just sell it."

I straightened up in my seat. I felt my pride come back in full dress parade, replacing my disappointment with flames of anger.

"Maybe it's no problem for you, Logan, but I'm a teacher," I said. "In my own way I am doing a great deal for the people in Winnerow. It was my dream to do something significant there, to continue to do something significant there." I sat back and pictured the hill and valley people in church during my wedding ceremony. I remembered the look of pride on their faces, the look of hope in their eyes. They saw something noble and caring in me and in my return, and now Logan was suggesting I simply walk away from my dreams.

"I realize that, Heaven," Logan said, standing up and moving around the desk. "And I explained that to Tony. He understands it, too, but he's made a wonderful suggestion, something that I'm sure will please you."

"And what's that?" I asked with ice in my voice.

"He wants to build a factory in Winnerow and have us develop some Tatterton Toys based upon the carvings the hill people do, the kind of whittling your grandfather used to do. Just think what that would mean for Winnerow and for the hill people. We would employ them to do the handicraft work. There would be jobs for people who presently barely scrounge out an existence. They'll be able to have decent homes; their children will wear decent clothing . . ."

"A factory? In Winnerow?"

"Yes." He started to pace the office, reciting with excitement as he did so. "One of the first things we're going to create is a miniature Willies with the hill people, little rocking chairs, old folks like your grandmother and grandfather sitting in them, him whittling, her knitting; little farm animals, the children walking off to school . . . we even thought about having a moonshiner's still . . ."

"So that's why he was asking all those questions about Winnerow last night," I said, more to myself than to Logan. He nodded. I had to admit to myself that this suggestion took the wind from the sail of my opposition. I sat back, once again in deep thought. Logan was encouraged and rushed up to me.

"Isn't it a wonderful idea? We're going to call the new set 'The Willies,' and just think of the irony . . . rich people buying replicas of the poor and the money finding its way into the pockets of the poor folks who will work in the Tatterton Toy Factory. Heaven," he said, some frustration coming into his voice, "how can you just sit there staring up at me? Doesn't it all excite you?"

"It's exciting," I admitted. "But it's just all coming at me so fast. I have a great deal to think about. I never expected anything like this. We were stopping here for a couple of days and then going on to Virginia Beach to continue our honeymoon. I had no idea this stop-over would result in a complete change of our lives."

"Sure, sure, I understand how you feel," he said. "It's a lot to take in at once, but big and important decisions always are."

"That sounds more like something Tony would say."

"He did."

"I thought so," I said. "Where is he anyway?" I looked to the doorway again.

"He had to see about some of the arrangements for our reception."

"How convenient," I said. "He knows what he's doing sending you to convince me."

"He didn't send me, Heaven. I insisted he let me speak to you first."

I shook my head, befuddled, not knowing whether I was being manipulated or presented with an opportunity of a lifetime. I always felt that way when Tony involved me in his desires.

"Men like Tony always get what they want," I muttered.

"Really, Heaven," Logan said. "What's wrong with that?" I looked up at him. I understood Logan's excitement and his ambition, but I didn't like the change that had already come over him. He was too infatuated with Tony and with all that money could buy. Logan had never been one to be interested in power and wealth. It amazed me how convincing and how influential a man like Tony could be.

"It's all right to get what you want," I said, "as long as other people aren't hurt in the process."

"Who will be hurt here? People will only be helped, Heaven," he said, taking a calmer tone of voice. "Sooner or later something like this would have come up. Whether you like it or not, you are the heir to the Tatterton empire and fortune. There simply isn't anyone else. I understand Tony's feelings, his reasons for being so determined to make us a part of it. How can you blame him for that?"

"I know," I said in a tired voice. "I don't blame him."

"Well, then?"

What could I say? If only I had grown up like a normal girl with a mother and a father who were with me and my brothers and sisters all our young lives, instead of being tossed from one abusive family to another, I wouldn't be so pained by such crises and decisions, I thought. Was I the Tatterton Tony wanted me to be or was I the Casteel I had been thought to be most of my life? Was I still running away from my true identity? I had hoped that by becoming Mrs. Logan Stonewall I would have put those problems behind me. I would simply be Logan's wife and we would raise our own family with no ties to the past. Now, looking up at Logan, seeing the excitement in his face, I realized that was a foolish dream.

"Let me just think, Logan. Please."

"Of course." He slapped his hands together. "And to enable you to do just that calmly and quietly, here's what I suggest—I suggest we cancel our reservations for Virginia Beach and continue our honeymoon here at Farthy."

"What?" I looked up quickly. Was it going to be one surprise after another?

"Sure. Think about it. We have everything anyone could have at a resort. Why, we have more. We have our own private beach. We don't have to mingle with the tourists. At night we can be driven into Boston in the limo and see some shows and shop, go to fine restaurants, and during the day we can go horseback riding here and lie around on the beach, or picnic. No one will bother us. Tony will be at work; your grandmother stays in her rooms. We'll have the place all to ourselves. What do you say?"

"I don't know. I . . ." I looked around. Everything was happening so quickly.

"At the end of the week we'll return to Winnerow and tell my parents our decision."

"Our decision? But . . . there are so many things to decide. For example, where will we live?"

"You'll live here, of course," Tony said. He materialized in the office doorway so quickly, he was like a spirit that had instantly taken shape. "Sorry to interrupt, but I came in to get something and just overheard your last question."

"Here?" I looked at Logan. He was smiling like a Cheshire cat. "What does he mean?"

"We were saving that as a final surprise," Logan said.

We? I thought. We were saving that as a final surprise? He was already thinking and acting like Tony's partner.

"What final surprise?" They looked at each other like two conspirators. Did Tony just happen to arrive at the right moment or had he been standing outside the office door throughout our conversation waiting for his we? I wondered.

"If you'll just follow along," Tony said, "I'll show you." Logan reached down and took my hand.

"Come on, silly. Let's see what he has to show us. Come on." He smiled at me.

I rose slowly, reluctantly, knowing I was being led to a view of my own future. We would all be filled with trepidation if we could suddenly see the rest of our lives, I thought. Right now I was being swept along, carried by a momentum that was not my own. Like a marionette, I held Logan's hand and we followed Tony up the marble staircase.

"You remember these rooms on the south wing," Tony explained as he turned right at the top of the stairway. "We never even opened them for guests. My grandfather and grandmother lived on this side of

Farthy. I always wanted these rooms to remain something special."
He turned and looked at me. "I hope you feel that way, too, Heaven."

"I don't understand what you mean, Tony," I said. He simply
smiled and a light sprang into his pale blue eyes, bright like the golden
flame of an oil lamp burning securely in its clear glass globe. Then he
went to the large mahogany doors that were usually kept closed and
opened them with a grand flourish, thrusting them back and stepping
away to let me see.

"The suite of Mr. and Mrs. Logan Stonewall," he announced.

"What?" I folded my arms across my body protectively and turned
to Logan. He stood there, still smiling like a Cheshire cat. "What is
this?" I walked forward and entered the suite.

Nearly everthing had been redecorated. The French Provincial furniture in the sitting room had been reupholstered in a striped silk cloth
in my favorite color: wine red. A large Persian rug had been placed
over the hardwood floor. The walls had been done in a floral-patterned
cloth paper, the colors in the petals picking up on the reds and whites
in the upholstery and rug. Over the two large windows hung antique
silk drapes, behind which were sheer curtains.

Tony moved ahead and opened the bedroom doors. Even the over-
sized king-sized bed looked lost in the enormous room, the floors of
which were covered with a thick, beige carpet so soft to the step it felt
as though I were walking over marshmallows. The windows on either
side of the bed had been redesigned, making them longer and wider,
thus providing the room with a great deal of sunlight and making it
look bright and lively.

The light oak posts of the bed with their hand-carved threads rose
to support a milk-white and apricot canopy. There was a matching
bedspread with frilly edges, and rust-colored throw pillows had been
placed at the center. To the right of the entry was a white marble
vanity table, resting in the middle of a marble counter that ran nearly
the length of the room. Under the counter were drawers framed in
wood the shade of the marble counter. Above it was a wall of mirror,
the edges of which were trimmed in gold.

The entrance to what would be my bathroom began at the end of
the counter. This additional bathroom had obviously been added recently, too. The fixtures were modern and plush, with the whirlpool
tub set in a caramel-tinted tile floor. All the knobs and faucets were
gold-plated. There were mirrors everywhere, which made the bathroom look larger than it was, although it was, in and of itself, one of
the largest bathrooms I had ever seen. Even Jillian's seemed small in
comparison.

I turned from the bathroom and went to the immediate right of the bedroom door, where there was one enormous walk-in closet so deep and so long I thought it had as much space as our entire cabin in the Willies. There were even new garments hanging on the racks, dresses and skirts and suits of the latest fashion. I turned to Tony in amazement.

"Went on a buying spree one day. Whatever you don't like, we'll send back. Don't worry about it." He smiled.

"I don't believe this," I said. There were even pairs of matching new shoes displayed on the bottom shelves. Tony always wanted to control everything—even to the clothes I wore, the way I dressed and put on makeup.

But the one thing that caught my attention the most was the painting hung above the bed, just under the canopy. It was an oil capturing a scene in the Willies with a shack set in the belly of a small hill. Two small figures sat in rocking chairs on the porch of the shack, looking remarkably like Granny and Grandpa.

"Of course, you can change anything you want," Tony said.

I stared at him a moment and then shook my head. Obviously, so much redecoration and renovation had to have begun some time ago. Tony had been planning this, hoping or expecting that Logan and I would live here. I wanted to be angry, to despise him for always getting his way, but the brightness and the richness of the rooms, rooms obviously built to cater to my taste, rooms created to make me feel happy and at home, tempered my indignation and smothered the sparks of my anger.

I looked at Logan, who stood beside Tony, beaming. For a moment another, more frightening thought occurred to me. Could he have known about this all along, even before we came to Farthy? Did he always know that Tony would offer him a vice-presidency and did he simply pretend his amazement and excitement? Was he capable of such deception? I didn't think so, but under Tony's guidance, anything was possible.

"How did you know we would even consider doing this?" I asked Tony. He shrugged. "It makes no difference. If you weren't going to live in this suite, it would still serve a purpose—it would be your personal guest suite, available only to you whenever you wanted to use it. I hardly think it was a financial gamble," he added, smiling. Logan laughed.

"I wasn't concerned about your money," I said. His blue eyes narrowed, but he kept his smile small and tight. I looked at the painting again. "Who did that painting?"

"One of my artisans at the plant. I sent him to the Willies and he returned with that. Rather good, I thought. What do you think?"

"It's wonderful," I admitted. I embraced myself again. It was a wonderful painting. Every time I looked at it, it would fill my heart with warmth and my mind with memories. I could almost hear the rocking chairs squeaking.

"So?" he said.

I looked at both of them again. Logan had begun to imitate Tony's posture, Tony's smile.

"I don't know. I feel like someone being swept along. I've got to think . . . about a great many things."

"Fine," Tony said. "Well, I'd better check on things outside." He looked at his watch. "With the reception coming up tomorrow, we haven't that much longer." He started out and then stopped in the bedroom doorway to turn back to me. "Don't be angry with me, Heaven, for caring about you and wanting you to be happy," he said and left before I could respond.

"Logan Stonewall," I said, spinning around quickly to confront him, "did you know anything about this before we came to Farthy? Tell me the truth," I demanded quickly.

"What . . . of course not . . . how could I?" He lifted his arms to plead his innocence. I studied him a moment and concluded he was telling the truth. "Why are you so upset, anyway? Look around you. This place is beautiful."

"I know that, but remember what I said downstairs . . . about men like Tony getting what they want. Don't you understand? He had to have begun this some time back; he had to have always planned for us to come here, for you to work for him."

"I don't believe that," Logan said. "How could he?"

"I do," I said. "But maybe it doesn't matter anyway; maybe it's all part of what's destined to be." I looked over the rooms again. "Come," I said, "let's get ready for dinner."

Logan, shaking his head in confusion, followed me out. How could I expect him to understand the forces at work at Farthy, the power of the ghosts and the shadows that Rye Whiskey feared, the mystery and the magic of the large house and its grounds, when I, myself, a blood descendant of the Tattertons, receptive to the voices from the past, did not comprehend the full extent of the power they had over me?

I should flee this place, I thought. I should rush out of here and return to the Willies, where I felt safe and snug in Grandpa's cabin

But the echo of that thought died quickly and was replaced by the echoes of Logan's and my footsteps as we hurried down the corridor.

Like a leaf in the wind, I felt myself being swept along, carried away by forces far stronger that I was.

❧ FOUR ❧
The Grand Reception

THE ROAD TO FARTHINGGALE MANOR HOSTED A PARADE OF LIM-
ousines, Cadillacs and Lincolns, Rolls-Royces and Mercedes. Tony
had pulled out all stops; he had invited every influential businessman
and politician and socialite within a hundred-mile radius. I knew that
all he had done to impress Logan and me up until now would pale
beside what he was about to present.

Every girl dreams of a wonderful wedding reception, but to see
something like this, an extravaganza beyond my wildest imaginings,
suddenly made all my dark thoughts about Tony and his manipula-
tions disappear and made me realize how incredibly lucky I was. I did
have a great deal to be thankful for. To know that all this splendor, all
these well-dressed people in expensive cars were gathering because of
Logan and me filled me with an excitement almost impossible to contain.

Suddenly, stepping out of one of the sleek black limousines, I spotted Our Jane and Keith. I ran toward them, my arms outstretched.
Our Jane had grown into a stunning eighteen-year-old. Only an inch
or so shorter than I was, Jane had developed a fuller figure. Her fiery
red-gold hair flamed about her small oval face, highlighted by a pair of
turquoise eyes so soft and vulnerable they could turn the hardest, most
cynical man into a blubbering schoolboy.

"Heaven!" she cried. "Oh, Heaven, I'm so happy for you."

Keith looked his part as well. As tall as Pa, his auburn hair deep
and rich, his brown eyes bright, he looked tanned, rich, and quite the
Harvard man, dressed in a light white-and-blue-striped cotton sweater
and dark blue slacks.

"Congratulations, big sister." He grinned, then replaced his pipe in
his mouth. What a handsome, self-confident young man Keith had

become! I knew he was an excellent student, a member of the prestigious rowing team as well as the highly successful debate team.

Looking at them now, it was hard to believe that they had once clung to me like two little monkeys, their faces pale with shadowed hollows beneath their eyes. It was almost impossible to resurrect the memory of their thin, little voices crying, "Hev-lee, Hev-lee" as they begged for something more substantial to eat during those days after Pa had deserted us and Tom and I were left to be both mother and father to them.

Maybe it was good I had a hard time remembering all that, I thought. Maybe it was best. I wished I had just as hard a time recalling other troubled memories as well.

"I just knew you two would marry some day," Jane said. "It's all so romantic. You two were just made for each other. Heaven, I . . . I'm just so happy for you. I'll bet the whole town of Winnerow went crazy when they heard the news."

"How is Winnerow?" Keith asked, a slight smirk in his face. His memories weren't fond ones, so he had no burning desire to return, even for a short visit.

"It's about the same," Logan said, suddenly appearing at my side. He looked so handsome in his tuxedo, his hair combed back, a white carnation in his lapel.

"Logan Stonewall!" Our Jane shouted. "How handsome you look."

"And how grown up and beautiful you look, Our Jane," he replied.

"No one calls me that anymore," she said, blushing.

Logan turned to Keith. "You certainly have grown since I last saw you. Heaven keeps me up to date on all your college success. She's very proud of you. Proud of you both. We're going to need young men like you in Winnerow now. There will be some significant changes there soon."

"Oh?" Keith said.

"We'll talk about it later," Logan said. "Right now, I'm going to get some champagne and something to eat, okay, Heaven?"

I kissed him and he went off, leaving me to chat with Keith and Our Jane.

"What a wonderful party this is going to be!" Jane exclaimed. The music down by the pool had just begun and the guests were beginning to dance.

"We must catch up on everything, Our Jane . . . I mean Jane. It's going to be so hard for me to remember not to call you that," I said, hugging her once again.

"You can call me Our Jane if you like, Heaven. I'm just so happy to see you!" She clapped her hands together, like she used to as a little girl when she was excited. "Oh, Heaven, I can barely stand still. Do you mind if I wander around? I don't mean to go off so fast, but look at all those flower arrangements, the pool, and—"

"You kids run off and have a good time, the time of your lives. We'll catch up later," I said.

They walked away together arm in arm. I stood for a while, watching them laughing with each other, whispering in each other's ear, joking and giggling. They were still very close, sensitive to each other's feelings and moods. In my secret and putaway heart, I couldn't help being envious of their relationship. Once, Tom and I had similarly strong ties. Just seeing them together suddenly made me feel small and lonely.

Would I always feel an orphan? Would I never feel I truly belonged anywhere? But I had to scold myself. Look at all this that Tony had done for me. Perhaps it was Farthy after all to which I belonged.

My eyes searched for Logan. I wanted him to stand by my side, to put his arm through mine, to be my husband always with me at our wedding reception, but wherever I spied Logan, there was Tony, dragging him from business acquaintance to business acquaintance, gallantly introducing Logan to the whir and flash of Boston society.

Feeling a little sad, I left Logan with Tony and turned toward the pool patio. Tony hated rock and roll, so the band he hired played only classics and easy listening music. It didn't have the spirit of the Longchamps, but the melodies were gay and upbeat and created the right atmosphere. Guests were jitterbugging to "In the Mood." Other were sitting at the small tables, shaded by colorful umbrellas, eating, while others wandered about from group to group, exchanging gossip.

Tony had hired two dozen additional servants for the reception. Waiters and waitresses dressed in red and white uniforms circled about the grounds, carrying trays of champagne in long-stemmed glasses and silver and gold trays of hors d'oeuvres. At least four hundred people had arrived, all richly dressed, modeling the latest fashions, originals by Saint Laurent and Chanel, Pierre Cardin and Adolfo. The warm breeze carried their laughter and conversation over the manicured grounds.

Some of the people I had met before, although I really recalled few. Despite their attempts at individuality, there was a sameness in their style of conversation, in the way they greeted one another. After my second glass of champagne, I giggled at the idea that a small army of mannequins had become animated and escaped from the windows of the most elegant Boston shops.

Suddenly I spotted Tony whispering something into the bandleader's ear.

"Ladies and gentlemen," the band leader boomed into the microphone, "before we continue with our festivities, I have been asked to play a special number. Would you all turn your attention to our lovely bride and to your wonderful host, Mr. Tony Tatterton."

The bandleader lifted his baton and the orchestra began a rendition of "You Are the Sunshine of My Life." Tony walked across the dance floor to me and held out his hand.

"This dance, princess."

I took his hand and he pulled me to him gently.

"Happy?" Tony asked, his face against my hair.

"Oh, yes, yes. It's a wonderful party." And it was. I truly appreciated how much Tony was doing to make me feel I belonged here.

"I hope you're really happy, Heaven," Tony said. "I don't mean to do anything but please you."

"I'm happy, Tony. Thank you."

"Having all of this is meaningless unless you have someone you love with whom to share it. Will you share it with me, Heaven?"

I looked at Logan, laughing and waving at me as he made one new rich friend after another. I looked at Farthy, the grand house looming above the party, its windows filled with the reflection of blue sky and soft cotton white clouds.

"Yes, Tony," I said.

He kissed me on the cheek and hugged me to him tightly, too tightly. I inhaled the strong, sweet aroma of his aftershave and felt his strong fingers pressed against my back. His lips grazed my cheek again, coming very close to mine, and for a moment, only a moment, a chilling sense of fear knifed through my heart.

"It's all just beginning," he whispered. "Just beginning. I want to do so much more for you, Heaven. If you'll only let me."

I didn't respond. He was holding me so closely and tightly, I could feel his need to have me with him always, a need that made me feel claustrophobic, a need so great it frightened me.

Midway into the dance, others began to join in. When the song ended, Tony excused himself to mingle with the guests. I stood simply gaping at everything. My heart was pounding so hard in my ears that for a moment all other sound was drowned out. I didn't hear the laughter, the music, or the conversations. I felt as if I were alone on the vast grounds, the sea of blue sky above, the breeze whispering around me like a warning. It took me a few moments to realize that Logan was at my side.

"Are you all right?" he asked.

"What?"

"You look lost."

"Oh, yes." I laughed to cover my trepidations, the pressure of Tony's arms still lingering on my back. "I was just in a daze. This is so overwhelming." Just then Jane and Keith walked over and kissed me.

"You looked absolutely radiant out there," Jane said.

"You did look beautiful, Sis," Keith agreed.

Logan took me in his arms. "You and Tony did make a splendid couple on the dance floor. He's quite a dancer for an older man."

"I suppose," I said a little coldly, hoping that somehow Logan would sense that something was wrong. But he saw only what he wanted to see, his bride, the start of a new life, the promise of a perfect future.

"I almost forgot, they asked me to get you and go down to the stage by the pool," Logan said. "There's about to be a presentation."

"Presentation?"

He shrugged.

"I know just as little as you do," he said, smiling, but it was such a self-satisfied smile that I doubted him.

Tony stepped onto the stage and walked up to the microphone. His eyes roved over the crowd until he spied Logan and me strolling toward him.

"Ladies and gentlemen," he began, "a special toast to our bride and groom." He held his glass up. "To a bright and wonderful future—"

He suddenly stopped. The crowd began turning their heads, trying to follow his line of vision. Jillian was stepping out onto the dance floor. A wave of astonishment rippled through the large sea of guests. Jillian continued drifting toward the stage, Martha Goodman scurrying like a duck behind her.

Jillian was dressed in her wedding gown. She had always had a beautiful, slim, and graceful figure. Even in her state of madness, she had no trouble fitting into it as perfectly as she had the day of her marriage to Tony. Her golden hair, bleached to the point where it looked like a mop of straw, was brushed down the sides of her face and the back of her head in stiff strands that curled at the ends. There were two blotches of dark pink rouge on the crowns of her cheekbones, and her lipstick, now the color of dried blood, was just as caked as it had been the first day I saw her in her suite.

She stopped at the bottom step of the stage and turned to look at the crowd of gawkers.

"Thank you all for coming. Thank you," she said. "This is the happiest day of my life, the day I'm to marry Mr. Anthony Tatterton. I'm so happy so many of you chose to share it with me. Please, please enjoy yourselves."

For a moment no one moved or said anything. Then Martha whispered something in her ear.

"This is my wedding, this is *my special day,*" Jillian said, turning to Martha with a ferocious look. She brushed back a strand of her wild, strawlike hair. *"These people came to see me! They came to be witness to my wedding, to my everlasting devotion to Tony Tatterton . . .* and I know," she said, her voice almost a whisper now, "I know that his love for me will always remain true." All the strength suddenly drained from her posture and she had to lean on Martha as on a crutch.

"Miss Jillian," Martha said tenderly, leading her back to her seat.

The crowd was dumbstruck. Tony regained his composure and stepped back up to the microphone as though nothing peculiar at all had occurred.

"Ladies and gentlemen," he began again, "a toast to Mr. and Mrs. Logan Stonewall."

"Hear hear," the men in the crowd chorused, trying to hide their embarrassment, and over four hundred people drank to our happiness and good health.

"Heaven, Logan, I wish you long life and happiness and as a token of that wish, I present you with this."

He raised his free hand to signal and the audience and Logan and I all looked toward where he pointed: a brand-new silver Rolls-Royce with ribbons wrapped around appeared. The crowd uttered one unilateral sigh of appreciation as it drove toward us. I looked up at Tony and saw the determination on his face.

There was no limit to what he would do to win my heart and devotion, I thought. His love for me was both ruthless and overwhelming. Once again that pang of fear I had felt on the dance floor returned. For a moment my handsome secret father looked like the Devil incarnate. I felt helpless before such power and wealth, such unyielding love.

I turned to Logan to see his reaction. His face was filled with happiness, his cheeks crimson, his eyes lit, his mouth opened in an expression of utter awe. He squeezed my hand, then dropped it and stepped forward to admire Tony's gleaming, extraordinary gift. I followed behind. Logan turned to me, his face so filled with happiness he nearly brought me to tears.

"Oh, Heaven," he said, "I don't think it's possible to be any happier than I am at this moment."

"I hope so, Logan," I said. "I hope so," His face was beaming so. How easy he was to please and make happy, I thought. His happiness was never clouded by dark suspicions as mine was. How I needed a man like him. I wanted to cuddle in his arms forever.

"Oh, Logan, I love you. Love me forever and ever like you do now," I pleaded as I fell into his arms.

"I will. I promise," he said.

When we kissed we were almost oblivious to everyone and everything around us. Then the crowd of well-wishers cheered again and the party continued. Logan and his new young companions inspected the Rolls-Royce and I turned to thank Tony as the music was begun again. Before he reached me though, Jillian got up from her seat and ran to him.

"Oh, Tony," she cried, "you do love me! Wasn't it a wonderful ceremony."

People stopped to stare and listen.

"Yes, Jillian." He put his arm around her to turn her back to her table. She leaned back and, looking over her shoulder, called to everyone nearby.

"Enjoy yourselves," she commanded. "Please, everyone, continue to enjoy yourselves."

I watched as Tony seated Jillian again and had Martha Goodman bring her something to eat. Then he started toward me. I couldn't help feeling sorry for Jillian, for the way people were looking at her and whispering.

"Why did you permit this to happen?" I demanded as soon as he was close to me and I could direct him to a place where we couldn't be overheard. "Don't you find it embarrassing?"

"Embarrassing?" He looked back in Jillian's direction as if he, himself, were back in time and hadn't realized what was going on in the present. "Yes, it's embarrassing, but it's more tragic to me than embarrassing."

"Then why permit her to come out here like that? In front of all these people. Most are surely laughing at her."

"She doesn't see it that way," he said, his face approximating a smile. I couldn't understand it. "In her eyes, mad eyes, she sees them all as having a good time at her wedding reception."

"But . . ."

"But what?" he said, his lips compressing into a tight thin line. "Whose embarrassment are you worried about, hers or yours? Should

I shut her up in her suite like some crazed animal? Should I let her
pine away within four walls? Or let her go crashing down the deep dry
well of her memories until she finds herself on the bottom, alone, in
the dark, forgotten?

"Don't you see," he said, his eyes moving off me and in the direction of the house, "I can't bear the thought of her shut away in some
institution.

"She was once very beautiful and very precious to me," he added,
turning back in Jillian's direction. "Like a fine, hand-painted piece of
china. Oh, she was terrified of getting older, of not being desirable and
beautiful, and I'm sure the realization that she couldn't prevent it
contributed to the way she is today, but don't you see?" he said, taking
hold of both my arms just under the elbows . . . "In a strangely
beautiful way, she has it . . . eternal youth and beauty. Her madness
has given it to her.

"So," he said, releasing me and taking a deep breath as he stood up
straight again, "I think we'll tolerate the embarrassment and put up
with the snickers. You can make that kind of sacrifice, can't you,
Heaven? You can do something totally unselfish, I'm sure. When you
want to," he added and started away.

"Tony . . ."

"Yes?" He waited. I looked back at Jillian seated comfortably by a
table, smiling and nodding at people, holding her fork like a toothpick
and pecking on her platter of food like a bird.

"What if she sees me?"

"What of it?" He smiled. "She'll just see you as Leigh, as young as
she was the day Jillian and I were married. She was twelve and she
wore a long pink bridesmaid's dress and carried a bouquet of sweetheart roses. I'll never forget how beautiful she looked that day." He
tilted his head with the reverie and then his eyes blinked and he looked
at me. "And you look just as beautiful today," he said and walked off
to return to Jillian.

I gave thought to what he had said and how he had said it. Tony
obviously still had a strong love for Jillian. Or was it something else?

The sad sight of Martha Goodman leading the grinning spectacle of
Jillian back into her room with its glassless mirror and timeless memories made me both sad and frightened.

"It's time to cut the cake." Logan came up and led me to the cake,
which was placed on a table at the center of the stage. It was a fairy-
tale cake, a five-tiered white confection bedecked with garlands and
flowers. It was almost as tall as I was. Beaming, Logan took my hand
and, holding the knife together, we cut a slice from the bottom tier of

the cake. As he opened his mouth and I popped in a small piece of cake, I couldn't help but remember that fantastic sundae he had made for me the day he had asked me to marry him. Our cake was a fantastic Tatterton creation, but I would always think of Logan's magical rainbow castle as my true wedding cake.

After everyone had been served cake and ice cream, and the waiters had made their way between tables bearing more champagne and cognacs and brandies and cordials, the reception began to wind to a close. Just as I was beginning to feel the exhaustion of the celebration weighing on me, I saw Keith and Our Jane wending their way over to my table.

"Heaven," Our Jane said, leaning over and hugging me, "Keith and I have to be going. I'll miss you so."

"You'll write me soon?" I asked.

"Every week."

I hugged Keith and watched them tread across the lawn together, arm in arm. Logan kissed me on the neck.

"You really love them, don't you?"

I melted into his arms. "Let's go up to our room, Logan, I'm so very tired."

"But everything's been moved into the new suite," he said.

"What? When?"

"While we were out here. I thought I'd surprise you. Is that all right?" I really didn't like the idea of him doing it without me, but I saw how important it was to him to surprise me.

"It's all right. Yes, it's all right." I sighed.

"What about the rest of our honeymoon, Heaven? Can we spend it here?" He seized my hand in his and pleaded with his sapphire eyes.

"Is that what you really want to do, Logan?"

"Yes, very much."

"All right, then," I said reluctantly. "Can we go up now? I feel as though I'm about to collapse from all this excitement."

"I'll be with you in a while," he said. "There are a few more people I want to say good-bye to." He kissed me and then went off to mingle in the dwindling crowd. I caught sight of Tony sitting like a king in a lawn chair, some of his business associates around him. He waved and smiled as he saw me head toward the house.

I met Martha Goodman in the upstairs corridor just coming out of Jillian's suite.

"How is she?" I asked.

"As happy as a button," she said. "Probably as happy as you are," she added, shaking her head.

Probably happier, I thought, but I didn't say it. Instead, I went on to our new suite.

Tony was true to his word during what remained of Logan's and my honeymoon week—he didn't discuss any business with him and, in fact, he was barely around. He was in New York for three days on business and had a number of meetings with his financial advisers in Boston, arranging for, I was later to find out, the establishment of a Tatterton Toy Factory in Winnerow. With Jillian cloistered in her suite, Logan and I really did have most of Farthy to ourselves.

We began each morning with breakfast in bed, after which we either went down to the beach or had the limo take us into Boston to shop, eat in fine restaurants, or go to shows. In the middle of the week Logan arranged for us to go horseback riding.

As Logan and I went to the stables to mount our horses, I couldn't help but remember that day. It was the day Troy and I had made love for the first time. But Logan didn't sense my reverie. We went down to the beach to ride by the ocean, which was a very beautiful and romantic thing to do. We brought a picnic lunch along, too, and spread out a blanket on the beach in a very private inlet Logan had discovered during his explorations. Making love to him with the sound of the ocean in my ears forced away all my painful romantic memories, and for a time I felt renewed and hopeful. Perhaps this decision to honeymoon at Farthy was a good one after all, I thought.

The constant pace of romantic and interesting activities Logan arranged during our honeymoon week and the devotion and love he demonstrated convinced me to close the lid on the trunk of fears stored in my conscience. The nagging feelings of dread that plagued me like a dull toothache, the worries about Logan becoming vice-president of Tatterton Toys and our moving into Farthy, I pushed aside. By the end of the week, when Tony had returned from his business dealings and Logan and I were preparing to drive back to Winnerow to get the rest of our things and to announce our new plans to his parents, we were both tanned, rested, and happy.

"You both look wonderful," he told us.

"I hope we honeymoon forever at Farthy," Logan replied, eyeing me with such obvious romance, I had to blush.

Tony grinned. "Keep every day a honeymoon, eh, Logan? That's the way to keep a marriage happy. But now we have a bit of work to do." How eager Tony was to claim Logan's attention for business again. "Heaven, both Logan and I decided last week that you should

choose the location for the new factory in Winnerow. Logan is autho-
rized to make a sizable offer for the property."

"Oh, Tony," I said. "I don't know. That's an enormous responsibility. What if I make the wrong decision?"

"You won't. You can't," he said. "We all know it's in you now to do
only what is best for Winnerow and for Tatterton Toys."

"I'll give you some suggestions about what to look for," Logan said.

"Oh? And since when do you have such expertise, Logan Stonewall?" I asked. Tony laughed.

"Well . . ." Logan, blushing, looked to Tony. "Tony has filled me
in on what to look for."

"That's another thing," I said.

"I'll never have to fear a coup d'état in this business," Tony said.
"Logan, Heaven will always keep you modest and aware of your limi-
tations."

"Don't I know it," Logan said, smiling like a boy. This time Tony
and I laughed together.

Logan and I packed only what we needed for the short stay in
Winnerow and set out in our new Rolls-Royce. As we drove down the
long, winding drive and out the main gate of Farthinggale Manor,
Logan looked into the rearview mirror and smiled as though he were
looking back at another woman he loved, one he knew he would soon
return to and embrace. Once again my heart fluttered in my chest as
though a butterfly had emerged from its cocoon within it. I couldn't
help it; I felt jealous of the power and beauty of Farthy.

"I'm glad we spent our honeymoon there," Logan said, "because to
us, Farthinggale will always be a place of love."

He looked at me and smiled, his face filled with such optimism, I
thought there might be enough for both of us. He reached out to take
my hand and caught my fingers greedily into his.

I tightened my grip on his fingers and he looked at me lovingly.

"You are happy, Heaven?"

"Yes, Logan. I'm very happy."

"I'm glad," he said, "because from now on, that's all that's going to
matter to me."

I prayed that he would always feel that way.

It was strange driving into Winnerow after the week we had spent
at Farthy. I felt as though I had moved from one dream existence into
another and back again. We had decided that we would spend our
time here in my cabin and would keep it as a place for us to use
whenever Logan or both of us had to return to Winnerow on business.

However, when we entered Winnerow, we went directly to his parents' home so that Logan could announce his new plans.

It was the dinner hour when we arrived, and when Logan opened the door to his parents' home, calling, "Mom, Dad, Heaven and I are back!" his mother rushed to the door to greet us, a flower-print apron tied around her dress, her hands still dredged with flour. "Why, Logan, Heaven," she declared, "you're not due back for a week." A frown wrinkled her brow. "I hope everything is all right?" She looked at Logan, anticipating news.

"All right? It's far better than all right. Mom! You are now looking at the executive vice-president of marketing and research of Tatterton Toys. And at the beautiful director of the board of the about-to-be-constructed local Tatterton Toys Willies Factory." Truly Logan seemed like a kid again, playing king of the mountain.

"I can't believe it." His mother's face fell. She wiped her hands on her apron, obviously trying to hide her shock and disappointment. Then she looked up again. "I must say I'm truly astonished. But what about the pharmacy?"

"Mom! This is the opportunity of a lifetime. Go get Dad and I'll tell you both all about it. I just know you're going to be thrilled for us, for all of Winnerow!"

At first Logan's dad was visibly upset. "Son, I was so looking forward to us being in business together," he said.

But when Logan described the salary he would be making and then described the proposed Tatterton Toy Factory and its economic potential for Winnerow, his parents changed their reaction. In fact, I thought his mother looked at me with new eyes. Suddenly she realized that her son was going to be far better off than he could ever have been if he had married one of the town girls and settled in Winnerow.

However, I sensed that her new warm feelings for me were not deep ones. She still wasn't impressed with me; she was impressed with the power and the wealth behind me. I couldn't blame her all that much for it. From what I had seen of the world during my short and troubled existence, her reactions were typical of most people.

Before we left for the cabin, I paid a visit to Mr. Meeks, the school principal, and told him of my intention to resign my teaching position. "The children will miss you," he said. "Especially the hill people's children. But perhaps you are right; perhaps you will be doing even greater things for them by bringing Tatterton Toys here and providing employment and opportunity. Goodness knows, there's not very much of that around here for them now. Of course, I wish you the best of luck."

I thanked him and then Logan and I drove to the cabin. No matter where I had been or how long I had stayed away, I knew the cabin would always be the same when I returned. Even though it was modernized, the woods around it wore the eternal face of the nature I had known as a child. I heard the same birds, saw the same crooked trees, walked through the same deep, cool shadows, heard the same silvery sounds of the rambling brook. This would forever remain sacred to me.

I made Logan a fine supper that first night in the cabin. We sat on the porch like Granny and Grandpa and discussed our plans for the future until we both grew tired enough to fall asleep in each other's arms. In the morning, after breakfast, Logan went back into Winnerow to tie up some business ends and I drove up and down the side roads, searching for what would be a perfect location for the Tatterton Toy Factory. Logan told me to look for a place that had access to transportation, a place that was close enough to the village so that the employees could easily spend their money there. Once the business interests in the town realized the benefits the factory would bring, there would be no opposition to it, he explained. I knew he was merely repeating Tony's instructions.

I found the perfect location rather quickly. It was a flat piece of land that provided a wonderful view of the mountains, yet was merely a mile or so from the downtown area. Anyone would be inspired working here, I thought. I rushed back to Winnerow to meet Logan and tell him, but his father said he had gone back to the cabin to find some papers he had left in a suitcase. I had unpacked the suitcases and organized everything on shelves and in drawers. Afraid that he wouldn't find what he was searching for, I decided not to wait for him to return. I drove back to the cabin myself.

As soon as I made the turn to approach it, I slowed down. Fanny's car was parked beside Logan's. I had decided not to call or see her until I had finished my business here, but she had obviously heard we had arrived and had come searching for us.

I parked my car and got out slowly. Before I reached the front door, I heard Logan's strange pleas.

"Please, Fanny, you can't parade about like that. Now do what you have to do and go. Please don't cause any problems for us. Please."

I heard Fanny's familiar tantalizing laugh and pulled open the front door.

There she stood near the bathroom, a towel wrapped around her naked hips, her arms folded over her bare bosom. Her hair was wild. She looked like some mythical sex creature, an enchantress tempting him to be unfaithful while his marriage was still in its infant stages. For a moment she stared at me with those dark eyes, her smile frozen on her face. But when she saw the look on my face, she only laughed.

"Why, Heaven, goodness sakes, ya can scare the devil out of a lost and lustful preacher with a look like that."

"Never mind my look. What are you doing standing here half naked?" I looked at Logan.

"She came claiming her plumbing broke and she wanted to take a shower in the cabin. Claimed she didn't know we were here."

"Well, I didn't, Heaven. You don't even have the courtesy to call ta tell me you're in town. How's I ta know you and Logan's livin' here?"

"We're not living here; we're just here for a day or two and then we're returning to Farthinggale Manor to live. But that doesn't explain why you're standing like that in front of my husband."

"I was only comin' out ta get a towel. I realized I forgot it and didn't want to embarrass Logan none by askin' him to bring one inta me."

"Didn't want to embarrass him? What do you suppose you're doing right now?"

"He don't look embarrassed," she said, smiling at Logan.

"Fanny!" I stepped toward her. "Get in that bathroom and take your shower properly."

"Sure, Heaven honey. Be only a few moments. Then we kin all have a nice little chat."

She reached down to open the bathroom door, exposing herself as she did so. After she went in, Logan shook his head and sat down. His face was flushed.

"Glad you came," he said. "She was getting impossible."

"You shouldn't have let her in."

"I couldn't keep her out of the cabin, Heaven. How was I supposed to do that?"

He was right; it was wrong to place any blame on him. Fanny was Fanny. She was the way she always was. She always had a need to take from me anything I really wanted for myself. This was just like the time years ago when Logan was waiting for me by the riverbank and Fanny showed up before I did and took off her dress and taunted him to catch her. Then he was just as embarrassed and as upset as he looked right now. He told me he didn't want a girl as loose and with as little inhibitions as Fanny. He told me I was his type. He liked his girls shy, beautiful, and sweet.

"You're right," I said. "No one but Fanny can be blamed for the things Fanny does. Your father told me you came up here looking for some papers."

"Yes, I wanted to close that checking account. I found where you put them in the dresser drawer and was actually just about to leave when Fanny showed up."

"I found a wonderful location for the factory, Logan. I want to take you to it later today."

"Fine."

"Why don't you take your papers down to the bank and I'll meet you at the drugstore in an hour. I'll stay here and see Fanny," I said. He looked back at the bathroom and nodded.

"Okay." He kissed me and then left. I waited for Fanny on the porch.

"Where's Logan?" she asked as soon as she emerged. She was wearing a bright red peasant dress, the top pulled down as far as it could be off her shoulders. It didn't surprise me that she wasn't wearing a bra and that half her bosom was revealed. I had to admit that Fanny was very attractive. Despite her wild life, she always had a rich complexion and the combination of her jet black hair and dark blue eyes made for a stunning appearance. "He's finishing off some business in town. What you did in there was horrible, Fanny," I said. I wouldn't let her put me off my purpose. "You're not a teenager anymore. Those kind of antics can't be excused. Logan is my husband now and you are not to behave like that in front of him again."

"Well, now," she said, her hands on her hips, her head cocked to the side, "I suppose ya think ya jus' gonna take ole Logan outta the Willies and make him one of ya Beantown dandies."

"He's not going to do anything he doesn't want to do."

She stared at me a moment, the anger in her face turning into sorrow. Only Fanny could change emotions instantly, the way you might turn faucets on a sink.

"Sure. Ya two is gonna go live high on the hog and leave me here with the pigs as usual."

"You decided to come back here to live, Fanny. You bought that house with the money from your ex-husband."

"But I thought I was gonna get my baby back. I thought ya was gonna help me do it, Heaven. Instead, that lowdown Reverend and his fallow wife still got her. What have I got? I don't have a family; I don't have respect. Why, ya didn't even invite me ta the reception at Farthy, but ya invited Keith and Jane jus' cause they're goin' ta some fancy college and look and dress like yer people."

"They're not my people," I said, but I realized she was right. I didn't want her at that party; I didn't want to risk the embarrassment, knowing the kinds of things she might say and do to deliberately humiliate me.

"I wanna come live at Farthy, too, then," she whined. "Why shouldn't I meet all those rich, frustrated old men and find me a sugar daddy like you did, Heaven."

"I didn't find any sugar daddy, Fanny." I shook my head. It was so frustrating talking to her sometimes. "And I can't just invite you to come live at Farthy so you can hunt for a rich man to marry."

"Ya always tried ta leave me behind. Ya still owe me, Heaven Leigh Casteel. Yeah, Casteel. I don't care what name ya take, ya still Heaven Leigh Casteel, a girl from the Willies, jus' like me, ya hear? When Ma left us, ya promised ta look after me and care for me, but ya didn't stop Pa from sellin' me ta that lustful Reverend, and when I asked ya ta help me get back ma baby, ya didn't do it. All ya had to do was offa him more money, but ya didn't do it. Ya didn't do it!"

"You're not the motherly type, Fanny. You'll never be."

"Is that so? Don't be so sure 'bout me, Heaven. Don' go around bein' so sure 'bout everyone else but yerself."

"I'm not sure about myself, Fanny. But we can never see ourselves as well as others can see us and you just don't want to see yourself for what you are. I'm sorry to have to say that, but it's true. Now, I have some business to tend to in Winnerow and then—"

"You jus' don' want me ta be near Logan. That's it, isn't it? Ya don' trust him."

"I have full confidence in my husband, Fanny. But you're right. I'm not happy to see you near him just because of the kind of thing you pulled in the cabin. I was hoping that all the things that have happened to you in your life would have helped you grow up some, but I see you still have a ways to go."

"Is that so? Well, let me tell you somethin', Miss Prim and Proper. Logan was enjoyin' ma little show up until ya drove up. I asked him ta get me the towel and he told me ta come out and get it myself. He changed his tune when he heard yer car."

"That's a lie, a terrible lie!" I yelled at her. Fanny always knew how to send me into a rage. "You're just saying these things now to hurt me."

She shrugged.

"Believe what ya want, but if ya believe in any man, yer a bigger fool than I think ya are, Heaven, and yer the one's got growin' up ta do." She pointed her finger at me and then put her hands on her hips and stood up straight and arrogant. I stared at her a moment.

"I have to go now," I said. "I can't waste any more time."

"Can't ya?" She laughed. I started toward my car. "Ya jus' can't go off and live in yer castle and leave me behind, Heaven. I ain't gonna fade into the Willies like ya'd like me ta. You and me ain't finished yet."

"I said I have to go." I hurried into my car and started the engine.

"We ain't finished yet," she called, coming down toward the car. I started away, watching her in my rearview mirror.

Despite her threats and her insinuations, I couldn't help but feel sorry for her. Jealousy was a sickness for her. I imagine it made her suffer a great deal. Right from the beginning, when Logan and I were sweethearts, she tried to take him from me, yet when Logan was no longer with me, she didn't pursue him. She didn't want him as long as I didn't have him.

How she must suffer in my shadow, I thought. Would she ever love a man for himself and want him not because she thought he was someone I wanted or would want, but because he was someone who loved her and whom she loved truly, honestly? Perhaps Fanny wasn't capable of that kind of love. Maybe that was what she inherited from our hard life in the Willies.

❧ FIVE ❧
Ghosts

IN A PRETTY GLADE IN THE FOREST, A CLEARING WHERE BRIGHT wildflowers grew, I found the perfect site for the Tatterton Toy Factory. I had remembered the place because, when Tom and I were children, we would sometimes walk by it after school and lie in the sun sharing our dreams. "Heaven," Tom would say, "if I ever make enough money, I'm going to build us a home here, with the biggest picture window you ever saw."

Logan loved the site. "It will be perfect for the new factory," he said, "with its proximity to power lines and roadways." I watched him step out the land and laughed to myself as he framed the building in his mind's eye by holding up his hands, the tip of his thumbs pressed against each other, to form the foundation of this imaginary building. Suddenly he had become a full-fledged entrepreneur, an overnight corporate executive. I didn't let him see me laugh because I knew how seriously he was taking himself. He wrote down some figures on a pad, drew a rough map of the site, and then drove us back into Winnerow to see a local attorney, Barton Wilcox.

There was no better way to spread the news of the upcoming economic investment in Winnerow than to start the negotiations for land. Before Logan and I left Mr. Wilcox's office I made sure I'd told a couple of secretaries, who in turn told their friends, and soon the Winnerow phone lines were buzzing with interest and excitement. Logan called Tony to tell him about the site and Tony wired a large sum of money into an account in the Winnerow National Bank. It was then that Logan felt a real sense of power and authority, for he had control over all that money. Tony couldn't have expressed his confidence in him and won his loyalty forever in any better way.

A meeting was set up in Barton Wilcox's office between Logan and the owner of the land, who practically swooned when Logan made his initial offer. Such sums of money rarely, if ever, were discussed in relation to anything in Winnerow. After a quick conference, Logan added an additional five thousand dollars to sweeten the deal and the negotiations were concluded. We had our factory site.

"Tony's going to be very happy with me!" Logan exclaimed afterward. He straightened his posture, standing tall and proud and with a flourish fluffed the monogrammed handkerchief in his breast pocket. "I think I fit into all this, Heaven. I really do. I have a real feel for it." He turned to me and smiled. "This is going to be wonderful," he said, taking my hand into his. "Together we are going to build the best dream this town has ever known. We're going to fill people with pride for Winnerow and put it on the map. And think of all the people we will help, people from the Willies who had no future and no hope at all before this."

I smiled at him. He was so excited. Sometimes I thought he could have enough excitement for both of us.

"You made a great decision when you decided we should live at Farthy and do this, Heaven. Really."

"I hope so, Logan." Despite his optimism, I couldn't help trembling every time I thought about our living at Farthy. The Willies still called to me. I almost felt as though I truly belonged there, despite my true heritage, that something was wrong with letting Tony change my dream. But I wasn't going to dwell on my fears. I was going to make this my dream, not Tony's. "We have a lot to do yet. What about the construction of the building?"

"Tony's bringing us to see an architect in Boston. He wants your input on that, as well as mine. Says you and I should best know what the people of Winnerow want and need. But after the factory is designed, we will use only local labor and buy materials locally. Good business sense."

"And the artisans?" I asked.

"I'll be back a number of times to search the hills for people with natural abilities. Of course, there will be a number of other jobs associated with the enterprise; there will be opportunities for many people. Just the way you envisioned, Heaven."

"I'm glad, Logan," I said. We drove back to the cabin so I could pack the rest of the things I wanted to have with me at Farthy, and Logan returned to his parents' house to gather up some of his things. At his parents' request we had dinner at their house and spent the night there. In the morning we started back to Farthinggale, both of us feeling our trip to Winnerow had been very successful. The only thing that left a bitter taste in my mouth was Fanny's lewd display. I expected it would fade away and be placed on the shelf on my memory, alongside other painful and unhappy moments. Let it stay there, I thought, and forever gather dust.

Tony was waiting for us at Farthy when we arrived. He sent the servants out to get our things and he, Logan, and I went into his office to discuss our trip and the plans for the factory.

"Logan and I will fly back to Winnerow the day after tomorrow with the architect," he said after hearing all the details. "Then, in about a week or so, we'll go over the first draft specs together. I imagine a good many of the local people got wind of our project."

"Oh, yes," Logan said. "News travels fast in small towns like Winnerow. My own parents probably spread most of it."

"I take it then they were happy with your decision to become part of Tatterton Toys."

"Very," Logan said. Tony turned to me, a self-satisfied expression on his face. How could Logan's parents not have been happy? I thought. Look how much Tony had showered on him already.

"You did very well, Logan. Very well. I think you're going to work in wonderfully here," Tony said. Logan was absolutely ecstatic. He sat back, his head held arrogantly high. "Tomorrow, let me take you into Boston to my tailor and get you fitted for some decent suits. A man with your responsibilities has to look the part."

"That sounds neat, thank you," Logan said and looked to me for my agreement. I wasn't sure I liked what Tony was doing. In a way he was making Logan over into his own image, and Logan, so infatuated with Tony and with himself, too, by now, was easy clay to ply and mold.

"How's Jillian?" I asked, eager to change the subject.

"The same," Tony said quickly.

"I'll stop in to see her. You two probably have more to discuss, but I'm going up for a rest."

"You all right, Heaven honey?" Logan asked. He heard the irritation in my voice.

"Yes, Logan. I'm just tired from the trip. Don't worry about me."

I left him in Tony's hands and went upstairs, stopping first at Jillian's suite. I found that Martha Goodman was not her usual unflappable self. I saw immediately that she was trouble and agitated.

"I'm so glad you've returned, Mrs. Stonewall," she said quickly, almost secretively.

"What's wrong, Martha?" Martha looked back at Jillian's closed bedroom door as if to be sure she wasn't there watching and listening to what she was about to say.

"She's been quite disturbed these past few days, quite different."

"How so?" I hesitated before opening Jillian's bedroom door.

"Well, you know how she's been living in the past, imagining herself young and beautiful again, talking about people long gone and making references to events that have long since passed."

"Yes?"

"She's hasn't been doing that these past few days and she hasn't made one attempt to put makeup on her face."

"But Tony . . . Mr. Tatterton just told me she was no different from what she was before we left for Winnerow."

"I'm afraid he hasn't really been here since you left, Mrs. Stonewall. He was out of town for three days and not here much when he was in town."

"Well, what does she do, then, if she doesn't act like she's in the past?"

"It's more frightening . . . she says the dead are coming back."

"Because she thought I was my mother, Martha," I said, smiling. "It's my hair color. I'm thinking of going back to my natural color and—"

"Yes, Mrs. Stonewall," Martha said, interrupting. "But before this, she was always in the same time period. She looked at you and saw you as your mother, but she saw herself as she was when your mother was alive. She was back in the past with you. Now she's in the present, but she swears the people who died in the past have returned. I can't explain it well, I know, but wait until you talk to her. She's very calm, very sensible, but terrified, like someone who has really seen a ghost. She really is somewhat in shock. I must say, Mrs. Stonewall, this is the first time I can remember being unnerved about taking care of your grandmother."

"But Martha—"

"And Mr. Rye Whiskey doesn't help things much, talking about ghosts and spirits all the time. All the servants are a little spooked." She looked down as if ashamed.

"I can see there's more, Martha," I said quickly. "Go on, tell me the rest of it."

"It's just silly, Mrs. Stonewall. I know it's because of all that's going on around me."

"What is it, Martha? Please, don't be afraid to tell me."

"Well, I woke up late the other night and . . ."

"Yes?"

"I heard music, piano music."

I stared at her, my body growing so cold, I thought I had lost all feeling in it. For a moment I couldn't speak.

"You must have been imagining it," I said, practically whispering.

"I know, Mrs. Stonewall. I didn't even mention it to anyone before now. But don't you see, it's all part of what's been happening to your grandmother. I don't like it. She looks at me differently and she spends hours staring out the window, looking toward the maze."

"The maze!"

Martha nodded slowly.

"That's what she's doing right now," she said and stepped back. I looked at the bedroom door and then back at her. The woman looked sincerely disturbed. How could Tony not realize what was happening here? Was he so deliberately oblivious to it? He was about to lose the services of Martha Goodman.

"Perhaps if I talk to her, Martha. I'll get her to come to her senses."

"Oh, I hope so, Mrs. Stonewall, because in my opinion it might just be better for her to be somewhere where she can get more professional assistance."

I turned the handle on the bedroom door slowly, then entered Jillian's bedroom. She was right where Martha said she would be—sitting by the window, staring out toward the maze.

The heavy scent of her jasmine perfume reached me immediately and I thought, yes, yes, that was what was so different about her in her madness. She spent hours before an empty mirror frame overdoing make-up, but she hadn't put on her favorite perfume, the scent I remembered so well. Now she had.

Unlike the other times I had seen her, she wasn't wearing one of her fancy nightgowns. She sat calmly, dressed in a black chiffon blouse and a black skirt. When she heard me and turned my way, she wasn't wearing any makeup at all, and her hair, although still overbleached, was brushed down rather neatly, the sides pinned back.

"So," she said. "You, too, have returned." She followed it with an efficient little laugh.

"Jillian . . ."

"From that hillbilly town. Only something like this would bring you back, I know. You ran out of here, gave all this up, to become a teacher in a backward school. And now you're sorry, sorry for what you lost."

She knew who I was! She wasn't looking at me and thinking she was looking at my mother. She turned back to the window to stare out.

Martha was right—she was very different. The tone of her voice was different; the look in her eyes was different. Just the way she sat there and held herself was different. Gone was the flightiness, the mad laughter, the strange ethereal way she moved her hands and flittered about her room. It was as though she had been given shock treatment and had come crashing back into reality.

"What are you looking for, Jillian? Why do you sit at the window all day and stare out at the maze?"

She spun around. Two small bright tears shone in the corners of her cornflower-blue eyes, eyes so much like my own they made me shudder.

"Everyone hates me," she said. "Everyone's turned against me, blaming me for all the bad things." She brought her lace handkerchief to her face and delicately touched her eyes. This was the Jillian I knew, acting, performing, playing her emotions like a musician would play an instrument. Her song was "Pity me, poor me. Poor Jillian."

I sighed. "Why does everyone hate you, Jillian? What have you done?" I asked in a tired voice.

"They said I chased your mother from this house. The servants used to whisper. Oh, I knew what they said. I used to hear them. They said I was too cold to Tony, living and sleeping apart from him, not permitting him to make love to me as often as he would have liked just so I could protect my youth and beauty. I wouldn't become worn and tired just to satisfy a man's hunger for sexual satisfaction, his need to prove his masculinity."

"Why should the servants have cared?" I asked thinking that it might be best to humor her. She smiled, but so coldly I felt the chill overtake me.

"Why do you think? They adored Tony. They still do. They think he's some sort of God walking around here. He can't be blamed for anything; nothing's his fault. When your mother threw herself at him and he didn't reject her, they thought it was because of the way I treated him. Don't you see? Everything's my fault. Everything. Even Troy's death."

"Troy's death!" I stepped closer to her.

"Yes, Troy's death. For what horse did he choose to ride? As though it were my fault that he chose it."

"Abdulla Bar," I said, repeating lines memorized ages ago.

"Abdulla Bar." She nodded. "My horse, the horse no one but I could ride. And so, it was my fault. Don't you see? My fault," she repeated, waving her handkerchief at me and turning back to the window. "And now they're all coming back to haunt me, to punish me."

"Jillian," I said, realizing now what she meant. "That's silly; that's foolish. Ghosts and spirits don't exist, they're merely the creations of uneducated and superstitious minds. People like Rye Whiskey rattle off such silly stories to entertain themselves. There's nothing out there, nothing but reality, hard and true. Please," I said, going to her and taking her hand into mine. She looked at me and I knelt beside her and looked into those troubled blue eyes, willing with all my might that she would hear and see me and understand, willing with all my might that I could be significant in her eyes, that for once I could be her granddaughter and we could share our deepest feelings with each other. "Please. Don't torment yourself. You're suffering enough as it is."

Suddenly she smiled and with her free hand she stroked my hair. It was the first time she had ever really touched me with any sign of affection.

"Thank you, Heaven. Thank you for caring. But," she said, turning away, "it's too late, too late."

"Jillian. Jillian," I repeated. "Grandmother." She didn't turn back. She was locked in a gaze now, locked in her maddening stare. I stood up and looked out the window, too, down at the maze.

A mist had blown in from the ocean. It looked as though the clouds had fallen from the sky to swallow up the secret and dark passageways. The sky was becoming overcast quickly. We were soon to have a summer thunderstorm. The darkness seemed appropriate.

I stood there by the window with my mentally tormented maternal grandmother and looked out at a continually evolving world below as if I, too, expected the spirits she thought were haunting her to come forth. It wasn't until Martha came to the door to see what had transpired that I realized how long I had been standing there, staring. I had been holding Jillian's hand the whole time. When I released her, she put her hand on her lap, and I went to Martha.

"You're right," I said in a low voice. "She is quite different." Martha nodded softly and looked at her, the sadness making her eyes heavy.

"I think she might become catatonic eventually, Mrs. Stonewall."

"I agree, Martha. I'll have to get Mr. Tatterton to send for her doctor."

"Oh, I'm glad you agree, Mrs. Stonewall," Martha said. "I mentioned the changes to Mr. Tatterton just a few hours ago and he said he would stop by, but he hasn't yet."

"He will. I'll see to it," I assured her.

"Thank you," Martha said. We both turned and looked at Jillian once more. She hadn't moved an eyelash.

"Guilt is one of the most difficult weights for the mind to endure," I said, almost in a whisper, more for myself than for Martha, but she overheard and quickly agreed.

I left the suite and rushed to ours. I didn't want any of the servants to see the tears of terror that had come into my own eyes. I knew that the things that Jillian had said, the things she felt people blamed her for and she had obviously come to blame herself for, had always been somewhere at the bottom of her thoughts, seemingly asleep, but merely waiting for the opportunity to rise and wield their power of destruction on the rest of her mind.

The same thing was true for me. Up until now I had been relatively successful in keeping those thoughts buried, but after seeing and hearing Jillian, I couldn't help but wonder when they would rise to haunt me, when I, like Jillian, would see a ghost as well . . . Troy's ghost. I should have done more to keep him from despair. Surely I shouldn't have left him and gone traveling about while he lingered here at Farthy, living in that cottage that had been our love nest, the site of so many happy hours for us.

How many nights had he lain awake thinking of me in that cottage, believing I had put him aside, believing I had accepted our fate? I knew how sensitive and prone to despair he could be. How easy it was for him to suffer, and yet I left him to endure the greatest pain of all . . . a broken heart. I left him without hope, thinking that all the dark thoughts he had had his whole life were meant to be.

Looking into Jillian's eyes, seeing the pain that made those orbs its new home, I felt the agony she felt. I fled from those reminders as much as I fled from her madness. Would guilt twist and torment me as it had her, until I, too, became mad and lived alone with my troubled thoughts?

Oh, Troy, Troy, surely you must have known you were the last person in the world I would want to harm.

But I had to drive the black thoughts of Troy from my mind. Now I was Logan's wife, and I wanted to make sure I never caused him to suffer the way Troy had.

I showered and dressed and went back downstairs to find Tony to tell him to go right up to talk to Martha Goodman.

Tony and Logan were not in the office. Curtis found me searching for them and told me they had left a message that they had gone into Boston.

"Something about plans for the factory in Winnerow," Curtis said, troubled that he hadn't remembered the message word for word.

"Don't worry about it, Curtis. Thank you." I didn't know whether to laugh or cry at Logan's monomaniacal dedication to Tatterton Toys. I knew he had to be tired from our trip, yet he wouldn't let that prevent him from showing his determination and drive to Tony. Tony should have known better, too, I thought. Why was he romancing Logan with the business so intently? He had what he said he wanted— he had us living here, sharing in his wealth, and he had Logan working for him. He should be paying more attention to Jillian and her needs.

"Well, they did say not to worry. They would be back in plenty of time for dinner."

Oh, how I wished I could be gay and happy at this moment, instead of troubled and melancholy. I decided it would be good for me to take a walk, to air out my stuffy, gloomy thoughts.

I was wearing a light blue, summer-weight blouse and skirt and almost turned back to get a cotton sweater, for the air had become cool and the salty sea breeze brisk. But I didn't. I walked on, embracing myself and distracted so by my worries that I didn't realize how fast and how far I had gone from the front entrance. I stopped at the entrance to the maze and looked back.

There, framed in the window, was Jillian. She looked like a mannequin; so still she was, so frozen in place. It was difficult to see the details of her face, of course, but I thought she wore an expression of fear. Suddenly her fear filled me and I was drawn into the maze, like a child who wants to be told the end of a scary fairy tale. The moment I entered the maze I recalled the first time I had done so, that first day I had come to Farthy, when I didn't even realize what the maze was. I was excited by the challenge of finding my way through the puzzle. Arrogantly, I had gone forward, taking the right turns and then the left turns. As the warm sunlight was absorbed by the tall hedges, I'd realized I had lost my prospective. I no longer remembered the way back. I had panicked, quickening my pace, nearly running.

Finally I had stopped to gather my wits and calm myself, straining to hear the pounding of the surf, hoping to use that as a reference point, but instead, I had heard the tap-tap-tap of someone hammering nearby. I had followed the sound until I heard a window close and the hammering cease. I had been walking just the way I was walking right now, with my arms folded pretectively over my bosom in Granny's way. I had made turn after turn until I stepped out of the maze and came upon Troy's cottage.

Just as I did now.

And it was just the way it always had been, a storybook house suddenly appearing out of the fog, comfortably nestled in the lap of the pine trees. Of course now there were no sounds of a hammer being used to construct those precious little Tatterton Toys; there was no light from any warm fire. There was nothing but the cold shadows and the darkened windows that looked like the eyes of a blind man, dull, gray, sightless, not even the reflection of the surrounding little crooked fence in its glass.

Yet the sight of it shattered my fragile heart.

Oh, Troy, I thought. How I wish I was once again coming upon your cottage as I had that first day, and after meeting you, I was once again trying to get you to talk to me. How I wish you were there once again to look at me the way you had—to see your dark eyes look over me so slowly, taking in my face, my throat, my heaving bosom, my waist, hips, and legs as though you feasted on me visually. How intently you looked into my face. I felt your gaze on my lips. I sensed how much I affected you and that filled me with a realization of my own potent femininity. Yes, Troy, you made me feel like a woman more than any man ever had before.

I realized I was embracing myself even tighter while lost in this reverie. What is happening to me? I wondered. I shouldn't be thinking of these things, for I had my true love with me and Troy was gone and gone forever. I shouldn't be letting Jillian's crazed dreams of ghosts affect and haunt me, too.

After a moment I got hold of myself and I brought my hands to the sides of my body and walked forward until I reached the cottage door. I was surprised to see how well the grounds around the cottage had been kept since Troy's death. The lawn was cut; the flower beds pruned. Even the panel windows looked clean.

After a moment's hesitation, when all the voices of caution sang out their warnings, I turned the latch and stepped inside, my heart beating in my chest like a bird ready to take wing. The moment I stepped in, I gasped. Troy's chair was just where it always had been, facing the fireplace. For a moment I expected that he would be in it and he would turn my way as he did that first day, but, of course, there was no one there and that silence and emptiness was more devastating than I had imagined it would be. I took a deep breath and held it as I looked up at the special tools he had used to construct those special Tatterton creations, each in its niche on the wall.

The floorboard to my left creaked as if a ghost had taken a step and I uttered a cry. Without any hesitation I turned and ran out the cottage door, sorrow and fear commingling in the tears that streamed down my cheeks. I fled back into the maze and ran mindless down the corridors, making one senseless turn after another. I tripped once, but caught myself before falling into the hedges. Finally, out of breath and exhausted, I stopped in the middle of a passageway to gather my wits.

Like the first time I had entered this maze years ago, I was once again lost. I had run in a panic, disregarding the pathways and directions I had once known so well. Right now, still emotionally overwrought, I couldn't think straight. Every opening and entrance looked the same. I wasn't even sure how to go back to the cottage.

I laughed at myself, more to calm myself than anything else. How silly and stupid you are, Heaven Leigh, I thought. After all these years and all those times you traveled the maze, to be standing here so confused. Take your time, think, gather your wits together. Imagine what it would be like for you to be wandering around in here when Tony and Logan returned, for them to have to rescue you. How could you explain such foolishness?

I ran through the corridors again, cursing the mystery. I was sure I had gone around in circles. What was the point of all this anyway? What distorted sense of humor created such things? I caught my breath and studied the various options. The more choices I had, the more confused I became. It was getting darker and darker. How long had I been wandering through the maze? All sense of time and place was suddenly lost to me. I couldn't calm my heart's pounding. Little cries were emerging from my mouth almost on their own. I tried desperately to calm myself, but it was getting to be harder and harder to do it.

I stared down one corridor, made a right turn and then a left. Everything looked as familiar as ever, but when I made what I thought were surely the correct turns, I found myself still deep in the maze, but perhaps far right of the exits to either Troy's cottage or the house. The shadows here looked darker, longer. Everything about this section was unfriendly to me. In my wild imagination I thought the hedges were taking revenge on me for solving their mystery years ago and moving from one world into another.

I finally decided that my only solution was to keep turning left once and then right once. Eventually I would have to come to the end of the maze, even though it might take me ten times the time it would take had I remembered the solutions. With my head down I proceeded. After a few minutes the sound of someone clipping caught my attention. I stopped and listened. Yes, it was definitely one of the grounds people working. I walked toward the sound and after making half a dozen turns came upon an elderly man trimming one of the hedges. I didn't want to frighten him, so I waited, hopeful that he would soon notice my presence. Even so, when he turned my way, I saw that he was quite shocked. He nearly fled.

"Wait, don't be afraid," I said. "It's only me, Mrs. Stonewall. Heaven." He was not familiar to me, so I imagined he was one of the many servants hired after I had left Farthy to go back to Winnerow to teach.

"Oh, miss," he said. "Oh, dear." He stood up, holding his right hand over his heart. "You gave me quite a start. I'm glad you're who you are; I'm glad you're of the living."

"I am, thankfully. But I must confess I wandered into the maze and lost my sense of direction."

"Oh, that's easy to do. Even I have done it a few times."

"Have you been working here long?" I asked. I thought a few moments of idle conversation might calm the moment and he wouldn't feel the need to exaggerate it when he related it to the other servants.

"Only a few months, ma'am."

"Enjoying it?"

"Most of the time, yes, ma'am. I wasn't a moment ago," he said and then laughed. "I thought for a minute there that one of Rye Whiskey's spirits had me."

"Oh, Rye Whiskey. Yes," I said, smiling. "He can spook anyone with his tales."

"Got me goin', ma'am. The other day I was sure I heard footsteps just on the other side of one of these hedges. I followed the sound and came out at a juncture just where whoever it was would have to come out, only . . ."

"Only?"

"There was no one there. I would have sworn on a stack of Bibles there was someone."

I stared at him a moment.

"Well, once someone puts ideas into your head the way Rye does, your imagination plays tricks on you," I told him. He nodded.

"That's what I think, too, ma'am. Well, then, if you're looking for the fastest way back to the house, just take this right turn here, go two left turns and then make a right. That should do it."

"Thank you. I feel a bit silly for getting confused."

"No reason to, ma'am. Have a good night now." He looked up. "It's almost too dark for me to go on working. I'm just going to finish this piece and be off myself."

"Yes," I said. "Thanks again." I followed his directions and stepped out on the grounds, a dozen yards or so from the place where I had first entered. As I walked quickly back toward the house, I looked up and saw that Jillian was still at her window.

Only now she was nodding slowly, as if my getting lost and emerging the way I had had confirmed something in her maddened mind, as if I had given flesh to her wild imaginings. She smiled at me and then pulled back from the window, satisfied.

I hurried on to reenter the house and bask in the warm security that lights and noise and other people would provide. I was happy to see that Logan and Tony had not yet returned. I went to my suite quickly and rinsed my face in cold water, finally calming myself and removing the flush in my cheeks. Shortly afterward Logan arrived.

"Where did you two go?" I asked as he undressed to shower and change for dinner.

"Oh, Tony wanted me to meet someone involved in marketing the toys abroad. Interesting man. Explained everything in great detail, and when I told him about our venture in Winnerow, he became very interested. He said Europeans have a driving curiosity about backwoods America. We're sure to prove successful. Tony became very enthusiastic about it."

"Did he?"

"Yes," Logan said, then paused as he studied my face. "Why do you look so unhappy?"

"I had gone down to see him about Jillian, right before you two left. She's in a very bad state and Tony's been ignoring it. Martha Goodman is disturbed enough about it to want to leave."

"Really? Oh, dear."

"Yes, oh, dear," I said. "I'll be downstairs in the living room. I have to speak with Tony."

"Okay. I'll be right along."

Tony was upstairs showering and dressing for dinner, too, but he appeared before Logan did, looking rather dapper in his blue velvet smoking jacket. There was a radiance and a brightness in his eyes. He looked happier than ever.

"Heaven. Would you join me in a cocktail before dinner?" he asked.

I was standing beside the piano, my right hand on the polished wood.

"No, Tony, not right now. I just want to talk to you before dinner."

"Oh?"

"Did you stop in to see Jillian and Martha Goodman?"

"No, I—"

"Why have you been avoiding it?" I demanded, stepping toward him. He stared at me a moment. Before he could reply, Curtis came to the doorway and he ordered a highball.

"Very good, sir," Curtis said and then eyed me.

"Nothing for me, Curtis," I said. "Well?" I asked as soon as Curtis left.

"I haven't been avoiding her. I've just been very busy. Why are you so disturbed about it?"

"I'm disturbed about it because she is not the same; she is quite different. Martha Goodman told me she has been asking you to come by to see for yourself. She's very upset about it and I believe she wants to leave."

"Martha?"

"Yes, Tony. If you weren't so oblivious to things around you, you would know that. You must go right up there and confer with her and call the doctor to come to examine Jillian."

"What's wrong with her?"

"She's changed." I ran my hand over the piano. "She's not living in the past; she's bringing the past into the present."

"Pardon?"

"She thinks she sees ghosts and she blames it on her own guilt."

"Oh. I see." His head was turned in a way that kept me from seeing his eyes, but I sensed the reason.

"It's something you don't mind letting her do—bear the entire guilt for my mother and even . . . for Troy."

"What?" He spun around, his blue eyes blazing like the blue tip of a gas fire. I felt the heat between us.

"I know what you're doing, I've done it myself, not only to her, but to Luke. When they carry all the guilt, it relieves us of our own burden. But it's not fair, Tony, and it's not right. Martha Goodman's right. Jillian is growing worse and worse with each passing day. Soon, she'll be catatonic, a vegetable. You can't ignore your responsibility any longer."

"This is ridiculous," he said, his lips curling. "I don't blame her for Troy's death, nor do I blame myself. I did all I could for him, under the circumstances, but you knew how unhappy and depressed he was, how he was convinced he would die because of those constant nightmares in which he saw his own death, even saw his own tombstone. He knew what he was doing when he chose Jillian's wild horse. In my mind he committed suicide," Tony said, following his words with a sigh.

We both paused when Curtis brought him his drink. He went to the couch and sat down, but I remained by the piano

"Now, as far as Jillian goes," he continued, "I've also done all any man in my circumstances could do. I kept her safe, warm, satisfied, even in her madness. But that didn't mean I had to sacrifice my own sanity, did it? She has a professional nurse twenty-four hours a day. I'm not neglecting her out of some ridiculous sense of guilt. I'm just busy, that's all."

"So busy that you haven't noticed what's happening here in Farthy. All of the servants are disturbed because of Jillian." I said. Tony smiled coldly and crossed his leg. He meticulously ran his fingers down the sharp crease of his dark blue trouser leg and stared at me.

"Are you sure it's not you who is disturbed because of Jillian? Does her presence here torment you?"

"Of course not," I said. "I'm thinking only of her welfare."

"I see." He sat back to sip his drink. "All right," he said. "I'll have the doctor come tomorrow. What shall I do if he recommends we commit her to an institution for the mentally ill? Should I send her away to keep the servants from telling ridiculous tales?"

"We'll have to do what's best for her," I said. I couldn't help myself. I was trembling now.

"Of course."

"Tony," I said, sitting on the piano stool, "Troy's cottage . . ."

"What about Troy's cottage?" He sat forward.

"It's . . . you've kept it just the way it was . . . like a living monument."

"You were there?" A quick glimmer of fear lit his eyes, then he banished it. "I see," he said, sitting back. "What would you have had me do, burn it down?"

"No, but—"

"You were right in one sense, Heaven," he said, all the anger and frustration gone from his face. "All of us have to come to terms with our own guilt . . . our own ghosts. I did what I could for him; I was angry at him for tossing his life away, but that doesn't mean . . . I don't miss him," he said.

I bit my lower lip to force the lump in my throat to stay down. I felt the tears well up in my eyes.

"In a way we are all a bit arrogant about our grief," he continued. "We think no one but we can suffer it as much. You weren't the only one who had a broken heart."

The long silence between us was shattered by Logan's arrival.

"I'm starving," he declared. He looked from Tony to me and back to Tony. "Something wrong?"

"No," Tony said quickly. "Nothing that's not going to be taken care of as soon as possible." He turned to me. "Right, Heaven?" he asked.

"Yes," I said. I rose from the piano stool, ran my fingers lightly over the keys, and followed Tony and Logan out of the room, the memory of Troy's music slowly dying away as we went in to dinner.

❧ SIX ❧

A Face in the Darkness

THE NEXT DAY JILLIAN'S DOCTOR CAME TO EXAMINE AND RE-evaluate her condition. He concluded that she was in remarkably good physical health, but she had indeed changed from a confused, disoriented state to a hypertense and volatile one. He prescribed tranquilizers. Martha Goodman was satisfied and agreed to stay on as Jillian's private nurse.

The day after the doctor's visit Tony and Logan went to Winnerrow with Paul Grant, the architect, to view the site for the factory. I accompanied them to meet with him a week later to discuss his preliminary plans for the structure and the grounds around it. I was immediately impressed with Paul and liked all of his suggestions. He had built a scale model of the planned factory and included the landscaping as well. It looked like an intricate Tatterton Toy.

"I'd like to keep the integrity of the woods here," he said, pointing to the right of the model, "and build a simple circular drive that branches off for deliveries here. Of course, the building should be all wood. A metal or stone building in this setting would be . . ." He looked up at me. "Quite out of character. Wouldn't you say?"

I didn't reply, but he knew I approved. He smiled and went on with his explanations. Somehow he had styled the factory after a cabinlike structure so that it looked like it belonged in the outskirts of Winnerow. There was a cafeteria for the artisans to have their lunch; there were large work spaces; there was plenty of storage and a good-sized delivery and packaging room. There was an office for Logan or Tony to use whenever they were there. He had even built an executive rest area.

"I'd like the model when you're finished with it," I said.

"Of course, Mrs. Stonewall. I'll deliver it personally," he said. I knew he was flirting with me, but neither Logan nor Tony seemed to notice.

Logan began to spend a great deal of time traveling back and forth to Winnerow. Tony accompanied him a few times, but most of the trips Logan made alone. He was truly in charge. I decided there was no reason for me to go back to Winnerow until the factory was completed.

A little more than a month after the start of construction, Logan began making his treks through the Willies in search of the natural artisans who would be solicited for work later on. Whenever he returned from one of these trips and described some of the people he met, I was always reminded of Grandpa. Some of the names Logan mentioned were still familiar to me. He wanted me to go along with him on this search, but I thought it might be too painful for me, might bring back too many vivid memories of all I had lost.

In the meantime I settled into a quiet existence at Farthy. When Logan was away, I took my dinners with Tony, who often talked about the Boston theater scene. He was always offering to buy tickets to this show or that.

"After all, we often decide whether or not they'll take their show to New York. We're very important to the theater world," he said. He tried everything to get me to accompany him to one of the new shows. I was content with reading, occasionally going horseback riding for exercise, and helping Martha Goodman with Jillian, who, with the help of the tranquilizers, had become quite subdued and rather like a sweet little girl. She rarely mentioned ghosts anymore.

Finally, part out of boredom and partly out of genuine interest in a new show opening in Boston, I agreed to accompany Tony one Saturday night. Logan was in Winnerow and wouldn't return until the following Wednesday. I went to my closet to decide what to wear and sifted through some of the dresses Tony had bought to fill the closet in my new suite. It had all been part of that surprise, but until now I really hadn't inspected the garments.

Near the end of the rack, I discovered a black satin dress with a pleated skirt and a sleeveless lace bodice. The bodice was to be worn off shoulder. The neckline was heart-shaped, which made it rather revealing. Tony had always had such a good eye for style and size, something I had discovered when he had taken me to purchase a wardrobe after I had been enrolled in the Winterhaven School, a private school for rather affluent girls. When I put the dress on and gazed at myself in the mirror, I felt the tingle in the small of my stomach that comes with the awareness of my own sexual allure. My bosom was lifted, deepening my cleavage. I felt positively tantalizing. I knew that in such a dress the ripeness of my womanhood was revealed. Gone was the soft, innocent look that had once been mine.

I pinned up my hair, showing the long line of my neck. My skin was smooth and soft where it dipped to meet my shoulders. I had a hand-knit, light wool shawl to drape over my shoulders, which I knew would suffice on such a warm summer's evening. I used a minimum of makeup, just a slight touch of eye shadow and some light pink lipstick.

After making these preparations, I stepped back and gazed at myself. It felt good to dress up; it felt good to be going somewhere. Since our honeymoon, Logan had been so wrapped up in his work and the factory in Winnerow, we had done very little together. I was glad I had finally given in to Tony's continual requests to join him for a show. The thought of moving about in Boston's high society and being entertained was invigorating.

A gentle knock on my bedroom door quickly pulled me out of my reverie. It was Tony, dressed in a black tuxedo, a white shirt and winged collar with a black bow tie. For a moment he simply stood there, staring in at me, a strangely troubled look in his eyes.

"What's wrong?" I asked.

"What? Oh, no, no, nothing's wrong," he stammered. Then he caught hold of himself, sighed, and beamed his warmest smile at me. "I . . . there's no color more flattering to you than black. It's the same with your grandmother. My God, Heaven, you're absolutely breathtaking. Your grandmother was beautiful; your mother was more beautiful; but you are the most beautiful."

"Thank you," I said, "but . . ."

"I was hoping you would wear that dress. But most of all I wanted you to wear these." He held up one of Jillian's most expensive diamond necklaces and matching earrings.

"Oh, Tony, I couldn't. I shouldn't." I shook my head my stepped back.

"Nonsense. I insist. They're simply fading away in a drawer."

He came around behind me and draped the necklace around my neck, fastening it quickly. Then he took hold of my shoulders and turned me to the mirror.

"Behold, how you flatter the diamonds and not vice versa," he said. The glittering stones felt warm against my skin and revived that tingling in the small of my stomach. I held my breath at Tony ran his fingers over the diamonds, his blue eyes sparkling almost as brightly.

"Thank you," I said, my throat nearly closing before I could utter the words. He had pressed his lips to the top of my head and closed his eyes.

"You're wearing jasmine, Jillian's jasmine. Leigh used to wear it, too," he whispered.

"Well, I . . . it was here and I . . ."

"I'm glad," he said. "The scent brings back only good memories. Don't forget the earrings," he said. He put them into my palm, holding my hand for a moment. "Don't be too much longer. I want to get to the theater a little early and show you off."

"Oh, Tony, please . . ."

"I'll be waiting downstairs. The limo awaits you," he said and was gone. He was so excited, he looked twenty years younger.

I put on the earrings quickly and took one more look at myself. I felt like a woman playing with fire by resurrecting Tony's memories of my mother, a young girl who, if I were to believe Jillian's mad utterances, seduced him, but found him a willing victim.

But I am not as young and as inexperienced about men as my mother was, I thought. Surely events couldn't run away with me as they had with her. I was in control; I knew what I was doing. I was going out to have a good time. It was good to feel beautiful and to be appreciated. What was so wrong with that? Didn't every woman want that? Long for that? Fantasize about being the center of attraction?

Yet wasn't it sinful to feel this way, to fall in love with your own image? That had been Jillian's sin, hadn't it: falling in love with herself, wanting to be forever young and beautiful? Was her madness her punishment? Would it be mine as well?

I scooped up my shawl and draped it about my shoulders, taking one last look at myself as I did so. For a moment, only a moment, one of the pictures of my mother in her photo album flashed before me. Her father, Cleave Van Voren, was gone. Jillian had divorced him and started up with Tony. There was Mommy with a new man, a much younger and handsomer man, twenty-year-old Tony Tatterton. And strangely, in this photograph, the beautiful, radiant girl who had smiled with confident candor into the camera lens before could not manage even a faint, false smile. Darkness troubled her eyes just the way they did in the flashing image I saw in my mirror.

Was I looking at a memory of her or of myself? The picture had been so prophetic. What did this image predict for me?

Refusing to permit anything to interfere with my warm, vibrant, and exciting feelings, I laughed at what I called my foolish imagination and ran from the room, my own laughter trickling behind and finally shut away behind the bedroom doors to linger in the shadows with all the other ghost sounds that haunted Farthinggale Manor.

The play was marvelous, a hilarious domestic comedy with not a single dry spot. It was a period piece about a young girl who had been promised in marriage to a doddering old millionaire. She was really in love with his son, but the marriage contract stipulated that if she didn't marry the old man, the son couldn't inherit a penny. The old man died before the first act ended, but the son and the beautiful young girl kept up the guise that the old man was still alive. He was always either asleep or napping in a chair. There were many opportunities for humorous situations. Of course, all ended happily ever after with the two lovebirds marrying.

"Don't you wish life could be like a play or a movie?" Tony asked me on the way back to Farthy. "Always ending happily ever after?"

"Of course," I agreed.

"You know, I sometimes feel all my money is like a fortress. It's true, you can't buy happiness, but you can buy away unhappiness, use your money to make things easier, more comfortable."

"Like you've done with Jillian?"

"Yes," he said. He turned to me in the darkness of the backseat of the limo. His eyes were obscured in that darkness, but occasionally a passing automobile or a passing street light flickered and revealed the sad look in his face. "Like what I've done with Jillian."

"And what you've done with me," I added.

"What do you mean?"

"Buying Logan," I said. I said it simply, matter-of-factly, as if it were something too obvious to deny.

"Why, Heaven, you don't mean to sit there and say—"

"It doesn't matter," I assured him. "I let it happen, so I must want it myself . . . this rich life, Farthy, surrounded by so many good things, and yet feeling as though I'm doing worthwhile things by sending Logan to construct that factory in Winnerow. I just hope it all has a happy ending, too," I added.

"It will," he promised and squeezed my hand for reassurance. "But let's not be maudlin tonight," he said, casting away the heavy tones from his voice. "The evening's been too wonderful. Did you see the looks you were getting? How jealous some of my friends were? They didn't know who you were at first." He chuckled. There was something about him that seemed very much like a little boy again. He was having fun, playing. Tony was such a serious man most of the time, absorbed in his schemes and in the business. It was rare to see this light, gay side of him.

For the first time I thought about him as a man and I wondered what was it like for him to be married to Jillian, to have a wife who was mentally ill. Never to have a companion, never to have anyone to take to dinner or to shows. In short, to have no one to love.

I remembered how gay and active he and Jillian had been when I first arrived at Farthy. All those exciting trips they took, to California, to Europe, all the big parties, the elegant dinners . . . suddenly all that had ended for him. All he had left was his work . . . and me.

Loneliness was the cruelest season of all, I thought; more damaging than all the frosts of winter, sending the heart into hibernation. It had no one to live for, to be awake for, to beat fast and furiously for. The lonely had only memories and hopes, dreams and illusions. Under their Christmas trees were beautiful fully wrapped empty boxes.

It was cruel of me to resent him for using his money to keep Logan and me at Farthy, I thought. With Troy gone and Jillian deranged, we were all he had now. I could understand his jealousy of anything that took my attention from Farthinggale. He wasn't like Luke. Pa lost his beautiful young wife in childbirth and then married another woman who bore him children. When she deserted him, he gave up and sold his family, but soon found a new woman and a new life. Tony was different. Even with all his money and power, he couldn't discard his past, cast off his memories, and start anew. I had to admire his steadfast devotion and loyalty, even though some might say my much poorer father who had become tied down to the circus he now owned was much better off.

"How about a brandy before going up to bed?" Tony asked me as we drew close to Farthy. "It always takes me a while to unwind and I'd like to get the chill out."

I agreed and we went directly to the living room, where Curtis had already made a fire in the fireplace. He brought us the drinks and Tony and I talked a little more about the play, about some of the people he had introduced me to, and about his plans for the further expansion of Tatterton Toys. Finally, feeling very tired, I excused myself and went up to my rooms. He remained sitting there, sipping his brandy, staring into the fire.

On the landing I looked in the direction of Jillian's suite and saw Martha Goodman beckoning me. She was dressed in a robe and slippers and appeared more than a little agitated.

"She's having a bad night," she whispered, coming out of the door-way as I approached. "Whenever the weather gets like this, she has a bad time."

"Did you give her the medication?"

"Yes, but it's not being so effective tonight." She frowned and shook her head.

"Restless, is she?" The wind coming off the sea picked up and even in the deepest parts of the big house we could hear it rush over the roof and windows, sounding more like the sea than the air.

"Yes. She's been muttering about Abdulla Bar. She claims she hears the horse galloping around the house, whinnying. She was so intent about it, so positive she heard it, she got to me, I have to confess. I actually sent Curtis out earlier to see if any of the horses had broken loose. Of course, none had."

"Oh, dear. Should I inform Mr. Tatterton? Perhaps we—"

"No, no. I just wanted to have a moment's conversation with someone, other than one of the servants. They sometimes get me more unnerved than Mrs. Tatterton does." She squeezed my hand. "It's all right. It will be all right. We'll all go to sleep now. Don't worry."

"Just call me if there is any problem. Don't hesitate."

"Thank you, Mrs. Stonewall. I'm so happy you've decided to stay here. It's comforting knowing you are just down the corridor," she said, an audible tone of relief in her voice.

"Good night, Martha." I patted her hand and went to my suite.

As I prepared for bed the rain began, heavy, hard, pounding and scratching at the windows. To me it sounded like so many small creatures scurrying up and down the glass. When I looked out, it was like looking into a black velvet curtain. Only an occasional streak of lightning permitted any visibility and when that jolt of heavenly electricity ripped across the cold, coal-black sky, it distorted everything below— trees, gazebo, lawn furniture. Everything looked liquid, oozing across my field of vision, changing shapes, elongating, heaving. It was a nightmare world. A night it would be easy to see ghosts in. I closed my curtains tightly and pulled back the quilt on my bed, anxious to go to sleep and wake up to the warm, morning sun.

I turned out the lights and pulled the quilt up to my shoulders, snuggled in the warmth, and closed my heavy eyelids. Fortunately, I fell asleep almost immediately.

But I wasn't asleep long before something woke me. It was pitch black in my bedroom, but I sensed another presence. What had awoken me, I realized, was the sound of the door being opened, the small click of the handle. For a few moments I stared into the darkness, vaguely making out a shape.

"Who's there?" I asked in a hoarse whisper. My heart began to pound. I felt cold terror creep up my body. "Is someone there? Tony?"

I heard the sound of footsteps and then saw the door open and close, getting only a glimpse of the figure who had entered and left. This mysterious person was too much in darkness for me to make out any identity.

I leapt out of bed, turning on the small night lamp on the table by my side. Then I put on my robe and went to the door. The lights in the corridor had been dimmed, so that all the shadows were wider, longer. I thought I heard a door close and I stepped farther out to listen and look, but there was no one in sight. Could it have been Jillian? I wondered. Had she gotten past a sleeping Martha Goodman and come down to my suite? Or had it been Tony, coming to tell me something and then changing his mind? I listened a little longer and then turned to go back into my suite, when I felt the dampness beneath my feet. I knelt down and touched the carpet. Whoever it was had brought the rain in with him.

Troubled and confused, I returned to bed. It hadn't occurred to me to lock my bedroom door before, but this time I did. Still, I remained awake for the longest time, and when I finally did fall asleep, it was a relief. I awoke to the sounds of the house coming alive—servants moving about, windows and curtains being opened, breakfast being prepared. I listened for a few moments and then quickly sat up in bed.

Had I imagined a nocturnal visitor last night? Dreamt it? Or had someone been here? I slipped into my robe and slippers and went to my bedroom door. It was locked. If I hadn't dreamt doing that, I couldn't have dreamt the other things. I opened the door to the suite and looked down at the hallway carpet. The dampness was gone, but there was other evidence. Someone had tracked in a little mud. Who had it been?

I dressed quickly, determined to solve the mystery, but I couldn't question Tony. He had already had his early breakfast and left Farthy for work. So I cornered Curtis in the dining room and asked him if he knew anything about it. Obviously, it was not a wise thing to do. The man became absolutely terrified. He obviously thought I had confirmed one of Rye Whiskey's tales of the supernatural.

"No, Mrs. Stonewall," he said. "I wasn't walking about and I didn't see anyone, but it's not the first time someone has been heard wandering about the house at night. Rye Whiskey says it's got to be one of Mr. Tatterton's ancestors. He says one might have been murdered and his soul's still lost."

"That's ridiculous. Tell Rye I want to speak to him."

"Very good, ma'am," Curtis said and disappeared into the kitchen. A few minutes later Rye appeared. The burly gray-haired black man looked as if he had been up all night himself.

"What is this about a murdered ancestor wandering through the halls at night? Don't you think that maybe you're taking these stories too far, Rye? You have Curtis believing it and Martha Goodman says many of the other servants shiver in their bones."

He smiled at me and shook his head.

"You heard him last night, is that it, Miss Heaven?" He nodded as if coaching me to answer.

"I heard something and saw someone, a glimpse, but it wasn't a ghost," I said, looking away.

"I heard him, too," Rye said.

"And you drank your fears away, drank yourself to sleep?" I demanded, turning back to him. "Is that it?" He didn't have to confess; I could see it in his face. "The servants are really becoming spooked, Rye. Do you want me to tell Mr. Tatterton what's happening here?"

"He already knows, Miss Heaven," Rye said, leaning toward me. "I've seen him up at night wandering about himself, listening, searching. Who knows?" Rye said, standing straight again. "Maybe Mr. Tatterton has met his dead relative?"

For a moment I just stared at him.

"That's ridiculous. What a ridiculous thing to say, Rye. I'm sorry I ever let you entertain me with your tales of superstition and the like."

"Sorry, miss. I got to be getting back to the kitchen to prepare Mrs. Tatterton's breakfast."

"Go on. You're absolutely no help." I watched him go and then looked at Curtis, who stood by as always, looking like a cigar store Indian. "I can't believe you listen to that gibberish," I said, but I didn't sound as convinced of my opinion as I should have. I left my breakfast and went outside to think.

Since that day I had gotten lost fleeing from the cottage, I had avoided the maze, but this morning, perhaps because of the strange events that had taken place the night before, I was inexplicably drawn to it again. The moment I walked outside I felt as if I had stepped into a dream. The morning sky took on a darker shade of blue as a large cloud blocked out the sun. Most of the mist and dew had been burned off, but that seemingly ever-present ring of haze lingered around the maze. I entered it as quickly as I used to when Troy was alive and I used to scurry back and forth between his little cottage and the main house. I closed my eyes and inhaled the rich scent of the flourishing hedges that perfumed the corridors. Then I entered the maze and followed the well-worn course I knew would take me to the little cottage. I walked as fast as I could, and when I finally emerged on the other side and faced the cottage, I was gasping for breath. The large cloud moved off the sun and the world around me brightened once again.

I looked back into the dark corridors of the maze, truly feeling as though I had passed from darkness into light, from sorrow into happiness, from despair into optimism. Yes, the maze kept more people from wandering through it, for most were afraid of its mystery, but I realized long ago one must take risks to find a deeper and truer happiness. Finding the courage was part of the cost, but it was well worth the expense.

The cottage was as I had last found it—frozen in time, well cared for, but hauntingly empty and silent. I folded my arms under my bosom and made my way slowly to the front door. There I hesitated. Why had I returned to the cottage? Why was I tormenting myself? Why had I agreed to live at Farthinggale Manor, where I knew all these memories would linger vibrant and true? I was tormenting myself with the sounds, the sights, and the scents. I was punishing myself for sins I hadn't committed.

Or had I? Wasn't I sinful to love Troy even though he was my uncle? Wasn't I sinful for filling his heart with hope and then permitting it to break, permitting him to suffer alone? Wasn't I sinful for not being here on the day he most needed me, the day he rode into the ocean to drown away his misery? I had strummed the strings of his heart and then left him as unused and as silent as the piano in the music room. Its music lingered only in memory; its usefulness was gone.

Yes, going into this cottage was another way to continue the torment, but I was like one driven by a passionate ghost. I opened that door again and stepped into the cottage that had once been the warm and comfortable setting for our love and promises.

The last time I had entered the cottage, I had been so shocked by the reality of it that I had run. I had expected it to be gathering dust, to look like something lost in the past, but Tony had been keeping it up and it looked the same as it had when Troy was alive. It was just as it was the last time I had been in it. It was just as it had been in my memory, just the way I had locked it in my heart. Only now that I stayed and looked about more carefully, I sensed something else. It wasn't just frozen in time; it was also alive in the present. I realized all of the antique clocks were on time. As if to punctuate this realization, the grandfather clock struck the hour and the light blue music box clock that was shaped like the cottage opened its front door and the tiny family within emerged and then retreated to the sweet and haunting melody.

I walked over to the work table upon which Troy used to make his Tatterton creations. On it were a half dozen or so tiny suits of armor and some bits of silver shaped like S's with holes at either end. There were tiny bolts beside them, ready to be fitted. When the silver links were tied together, the chain-link mail could move freely. They were so tiny and precious! What struck me as odd was how clean and dust free all these parts and pieces were. Some of the tools Troy used to use were still on the table beside them. I couldn't be sure, of course, because I had run from the cottage so quickly the first time I had returned, but it seemed to me that these tools had been neatly placed in their niche on the wall. I didn't remember seeing all this work on the table. Did Tony have another artisan living and working in Troy's cottage?

I decided to explore further. To my surprise I found the kitchen well stocked with food, fresh food. When I put my hand on the teakettle on the stove, I felt its warmth. Someone had made a cup just a short time ago. Why was Tony permitting the cottage to be used? Was that why he was so defensive about it when I asked, referring to the sorrow that he felt over Troy's death as a way of ending our conversation about it?

As I looked around the cottage, I saw there was even more new work, not just the tiny armor on the table. I saw the miniature medieval people that populated the precious little castles and straw huts lined up on the shelves. I saw a replica of an Old English cathedral partially painted, some of its tiny stained-glass windows not yet installed, and I saw the beginnings of a feudal battle scene with the knights on horses holding out their lances facing bowmen dressed in forest green. On a small hill was a beautiful young damsel, looking worried for her young knight, no doubt. Two ladies-in-waiting were there beside her, holding itsy-bitsy lace handkerchiefs to their faces.

Now I understood what Tony was doing and it chilled my heart. He had led me to believe that he had kept up the cottage as a living shrine to his dead brother out of some sense of guilt, when instead, he was only thinking about his business, his precious little toys. He had found someone as skilled as Troy and installed him in Troy's cottage! He was simply ashamed I should find out and know just what he cared for the most—making money and more money. Things that I thought had been as sacred and precious to him as they had been to me were not. I felt like a wife who had discovered her father had given away her dead husband's clothing and jewelry.

Enraged, I pivoted on my heels to rush out. I intended to return to Farthy to wait for Tony and confront him with my discovery. But something else caught my attention—the door to the cottage basement was nearly halfway open. I stared at it a moment and then smiled to myself. Of course, I thought. Whomever Tony had hired and permitted to use the cottage had heard me coming and had gone into the cellar to hide. Perhaps Tony had warned him about me after he and I had had that conversation about the cottage, and he had told him to avoid my confronting him. But I made up my mind I would confront this person so the evidence could not be denied.

I went to the door and descended the stairs, but I had forgotten just how dark it was below in the large, windowless room and through the tunnels that led back to the main house, so I went back upstairs and found a candle, just where they had always been, and then returned to the basement, determined to expose what I felt was a blasphemous violation.

The glow from the small yellow flame shivered on the cellar walls. As I turned from left to right the fragile illumination sliced gently through the darkness, revealing the floor and walls of the dark, empty room. He must have retreated into the tunnels, I thought, and continued on. I walked slowly, recalling how impatient I used to be with the slow pace that would keep the candle from blowing out. When Troy first showed me the tunnels, he told me he was always afraid to go through them as a small boy. Every time the tunnel made a bend, he expected monsters to appear, or ghosts to step out of the pockets of darkness.

But I didn't expect monsters or ghosts right now; I expected some frightened little man, afraid for his job, afraid that if I caught him, Tony would be angry and fire him. I knew it wasn't fair for me to take my own anger out on him, but I couldn't keep down the fury that had taken hold of me. That cottage and all that was in it was so much a part of Troy. It was painful to think that a stranger would sleep in his bed and touch his precious things.

Sure enough, I heard the sound of footsteps ahead. Whoever it was, he was retreating quickly, fleeing from the reach of my candlelight. I lowered the candle toward the floor and saw the imprint of footsteps. Some looked fresh; some looked like they might have been made the night before.

When I looked around, I realized I had traveled nearly half the way through the tunnels. How long could this go on? Didn't the fleeing man know he couldn't escape discovery? And wasn't he afraid to go charging through the darkness? Or maybe, since my return to Farthy, Tony and his new employee met surreptitiously down here in the tunnels.

"Whoever you are," I called, "you might as well come forward. I'll follow you right to Farthy and that will be most embarrassing for you. Come forward. I know you were in the cottage; I know you work for Tony."

I waited and listened. All was suddenly very silent.

"You're being very foolish," I said. "I saw the work you did; I know what you're doing. There is no longer any point in your running away."

I waited again. Still nothing.

"Okay, have it your way," I said. I continued forward.

I covered the flame with my left hand to protect it from the increased breeze caused by my quickening pace, not even hesitating as I came to a bend. I knew where I was and I knew just how much farther it would be before I reached Farthy. I would come to the bottom of steep, narrow steps that led up to the back of the kitchen hall. Breakfast was over. If everything was cleaned up, there might not be anyone in the kitchen, I thought. Tony's secret worker might escape into the house and leave by one of the side entrances before I reached him. I made a quick decision to forget the candlelight and rushed forward, remembering exactly how the tunnels turned. It was pitch dark, but using the walls as a guide, I moved on quickly. When I came around the final bend, I stopped. Someone was just a few feet away in the darkness, near one of the doors that led to nowhere.

He wasn't moving; I couldn't even hear him breathing. I stopped and listened, but he seemed to be just another shadow melding with the darkness, almost indistinguishable. My eyes, which had grown used to the absence of light, however, clearly made out his dark silhouette ahead of me. He looked like he was pressing himself against the wall, hoping I would simply go by him. There was something familiar about the shape. It made me think immediately about the dark figure who had entered my bedroom the night before.

"Who is it?" I asked in a whisper. "Who are you? Do you live in Troy's cottage?"

There was a long moment of silence and then I heard him respond in a whisper, too.

"Yes," he said.

There was something so familiar about the sound that my heart began thumping. I fumbled with the matches in my left hand, my fingers shaking so much I couldn't get one lit to touch the candle wick.

"Go away," he whispered in a raspy, obviously disguised voice now. "Don't light that candle. Just go away."

I saw him lift his arms before him as though to block me from his view. Then he turned and entered the tunnel that I knew went nowhere. I hesitated. Some part of me was telling me to do just what he had said, to turn around and go back. Sometimes we shouldn't challenge fate and destiny, this voice within me said. Sometimes we're too proud and too determined for our own good. This wouldn't be the first time that I had come to a fork in the road, only to take the more dangerous route.

But it was more than simple stubbornness that now drove me forward. And it was more than anger at Tony. No, there was another part of myself now at odds with caution. This part had been asleep, dormant, kept in storage on some back shelf in my heart. I felt this alter ego open her eyes and stir. I felt her heart beat once again with mine. I felt her emerge and then merge with me, and without any further delay I struck the match and lit the candle that would light my way through the darkness of my own mind and lead me to the answer.

I went forward into the dark end tunnel. The candle lifted the curtain of darkness around me to let me pass under, but I knew the curtain dropped like an iron door behind me as I went. I couldn't help but think about Rye Whiskey's tales of ghosts and disturbed ancestors. What better way for them to travel up from their restless graves than through the secret tunnels? All my childhood fears were sounded. Could Tom's troubled spirit have found its way to these dark veins in the earth? Would I walk into the pocket of darkness that housed my mother's young spirit as well? I looked back into the wall of black. Was it too late to change my mind? Had I already crossed the boundary?

I turned the first bend. The tunnel went a little ways farther and then the wall that Tony had built to shut it off from outside intruders loomed before me. Where was the dark silhouetted figure I had accosted only moments ago? Could I have walked right past him? I slowed my pace and lifted the candle higher, holding it almost at arm's length before me.

Suddenly I felt a breeze to my right and turned just as he stepped out of the darkest shadows. I brought the candle down and he closed his fist around the tiny flame to extinguish the light.

But he was too late. The glow had flashed over his face. The heat in my own must have made it just as bright. His eyes lingered in the darkness even after the candle had been snuffed and they were eyes I would know instantly and forever.

"Troy!" I cried.

"Heaven," he whispered.

And for a moment I was not sure whether or not I had come upon a ghost or an illusion of my own frightened and troubled mind.

I lit the candle again to discover the truth.

❧ SEVEN ❧
Troy

"YOU ARE NOT ONE OF RYE WHISKEY'S GHOSTS," I WHISPERED. I reached out slowly and touched his arm. A small, thin breeze traveled through the tunnels, making the small flame dance on a stage of darkness. The candlelight flickered over his face. His dark eyes which normally had the depth of forest pools looked even darker and deeper.

"No," he replied, "although there are times when I truly feel like one." A small smile played about his beautifully shaped lips. He was wearing a white silk blouse and tight black trousers, but in the darkness, with the tiny flame flickering, the white blouse took on a yellowish tint.

"I don't understand. What happened? What is happening?" I heard the hint of hysteria in my voice. He heard it, too, for he slipped his hand into mine and gently took hold of my palm.

"Let's return to the cottage," he said softly, "and I will tell you all."

I followed him through the dark passageways, feeling as though I had descended into some land of the dead and rescued him from the grips of eternal sleep. Together we were ascending, returning to the world of light and life. As we walked in silence our footsteps echoed behind us and fell back into the spongy blackness that absorbed all sound and quickly stifled it. My heart thumped so hard I was sure he felt the reverberations through my fingers. To me it was as if I were pumping life back into him, resurrecting him with every passing moment. Soon we were in the cottage cellar. He stepped back to permit me to walk up the stairway first. I looked back, hesitating, afraid I would lose him, afraid that the powers of darkness, once I released his hand from mine, would suck him back into the tunnels and into the past. But he remained right behind me, closing the door after we entered the cottage.

"Just before you arrived I was about to have a cup of tea," he said in a casual tone of voice. It was as if all the past two years had evaporated and this was just another one of my amorous visits. "Would you care for one?"

"Yes, please," I said. I sat down at the table quickly, my legs feeling wobbly. He went to the stove and started the flame under the kettle again. I watched him take out the cups and saucers and then get the teabags, not looking at me until he brought it all to the table. I shivered and my expression of pain and confusion must have troubled him.

"Poor Heaven," he said, shaking his head, "how I hoped to avoid this moment and how I longed for it at the same time."

"Oh, Troy," I said, "why?"

"You know why, Heaven," he said hoarsely, "in your heart you've always known. But I shall tell you anyway."

He sighed and sat at the table just across from me. The collar of his white silk shirt was open so that I could see the faint sprinkling of dark hair on his chest. For a long moment he simply stared down at the tabletop, his head lowered. Then he sighed deeply, raked his long fingers through his mass of waving hair, and lifted his heavy, troubled eyes to me. Although he didn't look sickly, he was thinner and paler than I remembered him. His hair was somewhat longer, the ends in the back still curling up. He looked as though he had been shut away from sunlight and life for ages. My heart cried out for him and I had the urge to reach out to comfort and embrace him.

"It was right here, right on this tabletop that I wrote that last letter to you," he began, "telling you how Jillian had come to me and told me that you were Tony's daughter and my niece, telling you how I realized then our love could never be. I told you I was going away to learn to live without you. I thought I could do that and eventually return to Farthinggale to go on with my life as it was before you arrived, as dreary as that life was."

The kettle whistled as if to punctuate his opening statement. We both remained silent as he took the kettle from the stove and poured the hot water. I dipped my teabag quickly, eager to get the liquid warmth into my system to battle away the icicles that had formed within. After a moment Troy sat down and continued.

"As it was probably told to you, I did return to Farthinggale while you were away on that trip to Maine right after your college graduation. I thought I had reached the point where I could return to Farthy and bury myself in the work once again, waiting patiently for my twenty-ninth birthday and what I believed would be my inevitable death before I reached thirty, a death," he said, raising his tired, tormented eyes to me, "I must confess, I now wanted. For to me, Death had become a doorway to a new world, an escape from the misery of living without you. For when I lost you so much of me died. I no longer lived in fear of death, just in quiet expectation."

He paused to sip his tea and looked off for a moment, a quaint, quiet smile coming to his face.

"As usual, Tony thought he could buy away my depression. I don't blame him for that. In fact, I feel sorry for him, knowing the frustration he must have always felt. He made this great party, just to cheer me up and keep me from thinking about my upcoming birthday. He promised he would see to it that I wasn't left alone for a moment." He laughed. "I must say, he had found this girl . . . she must have been part leech. I had to sneak away to go to the bathroom.

"Anyway," he continued, "she couldn't stand my indifference. Apparently, she had always been successful with men and I was proving to be a very annoying frustration. She became rather insulting. It doesn't matter what she said. I wasn't really listening to her anymore and I just wanted to get away from everything and everyone. I had realized that returning to Farthy was a mistake; I couldn't live here being close to you and never having you. I was already being hounded by the memories of your voice. I saw you everywhere around me. It was as if every girl at the party were nothing because she wasn't you. It was maddening, and Jillian knew it. Every time I looked at her she wore a sadistic smile of satisfaction.

"I had no plan; I never intended to do what I did. I think I went for the horses because I was driven by the happy memory of our horseback rides, but when I got to the stables, there was Jillian's horse, looking as defiant and as tormenting to me as Jillian. Impulsively, I decided to ride Abdulla Bar and show that horse it could be handled by someone other than Jillian.

"I know it was a silly, immature thing to do, but I was angry, infuriated at my destiny, enraged at a world that would permit such things to happen. Why was I singled out for such misery? I thought. Why, when I had finally found love and hope, was it ripped away from me and why had fate and destiny put it into Jillian's power to do it? The unfairness of it all was too overwhelming. I didn't care about anything anymore, least of all my own well-being.

"I saddled the horse and we burst out of the stables toward the beach. My fury found its way into the horse. He galloped as though he, too, were running from life, as if he were chosen to be the vehicle to carry me from this existence into the next. Don't you see," he said, some excitement in his eyes as he leaned toward me, "as I was riding that horse, feeling the wind through my hair, sensing the terror in its wide, wild eyes, I became convinced that the horse was meant to carry me out of this world, out of my miserable life. So I deliberately turned him toward the sea, and the horse defiantly charged forward as if it, too, were suicidal.

"We rode into the ocean until the waves lifted us and tossed both horse and man into the deep. I saw the horse struggling behind me, its eyes still angry, defiant, now accusing me of bringing it to this horrible death, and for a moment I did feel pity for it and hated myself. I could touch nothing without destroying or harming it, I thought. I was meant to be swept out to sea.

"I closed my eyes," he said, sitting back in his chair and closing his eyes as he spoke, "willing and ready to accept my inevitable death."

He opened his eyes, now cloudy with foreboding.

"But the ocean cannot be controlled or made to serve any man's desires. It is a slave to no one, even one as desperate and as determined as I was to use it as an instrument of death. Every time I went under, the waves lifted me up and out. I bobbed and floated. I was tossed and carried. I lost my boots. I saw Abdulla Bar lifted and washed back toward shore until he could touch the bottom and bring himself out and onto the beach.

"I closed my eyes and waited for the mighty ocean, the great waves I had often listened to and stared at alone at night, fascinated with their beauty and their strength, to take me down into their cold darkness.

"But instead I was cast about until I lost consciousness. When I awoke, I was some distance down shore, sprawled on the beach, alive, my appeal for a quick, painless death rejected. As I lay there feeling sorry for myself, I suddenly realized that the ocean had at least provided some relief—it had given me the opportunity to be considered dead. I could truly leave my identity and my life at Farthy behind. In a real sense I had effected an escape from some of my misery.

"So I gathered myself up and without permitting anyone to know what had happened to me, not even Tony, especially Tony, I returned surreptitiously to my cottage for what I thought would be the last time, and I took some of the things I wanted and needed and then went off to disappear into the night."

He sat back again, as if that had explained it all. My feelings of shock and amazement were quickly replaced with feelings of anger. Oh, oh, oh! All the pain he had caused—letting me think he was dead.

And now it was too late. Too late for us to be together! How could he let me suffer so when he was alive? Alive all this time!

"But what about the pain you caused in permitting us all to think you had died? Don't you know what it did to me?"

"I believed it was nothing compared to the pain you would have had to endure living your life knowing I was nearby, knowing we could never be lovers; nothing compared to the pain you would have knowing the torment I was going to endure as well. I realized it was selfish in a way, but I thought it was better.

"It was better," he added, nodding. "Don't you see, Heaven, you've pulled your life together and done significant things. Perhaps if you thought I was still alive, if I had continued to live here in the cottage, you would never have left Farthy. Perhaps you would be like Jillian. I don't know. I thought I was doing what was best for both of us. I hope you will come to believe that. It would be too painful for me to have you hate me now," he said. His dark eyes were filled with the fear of just that happening.

"I don't hate you, Troy," I said. "I can't hate you. I hate only what has happened. What did you do after you left that beach?"

"I traveled about." He sat back and tucked his hands behind his head as he spoke, remembering and reciting his secret existence. "I went to Italy and studied the great masters of art and architecture. I went to Spain and France. I sought relief in travel and in distractions. For a while that worked. I tired myself out moving about from one place to the next, and then"—he paused and straightened up in his chair again, again leaning toward me—"suddenly, I woke up one night in England. I was staying in an inn near Dover Beach. I had gone there because I couldn't stop thinking about that poem by Matthew Arnold. Remember it? I once read it to you. Some of the lines haunted me.

> "Ah, love, let us be true
> To one another! for the world, which seems
> To lie before us like a land of dreams,
> So various, so beautiful, so new,
> Hath really neither joy, nor love, nor light,
> Nor certitude, nor peace, nor help for pain . . .

"It seemed so true, especially for us. I lay there in my down-quilted bed listening to the sound of the sea and I thought I heard your voice; I thought I heard you calling to me from the ocean and I thought there was no longer any point in running away. I couldn't run away.

Not from you, not from the memory of your face and your voice and your touch.

"I made up my mind that night to return to defy nature and the gods if need be. I was coming back to you, to beg you to come back to me. I was willing to live as an outcast, to give up anything and everything if we could only be together, even if it was just to hold you in my arms while the winds of winter blew around the cottage. That would be enough, I thought, for if I were to die before my thirtieth birthday, as I had always feared, I would die in your arms. That was where I belonged."

"Oh, Troy, dear, dear Troy. Why didn't you write? Why didn't you try to contact me?" I cried.

"It didn't matter. By the time I had made up my mind to do this, you had already become engaged to Logan."

"But how did you know?" I asked. He smiled and finished the tea in his cup.

"I was in Winnerow just before your wedding. I came in disguise and actually was in Logan's parents' drugstore. I heard the conversations and learned of your engagement. So I turned around and left, but instead of returning to a life spent incognito, traveling abroad, I decided to return to the cottage to end my days and I've been here ever since.

"I saw your wedding reception at Farthy, watched it from behind one of the hedges in the maze. You looked so beautiful and Tony looked so happy. I even followed you and Logan about the grounds during your honeymoon, spied on you from afar, dreaming it was I who held you in his arms; it was I whom you kissed. For a while there, my imagination worked so well, I actually felt you beside me.

"It was wrong to do that; I know," he said quickly. "But forgive me. I couldn't help myself."

"Of course I forgive you. I understand how hard it must have been for you to watch without my seeing you." Oh, my own Troy, having to watch me marrying Logan! I couldn't bear to imagine it. Why hadn't he stepped forward, why?

"It was hard, painfully hard." His dark eyes flashed with life and light for the first time. "I wanted you to see me; I was working up the courage for that," he said. "Last night, knowing Logan wasn't here, I went to your room after you returned from wherever you had gone with Tony."

"I sensed something last night, although I didn't know it was you. I awoke and called out because I saw a body silhouetted in the darkness."

He stared at me for a moment.

"Why did you come here today?" he asked softly. "Because you thought it might be me?"

"No. I felt like someone under hypnosis, but I didn't know I would find you. When I realized someone was here, I thought it was someone Tony hired to work here. I thought he had lied to me and I wanted to confront this person, and then I suddenly had the feeling I was in the presence of something spiritual, maybe in the presence of a ghost."

"I am not a ghost, Heaven. Not anymore." He sat back and stared at me. "You've changed, grown older, wiser looking. Your beauty has matured. It makes me tremble to be this close to you, to actually hear your voice now."

He leaned forward and reached out to touch my face. I didn't move away, but I didn't feel his fingers on my skin. He sat back slowly.

"I feel like a little boy fascinated with a fire, wanting to touch it, even though I know to do so will only bring me pain."

"Oh, Troy," I said. The warm tears emerged from the corners of my eyes and zigzagged over my cheeks. He reached out again and this time I felt his fingertips caress my skin. I closed my eyes.

"How many times can I lose you, Heaven? Is this just another way for fate to torment me?"

I sat back in my chair, unable to speak. He handed me a handkerchief and I dabbed at my face. My sniffing brought a smile to his lips and then a small, gentle laugh. I shook my head, realizing what all this meant.

"Come into the living room," he said, "where it is more comfortable."

I nodded and went to the couch. Just like in the old days he sprawled on the carpet and looked up at me, his hands tucked behind his head.

"Troy," I said, shaking my head. "I can't believe that this isn't all a dream, that you're actually there looking up at me the way you used to."

"I know."

"When did Tony know you were still alive?" I asked.

"Actually, not until very recently. I was surprised when I returned to find the cottage just the way I had left it. I realized that Tony refused to accept my death. How ironic, I thought, and, of course, I realized what sort of pain I must have brought him. It made it all the more difficult to go to him to confess my ruse. I tried unsuccessfully a number of times."

"You wandered the house at night," I said, realizing now what the servants meant, that Rye Whiskey hadn't been imagining things when he thought there were spirits of the dead haunting the dark halls of Farthy.

"Yes. I even sat at the piano, hoping he would simply find me there, but when he didn't come upon me quickly, I lost my nerve. I thought I was recognized by the servants, but I imagine the sight of my darkened visage and body floating through those dimly lit hallways terrified them."

"You don't know just how much," I said, shaking my head.

"And then, one night, while you were away in Winnerow, I came upon Jillian just outside her suite. Apparently, her nurse had fallen asleep and she was free to wander about alone. I'll never forget that look on her face." He sat up, recalling the moment. "Her face seemed to age right before my eyes. She lost whatever semblance of youth she had managed to hold on to in her madness.

" 'No,' she said, 'it wasn't my fault. You can't blame me. I did what I had to do.' "

He turned to me, his eyes filled with pain and sorrow. He was compassionate and sensitive about hurting other people, even those who deliberately set out to hurt him. Oh, Troy, I thought, you are too good for this world. No wonder you were always haunted by fears of death.

"I reached out for her and called to her. 'Jillian, it's all right,' I said, but she was terrified and ran from me. One time after that I think she saw me from her bedroom window as I passed through the maze."

"But still Tony didn't know?"

"Shortly after that he came to the cottage. I imagine Jillian said something to him or to the nurse and it made him think of me and of coming here. Even though he had kept up the cottage, he apparently couldn't bring himself to come to it that often."

"He kept it as a shrine," I whispered and he nodded.

"But this day he came. I heard him approaching. I couldn't get myself to greet him at the door. Like a coward I hovered in that closet. I watched him come in and look about, his strong, dignified face weakening. He went to the rocker by the fireplace and stood by it, his hand on the back, rocking it gently and looking down at it, imagining me in it, I'm sure. Then he turned about and started to leave.

"But you see, all the while I was here, I couldn't help myself . . . I had started new work. It just seemed to be a natural thing for me to do. I was in the cottage. The tools were there; the materials were there. I had ideas, so I worked. He saw the new things and went to them. For a few moments he handled everything, looking like a gold panner who had finally discovered nuggets. Then he raised his head and spun about.

" 'Troy,' he called. 'Troy.'

"Whatever fears I had fell away. I saw the happiness in his face and could deny him the truth no longer. You know what Tony's and my relationship has been, since my mother died before my first birthday and my father before I was two years old. Tony was really the only parent I can remember. He was my world. I adored him and he loved me, protected me, worried over my every illness. Things changed between us only after he married Jillian. I was jealous of her and she was jealous of me.

"But seeing him there, the realization that I might still be alive on his face, I couldn't bear myself for having held back this long. I stepped out of the closet."

"What did he do?" I asked breathlessly.

"He burst into tears and embraced me. For a long while we just held on to each other, and then, when things calmed down, we sat here and I told him the story I told you."

"And what was his reaction to all that?"

"He was angry at first, just like you were. I kept apologizing and trying to make him understand my motives. After a while he did."

"But he didn't bring you back to the house and he didn't tell me you were still alive."

"No. We made promises to each other."

"Promises?"

"Naturally, he told me all about you, told me about your marriage and how Logan was becoming part of Tatterton Toys and how he had gotten you to move back into Farthy and be part of the family again. He's terrified that you'll leave him now. I can't say I blame him for that. If you do leave him, what does he have? Jillian's mad as a hatter, and I, I'm more convinced than ever that I can't remain here much longer."

"So what did you promise?" I asked.

"To keep myself away from you, so as not to ruin your marriage and your life at Farthy. And truly, Heaven, much as I longed for you, to speak to you, to see you again, I, too, thought that best. Tony promised to keep my existence a secret from everyone, not just from you, so I could go on living a new life.

"We made plans for me to establish myself somewhere else and do my work under a different name. It's painful for both of us, but we both realize why the sacrifices have to be made."

He looked up at me, his dark eyes pleading for understanding. I nodded slowly, so many realizations were crowding into my mind all at once.

"I see," I said. "So now he realized also that Jillian wasn't talking madness when she described the ghosts."

"Yes."

"And that explains why he wasn't so concerned about the changes that had come over her. He didn't panic because he knew she wasn't really getting worse. In fact, the prescription of tranquilizers was the best thing, under the circumstances. It would keep her from talking more and more about you, imprison her in her own madness."

"I don't care," Troy said, with a sudden uncharacteristic note of contempt. "Jillian never liked me. She couldn't wait to do something to hurt me deeply. What's happened to her is poetic justice. I don't want to inflict any more pain on her, but I don't want to feel sorry for her. I think Tony has come to feel the same way."

"Maybe," I said. We stared at each other. Once again I was plunged into Troy's world, with reality far beyond the door. Here in his safe, snug, and warm home, there was only beauty and kindness for me. His soft, dark eyes caressed me and flooded warmth into my face. I felt my lips being drawn to his, but I resisted. Logan's image danced before my eyes. Logan. My husband, my forever true love.

"Oh, Heaven," Troy said, as if he could read my thoughts and understand. "Why is it that for us to be happy, so many others must be made unhappy?"

"I don't know. It does seem as though fate is playing with our hearts and lives." I stood up quickly and went to the window that looked out on the maze, my heart tormented by love for two men. For a long moment we were both silent. "Logan is so excited about his new life," I said. "He's off in Winnerow overseeing the construction of the new factory."

"Tony told me all about it. It sounds like a wonderful project. I've even thought of contributing a new toy or two."

"Really?" I turned back to him. The walls of my heart quivered. I held the tears within and swallowed the cries that threatened to emerge from my throbbing throat. "Logan adores me," I said. "He's sensitive to my every mood and feeling. He was there when I needed love and comfort the most. He's always been there."

"I know," Troy said. "Heaven, you know I didn't want to do anything to bring you any more pain and agony. If I hadn't been so weak, I would have left before you discovered me and followed the plan Tony outlined. As usual, he knows best. And now I've only succeeded in putting you into an emotional turmoil. It seems I can't stop hurting the ones I love."

"Oh, no, Troy. You mustn't think that way," I said, going to him. "I'm not in pain; I won't be in pain. I promise you."

He nodded even though we both knew what I said was untrue. Why was it that life demanded us to lie to ourselves so often? I wondered. Wasn't it ironic that in order to be happy, we had to be self-deceptive, we had to live in illusion?

"I'll be leaving soon now anyway."

"When?"

He stood up and walked slowly toward the front door. "I'm not going to tell you and I'm not going to tell you where I'm going. Don't force me to do that," he said and smiled softly. "Let's just think of this as an interlude, a gift from the gods, a few moments when we cheated Death and leave it at that. Don't tell Tony what you've discovered. He doesn't have to know I've broken my promise."

"Of course I won't tell him. But Troy, do you really expect me simply to walk out that door and forget you?"

"No, I don't expect you to forget me, but it's best that you think of me as I was . . . gone. Funny," he said, widening his smile, "I've passed my thirtieth birthday and I'm still here. I guess you were always right to be optimistic."

We stared at each other.

"Troy . . ."

"If I kiss you I'll never let you go and we'll only bring about more sadness and tragedy, for you'll be losing a life and a marriage that promises to be productive and replacing it with a forbidden, sinful love that leads to nothing but our own selfish pleasures. You know that as well as I do," he said. I nodded and lowered my head. He reached out and lifted my chin. "Let me remember you smiling," he said.

I smiled through the tears and the pain like sunshine in the rain. He opened the cottage door and I passed through. He stood there for a moment looking out at me and then he closed the door. I felt the walls around my heart collapse. My tears poured forth. I clenched my hands into fists and turned to run down the walkway and to the maze, charging into it and through its corridors like a wild and frenzied animal, like Abdulla Bar, his eyes red and wild, charging toward the sea. My cries were like long, thin scarfs blowing behind me. I didn't stop until I burst out of the maze to face Farthy.

I ground away the tears with my fists and continued forward, pausing once to look up toward Jillian's window. Once again there she was, looking out. This time she wore a look of satisfaction. In her madness she knew the painful truths, truths that had begun years ago when my mother had pressed her body against Tony's and begun a sinful love whose insidious tentacles, like the vines along the walls of Farthy, crawled in and out of the lives of all of us and would continue to do so until our dying days.

I intended to go right up to my suite to lie down, but Curtis greeted me with the news that Logan had been calling. With his usual cigar store Indian stiffness, Tony's butler waited in the hallway with Logan's message on a slip of paper. I had the impression he had been standing there ever since Logan called, waiting for my return.

"Mr. Stonewall has phoned twice, Mrs. Stonewall. The last time was only minutes ago. He gave me this number for you to call."

"Thank you, Curtis," I said. I went directly to the living room to use the gold antique phone and dialed the number. My hands were trembling. A man answered.

"Mr. Stonewall? Yes, ma'am. Right away," he said in an excited tone of voice. I heard a buzz of activity in the background—people talking loudly to one another, a typewriter clicking, another phone ringing, and the sound of bulldozers and other construction equipment just outside a nearby window.

"Heaven, where have you been?" Logan asked as soon as he got on the line.

"Just walking about the grounds." I was desperate to envision him, to feel close to him, my husband, my anchor. "What's all that noise?"

"Oh, this is my headquarters," he said, the pride in his voice so obvious I could imagine him pulling his shoulders back, holding his head high, and smiling. "I set up a small trailer on the factory site. I have an assistant. That's who answered the phone. Maybe you remember him—Frank Stratton, Steve Stratton's youngest boy. Stratton's Lumber Company," he added when I didn't respond.

"Sounds like you're very busy," I said.

"It's going well, Heaven. I wish you had decided to come along this trip, just so you could see the progress. We're well past the midway point and I've found two artisans in the Willies who could carve a Madonna out of a birch branch."

"That's wonderful," I said, trying to sound enthusiastic, but I was still in a state of shock. All I could think about was Troy. Troy still alive!

"Anyway, I was calling to tell you I can't come home today. I'm going to have to stay until the weekend. We have too many problems to solve on the site."

"Oh, Logan."

"I know. I never intended to leave you alone so long, but everyone's afraid to make a decision without my okay," he said. "Maybe you should fly down here."

I thought about it. Maybe I should leave immediately, run to the harbor of Logan's arms, where Troy was only a dimmed memory. Yet . . . yet . . . I wanted to be at Farthy, more than ever now.

"No, it's just another day and a half," I said, trying to sound cheerful and self-controlled.

"You're upset. I'm sorry. It's hard for me, too, being away from you, but I keep telling myself, all this is really for Heaven."

"You're getting to be some smooth talker, Logan Stonewall," I said. He laughed. "I spoke to Tony this morning. He told me you went to a wonderful play last night."

"Yes."

"I'm sorry I wasn't there to go along, but I promise you, as soon as this is finished—"

"Don't make promises, Logan. Let's just take every day as it comes and goes," I said. There was a moment's silence.

"You sound very sad, Heaven. Is anything wrong? I mean, other than my having to stay over?"

"No," I said quickly. "I just don't want to suffer any disappointments."

"Sure. I understand," he said. "Mom and Dad send their regards."

"Thank them. Have you seen Fanny?"

"Fanny? No. She's . . . I think she went somewhere with Randall Wilcox this week."

"She's still seeing him?"

"Now and again," he said quickly. "I'll call you tonight," he said. "Please, remember how much I love you."

"I will," I promised. After we ended the conversation, I just sat there for a while staring at the piano.

Haunted by love and confusion, I rose and went up to my suite. I must have fallen into a deep sleep right away, for when I awoke, it was almost dark and there was a gentle rapping at my door. It was Tony.

"The servants informed me you have been in your suite all day. You didn't even come out for lunch. Is anything wrong?" he asked, narrowing his steady gaze. I looked away, fearful that Tony, with his penetrating eyes, would see into my heart and find Troy's image there, vibrant and alive. Would I be able to keep the promise I made to Troy, the promise not to let Tony know I had seen Troy! How could I continue to act the same toward Tony, knowing that he had known

Troy was alive and kept it from me? I resented him for not telling me the truth, yet I realized he was only trying to protect me.

"Just a summer head cold," I said. "I took a few aspirin and fell asleep."

"You must have gotten a chill last night after we left the theater. Feeling better?"

"A little."

"Is it warm enough in here?" He looked around the sitting room.

"Oh, yes."

"Well," he said. He appeared uncomfortable, standing in the doorway, but I hadn't invited him in. All I could think of was closing the door and returning to my bed. "You spoke to Logan, I assume."

"Yes. Sounds as if everything's going well."

Tony shrugged. "There are a few glitches. I'll probably fly down there tomorrow just for the day. Want to go along?"

"No, I don't think so. If it's nice, I'd rather sunbathe here for a while."

"Okay. See you at dinner?"

"If you don't mind," I said, "please have something sent up. I'd rather take dinner in the suite tonight. I'm still not feeling a hundred percent."

He raised an eyebrow and studied me even more intently. Surely now he will realize what I have discovered, I thought. I didn't have his inscrutable face. I was more like Jillian. My emotions were usually undressed, parading about my eyes and lips, ready to announce each and every feeling within my heart.

"Perhaps I should send for Doctor Mallen," he suggested.

"No, no."

"But—"

"I promise. If I don't feel better in the morning, I'll have you do so," I said quickly.

"All right. I'll instruct Curtis to bring your dinner up here. It'll be lonely for me, though," he said, smiling. "You know what it's like eating in that big room with Curtis standing right behind me waiting for me to drop a spoon."

I laughed. How well I knew that!

"That's better," he said. "I'll check up on you later," he promised and left.

Oh, Tony, I thought after he closed the door, I don't know whether to pity you or to hate you. I felt like someone riding a merry-go-round, all the horses constantly moving up and down and around, nothing still enough to afford a point of reference, to show where, in fact, solid ground could be found. All my feelings, like those fanciful ponies, were being pulled from both directions, up and down and spun around until I felt dizzy inside.

I wanted to be alone to try and sort them out, and yet I was afraid to be alone. Lying there in the silence of my bedroom, I fought back thoughts of Troy, thoughts that were now more forbidden than ever. It was on this bed, wrapped in Logan's arms, feeling his kisses on my lips and cheeks, that I had uttered promises of love and devotion to him as he had uttered them to me. It seemed a terrible betrayal to rest my head against the pillow and envision Troy's eyes, Troy's lips, Troy's kisses, while the scent of Logan's cologne lingered on the sheets.

Trying to fight back these invading images of Troy, I tried to picture Logan when he first came to Winnerow, for first love, young love, is something a woman can never forget. It carries special charms that linger forever and forever. Even when I became an old lady, older than Jillian, older than Granny, I knew that I, like every woman, would stop in my rocking chair, senile or not, and recall the special excitement I felt when my heart first fluttered because of a boy's look, a boy's touch. Such memories can warm the loneliest heart and turn the saddest eyes into gleeful ones. They were like the perennial fruits —apples, peaches, plums—that blossomed on the trees over and over again every year. No matter how old the trees were, there was always some fruit, something fresh and wonderful. Good and happy memories, especially memories that made you more aware of life's thrilling moments, were the fruits of life's labor.

And so it was with Logan and me when we were both young and fresh in the Willies. I could draw the images from my precious trunk of recollections and once again picture Logan that first time I set eyes on him in school. He stood out like a prep school boy in his sharply creased gray flannel slacks and his bright green sweater worn over a white shirt and a gray-and-green striped tie. No one ever came to our school dressed up as Logan Stonewall did.

I could still hear my brother Tom first introduce us.

"And this is my sister, Heaven Leigh." There was so much pride in Tom's voice.

"What a pretty name," Logan said. "It suits you very well. I don't think I've ever seen more heavenly blue eyes."

After he said that our eyes seemed to cling and strike a gong that would resound throughout our lives.

Logan Stonewall, my beautiful first and forever boyfriend, good-looking in the kind of way I'd seen in books and magazines, like someone with years and years of cultured background that had given him what none of us in the hills had—quality.

As if they were a protective cape, I wrapped the memories of these early days around myself to keep out the feelings and temptations knocking at my door and for a while, a long while, that worked well. Curtis brought me my dinner and I ate most of it. Afterward, Tony came, as he had promised, to see how I was doing. Satisfied that I was merely sleeping off a minor head cold, he left, telling me he would be leaving early in the morning to catch a plane for Winnerow.

"I won't see you before I leave, but I'll call during the day," he said, "to see if you're indeed all right."

He lingered before saying good night, as if he wanted to say more or ask more, but there was a fog of silence between us best not penetrated. I think he sensed that.

"Good night," he said.

I closed the door after him and once again retreated into my own thoughts, reaching back through time to find diversion in the happier memories.

Only this time my mind betrayed me. Instead of remembering the wonderful early days with Logan, I recalled Troy coming to my graduation from the Winterhaven School. I had been terribly disappointed to learn that Jillian and Tony would be in London that day. I would have no one to see me reach the accomplishment that had once seemed so distant and impossible when I lived in the Willies.

In single file the graduates paraded in to take their seats. I was eighth from the front girl and at first I saw only a blur of unfamiliar faces. Then I saw Troy, seated out there, looking up at me with such an expression of pride and delight. I had felt a rush of happiness such as I'd seldom known before because Troy had come and had asked several of Tatterton Toy Corporation officers and their families to show up as my family.

"Did you really think I wouldn't come?" he had teased as we drove home that night after the school dance. "I never knew a girl who needed a family more than you, so I wanted to give you a huge one."

How I had wanted to hug and kiss him then. I think that was when I first realized I was falling in love with him, slipping and sliding down a tunnel of affection, the walls of which were greased with sympathetic words, loving phrases and touches, soft, compassionate eyes, and hopeful promises.

I recalled how we had walked quietly in the garden and talked until it began to rain and how he had fled from me that night. When I had asked him why he was leaving me so early, he told me it was because I was young and healthy and full of dreams he couldn't possibly share.

How prophetic he was.

Oh, Troy! I crushed the pillow against my face, smothering the sound of my sobs. Can I let you die a second time?

❧ EIGHT ❧
Forbidden Passions

IT WAS AFTER TWO A.M. I FELT AS IF I WERE IN A DREAM. FOR hours I had dwelled fitfully on the rim of sleep, tossing and turning, moaning and crying softly. Finally I fell more into a state of troubled unconsciousness than the peaceful oblivion I had so desperately sought. I saw myself hanging from the edge of a sharp cliff, dangling hopelessly above the darkness. The jagged edges of the rock to which I clung cut painfully into my fingers until I had to let go. I felt myself endlessly falling and awoke with a start.

I sat up quickly. The illusion of hanging from that cliff had been so vivid that I actually felt pain in my fingers. I opened and closed my hands and looked about the room. Moonlight cast a thin white beam through the curtains. I felt as though I were looking through gauze.

Suddenly the silence around me was pierced by the silvery soft notes of the piano below. Was it my active imagination at work, or had Troy taken another of his nocturnal, ghostlike walks and made his way back to the past? Was this his way of mourning for our lost love, crying through the music, or was this his way of calling to me? If he was calling to me, why was he haunting me with impossible promises?

I got out of the bed, put on my velvet slippers and went to the door of the suite. My fingers trembled as I turned the brass handle. When I opened the door and looked down the corridor, all was silent and dark. The piano music had to have been a trick my mind was playing, I thought. No one else had been lured out of sleep by it. Yet I didn't close the door and return to bed. I stepped forward, like a sleepwalker, feeling as if I were floating over the carpet, and continued down the dimly lit hallways.

For a moment I lingered at the top of the stairway and looked down at the empty rooms below. The great house seemed to be holding its breath. I took one step and then another and another, still feeling as if I really hadn't awakened, as if this was all part of that tumultuous nightmare that had seized hold of me. I paused at the doorway of the living room and looked in at the piano. No one was there. The keyboard was closed. All was still; all was quiet, yet I felt a flush come into my cheeks and throat as if I had discovered Troy waiting, pleading for me to come to him. I wanted it to happen so much that I couldn't admit to myself that he wasn't calling to me.

I didn't return to my suite. That secret part of me that had been stirred was now in command. I proceeded on through the dining room to the kitchen and the pantry that led to the doorway which opened on the stairway leading down into the tunnels. I took up the candle and its holder from the shelf by the door and lit the flame, which, like a gentle hand, parted the darkness below, laying out a flickering yellow pathway for me to follow.

Each step I took was accompanied by the imagined voices, some whispering warnings, some beckoning me softly. As the light washed the blackness from the tunnel walls, I saw a gallery of faces there from past and present, each animated, each offering words of advice or condemnation. There was Granny telling me to be careful, warning me about unseen evil spirits. There was Luke scowling and nodding as if to say I was doing what he expected I would do. There was Tom, beautiful, graceful Tom, urging me to think of Logan; there was Fanny laughing lewdly, urging me to go forward to satisfy myself. And there was Jillian, heavily made up, warning me that I was only going to grow old before my time. Finally there was Tony, looking scared and jealous, pleading with me to turn back.

I moved around a bend in the tunnel and all the faces drew back into the darkness behind me. I was alone once again, surrounded by silence so deep I could hear the thumping of my own heart. After a moment that was replaced by the melodious tinkling of the piano. Was I still dreaming? Was I really here?

I paused when I reached the cellar of the cottage. There was still time to turn back, I thought, and hesitated before going any farther. But a breeze coming from behind me made the candle flicker and before I could cup it protectively, the light went out, leaving me in pitch darkness. I saw a dim glow emanating from the door upstairs. When I peered up the stairway, I saw that Troy had left the door open.

Was he expecting me or was he merely hoping I would come to him? Or had he indeed just returned from playing the piano in Farthy and left the door open, knowing what the magic of our past memories could do? I looked back into the darkness behind me and then, with my heart thumping harder than ever, began to ascend the stairway. Just before I reached the doorway, his silhouette appeared in the light of a small lamp behind him. His face was masked in shadows, but I saw his hands reach out for me.

"Oh, Heaven!" he cried. "You shouldn't have come."

"I know," I whispered. As my eyes drank in his precious beauty, I took his hand.

"You should turn back before it's too late," he whispered, but his eyes belied his words.

"It's already too late," I insisted, putting all my love and passion into my low raspy voice.

"We must not do this," he said, but he pulled me closer to him and caught me up in his arms and pressed me against him. "Oh, Heaven, how can I turn you away?" He swung me up into his arms and carried me to this bed.

Many times since that fateful day when I had found Tony by the beach and he had described Troy's death to me, I had made love to Troy in my hungry imagination. It was my way of bringing him back to life. I had longed so for this moment, even during the time Logan began to court me again. And now, in Troy's arms with his eyes gazing lovingly into mine, this all seemed more like something imagined, something dreamt.

He continued to offer frail statements of protest, even as we clung to each other, but I was protective of our stolen moments of passion and joy and I kissed him into silence again and again until all the hesitation in him disappeared.

A part of me still wanted to resist, a part of me remembered that for better or for worse, I was married to another man. But in Troy's arms, and with his lips against mine, tasting his passion caused whatever resistance that lingered to quickly die.

I didn't care. I loved him, I would always love him. I wanted him to consume me just as a flame consumed that kindling that fueled it. It seemed appropriate that we would die in each other's arms and go up in the smoke of our demanding passion. Never had I felt such passion for a man. Never had our lovemaking been as intense and exciting as it was at this moment, perhaps because it was so forbidden. I surrendered myself completely to our love.

"Oh, Troy," I whispered, "I've dreamed of you, longed for this moment so much."

He kissed me deeply. "I love you still, Heaven. Still and always my heavenly Heaven."

Our lovemaking was so wonderful, it brought tears of happiness to my eyes, tears he eagerly kissed away. Over and over we reached an ecstasy from only of the truest, deepest passion, a passion that knew no right or wrong.

After it was over we lay in each other's arms, satisfied, spent, like two small boats caught in a hurricane after they've come home to harbor.

"Heaven," Troy asked as he caressed my hair, "how can something so wonderful and good be sinful? It's a cruel joke that's been played on us."

"I don't care," I said defiantly. "All I care about is being in your arms and having you hold me tightly to your body. Let's stay like this until we die."

He laughed and kissed first my right eye, then my left.

"How much you sound like the Heaven I first met," he exclaimed, "wildly hopeful and willing to challenge any obstacles to our love. But it's all different now; it's all changed," he said sadly. "I shouldn't have allowed this to happen. I'm afraid you're going to be sorry when you think about it later on. I'm sorry."

"Oh, no, Troy!" I cried and held him more tightly to me. "Never. I'll never be sorry about loving you, about wanting you, about giving myself completely to you."

He sat up in the moonlight and combed his fingers through his long hair, his beautiful, sensitive face erased by the silvery light filtering in through the window. Then he turned to me.

"Perhaps you don't know yourself as well as I know you, Heaven." His voice was low and gravelly, and sadder than tragedy. "Think about Logan, about what you've started together. Can you just cast all that aside for a few stolen moments of pleasure with me?"

"I don't care," I insisted. "I will treasure this moment for as long as I live."

"Yes, but what about Tony? He might find out; he would be furious and would end the construction of that factory in Winnerow. And if the folks in Winnerow found out why, you could never, ever go home to the Willies again, Heaven. You, yourself, know how much incest goes on in the hills. People there would condemn you as just another hillbilly. The people in the Willies would resent you for destroying their newfound hope, their only chance to better themselves. You would be more alone than ever."

"I wouldn't be alone if I were with you," I pleaded, clinging to him as if for dear life.

"Could you live with yourself, knowing what kind of pain you imposed on poor Logan? None of this is his fault. You admit yourself that he is devoted to you, that he loves you dearly. Is this your way of repaying him?"

"Oh, Troy." His arguments tore at my frail bubble of joy. I felt crushed, my rainbow world crushed by truth and reality, and I hated it. I searched my thoughts for a way to overcome the inevitable end.

He got up from the bed and walked to the window. I watched him staring out at the dark world in silence, hot tears now streaming down my face.

"Don't think there isn't a part of me that wants to encourage you to do it. I told you, I came back hoping to spend the rest of my life with you, no matter what the consequences, but that was before all this. There are too many people to hurt now. Oh, we could be happy for a short while, but Heaven"—he sighed, turning back to me—"neither of us is insensitive enough to live with the pain we would cause. You know I am right about that, don't you?" he asked softly. I nodded and he came to me. He kissed away my hot tears and stroked my hair.

"I can't give you up. I can't!" I cried.

"My poor, precious Heaven," Troy soothed.

"Troy," I said, straightening up quickly, a childlike excitement returning to my voice, "why can't we have it both ways? Don't leave the cottage. Don't leave Farthinggale. I'll come to you whenever I can. No one need ever know. The tunnels our ancestors built will become a blessing, a way to link us forever and ever."

"Oh, my darling," he said. "Don't you realize that would be even more painful for us? Every time you left me to go back to Logan, every time we heard some sound near the cottage and jumped in fear, we would suffer additional agony. And how long would it be before Logan would realize that your kisses were restrained? That you were holding yourself back for another man?

"A man can sense that, you know. I don't care how busy he is, when he comes home at night and looks for tenderness and love, he will feel that your heart is somewhere else. There you will be denying his accusations, covering up, living like some sort of criminal or spy. Maybe he would employ one of the servants to watch you while he was away. Maybe he would complain to Tony, who would soon realize what was going on.

"And after the truth was revealed, how would you feel about yourself? How could you face Logan? No, darling Heaven. It would be even worse for us to carry on in secret, traveling through the underground tunnels, meeting when Logan was away or you could steal an hour here, an hour there

"Our love, our precious, beautiful love would become something sordid, sneaky, even ugly."

"And do you know what would eventually happen? Eventually you would come to resent me for it," he said. Then he gently ran the palm of his hand down the side of my face. I closed my eyes at his touch.

"What makes you so wise?" I asked him.

"I'd rather not be, believe me. You know that the things I am telling you are true, don't you? You realize how painful it is and will be for me to deny you?"

"Yes," I said. "I know because I know how painful it is for me."

We stared at each other in the darkness, our eyes lit by the moon. We were like two stars blinking at each other in the night sky, so bright, so eager to touch and become one, and yet so distant.

"Go back, Heaven," he whispered sadly. I reached out and touched his lips with the tip of my fingers to silence him.

"Not yet," I said. "If we have stolen one precious time, one night more together, let us enjoy it together until the end. I want to lie here beside you until the first light of morning. Then I will rise quietly and leave your bed forever."

He said nothing. He didn't resist. He kissed my neck and drew me back down to him. We fell asleep in each other's arms afterward, but I awoke at the break of day, just as I had promised. I was facing the window, and I watched as the morning light began to lift away the veil of darkness. I had hoped the night would go on forever, but morning had come, just as truth and reality had, just as all the things Troy had said would happen would come. There was no denying time. Our love was too fragile, too private to hold back the flood of minutes and hours, days and months, all the years we would be without each other.

My heart felt like a brick in my chest. Gently I untangled myself from his embrace. Troy was locked in sleep. He looked like a little boy, dreaming of holiday happiness, perhaps dreaming of some tiny new Tatterton Toy. Maybe it was a toy world in which two people like us could share their love without restraint.

I slipped silently from the bed and put on my nightgown and peignoir. I got back into my slippers and went out to the kitchen to get a match to light the candle in my holder. When I looked back at Troy, he was still asleep, his eyes shut tight, his lips closed gently. I thought about going to him and kissing him once more, but I was afraid to wake him. It was better for him and for me that I simply go. Perhaps when he finally awoke, he would think it had all been a dream. Perhaps after I got back to my suite and into my bed, I would think it had all been a dream. Perhaps it had all been a dream.

I closed the door behind me and made my way down the stairs into the cellar and then started through the tunnels. All was quiet. The voices that had escorted me during the night had been silenced by our lovemaking. There were no faces on the walls. I passed through the darkness swiftly and made my way up the stairs, through the back of the kitchen and into the great house. It was still early enough for all to be quiet. No one had yet stirred.

I went up the stairs and paused in the corridor. The strong morning sun was beginning to lift away the dimness and the chill that accompanied it. Without further hesitation I went toward my suite. But just before I reached the door, I heard a horrible scream echo down the corridor. I turned as Martha Goodman came running out of Jillian's suite, her hands pressed against her cheeks. She turned in a circle until she saw me standing there.

"Heaven!" she screamed. "Come quickly! Quickly!"

I rushed down the corridor just as Tony, dressed in his blue silk robe, emerged from his suite. He looked at me and I raised my arms to indicate I knew nothing. We both followed Martha into Jillian's bedroom and discovered what it was that had caused her hysteria.

Jillian was slumped in her soft velvet vanity chair facing the empty mirror frame. Her arms dangled over the sides. She was dressed in her black wool crepe suit trimmed with a mink collar and cuffs. From beneath her jacket peeked a glittering black chiffon blouse. I remembered her in that outfit. I remembered how beautiful she had looked, how stunning, how like a diamond set against black velvet.

The room reeked of her jasmine perfume, suggesting she had bathed herself in it. Her hair was pinned up with pearl combs and she had been at her face again, caking it with makeup, staring into an illusion of herself and going through those long, intricate beauty rituals that used to take up so much of her time.

Only this time she had been preparing herself for her final gala affair. I gasped and seized Tony's arm as we both stared down at what was obviously a dead Jillian. On the floor, just beyond the reach of her dangling fingertips, lay the bottle of tranquilizers.

Martha Goodman was weeping hysterically. I went to console her. "What happened?" Tony asked, as if hearing it said by someone else would be the only way it would register in his mind as real. Slowly he went to Jillian and knelt at her side. He took her hand into his and looked into her silent face. Death made the smile under her mask of makeup look even more grotesque. He turned to me and Martha Goodman. "What happened?"

"Oh, Mr. Tatterton, I didn't know she even understood what it was she was getting whenever I gave her the pills. I told her they were vitamins, just so she would take them willingly. She always smiled and nodded and looked eager to take them."

"Yes?" he said. Martha looked to me. Why wasn't he understanding? She turned back to Tony.

"Well, she must have always known what they were. Sometime during the night she snuck into my bedroom and stole the whole bottle. Then she came back in here, dressed herself like that, and made herself up like that and . . . and she took the entire bottle of tranquilizers. I never heard her; I never knew what had happened until I got up to see how she was and found her like this. But it was too late. Oh, dear, it was too late," Martha said and started to cry again.

I tried to comfort her. "Martha, it's not your fault. You can't blame yourself," I said.

"My darling," Tony said tenderly, wiping off Jillian's makeup. "You'll be able to rest now. There will be no more ghosts to haunt you."

He fell to his knees and pressed Jillian's limp wrist and hand to his forehead. His body shook with silent sobs. Martha stopped crying and both of us stared down at him. Somehow I hadn't thought Tony capable of such a show of emotion. Most of all I thought he had lost his love for Jillian once she had become mentally ill, but he was crying for her now as if she had died at the peak of their love. I suddenly realized that in a strange and eerie way he had refused to see her as anything but the beauty she'd been. Perhaps that was the real reason why he decided to keep her at Farthy, hoping that, even miraculously, the woman he'd once loved would return to him.

"I can't believe she's gone," he repeated over and over. "I can't believe she's gone."

He looked at her the way he used to, when I had first come to Farthy and found them active and vibrant and alive, when Jillian was one of the most beautiful women I had ever seen and Tony the most elegant man I had ever met. They were some kind of dream couple, the younger husband and his princess living in a castle built from dreams and rich make-believe.

"Jillian," he moaned. "My Jillian." He turned to me, his watery eyes pleading to hear the words, "This isn't so."

"Oh, Tony," I said, "perhaps this is what she wanted the most; perhaps she couldn't live the way she was living any longer. At least she put herself to sleep, seeing herself the way she was—forever young and beautiful. I'm sure she was happy until the end."

He nodded and looked back at her.

"Yes," he said. "Of course, you're right." He kissed her hand and then stood up, pressing his palms against his eyes, then running his hands over his hair as he straightened his posture. "Well," he said, a harder, more formal tone coming into his voice. "We've got to call the doctor anyway. There is always an inquiry whenever there is an unattended death."

"Oh, dear me, dear me," Martha Goodman said. "The poor woman."

"Now, no more of that," Tony said quickly. "Let's do what we must. There are arrangements to be made. People to inform." He turned to me. "Will you be all right? Can you . . ."

"Yes," I said. "Martha and I will comfort each other. It will be all right here, Tony. Do what you have to do. I'll help with anything you want."

"Thank you. Well," he said, looking back at Jillian once more, "I'd better go inform the servants and call the doctor."

Martha's sobbing grew harder and louder as he left the room. I walked with her back to her own bedroom and advised her to get dressed.

"I'll go do the same," I said.

"Yes, of course. You're right. I have to get myself together. Thank you, Heaven. You're so strong."

I left her and went back to my suite, stunned by Jillian's death, so hard on the heels of Troy's resurrection—and the resurrection of my love for him. I was not a stranger to Death.

I thought about Jillian passing from this world to the next; I didn't pity her as much as I pitied Tony. He had tried to cling to a part of his life that had been happy and wonderful, but now there it was irrevocably gone. Never before had he been as alone as he would be now.

After I dressed I called Logan in Winnerow to tell him the news. He promised to be on the first plane to Boston.

"How's Tony taking it?" Logan asked.

"He's keeping himself busy right now with all the arrangements. The hard times will be afterward," I said, speaking from experience.

"And how are you?" Logan asked.

"I'll be all right."

"I'll be there as soon as I can," he promised. "Whenever you need me, I'll always be there," he added before hanging up.

Perhaps it was Logan's promise, more than anything else, that opened the floodgates for my tears to rush out. I knew he meant what he said, and the softness in his voice reminded me of how much I needed and wanted family. I had once hoped that Jillian would be more like a mother than a grandmother to me. She turned out to be neither and I resented her for that, but I had never stopped wanting her to love and need me.

I thought about all the family I had lost—the mother I had never known because she died giving birth to me, the father I thought I had, but who resented me because my birth took away the young wife he adored, my granny, who was old far before her time, worn down and haggard by the hard life in the Willies, my grandpa, who had come to love and rely on me, but who was lost in his own imaginary world until the day he died, and my gentle and loving brother Tom, the victim of a cruel freak accident, an accident caused by my need for love and retribution.

For me love had always been like a small cloud of smoke drifting through my life. I reached out to touch it, my hands plunged right through it, and it drifted on, farther and farther until it disappeared in the distance. Only Logan had remained constant as the sun. Only Logan promised always to be there. And Troy . . . at the thought of him all I could do was cry. I cried for myself as well as for Troy and for Jillian. I cried for Granny and Grandpa and Tom and the mother I never knew. Finally I cried only for Jillian. Perhaps as she sat before that false mirror and put on her makeup for the last time, she came to know the truth. Perhaps she turned to a dark corner in her suite and saw Death standing there, waiting patiently, smiling gently as Granny had smiled when she died. I could almost hear her talking to Death, as if He were someone who had come to escort her to the most gala affair of her life.

"Oh, dear," she would say, "are you here already? You must be patient; you must give me time to prepare myself properly. There are distinguished people to meet and see. I must refuse to go anywhere until I am ready," she would insist. Then she would have gone to her closet and sifted through all the garments until she settled on that black suit, thinking it was perfect for this particular occasion.

"And anyway, Tony always tells me that black is my best color. What do you think?" she would ask, turning to Death and showing Him the outfit. Death would nod and smile and she would put it on, splashing the jasmine perfume over her breasts and arms beforehand. Then she would have worked on her hair, choosing those beautiful pearl combs. "These Tony gave me years ago. As a surprise, you know. He was always coming home with some surprise or another. He loves me so. Worships me, you know."

Yes, Death knew.

She made Him wait as she worked on her makeup, perhaps for

hours, until she was satisfied. Then, rising from her seat, she turned and spun and studied herself from every angle. Finally she went into Martha Goodman's room and found the bottle of tranquilizers.

Back in her suite she swallowed pill after pill, chattering away about this friend or that, about something this one wore that was in style, something that one wore that was out of style. Death was patient, a good listener. How happy He made her right to the end.

"I'm very tired," she must have finally told Him and He finally came out of his corner. Perhaps she lifted her hand as He approached, and when He took it, she closed her eyes. His wait was almost over.

In her mind she must have heard music and long strings of thin laughter. There were people all around her, fine guests dressed in elegant clothing, and Tony standing off to the side as usual with his business associates watching her proudly, for she was his forever young and beautiful wife, even to this moment, this final, wonderful send-off party at which she was the guest of honor.

As it should be, as it always would be.

I sighed, rubbed away the tears with my fists, and rose to go to the bathroom and wash away the evidence of my mourning. I had to be strong for Tony and for Logan and for the servants. I had a responsibility now. I couldn't be a little girl from the Willies.

The doctor had already arrived, examined Jillian, and declared her dead by the time I joined everyone downstairs. An ambulance had been sent to take her body to the nearby hospital where an autopsy would be performed immediately. Since it was a suicide, the police had to be called in. Tony submerged himself in all these things eagerly, grateful for the distractions.

Of course, the servants were depressed. There was a heavy, mournful pall about the great house, even though it was a bright, warm day. Curtis kept the curtains closed; everyone spoke softly and looked at one another with sad, drooping eyes. Martha Goodman remained in her room most of the day. I visited with her twice. Her plan was to remain at Farthy until the funeral and then leave.

Jillian still had two living sisters and a living brother. Her mother, Jana Jinkins, whom I had met when she was already eighty-six years old, was now quite senile and in a nursing home. Tony called the sisters, who lived together, and they said they would call their brother and all be at the funeral. He told me that from the tone of their voices, it was pretty clear they were all expecting some inheritance.

"They're going to be terribly disappointed," he said. "Jillian was never close with them. In fact, she despised them. There is nothing in her will for them. But there is something for you," he said.

"Please, I don't want to talk about it now," I insisted.

"But we must, Heaven. It was something she decided to do shortly after the incident with Troy, when she told him about Leigh and me and who you really were. She made me promise never to mention it to you. She wanted to be sure that you didn't think she was trying to buy back your love and affection for her. Of course, after she became the way she was, I never gave it much thought and until now I forgot all about it."

"I guess she was a little more complicated than I had thought," I said. He nodded. "We all seem to be torn between our loves and our hates, pulled in two different directions much of the time, tormented by our feelings. It's almost better to be . . . to be . . ."

"To be like she finally was," he offered. "Lost in a comfortable illusion." He stared at me. "How much you look like her now, like her when she was young and very, very beautiful," he said.

I couldn't remember when he had last looked at me so intently. It made me uncomfortable.

"Is there anything else I can do?" I asked quickly.

"What? No, no." The phone rang. "I'll be all right. Logan should be here soon," he said, picking up the receiver.

Tony remained in his office most of the day, refusing to take anything but tea. As the news spread, phone calls came from his business acquaintances and friends. I left him alone when I realized there was still a good hour before Logan's arrival and I had time to go to Troy and tell him the terrible news. I didn't imagine that Tony would have thought to inform him.

This time I went quickly through the maze, threading through the corridors automatically, without so much as a thought about this turn or that. As usual this time of the day, the front of the little cottage was bathed in sunlight, its storybook appearance an inviting respite from grief and sorrow. Once again I thought of it as an escape from reality, this time very sad and tragic reality.

I knocked on the door softly and turned the handle, surprised to discover that the door was locked. I knocked harder. It was unusual for Troy to lock his cottage door. He never worried about thieves or intruders, even when he left the cottage for a prolonged period of time. Since I didn't hear his footsteps, I peered into a front window. The cottage looked empty, quiet. There seemed to be no sign of him.

"Troy," I called. "Are you in there?"

There was only silence in response. I went around to the side and peered in another window, a kitchen window. I didn't see him, but something else caught my attention. There was an envelope propped against the salt shaker at the center of the table, and I could make out *Heaven* written on the front of it. I could also see that the door leading down to the basement had been left open. Troy had assumed that I would come to his cottage only through the tunnels, I thought. I tested the window to see if it would open, but it had been latched shut. All of the windows were latched shut.

Frustrated and with mounting dread of what I would discover in that letter I went back through the maze to Farthy and snuck behind the kitchen to the doorway to the tunnel. I hurried through it to the cellar of the cottage and up the stairs into the kitchen. Catching my breath, I scooped up the envelope.

My heart was beating so hard, I had to sit down before tearing the envelope open. Then I pulled out the sheet of stationery within and began to read.

My dear, dear forbidden love,

Now, more than ever, last night seems like a dream. So many times this past year I had the fantasy, that now, now that it actually came to pass, I find it hard to believe it really happened.

I sat here thinking about you, recalling our precious moments, your warm embrace, the softness in your eyes and in your touch, I had to get up and go to my bed to search for strands of your hair, which, thank God, I found. I shall have a locket made for them and wear them, close to my heart. It comforts me to know that I shall have something of you always with me.

I had hoped to remain here a while longer, even though I recognized it would be a torture, and from time to time spy on you at Farthy. It would have brought me pleasure as well as some pain to see you walking over the grounds or sitting and reading. I would have been like a foolish schoolboy. I know.

This morning, not long after you left me, Tony came to the cottage and told me the news, news I expect you will be bringing to me, too. Only by the time you arrive I will be gone. I know it seems cruel of me to leave Tony at a time like this, but I gave him all the comfort I could while he was here and we had a chance to talk.

I did not tell him about us, about your visit last night. He does not know you know of my existence. I couldn't add that to his troubles at this time. Perhaps there will be a time in the future when you feel he should know. I leave that to you.

You are probably wondering why I feel it necessary to leave so quickly after Jillian's death.

My dear Heaven, as hard as it may be for you to understand, I feel somewhat responsible. The truth is I enjoyed tormenting her with my presence. As I told you, she saw me a few times and I knew it shocked her each time. I could have told her the truth, that I was not dead, that I was no ghost, but I chose to let her believe she was seeing a spirit. I wanted her to suffer some guilt, for even though it wasn't her fault you were born Tony's daughter, I always resented her for telling me, for exposing that horrible truth between you and me. She was always a very jealous person, resentful of the affection Tony had for me, even when I was just a little boy.

Now I feel terribly guilty about it all. I had no right to punish her. I should have realized it would only bring pain to Tony and even to you. It seems that I bring sadness and tragedy to everyone around me. Of course, Tony doesn't feel this way. He didn't want me to leave, but in the end I convinced him it was best.

Please stand by him during this time of great need, and comfort him as best you can. You will be acting for both of us.

I expect you and I shall never set eyes upon each other again or touch each other the way we touched each other last night. But the memory of you is so engraved in my heart that I take you with me no matter where I go.

Forever and ever,
Troy

I folded the letter neatly and put it back into the envelope. Then I stood up and went to the front door. I unlocked it and turned to look about the cottage one more time, then I left, locking the door behind me. Without turning to look back again, I rushed into the maze and ran through the corridors of hedges, pursued by the sound of my own sobs, running harder and faster in hope of fleeing that part of me that had lived in the dream. Now it was cursed to wander forever, lost in this maze.

❧ NINE ❧
Old and New Lives

I WAS IN OUR SUITE LYING IN BED WHEN LOGAN FINALLY ARRIVED.
I had cried myself to sleep, and awakened with my throat raw, my
heart like a stone in my chest. I just lay there staring up at the ceiling.
Sorrow had seized me and made me its own silent creature. I didn't
even turn to greet Logan as he came through the bedroom door.

"Heaven!" He rushed to my side and hugged me. Even though I felt
limp in his arms, I welcomed the feel of his strong, comforting embrace and the rich scent of his manly cologne.

"Poor Heaven," he crooned, stroking my neck.

I lowered my head to his shoulder. I felt false, betraying him, knowing he thought he was soothing sorrow brought about solely because
of Jillian, but I let him go on. He pressed his face to mine and kissed
me.

"It must have been terrible for you," he said. "I'm sorry I wasn't
here when you found her. Tony's taking it very badly," he added. "I
stopped by his office to see him on my way up to you and he would
barely talk. Is there anything left to do? Anything I could help with? I
couldn't get him to say."

"I don't think so," I said, shaking my head. I looked at him, my
faithful, devoted Logan, energetic, optimistic, and determined. He was
healthy and strong and vibrant. He seemed incapable of being depressed or diminished. His sapphire eyes were full of hope and life.
Even now, even during these troubled times, he still possessed the
same demeanor of assurance he had when I had first set eyes on him.

How different in temperament he was from Troy, who always lived
under a threatening cloud of sorrow. True, Logan wasn't as sensitive
or as poetic, but at this time I welcomed his sunshine like the grass
and the wild flowers in the Willies welcomed the sun's rays that

slipped through the gloom of the forest. I knew he would always be there to lean on, should I need to or want to. He was my source of strength, my Rock of Gibraltar.

During the days of mourning, Logan kept in constant contact with his office in Winnerow, but he had the decency to carry on his business out of sight and hearing and rarely, if ever, mentioned it. Tony didn't want to talk about anything but Jillian.

Visitors began to arrive the day after Jillian's death. It fell to me to be the hostess to greet and thank them. The day before the funeral there were over a hundred people at Farthy. Rye Whiskey prepared trays and trays of food and drink. All the servants were wonderfully supportive and terribly concerned about Tony. I saw how much they respected and even loved him.

Logan remained constantly at Tony's side, looking more and more as if he, and not Troy, were his younger brother. I was proud of him, proud of the way he conversed with people, and proud of the affection and comfort he was able to give to Tony.

Jillian's two sisters and brother didn't arrive until the morning of the funeral. As soon as they came to Farthy, Tony got up from his chair and took them directly into his office to show them Jillian's will and make it very clear that they weren't going to leave with any inheritance. He took the wind out of their sails of greed, gathering some pleasure from their gloomy faces of disappointment. Afterward, he told me this was something Jillian would have loved to have seen.

"They were always jealous of her," he explained, "especially her two sisters. They were so plain and homely looking it was no wonder they couldn't attract a man. They became so sour and so bitter, Jillian hated to be in their company. They never even informed her they had put her mother into a home until months after they had done it."

The elegant Boston church was packed for the funeral; there were even people standing in the rear by the door. Afterward, the funeral procession of fancy automobiles and high society that inched along the highway to the cemetery reminded me of the parade of people who had come to Logan's and my wedding reception. When I looked back at the way these people greeted one another, the men dressed in expensive suits, the women in costly dresses, bedecked in rich jewels, I couldn't help but compare them to people in the Willies at the burial of their own poor and distraught, their faces cloaked in gloom, as they stood by and watched one of their young 'uns or old ones lowered into the earth.

As poor and as unsophisticated as the people in the Willies were, they felt sorrow for one another in a way that suggested they were all of one family. Perhaps all the hardships, all the struggles tied them so tightly together that it was impossible for them to come to the funeral of one of their neighbors, whether he be young or old, and not feel as though one of their own had passed on.

Afterward, they would return to their own shacks to ponder their own fragile, vulnerable existence. Death had a freer hand in the Willies; there was less resistance. Being poor made them weak. And yet, I thought, how foolish these rich people were to move about with such arrogance. Did they have no feelings, no empathy? Jillian's death should have put in their hearts the same kind of cold fear as was put in the hearts of the people in the Willies to see one of their own, a woman as rich and as protected as Jillian, so easily claimed by death.

I stood by Tony's side and held his arm as they lowered Jillian's coffin into her grave, and I thought about Troy's plea in his final letter to me to give Tony enough comfort for both of us. His hand tightened around mine, but he did not weep openly. I felt him shudder and then we all turned to leave the cemetery.

"Well," he said stiffly, "now she's finally at peace. Her struggle is over."

Neither Logan nor I said anything more. We all got into the limo and Miles drove us back to Farthy. Rye Whiskey had prepared some hot food, but Tony ate little. He left the mourners and went to his suite to sleep and it remained for Logan and me to greet, entertain, and finally say good-bye to people.

One of the mourners who came to pay her respects was a girlfriend of mine from the Winterhaven School, Amy Luckett, who had been the friendliest to me of all the rich, arrogant, and snotty girls who made my life miserable there. Amy wasn't married. She had been traveling a great deal through Europe and had only recently returned. She promised to come to Farthy in a day or two to visit. I thanked her; she was one of the last to leave.

"Tired?" Logan asked me when we were finally alone.

"Yes."

"Me, too." He put his arm around my shoulders.

"You go up," I said. "I'll be right along."

"Don't be long," he said and left me. I went outside to get a breath of air before going up to our suite. It was that time of the day Granny used to call the gloaming. Darkness had fallen; most of the natural world was preparing to sleep. I looked off at the maze and thought about Troy, wondering where he had gone and what he was thinking at this moment. Somehow, I was sure his thoughts were of me. My thoughts were interrupted when Miles drove the limo up front. Curtis appeared at the front door with two suitcases and Martha Goodman followed him out of the house.

"Oh, Martha," I called, walking over to her. "I had forgotten you were leaving tonight." I took her hand and then we embraced. "Where will you go now?"

"Oh, the employment agency has already offered me another position in Boston. I'll write to let you know where I am and maybe sometime when you are in the city . . ."

"Oh, of course. I'll take you to lunch," I offered. She nodded, smiling, and then her face saddened.

"I knocked on Mr. Tatterton's door to say good-bye, but he never responded. You'll tell him for me, please."

"I will. Take good care of yourself, Martha," I said. We kissed and she started for the car. Then she paused and turned back to me.

"That piano music," she said. "It wasn't in Mrs. Tatterton's imagination and it wasn't in mine, was it?" We stared at each other for a long moment.

"No, Martha," I finally said. "It was real." She nodded and went on to the limo. I watched it drive away and then I went inside to go up to Logan.

It was that night that I learned that a man and a woman sometimes make love out of a need to comfort each other, and not only out of sexual passion and desire. Logan was already in bed when I arrived. I prepared myself for sleep and got into my sheer nightgown. As soon as I got in beside him he put his arm around me and kissed me. I pressed my face against his shoulder and chest and began to weep. It was true I was weeping for Jillian and for Tom and for Troy, and for all the people I had loved and lost, but I think most of all I was weeping for myself, and even for Logan.

I was weeping for that little girl in the Willies, that wide-eyed, blue-eyed girl who had been forced to grow up too quickly, who had been forced to be a mother to her younger brother and sister and who had seen even that hard, often overwhelming life torn apart by the devastating sale of her brothers and sisters to other families. I was weeping for that yet innocent child victimized by the insanely jealous Kitty Dennison and then befriended and seduced by her husband, Cal. I thought that would be all the love and tenderness there could be for me and was so confused as to mourn the loss of it at first. Most of all, I was weepy for Troy, for the love I should have been able to claim as mine forever.

Logan kissed away my tears the way Troy had and I found myself kissing him back. I needed to be loved. I needed to be reassured and to know that I was alive and that I was cherished. Every kiss, every caress, built the foundation of my fortress of faith in the future. I didn't want loneliness and sorrow. I wanted an end to tears. I wanted to feel something other than sadness, and I knew that through the act of lovemaking I could do that.

I could make my body feel alive; I could make it tingle and send thrilling electricity up and down my spine until the very tips of my fingers sang. I wanted Logan to kiss me everywhere, to touch me everywhere. No part of me was to be left out; it was to be a complete surrender of myself to the ecstasy of our lovemaking. My demands excited him and made him more passionate than he had ever been. I knew the intensity of my kisses surprised him, and he was surprised by how hard and how long I held on to him.

But I couldn't control my urgent need. Our lovemaking was so intense that after it ended, neither of us could speak right away.

"Heaven," he finally said, putting his hand on my shoulder, "there is something . . ."

"Shh," I told him. "Don't break the spell," I said. I wanted only to turn over and drift into a deep, peaceful sleep. I did. I barely heard him say good night. My eyelids shut and darkness came thundering down like a heavy black curtain falling with the weight of stones to punctuate the end of a performance.

But I knew that tomorrow it would all begin again.

Right from the morning after Jillian's funeral, a dramatic change came over Tony. He suddenly seemed much older, even though he was twenty years younger than Jillian had been and shouldn't have been showing such signs of age. His hair looked grayer, his eyes looked darker, the wrinkles in his forehead looked deeper, and he seemed to move more slowly. That aristocratic posture I had always seen somehow seemed stooped.

He didn't dress as impeccably, either. Before, he rarely came downstairs without a jacket and tie. Now he wore an open shirt and trousers that needed pressing. He didn't brush his hair or shave, and he was consumed with a desire to rifle through old documents, old pictures, all sorts of memorabilia. Immediately after breakfast, which now for him consisted of little more than coffee, he cloistered himself in his office and spent hours and hours going through old cartons and old files. He could not bear to be interrupted by anyone or anything and was very short with both me and Logan.

Calls were coming in from the Tatterton stores and offices, but he neglected them. Logan did what he could, but he didn't know anything about the business and he had his own responsibilities in Winnerow. I knew he was champing at the bit to get back to the project. Finally I told him to return.

"But I hate to leave you here the way things are now," he said. "Can't you come with me for a few days? I want you with me. It's important to me and—"

"I don't think I should go anywhere just yet, Logan. Don't worry about me. I'll be all right. It's Tony who is going through the hard time."

Logan nodded silently. "Don't I know it. I went in to talk to him about some of the decisions that have to be made in Winnerow and do you know what his response was?" I shook my head. "He acted as if he'd never heard of the project. Which project is that? he said. I didn't know what to do. A moment later he was back at those cartons. I wouldn't have thought Tony was a man comfortable living in an illusion," he said. "He's too much of a realist; he's too practical."

"Maybe when it came to others, but not himself. We all have our private illusions, Logan."

His eyes widened. "Oh?" He stared at me for a moment, a rather strange look on his face. Then he shrugged. "I guess I'm just going to have to make all the decisions that have to be made, myself."

"Tony expected you would anyway," I said. "He wouldn't have given you the responsibility if he hadn't trusted you."

"I suppose you're right. Yes. Okay, I'll be back by the weekend," he said. "I'll call every night and you don't hesitate to call me if there are any problems."

"I will. Don't worry," I told him. He made his arrangements to return to Winnerow and then went up to pack his bag. I was sitting in the living room by myself when he stopped to say good-bye. We kissed and he left. I couldn't blame him for wanting to leave this gloomy house right now.

I stopped in to see Tony a few times, each time finding him absorbed by a document or a photo album.

"You've got to start eating regularly again and get back into the swing of things as soon as possible, Tony," I told him the last time I looked in on him. "It's the only way to overcome grief."

He stopped reading and looked up at me as if just realizing what had taken place. The curtains on all his windows were shut tightly, so that the bright afternoon sunlight couldn't warm the dull, dark, and dismal room. The only light on was the lamp on his desk and it cast a pale, yellow glow over him. He looked about the office, down at his documents and pictures, and then back at me. Then he sat back in his chair and pushed his reading glasses up over his forehead.

"Well," he said. "What time is it?" He looked at the grandfather clock in the corner to answer his own question. "I guess I've been in here quite a long time."

"Yes, you have. And you've not eaten anything substantial."

"I like it when you worry about me," he said, smiling, suddenly animated. "Your mother never really worried about me," he added.

"My mother?" Why would he even bring up such a thing? I wondered. My mother had been too young to have such concerns. She ran away when she was barely old enough to bear mature responsibilities. "My mother?" I repeated.

The half smile on his face slowly faded and he sat forward, shaking his head as he did so. Then he scrubbed his cheeks with his palms and rubbed his eyes with his fists as if wiping away tracks of sleep made by the sandman. He took a deep breath and looked up at me.

"I'm sorry," he said finally. "I lost myself in time for a moment there. You're standing in the shadows and I was reliving a moment when Leigh had come through that door. I guess I am concentrating on the past too much. You're right. I should shower and dress and eat a decent meal. I don't know what I'm doing or why I'm doing it. Heaven, I feel so guilty about what happened to Jillian," he added in a confessional tone.

"But Tony," I said, "you shouldn't feel responsible. You provided everything she could need . . . Martha Goodman, doctors, medicines . . . you made her comfortable . . ."

"And kept her in a world of insanity," he said. "For my own benefit, hoping, always hoping she would somehow snap out of it and return to me. It was wrong. Perhaps if I had given in and put her in an institution . . ."

"Tony, she wouldn't have been any happier. Maybe she wouldn't have taken the pills, but she would have died in so many other ways."

He looked at me, considering my words. Then he nodded.

"You have become a remarkable young woman, Heaven. As I sit here looking at you, I can't help but remember our first discussion in this office, when you told me the truth about your past and about Leigh's death and I dictated all those rules and commands to you. I thought you were something wild, undisciplined, backward. I wanted to make you over into my kind of person, to bend you and mold you.

"As it turned out, you had a firm spine and a strong mind of your own. You would be what you were destined to be, what you wanted to be, and nothing I gave you or told you changed that absolute fact. I misjudged you." He laughed. "I should have had more faith in my own genes, eh? I should have told you the truth about your parentage then."

"Maybe," I said. And then I thought, in this house the truth is often misplaced. I was tempted to tell him that I knew Troy was still alive, but I held back. It was still too tense and too emotional a time. Wounds were still raw. Anyway, I couldn't help but be angry at him for keeping it a secret from me, no matter what his reasons were, and I thought it would be unfair to accuse him and express anger now.

"Where's Logan?"

"I sent him back to Winnerow," I said. "He was calling there every five minutes."

"Right, Winnerow. Everything seems so vague in my mind right now. I feel like someone who has been struck in the head and left numb."

"In a way you were."

"Yes. Well, I'd better try to get myself together. I'll go up and shower and dress and then come down to eat. Let Rye know for me, will you?"

"I will, but I'm sure he has something ready. He's had something ready all day."

Tony nodded.

"I want to thank you for being such a strength and comfort to me, Heaven," he said. "You've proven yourself capable and quite dependable. It makes me happy to know that when the time comes, you will be able to move right into my position and run our financial empire."

"There's quite a while to go yet before I'll have to do any of that," I said. He didn't respond. He just looked at me and then came around his desk. Suddenly he embraced me and held me tightly to him.

"Thank God you're here," he whispered. "Thank God you returned." He kissed me on the forehead, held me a moment longer, and then left. For a moment I just stood in his office thinking how complicated men could be. Just when you thought they were insensitive and hard, coldly practical and ruthless, they revealed their deep, innermost feelings and brought you to tears. None of the men in my life were easy to understand, I thought, and wondered if that was how it was for every woman.

I left Tony's office to give the servants instructions and then went up to my suite to rest. Logan called that night, all excited about some of the things that had taken place while he had been away. He talked on and on about the project in Winnerow, finally remembering to ask about Tony. I told him I thought he was starting to get back to normal, even though I wasn't sure about it. Logan seized on my words to tell me he thought he might have to stay over until Saturday. He had talked the electricians into doing some work Saturday morning and wanted to be around when they started, he explained.

"And since everything seems to be settling down there."

"Do what you have to do, Logan," I said. Like any other man, he heard only what he wanted to hear. I was short with him. But he chose to ignore it.

"I will and then I'll hurry home," he said.

The next morning Amy Luckett called to ask if she could come to visit me. I welcomed the distraction and invited her to lunch. Tony did get up to go to work, but a few hours after he left, his office called to ask him some questions. I told his secretary I had assumed he was going there. I had no idea where he was. She promised to call the moment he arrived. I was worried about him, but after Amy arrived, I got so involved with her that I didn't think about the fact Tony's secretary hadn't called until after Amy left.

Amy had gained considerable weight since we were students together at the exclusive Winterhaven School for Girls. Now she was a round-faced woman with a small bosom and wide hips. She still had a soft, gentle smile with friendly brown almond eyes and she still kept her hair wrapped in a bun and pinned up tightly just behind the top of her head. She had clusters of peach-colored freckles under her eyes and just over her eyebrows. I remembered her as a short, chunky girl, timid, always a step back in the shadows of the others. But unlike the others, she didn't seem as taken with her wealth and position.

It was a clear, bright sunny day with a gentle cool breeze coming in from the ocean, so I had our lunch set up on the patio that overlooked the pool and the gazebo. Curtis fixed up some umbrellas and we sat munching on small sandwiches of ham and tuna that Rye had prepared. I listened to her describe her travels, the sights she had seen, the people she had met. Then she changed the subject.

"Some time ago I received a letter from Faith Morgantile," she said, "while I was touring in London. The letter was totally devoted to you."

"Really? Faith Morgantile? In school she treated me like a leper."

"Well, the truth was she was always jealous of you. She told me you had been married and had moved back to Farthinggale. You could just see the lines on the paper dripping with jealousy. If she could, she would have written it in blood."

We laughed.

"I try not to think of those girls very much now," I said. "I get so angry when I do. I'll never forget the things they did to me." I embraced myself as I recalled the embarrassment and pain. Young girls could be very cruel to one another, I thought, especially spoiled-rotten rich young girls.

"It was cruel, but they were jealous!" Amy repeated, her eyes wide. I knew that in the beginning she had to have been part of anything they did. If she hadn't been, they would have turned on her. They despised anyone who was in any way different. I was at a disadvantage immediately because I hadn't traveled as they did and Tony had bought me the wrong sort of wardrobe—rich, conservative clothing.

"I guess so. Although I don't know why they should have been so jealous. They were all rich and all came from good families."

"They couldn't help it," Amy said. "Especially when they saw you with Troy Tatterton and you told them he was too sophisticated to go out with any of them."

I pushed away the stab of pain at the mention of Troy and forced myself to be light and airy.

"I remember. And I remember it was shortly after that that they vandalized all my good clothes and tore all my sweaters. How arrogant they were when I told them I was going to Mrs. Mallory. They knew she wouldn't do anything to risk the loss of their tuition money."

"Yes, they knew," Amy said, biting into her third finger sandwich.

"And then, when I went to the dance and they pulled that horrible trick on me, spiking the tea and fruit punch with a laxative." I clutched my stomach, recalling the pain, the agony, and the embarrassment, knowing everyone at the dance was in on it.

Amy stopped chewing.

"I tried to warn you, I told you not to go to the dance as soon as I saw you had put on that revealing red dress."

"Yes, I remember."

Amy shook her head sadly. Then she smiled.

"But you got back at them, sending Pru down that chute into the messy clothing."

"A funny way to win their respect. I never became one of them, but at least they left me alone."

Amy nodded, anxious to get on with her topic.

"Now, from the letters I get and the things I hear when I see some of them, they're even more jealous of you than ever. They think you're the happiest, luckiest girl in the world."

"Do they?"

"Living here in Farthinggale, married to a handsome man, heir to such a huge fortune . . ."

I looked at her. It seemed obvious to me that it was she who was jealous. Despite her wealth and her good breeding, her fancy schools and her colleges, her clothing and her traveling, she was alone, still searching for something romantic to happen to her. The frustration led her to overeat and the overeating made her unattractive.

"You've gained a lot of weight, Amy," I said when she reached for her fifth finger sandwich. "Shouldn't you be concerned?"

"Oh, I am. I try, but sometimes I just get so . . . hungry," she said and laughed. "But you're so right," she said and put the sandwich down. She sat back and smiled. "It's such a beautiful day, isn't it?"

"Yes, it is."

"Do you ever go into that English maze?" she asked. "I would be too frightened."

"Sometimes."

She paused and then leaned forward. Obviously, what she was about to ask next was the real motive for her visit. It had simply taken time for her to work up the courage. I knew what she was after was intimate information that would make her valuable to the girls of Winterhaven once more. They would phone her and invite her to their homes and she would feel important and wanted. It both saddened and annoyed me.

"Tell me," she said, "now that so much time has passed. What was the reason that Troy Tatterton committed suicide?"

"First," I said in a stiffly formal and correct voice, "it wasn't a suicide. It was a tragic accident. His horse went out of control. And second, I wasn't at Farthinggale to serve as an amateur psychiatrist, analyzing everyone like some of those horrible girls at Winterhaven did and most likely still do, just because they took an introductory psychology course."

"Well, of course, I—"

"I don't care to contribute to that sort of gossip anyway, Amy. It's not ladylike for you to do it, either. It should be beneath you by now."

"Oh, it is, it is," she said, widening her eyes for emphasis. "I was just . . . personally curious."

"We shouldn't depend on other people's tragedies for our entertainment," I said curtly and looked at my watch. "I'm afraid I'm going to have to excuse myself," I said. "I have so many things left to do. I'm sure you understand."

"Oh, of course. Perhaps we can spend time with each other again in the near future. I'm not due to leave for Paris until the fall. I'm going to study art," she said proudly.

"That sounds wonderful. Yes, I'll phone you as soon as I can," I lied. I was glad to get rid of her. Even though she was not as cruel as the others, her arrival and our conversation had brought back too many unpleasant memories of my time at Winterhaven. I had succeeded in burying most in my trunk of sorrows and was unhappy to see some of it pulled out for display, even if only for a few minutes.

After she left I asked Curtis if Tony had returned or called. When he said no, I called his office and his secretary told me they still had made no contact with him. Now, more worried than ever, I wondered what I should do. He had been acting so strange since Jillian's death.

Why it should finally come to me, I do not know. I was sitting in the living room thinking about him when the possibility occurred to me. I stood up sharply and then hurried out of Farthy and across the grounds to the maze. I walked quickly through the corridors of hedges until I reached the cottage. A cold chill gripped my heart when I saw Tony's car parked in front. Slowly I approached the front of the cottage and peered into the small panel window behind the rose bush.

There Tony sat in Troy's rocking chair facing the small fireplace. He barely moved. He had probably spent most of the day here, continuing to mourn in private. Although Troy was no longer there, for Tony, being in his brother's little home among his things, sitting in his chair, was enough to give him some brotherly comfort. I thought about going in to him, but changed my mind. Sometimes privacy is very important and very precious, I thought. I was sure that Tony didn't want to be discovered in the cottage at this time. All sorts of things would have to be said and confessed, not only by him, but also by me. I turned away and returned to Farthy.

Just before dinner Tony came home. He pretended he had been working hard. I didn't have the heart to tell him his office had been calling all day. Curtis gave him some messages, which he took without speaking. Then he went directly up to his suite. He said he was hungry and he would be down to dinner, so I went to my own suite to shower and dress.

Right after I showered, my phone rang. I lifted the receiver, expecting it to be Logan. It wasn't. It was Fanny. I hadn't spoken to her since our argument in the cabin, and I knew she would accuse me of avoiding her, but it seemed she had other things on her mind, worse things. She had finally found a way to pierce my heart.

"I was sorry ta hear 'bout yer granny," she said. "Or didn't ya call her granny? Probably had a fancier way now that yer one of them Beantown high and mighty."

"I called her by her name," I said. "Or I called her Grandmother. So, how have you been, Fanny?"

"Took ya long enuf ta ask," she said. There was a slight pause and then, with a musical tone, she asked, "So tell me, Heaven Leigh, are ya pregnant yit? If you were still in the Willies ya would be."

"No, I'm not, Fanny. I'm not ready yet to start a family."

"Oh . . . well, I got some news fer ya. I am," she stated gleefully.

"Really?" I sat down. I knew that in a moment she was going to tell me all about Randall and how she had been carrying on with him and how he had now made her pregnant, but she had other surprises in mind.

"An' it's not my fault, Heaven. It's yer fault."

"My fault?" I was getting ready to hear how I had left her all alone back in Winnerow after I had made promises when we were younger to always look after her. She always accused me of letting Pa sell her to the Reverend and his wife and told me I should have done more to stop her from selling him her baby. Whatever she was now, whatever happened to her now, was my fault because it was the result of all that.

"Ya shoulda been here; ya shoulda had more interest," she sang. I didn't like the light, happy tone in her voice. There was something in it, something quite unexpected.

"Interest? Interest in what? What are you talking about, Fanny?" I asked, trying to sound as bored and disdainful with her little games as I could.

"Interest in yer own man, in Logan," she declared.

"Logan? What does this have to do with Logan?" I asked her, my heart beginning to pitter-patter.

"It's Logan who made me pregnat, that's what," she said. "I'm the one havin' yer husband's baby, not you."

❧ TEN ❧
Fanny's Game

GOOSE BUMPS BROKE OUT OVER MY ARMS AND LEGS. I FELT AS IF two arms carved from ice had embraced me. Fanny's short laugh sounded like static on the line. The sounds stung, yet even though I wanted to, I couldn't pull the phone away from my ear. It was stuck there like maple syrup frozen on a winter tree in the Willies. My silence encouraged her. I could envision her looking hateful and vicious, her eyes burning, her small white teeth flashing. Fanny had always been able to turn her emotions on and off, to change from one to another as easily as she changed channels on a television set.

"If it's a boy, I'm a gonna name him Logan," she said. "And if it's a girl, I think I'll name her Heaven."

For a long moment I didn't respond; I couldn't respond. My lips were sewn shut, my teeth pressed so hard against each other, I was afraid I'd break one. I could feel the veins in my neck straining as I made a tremendous effort to swallow. How my throat ached.

Thoughts ran frantically through my mind with lightning speed. Perhaps Fanny was lying because of her jealousy of me. Not that I didn't believe she was pregnant. I believed that, but I believed the child had to be someone else's and not Logan's. Probably it was Randall's, but once Fanny discovered she was pregnant, she came up with this plan, taking advantage of the fact that Logan was in Winnerow so much and we were separated so much.

"I don't believe you," I finally told her, my voice so thin and sharp I hardly recognized it myself. "You're lying and it's a horrible and mean thing to do! But I'm not surprised at you, Fanny," I continued, getting more control of myself. "It doesn't surprise me that you would still try to come between me and Logan. You've been trying to do that from the first day I met him," I accused, "and he showed that he wanted to be with me and not with you."

She laughed again, sounding as if it were I and not she who lived in a world of pretend. For the first time she appeared to be the superior one, her tone of voice condescending. I was the one who had to be humored; I was the one who had to be treated like a child. It made me so angry, I wished she were there in front of me so I could pull out her hair or slap the arrogance out of her face.

"Go on, laugh. You want me to remind you? Shall I remind you of the time Logan was waiting for me by the river and you took off your dress and went running up and down naked to try to get him to come after you before I arrived? He didn't go after you, did he?"

"Only because he heard you was comin', Heaven. He asked me ta take off my dress. I said I might an' he said, go on, I dare ya ta, so I did, an' then he got scared when he heard ya comin'.'"

"Another one of your lies," I retorted. "Why, that first time he ever came to our cabin, you paraded about in your panties with nothing covering your breasts but a few of Granny's old shawls. Did he ask you to do that, too?"

"No, but he was lookin' pretty good, wasn't he? He was always lookin' at me, jus' hopin' fer the chance."

"That's ridiculous. That is the most ridiculous thing . . . why . . . why didn't he choose to go with you instead of Maisie Setterton then when he had the chance, huh?" I asked. I hated the whiny sound in my voice and I hated playing this childish game with Fanny, but she had me in such a rage. I couldn't help it.

"He was jus' tryin' to get ya jealous by goin' with Kitty Dennison's sister because he thought ya still liked Cal Dennison. He told me," she said. "So there. Ya made me tell ya the ugly truth about him, but I ain't gonna hide any of it no more. I'm thinkin' only about myself."

"You're lying," was all I could say. Why was it that Fanny was always able to find the weak spots in my walls of defense? All our lives, as long as I could remember, she either played on my fears or my conscience.

"I'm not lyin'. You'll see when ya ask Logan and make him tell ya the truth. I'll tell ya jus' what ta ask him. Ya ask him why he was so nice ta me when I went over to the factory site. Ya ask him why he didn't say no when I offered ta bring him somethin' ta eat at the cabin that night. Then ya ask him why he didn't send me home.

"Ya don't hafta ask him," she said quickly. "I'll tell ya. He always wanted me, but he jus' thought I wasn't as good as you. Well, yer good, yer smart, and yer refined, but yer not with him when he wants ya to be. A man likes his woman at his side, don'tcha know that? Funny thing is yer suppose ta' be smarter than me and ya don't know half as much as I do when it comes to men."

"I don't believe you," I said weakly.

"Don'tcha? He told me all about yer wonderful suite at Farthy, 'bout that picture of the Willies ya got hangin' over the bed, 'bout—"

"Shut up," I said. "I don't want to hear any more of this."

"Okay, I'll shut up, but only fer now. I'm havin' Logan's child and he's gonna be responsible, ya hear? I want him ta take care of me forever and ever." She paused. I could hardly breathe. "He didn't even ask me if I had any protection that night. He jus' took me inta his arms and—"

I slammed the phone down, but I imagined that instead of being angry about it, Fanny was probably laughing. For a few moments I just sat there staring up at the picture of the Willies hanging above the bed. Then I crumpled on the bed and cried. My body shook so hard with the spasms of grief and pain, the whole room seemed to be vibrating.

Betrayed again, by the one man I thought I could always believe. By the one man who was always there. He was just like the others! It was unfair. Why was I cursed to try and trust and believe in the men whose love I needed, when they always betrayed me in the end? Fanny was right—I was dumber than she was when it came to men. Oh, Logan, how could you! How could you!

Slowly my tears wound down until I sat up, sniffling and rubbing my eyes red with my fists until they actually burned. I took deep breaths until I felt my heartbeat slow down. Then, gathering my wits together, I chastised myself for permitting Fanny to get to me. There was still a good chance she had made it all up. I had to hope for that.

With my fingers trembling, I dialed the number of the cabin in the Willies. The phone rang and rang and rang, but Logan didn't answer. I called the factory site, but again, no one answered. He might be at his parents' I thought, and dialed their number. His mother answered.

"Why, no, dear," she said, "he's not here right now. We invited him for dinner, but he's at the diner, having dinner with his foreman and one of the contractors. Is something wrong? Can we be of any help?"

"Tell him I want him to call me as soon as he returns," I said. "No matter what time."

"I will. Right away, dear."

Not more than five minutes later the phone rang. It was Logan calling me from the diner in Winnerow.

"What's wrong, Heaven? Something with Tony?"

"No, Logan. Something with Fanny," I said coldly.

"Fanny?" I heard him swallow deeply on the other end of the phone, heard the hesitation in his voice. My heart closed like a clam shell. "Ah . . . ah . . . what are you talking about?"

"You know what I'm talking about."

There was silence on the other end of the phone. "Heaven, I don't. What's wrong with Fanny?"

"You had better come right home, Logan," I said.

There was another long pause. "Heaven, what has Fanny been telling you? You know she wants to poison things between us."

"She's pregnant," I said. I wasn't going to add anything more.

"Pregnant? But—"

"I'm not going to discuss this over the phone, Logan," I said.

"All right," he said and sighed. "I'll start out immediately."

It was as good as a confession. I cradled the phone gently, as if it were a fragile baby bird and then turned and saw myself in the wall of mirrors. My neck and chest were covered with red blotches, a rash that had broken out because of my nerves. My face was so flushed I looked as though I had a terrific fever. My eyes were bloodshot and my hair, still wet from my shower and shampoo, drooped down the sides and back of my head. I looked like Jillian during one of her moments of madness.

As I sat there staring at this strange image of myself, my feelings raced from anger to outrage to self-pity. My husband had slept with my sister. Fanny had at last found some satisfying revenge and given voice to her aching jealousy. I was hurt, mortally wounded. How much could love withstand? How much? People who came to Farthy would take one look at my face and see that I was a woman whose husband had betrayed her. Imagine what such information would be in the hands of someone like Amy Luckett. I imagined the vicious and arrogant girls of Winterhaven gathering around me to chant: "Heaven was betrayed! Heaven was betrayed!"

And then, as suddenly as it had come, the self-pity slipped off my image like a cellophane wrapper on a forbidden chocolate and was replaced with the heavier, darker wrapping of guilt. Troy. My beloved, beautiful, passionate Troy. I had betrayed Logan with Troy. But it wasn't the same, no, not at all. For I loved him, truly loved him with all my heart and soul even though he was more specter than flesh and blood. How could I refuse him, how? And it wasn't wrong, wasn't the same, it wasn't, because he was only a ghost of my love come back for a precious fleeting moment. My love was his life blood, and to have denied him that would have been to have denied who I was, the spirit that was purest and noblest in me. He had come back and then had returned to that unknown, unclear, mysterious world of oblivion, never to be heard from or seen again. Surely that made what I had done different from what Logan had done. I couldn't believe that Logan had any deep feelings for Fanny. It was lust, simple lust that drove him to her, and it was not love, but revenge and hatred that drove her to him. She was merely an object of pleasure, a sexual distraction, a sorceress. At this moment I hated her for making my life tawdry, for turning what was pure into something soiled and base, and my hate for her gave me the strength to face the crisis.

No, I decided, I would not equate my love with Troy with Logan's carnal act. Logan was a man of flesh and blood, Troy a man of spirit and dreams. Fanny was right—she knew more about men than I did. But I knew more about survival.

I said nothing about the situation with Fanny to Tony that night at dinner. I decided to let Logan explain his sudden return to Farthy himself. In any case I didn't want Tony ever to know. At dinner that night, as I tried to remain composed and seemingly serene, I saw that Tony looked somewhat revived, dressed in one of his light blue summer suits, his hair neatly brushed, but he made little conversation and from time to time simply stared across the table at me, his eyes taking on a glazed, far-off look like someone whose eyes had turned inward and who was really looking at some image or memory from his past. Between courses he sat with his elegant, well-manicured hands templed under his chin, saying nothing, and then he lowered those fingers and drummed a mindless beat on the lace tablecloth and on my nerves.

The little I ate, I ate because I didn't want to draw any attention to my state. Our longest conversation came when I suggested Tony consider taking a short vacation.

"A change of scenery might do you a world of good," I insisted.

"Would you come, too?" he asked quickly.

"Oh, I couldn't," I said. "Not with Logan so involved with the new factory in Winnerow. I'll have to spend more time with him. Just like any man, he doesn't know when he's working too hard or too long."

Tony smiled and nodded.

"Jillian used to constantly complain about that. She was always after me to take her on a special honeymoon and if I protested about the work I had, she would tell me to leave it to Troy. Troy was creative; he was a creative genius, but he was no administrator, no manager.

"Still, if it hadn't have been for Jillian, I probably wouldn't have taken the holiday trips I did take, or gone to the parties, or held the dinners here. She could be such a bright spot, such a jewel, so full of energy, moving through this house with a trail of laughter behind her, her jasmine scent left lingering in the air.

"Oh, I know she doted on herself far too much, but it was nice to have something soft and beautiful, and even if only illusionary, someone forever young. Funny," he said, sitting back and smiling to himself, "but even when she was shut away in her suite, caking herself with makeup and dousing herself with perfume, I felt good knowing she was there. I could walk past her doors and inhale her scent, and remember." Then his voice became mournful, and his faraway eyes focused on me, the pain returning to them, bright and piercing.

"Now the doors are shut, the hallway smells like any other hallway in this big house, and there is only the silence." He shook his head and looked down.

"Tony, this is why I think you need a change of scenery, if only for a short while. Tell me some of the things that have to be done over that time, and I'll look after them for you. I can do it," I assured him.

He looked up, smiling. "I know you can. I don't worry about that anymore." He took a deep breath and sighed. "I'll see," he said. "Maybe."

After dinner he retired to his office to work. I tried to distract myself by reading, but Fanny's laughter kept echoing in my memory and pulling my eyes from the pages and lines. Finally I went upstairs to wait for Logan in our suite.

It was very late when he finally arrived. I had fallen asleep in my clothes, but my eyes snapped open instantly the moment he walked into the suite.

He stood there looking at me. He looked liked he had run all the way. His eyes were bloodshot, his shoulders sagged, and his hair was disheveled. It looked as if he had been put through an electric mixer. He hadn't shaved and his full-faced beard looked scraggly. His suit was wrinkled and his tie loosened, the collar unbuttoned. It was as if Fanny's hold on him was still visible.

For a moment we just looked at each other. Then I sat up, brushed back my hair with the palms of my hands, and took a deep breath.

"I want you to tell me the truth, Logan," I said, my voice seemingly devoid of emotion. "Did you make love with my sister?"

"Make love," he repeated, sneering. He took off his suit jacket and draped it over a chair by his closet. "I'd hardly call what happened between us love."

"I don't want to play word games with you, Logan. Fanny called to tell me she was pregnant and to tell me the child was yours. Is the child yours?"

"How would I know? How could any man be sure when it comes to Fanny?"

"Tell me what happened, Logan," I said, turning away. I looked down at the floor. I felt stunned. My whole body became as numb as if I had slipped and fallen into one of the forest ponds in the Willies when they had only a paper-thin sheet of ice on the surface. How deeply were Logan and I about to sink now? I wondered.

"It happened when we first started work on the factory," he began. "I was just so wrapped up in everything, I didn't think clearly. She came there a few times and just hung around, watching me work, talking to the laborers. I didn't think much of it. I certainly wasn't going to chase her away, although once or twice I did ask her not to distract the men when they were busy."

"Go on," I said. He walked across the room and stood by the mirror, his back to me.

"One day she said she was going to come over to the cabin with a hot home-cooked meal. She said she only wanted to make up for some of the trouble she had caused us; she only wanted to be thought of as a sister again, to be part of the family." He spun around.

"I believed her, Heaven. She was very convincing and seemed very pathetic."

"Fanny is a wonderful actress," I said.

"She cried to me about her lost child, talked about how hard it was to live in the same community with her, seeing her from time to time, but unable to be a mother to her. Then she talked about Jane and Keith and how they won't have anything to do with her. She told me about her marriage of convenience to old Mallory, how she got a nice house and some money out of it, but how she was all alone, how she was without any family. She seemed so sincere that I thought maybe she was changing. Maybe time and maturity had made her see things."

"So you made love to her?" I asked, turning on him. He shook his head.

"Not because of that. That's not what happened. She did show up with the hot meal and we were having a good dinner together. She had me laughing at stories about the old days, about some of the naughty things she had done in school." He stared at me a moment, as if deciding whether or not to go on. I would be spared no ugly details, I thought.

"And?"

"Well, she had brought a few bottles of wine along. I didn't think anything of it. We had them at dinner and kept talking and drinking and talking. I guess I got a little intoxicated. And I'd been missing you so. But I'm not going to make that my excuse," he added quickly. "I know that's not a justifiable excuse . . . I just want you to understand what happened and how it happened."

"I'm listening," I said. I was cold-eyed, stern, and determined. He had to look away.

"Well, it was a hot night to start with, and as usual Fanny was wearing this very loose, off-the-shoulder thin, cotton dress. I didn't realize it at first, but as we were talking and drinking, that dress slipped lower and lower until . . ." He shook his head. "I don't know how it actually happened. One moment we were sitting by the table and the next she had her arms around me and she was half naked.

"She kept talking about how lonely she was and how lonely I must be and how much she needed to be loved and how one night wouldn't matter. The wine had made me dizzy. Before I realized it, we were in bed.

"I tell you, it was more like I was raped than I made love to her," he pleaded.

"Oh, how you must have suffered," I said sarcastically. He pulled his hands back and nodded slowly.

"I know. You're not wrong. I can't make up any excuse that would justify what happened, but believe me, it was that one time only. After I realized what was happening and what we had done, I felt terrible and I demanded she leave the cabin and not come around the site anymore.

"I thought that was the end of it . . . a one night's indiscretion. I put it out of my mind, convincing myself it was a nightmare. I thought that if I thought of it that way, I could live with it and eventually forget it.

"Please, Heaven, believe me. There is nothing more to it. I don't love Fanny. I don't even like her. But . . . but I'm only a man and she knew how to take advantage of that fact, just as the devil would," he added quickly.

"I've avoided her like the plague ever since. She came back to the site a few times, but I wouldn't even look at her." He sat down beside me. "I know it's asking a lot to ask you to forgive me, but I am asking you to do that," he said. He reached for my hand. I let him take it, but I didn't look at him. "I don't know what I can do to make it up to

you. I can only tell you that you are my life now, and if you turn from
me or want to leave me, I don't know what I'll do. I mean that."

I didn't say anything. He lowered his head. He couldn't know it, but
there was a war going on inside me. It was as if there were two of me.
One wanted to be hard and mean, wanted to say all sorts of vicious
and angry things and chase him from the suite. Men, I thought. How
false they could be. They never stopped being little boys, selfish little
boys. This part of me knew Logan was trying to twist and connive
events, trying to make himself out to be the real victim here. As if it
could be all Fanny's fault.

Then the second part of me, the softer, forgiving part, saw the
agony in Logan's eyes, the torment in his face. He was afraid of losing
me. Perhaps he was telling the truth; perhaps he was guilty of only a
single indiscretion. Maybe he had been lonely and I had been wrong
not to accompany him to Winnerow.

And what had kept me from doing that? my second self asked.
Wasn't it my longing for Troy, my infatuation with the past, my effort
to make the impossible possible? I did bear some guilt here. It was
only just that I be forgiving.

"Heaven," he said again, pressing my hand to his cheek. "Please,
believe me. It was a mistake and I'm sorry for it. I didn't want to do
anything to hurt you."

"She says the baby is yours," I repeated.

"What should I do? You tell me what to do. I'll do whatever you
think is right."

"When it comes to Fanny, you can't be concerned with what is right
and what isn't. Fanny will get her way. What she will do is make it
known that you and she slept together."

"But everyone in Winnerow knows what she is," he said. "Surely
because of that—"

"Because of that they'll believe her," I said. "If every Tom, Dick,
and Harry is sleeping with her, why not Logan Stonewall, too? Many
of those people are eager and willing to believe bad things about us,
either because they are jealous or because they still can't stomach a
Casteel being so wealthy and powerful in their hometown."

"Are you saying we should let Fanny blackmail us?"

"It might be your child, might it not, anyway?" I asked. He closed
his eyes and pressed his lips together. "I'll handle Fanny," I said.
"She'll be happy once she knows she's going to be taken care of, once
she knows she's hurt me deeply."

"Oh, God, Heaven. I'm so sorry. So sorry," he wailed, pressing his hands to his face. A part of me wanted to comfort him, but a stronger, harder part of me wouldn't let me.

"Think of an excuse for your sudden return," I said. "I don't want Tony to know about this right now."

"All right. I'll just tell him I missed you and—"

I spun around so fast he swallowed the rest of his words.

"I don't want to hear any of that right now, Logan. I just want to go to sleep and see what I can do in the morning to pick up my self-respect. Do you understand?"

He nodded, looking so weak and insecure and regretful I was almost unable to continue my hard demeanor.

"Good," I said and prepared for bed.

Afterward, he crawled in beside me, taking great care not to touch me. He crumpled up as far away as he could on his side of the bed. When I looked over at him, he did look like a little boy, a little boy who had been naughty and sent to bed without any supper. He would try not to breathe too loud, afraid he might bring on some further chastisement.

I couldn't help wondering how it would have been, had it been the other way around. What would have been his reaction had I confessed to him about my meeting with Troy and our lovemaking? Would he have forgiven me or hated me? Would he have understood? Would he have forced me to sleep far away from him in the bed and not touched me, not given me any hope of redeeming myself?

I cried silently that night for all of us, even for Fanny, who was so filled with jealousy and hate that she was willing to destroy herself just to get back at me. I knew that in years to come she would use this new child like a whip, stinging me whenever she could by reminding me whose child it was. My only hope was that it would look so much like Randall Wilcox that the question as to who was the father would be obviously answered. But in my heart I knew it really wouldn't matter anyway. Once I sent that first check to Fanny, she would have her hold over us.

Oh, well, I thought, rationalizing, at least it would all go to family.

Family. How strange and ugly that word had become. Perhaps that was the saddest thing of all.

Tony was still in such a daze the next day that he didn't even think much about Logan's sudden return. Logan said he only half listened to anything he told him. In a way it worked out for the better that he had come home, for he accompanied Tony to the Tatterton offices and stores and was able to take over some of the duties Tony was either not able or willing to assume yet.

Every day for the remainder of the week Logan brought me some gift before dinner. I knew he was trying to win his way back into my heart. He brought me flowers and clothing, candy and jewels. He didn't press hard for my forgiveness. He simply gave me his gifts and waited hopefully for a sign or for a warm word.

Finally, one night when he came to the suite after spending the day with Tony, he found me crying. I let him embrace me and kiss me and stroke my hair. I listened to his pleas and his words of love. I let him make eternal promises and beg me for my forgiveness and love. And then I let him kiss me hard on the lips.

I was afraid myself that we would never make love again, or that when we did, it would be so mechanical and impersonal it would mean nothing. But my hunger to be loved and to put aside all the hardship and misery I had experienced was greater than I had realized, and Logan's need to be forgiven was all-consuming. We made love passionately and before it was over, both of us were crying in each other's arms.

"Oh, Heaven," he said. "I'm so sorry I hurt you, so sorry I gave you any pain. I would run through a hall of fire rather than have done this to you."

"Just kiss me and love me and never let me out of your mind again," I whispered breathlessly.

"Never. I'll make you so much a part of me that when you're sick, I'll be sick; when you're tired, I'll be tired. When you laugh, I'll laugh. We'll be like Siamese twins, connected by a love so strong even Cupid will be amazed. I swear it," he said. He kissed me so many times, he made my body tingle and sing. He was so grateful for my love and forgiveness, he made me feel like a princess again, bestowing the gift of life and happiness upon him.

That night we both slept more soundly than either of us had the entire week. In the morning when we went to breakfast, it was as if the pall of mourning had been lifted from the house. Even Tony seemed more alert and eager to begin the day. He and Logan walked about Winnerow again. An old energy and excitement returned. We all decided to leave that afternoon for Winnerow and visit the site. And while we were there, I was going to pay a visit to my sister Fanny.

Logan knew that was what I was setting out to do when I left him and Tony at the site. Fanny had a contemporary-styled house that sat high on a hillside, directly across from the mountain where the log cabin was. She had built it with the money she had gotten from Mallory, the elderly man she had married and then divorced. He had been paying her alimony all this time. Her two Great Danes came barking around my car as I drove up. She had to come out to put them into their pen before I would get out of my car. She thought that was very funny.

"They're good watchdogs," she said. "Neva know who's comin' up here, know what I mean, Heaven?"

"Just keep them away from me," I scowled. They looked scraggly and poorly cared for. Fanny never liked animals. She said she kept them only for protection, but even guard dogs needed some love and affection.

"Ain't this a pleasant surprise," she said when I finally got out of my car.

"It's no surprise, Fanny. Not to you."

She threw her head back and laughed.

"There shouldn't be no hard feelin's betwixt you and me, Heaven. Sistas got ta stick togetha, don't they?"

"Yes, they do. And sisters don't try to steal husbands, either."

That made her laugh again.

"Ya comin' inside or ain't my home good enuf for ya now?"

Without replying, I walked into her home. She hadn't done much to it since I had been in it last. Her eyes were on me as I looked about.

"Not too fancy, but comfortable," she said. "Maybe now I kin afford ta git some fine, rich things."

"What happened to your alimony?"

"Didn'cha hear? Ole Mallory kicked the bucket an' the ingrate left everythin' ta his children. Lot they cared 'bout him, but he was blind ta truth, jus' like most men."

"I see."

"I'm not goin' ta offa ya anythin' ta eat or drink. Ya probably don't think I'm clean enuf now that ya live in a palace an eat offa silva dishes and outta silva bowls."

"I'm not here to pay a social call, Fanny. You know that. You know why I'm here." I sat on the couch and looked at her. No matter how I felt about her, I had to admit that Fanny was an attractive woman. She wore her jet-black hair cut stylishly about her neck and her dark blue eyes were more vibrant and sparkling than ever. Her complexion was as rich and as flawless as I had ever seen it. She saw the way I was looking at her and put her hands on her hips. Her pregnancy didn't show yet, so she still had a perfect hourglass figure.

"They tell me pregnancy makes a woman look healthy," she said. "What d'ya think?"

"You look fine, Fanny. I suppose you're seeing a doctor."

"Ya suppose right. I'm seein' the fanciest, most expensive docta I kin. This baby's gettin' only the best. I already told him where ta send the bills.

"So." She smiled and sat across from me. "I take it ya had yer little talk wit' Logan."

"I'm not here to argue with you, Fanny. What happened, happened. There's no way we can be sure this early that the baby is indeed Logan's, but—"

"Fancy talkin', aren't ya? No way ya kin be sure. Suppose ta mean I sleep around wit' jus' anyone, huh? Well, I don't care how fancy ya kin talk now, ya can't talk yer way out of the truth. I haven't seen Randall for nearly a month a Sundays an' I haven't been wit' any man other than Logan. Doctor's kin tell when a baby's been made, Heaven. An' Logan Stonewall made this one," she said, jabbing her stomach. I winced.

I had come here hoping to be tough and determined, to present her with an offer and leave with some dignity, but as usual, Fanny was beyond being embarrassed or frightened. Her eyes burned back at me with stubborn, arrogant pleasure.

"I don't propose we go through any test to see what is true and what isn't, Fanny. It would only hurt everyone."

"Ya don't propose . . ." She sat back, smiling like a mad wildcat. "Well, what do ya propose, Heaven Leigh?" Her black eyes narrowed until the whites were only glimmers between her heavily lashed lids.

"Naturally, we'll take care of all the medical bills."

"Naturally. And?"

"And provide a sum to support the child and its needs . . ."

"And its needs includes me," she said. "I ain't a pin cushion ta prick and poke and forget about, ya know. I mean ta be treated like a woman with class, jus' like you," she said, putting her fists on her hips and spreading her legs. "Who do ya think ya are, anyway, comin' in here and offerin' jus' ta take care of the baby's needs? Yer husband comes ta me becuz ya ain't there when he needs love and tenderness and now there's hell ta pay. I gotta live with the child, don't I? I gotta be tied down, don't I? I ain't gonna be able ta go around lookin' for a new man."

"Fanny," I said, smiling at her, "are you sure you want to keep this child?"

"Oh, I see what yer gettin' at. Think ya kin come in here and make me a single, one-time offa, huh? Get the baby and pretend it's yers, maybe, huh? An' then I'd have no claims ta anythin' more, right?

Smart . . . only I ain't dumb no more, not dumb as I was when the Reverend took my Darcy."

"But you just said yourself how difficult it's going to be for you to have a child, and you're right. It will restrict you."

She smiled, and when Fanny smiled, even a wicked, hateful smile, her white teeth flashed brilliantly in contrast to her Indian coloring.

"I'll take that chance," she said.

"But what kind of a mother will you be for this child?" I asked, taking the most reasonable tone I could, even though it took great effort to control my anger.

Her dark eyes narrowed again.

"Now, don'cha go and start that stuff again, Heaven Leigh. It was an excuse ya had when ya couldn't get my Darcy back from Reverend Wise."

"It's not an excuse, Fanny," I said, still speaking softly. She sat back and studied me. Then she shook her head.

"Ya jus' like Pa, ain'cha? Ready ta buy and sell children, do anythin' that'll make things easier for ya."

"That's not it, not it at all," I said. How could she suggest such a thing? I wasn't looking out for myself, I was worried about what she would do to a child.

"Sure it is. Ya'll pay me a sum for the child and then go and give it away, won'tcha? Won'tcha?" she demanded.

"No. That wasn't my intent."

"Well, I don't care what ya intent was. The answer is no. I'm keepin' the baby and Logan and ya are payin' me ta keep it well. It'll be as good as any of yer kids'll be and it'll go ta the finest schools and wear the finest clothes, ya understand me, Heaven?"

"I see," I said. "So what do you propose?" I asked. The question, demanding something specific from her, took her off guard. She just blinked at me a moment. "How much do you think we should send you a month, Fanny?"

"I don' know. I suppose . . . fifteen hundred. No, two thousand."

"Two thousand dollars a month?"

She studied me to see if I was happy or sad about the amount, but I kept my face expressionless.

"Well, ole Mallory was sendin' me fifteen hundred, but that was me without a child. Better make it twenty-five hundred," she said. "I want it on the first of the month, promptly. Shouldn't be no hardship for ya, Heaven. Not with ya all buildin' this big factory here in Winnerow and all."

I stood up abruptly.

"You'll get your twenty-five hundred a month promptly, Fanny. An account will be set up for you and the child in the Winnerow bank, but I'm warning you now, if you ever, ever try to blackmail us further by threatening to tell the people of Winnerow stories about you and Logan . . . I'll cut off every penny and let you fend for yourself.

"And I don't want you talking to Logan or trying to see him or contacting him in any way. If you have any problems, you'll call me directly, understand?"

She stared up at me, her dark eyes brilliant, fired by hate and jealousy. Then her expression became a pained one. No one could discard one emotion and replace it with another as quickly as Fanny could.

"I'm so disappointed in ya, Heaven. I woulda thought ya'd feel sorry for me. I was the one taken advantage of, ya know. That's all men kin do is take advantage.

"Ya come ta my house, where I live all alone, jus' wit' two dumb guard dogs, come from ya place where ya got all those servants an' some family and a husban' an' all those fancy things, an' what do you do, treat me like some thief, instead of the sista who suffered wit' ya in the Willies. Ya shoulda come here offerin' ta do a whole lot more fer me."

"Life has not been as sweet for me as you think, Fanny. You're not the only one who has suffered and when I suffered, you were nowhere nearby to do anything for me. I had no one but myself."

"Ya had Tom. Ya always had Tom. He loved ya and never loved me, never cared fer me one bit. An' Keith and Jane don' care fer me, either."

"You'll get your money," I said. I started for the door. She got up to chase after me.

"They care fer ya becuz yer rich and fancy. Even when ya was poor and had nothin' but rags, ya acted rich and fancy and treated me like some poor relative. Ya neva wanted me fer a sista; ya neva cared fer me!" she screamed.

I went out the door and hurried toward my car. She followed down the sidewalk.

"Ya always wished ya neva had a sista like me. Ya neva wanted ta know me in school or afterward or ever. Heaven!" she yelled.

I turned to her. We stared at each other for a moment. I couldn't hide the truth. She was right.

"Truth was ya was jealous of me, Heaven, becuz Pa liked me, Pa held me; Pa kissed me. Right? Right?" she demanded. "Cuz yer birthin' killed his Angel and ya can't ever run away from that,

Heaven. Neva, not by livin' in a palace or by buildin' factories, or nothin'."

She folded her arms across just under her breasts and smiled.

"I feel sorry for you, Fanny," I said. "You're like a flower planted in manure."

I turned and got into my car, but it was her laughter that followed me down the driveway and propelled me away as fast as I could go.

❧ ELEVEN ❧
Life and Death

THAT NIGHT I TOLD LOGAN ALL THE DETAILS ABOUT MY MEET-
ing with Fanny and what I had agreed to. He sat at the kitchen table
listening, his eyes fixed on a waterglass that he kept turning and turning in his hands. I spoke quickly and pointedly, realizing the discussion was painful for both of us. He didn't disagree with anything or
ask any questions. When I finished speaking, he sighed deeply and
then sat back.

"Heaven," he said, "I don't want to come down to Winnerow any
more without you. I miss you too much. What do you say we buy a
house down here. Something that will be so grand it will be the talk of
the town. I need you with me, Heaven."

"What's wrong with our cabin?" I asked. "It's always been home to
me. Why do we need a house?"

"Don't you think the owners and managers of what will be the
community's biggest enterprise should have their own home, the kind
of home where they can entertain important guests, hold dinners and
parties? We can keep the cabin as a weekend retreat." Then he stood
up. "I just think we need a fresh start here, Heaven, for both of us."

I thought about it. The cabin was tainted by what Fanny had done.
Living somewhere else would help put that incident behind us. Besides, I knew that buying a fancy house was something his mother had
been pushing for him to do ever since Logan and I were married. No
amount of money or power mattered as long as we continued to spend
our time in the Willies. Staying in the cabin in the hills, surrounded by
the poor people, was degrading in his mother's, and in the other
townspeoples', eyes. It made people think I had won him over to my
world, rather than him winning me to his.

Power and money were changing Logan. He never went anywhere

now without putting on a suit and tie. He bought a very expensive watch and a diamond pinky ring, had his newly grown beard trimmed every other day, and even went for manicures. When I asked him about it, he explained, "A man who steps out of a Rolls-Royce has got to look like he belongs in it."

I knew the real reason for my feelings had to do with what had happened between him and Fanny. I didn't like the idea of his staying in the isolated cabin, which had been the setting of their lovemaking, or whatever Logan chose to call it. And I thought Fanny might have been right when she blamed me for not spending enough time with Logan in Winnerow. If we had our own home there, there would be more reason for me to go along.

"I suppose you're right," I said. "What did you have in mind, building a house or buying one?"

"Buying." He sat forward, clasping his hands on the table and smiling like a Cheshire cat.

"You've already looked into it, haven't you?"

"Uh-huh." There was an impish dazzle in his blue eyes and his smile widened.

"Well? What house?"

"The Hasbrouck House," he announced.

"What? You're kidding!"

He shook his head. "It's up for sale," he said.

The Hasbrouck House was a beautiful, colonial-style home a half mile east of the factory site. It was owned by Anthony Hasbrouck, who was considered "old money"; his family went back to pre-Civil War times.

"I don't believe that Anthony Hasbrouck would sell that house."

"His investments haven't been doing well lately and he is desperately in need of cash." Logan seemed to know a lot about Anthony Hasbrouck.

"I see." I imagined that Logan, who now hobnobbed with all the power brokers of Winnerow and the surrounding area, discovered this. By the way he was smiling, I thought he had probably already made Hasbrouck a handsome offer for the property.

I couldn't hide my excitement about it; I knew the home. Tom and I had often walked past it when we were children. To us it always looked like one of those mansions described in great novels, with its sprawling, beautifully landscaped grounds and tall pillars in the front. There was an enormous carved-oak double door that looked as if it would take a giant butler to open. It was easy to imagine wonderful dinner parties taking place in this mansion. All sorts of romantic adventures would go on behind those great oak doors.

We used to dream about living in it. Everyone in the family would have his or her own room. As the oldest daughter, I would dress like a Southern belle and take visitors out to the garden to drink mint juleps. . . . Tom would pretend he had his own string of racehorses. I smiled, remembering our silly, childish dreams that suddenly looked like some sort of prophecy. Oh, Tom, Tom, I still miss him so. My bright dreamer brother. And now every dream, one after another, was coming true, but never the way we had imagined it, never quite as bright and shiny and golden as the dream meant it to be. Logan saw the wistful smile on my face and brightened.

"I'd hoped you would agree to the idea," he said, warming more to his plan, "and went ahead and made us an appointment to view the house tomorrow morning. Is that all right?"

"Yes," I said, a little disappointed he hadn't spoken with me about it first. It reminded me too much of the way Tony did things. Logan was too much under Tony's influence, too eager to emulate him in every way. And though I was impressed with how quickly Logan was becoming a take-charge businessman, it was the soft, sweet, caring boy I had fallen in love with that I needed and missed.

The next morning Anthony Hasbrouck, a man who wouldn't have given me a second look when I was a little girl living in the Willies, who had once chased Tom and me away from his front gate, now put out the red carpet for me as he guided us on a tour of the mansion. He wore a black velvet smoking jacket, black slacks, and velvet slippers and spoke with a syrupy thick Southern accent, calling me "Heavenly," instead of "Heaven."

"Why, thank you for showing us your place, Mr. Hasbrouck," I said.

"You call me Sonny, all my friends do."

"Sonny it is, then," I said, turning to Logan. "If we take this house," I whispered loudly enough for Mr. Hasbrouck to hear, "we're going to have to have the whole place redecorated. It's just been allowed to fall to pieces." I enjoyed going on and on about how much more glorious his house would become in my care, how many more rugs there would have to be, how the old kitchen wouldn't do at all. I rarely enjoyed flaunting my wealth, but with people like Mr. Hasbrouck, people who had looked down on us Casteels, who had chased my lovely Tom away from his dreams, I truly did enjoy it.

"And most of all," I said, taking Logan's arm as we strolled through the grounds, "we are going to have to have a lot more servants and gardeners—I just can't believe what has happened to this old estate."

Mr. Hasbrouck turned bright red. He kept twirling his mustache and gritting his teeth. I knew he couldn't stand to have to sell his house to a Casteel, but as Logan assured me, he needed the money.

"Sonny," I said, smiling brightly and acting as charming as I could, "I do like your home, but I'm afraid the price is just too high for what we'll be getting." I forced my face into a frown.

Logan was flabbergasted. He reeled around. "But, Heaven, darling—"

"I suppose your pretty little wife is right," Mr. Hasbrouck said. His face was now as red as a tomato. "Heavenly, you sure do strike a hard bargain."

As soon as we got into the car, Logan swept me into his arms. "Not only do I have the prettiest wife in town, but I have the smartest. I can't wait until we get back to Farthy so I can tell Tony how you handled this."

It was three days later, when Tony ushered Logan and me into his office for a welcome-home drink, that Logan announced the news. "Tony," he began, his eyes glittering with pride and excitement, "Heaven and I have taken the first big step of our marriage. We've bought our own home."

At first I could barely read Tony's response, it was such a mixture of muted surprise, sadness, loneliness. Then he simply looked bereft.

He didn't say anything one way or the other about it, but I sensed he wasn't happy that we had bought the Hasbrouck house. It was too much of a home away from home, and the reality that we had another life, apart from the one at Farthy, was not something he liked. I felt sorry for him, knowing he feared being lonely, especially now, with Jillian gone.

As the weeks passed, while I should have been absorbed in ordering wallpaper and draperies, rugs and furniture, and inquiring into household help, I found myself barely able to get out of bed. Tiredness had become my constant companion, and I felt somehow distant from myself, as if I didn't really know who I was or what I wanted. Had it been a mistake to buy the house? Why was I feeling so confused, so listless? I made several trips into Boston, to the posh department stores, to order things for our new home, only to return to Farthy wrung-out and exhausted.

"Heaven," Logan said one night after dinner, when I told him I was going to bed early, "you seem too tired these days. Is something wrong? I hope this new move isn't going to be too much of a strain on you."

"I'm fine, darling," I murmured.

"I want you to see the doctor tomorrow, Heaven. This isn't like you."

The doctor's conclusion nearly left me speechless.

"Pregnant?"

"No doubt about it," he said, smiling.

This was wonderful! Why hadn't I suspected it myself? I had to giggle to myself. Of course, this explained everything! A baby! I had always dreamed about having my own family, and now that dream was coming true. Oh, I was so happy! How I would cherish and love and protect my own little one! She would never see any of the pain and agony I and my brothers and sisters had endured. Although Logan and I hadn't sat down and planned it, it did seem to be the perfect time to have our first child. We would have the new factory; we would have the new house in Winnerow, and we would have a new baby. Fatherhood, I thought, would return to me the joyful, boyish Logan I had married, it would bring him back to earth, down from his business pedestal.

"Mrs. Stonewall," the doctor said, bringing me back to earth, "I'm going to examine you so we can determine exactly how long you've been pregnant."

My heart skipped a beat.

"It's important that we know so that we can prepare properly for the little one's arrival."

With great care and thoroughness the doctor examined me.

"Why don't you get dressed now and step into my office," he said when he was finished, "so that we can go over everything."

I was trembling so. "Please, Dr. Grossman, could you tell me how old the baby is?"

He told me.

I felt the blood drain from me. The baby was already two months old, it seemed. Two months. Two months ago was when I had visited Troy in the cottage. Oh, my God! Whose baby was it? I didn't know. Whose baby was it? Logan's . . . or Troy's?

"Mrs. Stonewall, Mrs. Stonewall." The doctor's voice brought me back to the room. "Are you all right?"

"Oh, forgive me, Doctor," I said, trying to gather myself. "I just felt a bit dizzy. It's such happy news, so unexpected. I just don't understand why I didn't suspect. Why I didn't keep track. There's been so much . . ."

I drifted off as he ushered me out of his office. I was happy to be alone in the back of the limo, as the same fear pounded and pounded through my brain. Whose baby was inside me? Logan's or Troy's? And worse, though God might look down and strike me dead, I didn't know whose I wished it to be.

But by the time we pulled up to the front gate at Farthy, I knew I didn't care—I loved them both. And I knew in my heart that Logan would worship our child and be the best father in the whole world. I may not have known who my real father was, but the father who raised me, Luke, didn't love me the way I needed to be loved. Should I confess the truth to Logan and tell him that the child might be Troy's and take the risk that he would become as angry and bitter as Luke had been and treat our baby the way I had been treated? No, I couldn't let that happen, I couldn't do that to my baby. If I did confess the truth to him, and we couldn't tell whose baby it was when it was born, he would always have doubts and he wouldn't love the child as much as he would if he were sure. It wasn't a fair thing to do to Logan. Besides, it might be his, it might well be his! No, I decided in my heart, this secret would remain beside the others that remained locked there by sealed lips.

Logan was in Tony's office, speaking on the phone, when I returned from the doctor's.

"Could you please come up to our suite, Logan? I have something to tell you."

He covered the phone with his hand. "Can't it wait a half hour or so, Heaven? I'm in the middle of an important negotiation."

"Logan Stonewall! You be up in our suite in two minutes!" I ordered. "You're about to get the biggest acquisition of your life!" I turned and hurried from the room, not wanting him to guess the truth from my excited eyes.

A couple of minutes later Logan stood in the doorway of our suite, his arms crossed, looking a little perturbed at my interruption. "This better be good, Heaven," he warned.

I walked over to him, threw my arms around his neck, and looked deep into his eyes. "You're going to be a father," I announced.

His face reddened with excitement; his sapphire eyes brightened like the morning sky on a clear summer's day, and he smiled from ear to ear.

"Heaven," he said, "how can you stand there so calmly and say that?" He held me away from him and up and down his eyes scanned me, searching for some difference. Then he laughed and gave a boyish leap and hugged me again. "This is wonderful news! Wait until we tell

Tony! Wait until we tell my parents! This is a cause for celebration! Let's all go out tonight and have the finest dinner possible! I'll go tell Tony and tell Rye to cancel the meal he's preparing. Oh, I'm so happy we bought that big house now. I'll have the contractors prepare a nursery room immediately, and we'll hire a nurse to help you when you're in Winnerow and when you're here, too."

He clasped his hands together and raised them over his head. He looked like he was about to break out into one of Grandpa's jigs.

"When the baby is born, we'll have two big celebrations—one here at Farthy for all our Boston friends and one in Winnerow. You're going to be a mother and I'm going to be a father!" he exclaimed. "Heaven, you look beautiful, radiant. What a wonderful surprise. Thank you, thank you," he said and embraced me again, falling on his knees and pressing his head against my belly. Suddenly he burst into tears. He couldn't stop crying as I caressed his head over and over.

"Heaven," he sobbed, "I am the happiest man on earth, I am—" Then he looked up, his blue eyes all watery, tears streaking his face. "I don't deserve this happiness," he said, "forgive me."

I wanted to be as happy as he was and join him in his excitement, but the more he poured out his joy, the more I wondered if I were going to present him with another man's child. It seemed so deceitful, but I couldn't say anything. It was time for us to have happiness in this house anyway, I thought. It was time to have new beginnings. I would do nothing to put a damper on that, not when we all needed it so.

He was so elated, he rushed out of the suite half dressed. I laughed at him and pushed aside my dark worries and forebodings. I decided I would be just as excited and just as happy. Moments later Tony appeared at the door beside him.

"What is this Logan babbling about? I'm to be a great-grandfather?" Tony asked, his eyes glittering with pride and happiness.

"It seems so," I said.

"Congratulations, Heaven," he said and he came forward to embrace me. "Your timing couldn't be any better. It's like a jolt of new energy and hope; it's truly a spiritual gift."

"We're going to the Cape Cod House," Logan announced. "I just made the reservations. Champagne, lobster dinners, the works, eh, Tony?"

"Of course." He smiled as if Logan had hit on the most brilliant idea. "We must celebrate. It's good to hear good news for a change. And won't it be wonderful to hear a baby crying and laughing in the halls of Farthy once again! The Tattertons indeed will go on."

"Yes," I said and then fear wrung my heart. Maybe the Tattertons would go on even more pure than he realizes, I thought. But I pushed the thought away. Instead, I let myself be carried off by Logan's exhilaration and energy. We all dressed like fashion plates, got into our limo, and went off to celebrate the coming of my new baby, all of us already intoxicated by happiness before we raised our first glasses of champagne to toast the future.

We had had a wonderful time at the restaurant. Tony and Logan drank a bottle and a half of champagne. Every time I reached for my glass, either one or the other would say, "Now, now, you've got to be careful what you eat and drink . . . little mother." For some reason just saying it would set them both off, laughing hysterically. Before long, everyone in the restaurant was watching us.

That light, carefree abandon remained with us throughout the evening and all the way home. We had taken the opportunity for happiness and used it like a salve to cover and heal our scars of sorrow and bereavement. We got into a discussion about names for the baby, and Tony complained that modern-day parents just didn't seek dignified names for their children anymore.

"They're naming them after everything nowadays, from soap-opera characters to racehorses. If it's a boy, I'd love to see you name him Wilfred or Horace, after my great-great-grandfather and great-grandfather. He should have a middle name with equal dignity . . . say, Theodore or . . ."

"Or Anthony," I interjected.

"Wouldn't be so bad," Tony agreed, quirking an eyebrow and smiling. Logan laughed nervously.

"If it's a girl, I'd like to name her after my granny—Annie," I told him.

"Annie? Shouldn't you call her Ann?" Tony asked. Logan nodded. He would agree with anything at this moment, I thought. The champagne had gone to his head.

"No, I think Annie is perfect," I pronounced emphatically.

"Oh, well, as long as you don't call her 'Late for dinner,'" Tony said and he and Logan fell into another fit of boyish laughter.

We were all still in a gay and celebrating mood as we entered Farthinggale Manor. Curtis's face sobered all of us immediately, however. He greeted us with a formal nod, sadly shaking his head.

"What is it, Curtis?" Tony asked, a worried frown crushing his smile.

"A telegram arrived for you, sir, and then shortly afterward, there was a phone call from a Mr."—he looked down at his note pad— "J. Arthur Steine, an attorney representing Luke Casteel."

"Luke Casteel!" I looked at Tony, bewildered. His face blanched as he stepped forward to take the telegram from Curtis. What was this? My mind roamed like a blind beast, trying to find a familiar landmark. Why would Pa's lawyer be sending a telegram to Tony? Logan grabbed my hand and I waited at his side while Tony ripped open the envelope and read the contents. His face drained of color until it looked like the pale mask of a ghost.

"My God," he said softly and simply handed me the telegram. It was addressed to Anthony Tatterton. It read:

TERRIBLE AUTO ACCIDENT STOP LUKE AND STACIE CASTEEL FATALLY INJURED STOP DETAILS TO FOLLOW STOP J. ARTHUR STEINE

"What is it?" Logan asked. Without speaking, I handed him the telegram.

"Oh, my God," he said. He put his arm around me. "Heaven . . ."

I raised my hand to indicate I would be all right and ran directly into the living room. It felt like my heart had stopped beating and my blood had frozen in place. I no longer felt the floor beneath me.

"Curtis, bring Mrs. Stonewall some water," Logan ordered. He followed me in and Tony went off to his office to call J. Arthur Steine. I sat on the couch and leaned back, closing my eyes. Logan sat beside me, holding my hand.

"I know it's terrible news," Logan said, "but you've got to think of your own health and the baby's."

"I'll be all right, Logan," I whispered. "I'll be all right."

Pa. Luke Casteel. The man whose love I had craved but never won. But now only good and happy scenes came to mind. I saw him outside our cabin pitching a baseball to Tom and Tom swinging with the bat, the only plaything left over from Luke's own childhood. I saw him out in the yard on a warm summer's day, his ebony-dark hair shining. He was handsome enough to be a movie star when he was clean shaven and neatly dressed. How the women would gaze at him! I remembered how much I longed for him to look kindly and lovingly at me, and when I was lucky enough to catch him staring at me, probably seeing his beloved Angel Leigh in my face, I remember how it filled my heart with such excitement and joy.

Pa, the beautiful, unattainable man I loved and hated, now gone and lost forever, no chance of us ever meeting on some quiet day and forgiving each other for our hates and our loves, no chance to explain or to understand, no chance to mend things or heal wounds, no chance for soft words.

How many times in my deepest thoughts had I rehearsed the scene.

Luke would look at me and I at him and we would know the time had come to make our peace. We would go off together, I and the father I never had, and we would walk, silently at first. Then Luke would begin. He would tell me how bad he was when we had all lived in the Willies. He would confess his sins and apologize for his negligence. He would speak honestly to me and he would finally tell me that he had been unfair to dislike me simply for being born. He would beg my forgiveness and then I would beg his.

I would beg him to forgive me for my mad pursuit of vengeance, for trying to look just like his Angel Leigh and haunting him at his circus. And I would tell him once and for all that Tom's death wasn't his fault . . . it was mine.

And then we would comfort each other and hug each other while the sun began to fall over the horizon and sink into the sea, and my heart would be so full of joy it would feel like it would bust.

We would walk back hand in hand, renewed, reborn.

Now I would walk alone and the words that should have been said would never be uttered.

The tears silently climbed over my lids and began their descent down my cheeks. Logan held me closer to him and we sat there quietly. Curtis brought me some water and then Tony appeared. I wiped my face and looked up at him. He shook his head and sat in the high-back chair across from us.

"It was a head-on crash. A drunk driver crossed the highway and ran smack into them. They were coming home from the circus site just outside of Atlanta when it happened. The lawyer says from the police report it looks as if they didn't know what hit them. The other driver must have been going ninety."

"Oh, God," I said. My stomach felt wobbly. It was as if dozens of butterflies had suddenly burst their cocoons and beat their wings within me. "What about Drake?" I asked.

"Thank God he wasn't with them at the time. They had a live-in maid and nanny, Mrs. Cotton. She's with the child now. Luke's wife had no brothers or sisters and only her mother is alive, but living in a nursing home."

"I've got to go immediately to Atlanta," I said. "To make the funeral arrangements and to get Drake. He'll live with us now," I said, turning to Logan. There was no opposition in his face.

"Of course," he said. "I'll go with you."

"I've already taken care of the funeral arrangements," Tony said. "Through this attorney."

I stared at him a moment. There were a dozen questions colliding through my mind, not the least of which was why the telegram came to him instead of to me, but I didn't feel like asking questions now. I wanted to set out immediately for Atlanta and get Drake.

"I'll have to contact Keith and Jane and . . . and Fanny," I said. "When will the funeral be?"

"Under the circumstances, I thought it best to be as soon as it can be," Tony said. "Day after tomorrow. Should give us enough time to see to any business problems and . . ."

"I'll meet with this lawyer tomorrow," I said. "And do whatever has to be done."

Tony stared at me for a moment and then looked quickly at Logan.

"Don't you think, considering your condition, you had better leave that business to us? I'll fly down to Atlanta and—"

"I'm pregnant, Tony," I interrupted, "not sick or helpless. It's my obligation, my responsibility," I insisted. "I want to do all that I can now for Drake and . . . for Luke. I want to do it," I repeated, my eyes blazing.

Tony simply nodded. "Whatever. I'll be here to help if you want me. Just call."

"Thank you," I said. "I'd better start calling my brother and sisters. Logan, will you make the travel arrangements, please?"

"of course," he said.

"Use my office if you like," Tony offered. I nodded and went there to make my calls.

Keith and Jane took it as calmly as I expected they would. After all, they'd never really known Luke. They both wanted to know if I thought they should come down to Atlanta to attend the funeral, but I thought it was not necessary. After all, what was Luke to them, but a man who had sold them when they were little children. It was more important that they continue working toward their goals, staying in their new lives that were better than anything Luke had ever thought of giving them. They were relieved to hear me say it.

Fanny was another story.

"Pa's dead?" she asked after I told her the details. She sounded shocked, as if she needed to hear the whole story again before it seemed real. "How'dja know he's really dead? Maybe he ain't dead, Heaven," she insisted. "Maybe he's just hurt bad. Maybe—"

"No, Fanny. It was a fatal crash. There's no sense getting up false hope."

"Pa . . . Oh, Jesus." I heard her sob. "I was goin' ta go see him soon, let him know how good I was gettin' on."

"The funeral's the day after tomorrow," I said. "I'm going down tonight to see after Drake."

"Drake," she said. "Poor li'l Drake. He'll need a new mommy now."

"I'm going to take care of it all, Fanny," I said.

"Sure ya are," she said, suddenly turning bitter on me again. "Yer Heaven Leigh Stonewall, the Tatterton Toy Queen. Ya kin take care of everythin'."

"Fanny—"

"I'll see ya at the funeral, Heaven."

I was sitting with the dead receiver in my hand when Logan appeared in the doorway.

"If we hurry, we can catch the next plane out of Boston to Atlanta," he said. "I told Miles to bring up the car."

I ran up to our suite to get what I would need for the funeral. Logan did the same, and in less than twenty minutes we were back in the limo heading toward the airport in Boston.

How fragile, quick, and unpredictable life is, I thought. One moment we were all happy and silly, and the next we were in mourning, saddened and distraught. "Life is jist like the seasons, chile," Granny once told me. "It's got its springs and its summas and ya got ta cherish every moment of the spring when it comes ta ya, cuz nothin' stays fresh and young and pretty foreva, chile, nothin'. The frost gets inta people, jist like it gets inta the ground."

The frost had gotten into me. I felt cold and empty—even now that I was filled with a new life! I shuddered, curled up against Logan, and slept most of the way to the airport and most of the way on the plane. By the time we arrived in Atlanta and got to Luke's house, it was dawn. Even so, Mrs. Cotton was waiting up for us.

She was a tall, stout woman with large, almost manly features. She looked like someone who had done hard manual labor most of her life, a woman aged beyond her years by her hardships. She had dull brown eyes and coarse, dark pink, full lips. She had an old coverlet draped around her shoulders when she came to the door.

"I'm Heaven Stonewall and this is my husband, Logan," I said. She nodded and stepped back. "We came as soon as we could. Mr. Casteel was my . . . my father," I said, thinking that was the easiest way to explain things.

"I know," she said. "Mr. Steine called to tell me all about you. There's a guest room you can use. It's right past the kitchen on the right."

"How's Drake?" I asked.

"He's asleep. Doesn't know nothin' yet," she said. "I didn't think it was necessary to wake him to tell him the ghastly news. He'd be too tired to understand anyway."

"You did the right thing," I said. She didn't seem to need my approval though. She shrugged and started away.

"I gotta get some sleep myself," she said. "The boy gets up very early."

"Oh, I'll look after him," I told her.

"Suit yourself."

"In fact," I said, liking her less and less, "you can leave as soon as you want tomorrow. Just let me know what Luke owes you and—"

"That's all been taken care of."

"Oh?"

"By Mr. Steine," she said. "I'll leave sometime in the afternoon. Got someone pickin' me up."

"Okay." She wasn't wasting any time, I thought.

"Right past the kitchen," she said again and went off to her own quarters.

"Sweet soul," Logan said, shaking his head.

"Imagine that as a nanny," I said. Logan took our things to the guest room and I looked in on Drake. It had been years since I had seen him, but even when he was only a little more than one, I thought he was Luke's lookalike with his huge brown eyes framed by long black lashes.

I tiptoed to the side of the dark pine bed and looked at his tender little face. At a little more than five years of age, he had Luke's ebony-dark hair and deep bronze skin, skin that revealed Luke's Indian ancestry. I brushed a few strands of hair off his cheeks. He smacked his lips and moaned softly, but he didn't wake. My heart went out to him when I thought of the sorrow that had to be made clearly his tomorrow. To lose your mother and your father in one day had to be an overwhelming emotional blow, one from which you can never fully recuperate. I knew. For even though I'd never known my real mother, I'd always longed for her and missed her. And Pa, Pa, the only father I had known, had been a true father to little Drake. From tomorrow on, he would never be the same, but I was determined to use all my wealth and power to make his life as comfortable and as happy as would now be possible.

Logan and I managed to get a few hours of sleep before Drake wakened in the morning. I heard him moving about in the hallway and then I heard Mrs. Cotton making his breakfast. She hadn't told him we were here. I heard him ask, "Where's Mommy?"

"Your mommy's not here," she said. I put my robe on as quickly as I could. That woman was not whom I would want to break bad news to a child.

"Where is she?" Drake inquired. "Sleeping?"

"Oh, yes, she's sleeping. She's—"

"Good morning," I interrupted quickly. Drake turned abruptly and inquisitively gazed up at me with his big brown eyes. I thought he would grow to be just as handsome and cut just as manly a figure as his father. Already he had strong-looking shoulders for a young boy, and his face had the same firm chiseled lines that Luke's had had. "I'm Heaven," I said. "Your older half sister. You don't remember me, but I was here many years ago, when you were just a little baby. I gave you some toys."

He just stared at me. Mrs. Cotton shrugged and went back to preparing breakfast.

"I don't have any new toys," he said, lifting his arms. He was so cute I couldn't help but kneel down and hug him.

"Oh, Drake, Drake, my poor little Drake. You will have toys, hundreds of toys, big toys and small toys, toys with motors, toys you can ride, and you'll have a big place to ride them."

My emotional outburst frightened him. He leaned back and looked past me down the corridor.

"Where's my mommy?" he asked, worried now. "And my daddy?"

Logan appeared in the hallway and Drake's eyes widened with more surprise.

"That's Logan," I said. "He's my husband."

"I want my mommy," he said, getting off the chair, starting past me. I couldn't stop him. I looked at Logan and shook my head. When it came to little children, sorrow was like a large wild bird caged. It was too big to live within them.

Drake opened his parents' bedroom door and stood staring at the empty, untouched bed. I came up beside him. He turned and looked up at me, his eyes filled with fear. At that moment he reminded me of Keith when Keith was his age. Keith had such expression in his eyes, too. I took him in my arms and held him close to me again, kissing his cheeks, just the way I used to kiss away the tears on Keith's soft, little face.

"I must tell you something, Drake," I said. "And you must be a big boy and listen, okay?"

He brought his small, closed fist to his eye and rubbed back the beginning of his tears. I was sure he had inherited Luke's inner strength. Only five and he didn't want to show his fear and sorrow. I sat down on the bed with him still in my arms.

"Do you know what it means when people die and go away to Heaven?" I said. He looked at me funny and I realized the confusion. "Yes, my name is Heaven, but there is also a place called Heaven, a place where people go to be forever and ever. Did you ever hear about that place?" He shook his head. "Well, there is such a place, and sometimes people have to go there sooner than they expect," I said.

Logan came to the doorway and looked in on us. Drake eyed him cautiously and Logan smiled as warmly as he could. Then Drake turned back to me, eager to hear the rest of my story. I saw that he was treating it like a story, and I imagined that Stacie often had held him like this and either read to him or told him fairy tales. Only he must not think of this as a fairy tale, I thought. Somehow, I had to make him understand.

"Well, last night God called your mommy and daddy to Heaven and they had to go. They didn't want to leave you," I said quickly, "but they had no choice. They had to go."

"When are they coming back?" Drake asked, already sensing something very disturbing.

"They're never coming back, Drake. They can't come back, even though they want to. When God calls you, you have to go and you can't return."

"I wanna go, too," he said. He started to struggle to get out of my arms.

"No, Drake, honey. You can't go because God didn't call you to go. You have to stay on earth. You'll come with me and live in a big house and have so many nice things, you won't know what to play with or to do first."

"No!" he cried. "I wanna go with my mommy and daddy."

"You can't, honey, but they would want you to be happy and to be well cared for and to grow into a fine young man, and you'll do that for them, won't you?"

His eyes narrowed. I felt his arms tighten and his anger rise as his cheeks reddened. He had Luke's temper, all right, I thought. Looking into his eyes, I thought I could look back through time, beyond Death itself, and see Luke staring at me.

"Don't hate me for telling you these things, Drake. I want to love you and I want you to love me."

"I want my daddy!" he yelled. "I want to go to the circus! Let me go! Let me go!" He struggled against my embrace until I released him. Instantly, he charged out of the room.

"It's going to take time, Heaven," Logan comforted. "Even for a boy that young."

"I know." I shook my head and looked around the bedroom. On the small night table there was a picture of Luke and Stacie standing just outside the house embracing each other. How young and happy Luke looked. How different from the man I knew as my pa in the Willies. If only life had been happy for him then, it would have been happy for all of us.

"We'd better have some breakfast and get dressed, honey," Logan said. "You want to see that lawyer and then go over to the funeral parlor."

I nodded and rose slowly from the bed upon which Luke and his bride had made love to each other and pledged themselves forever and forever to each other. Now they would be lying side by side in the cold, dark earth.

I hoped that I was right; I hoped that what I had told little Drake was true. I hoped they were called to a happier place, a real heaven.

❧ TWELVE ❧
Good-bye, Pa

DRAKE WAS STUBBORN AND SULKED. HE REFUSED TO EAT ANY breakfast and wouldn't let me dress him. Mrs. Cotton had to do it. It was the last duty she performed for Luke and Stacie Casteel. Even though he was reluctant to go, we took Drake with us to the law office of J. Arthur Steine, which was located in downtown Atlanta. The sights and activity soon attracted little Drake's interest, and before long he permitted me to hold him on my lap while he gazed out the window. I brushed back his silky ebony hair with my fingers and studied his face. Stacie had kept his hair long, something I couldn't blame her for doing. It was so thick and rich-looking. I kissed him softly on the cheek and held him snugly to me, but he was too involved with the things he saw to notice or care.

J. Arthur Steine's office was in a posh modern building. I was surprised that Luke had chosen this firm, because it looked like one associated with big corporations and wealthy people. His circus wasn't an insignificant venture, but it was far from being a P.T. Barnum. He had spent most of his time going from one small town to the next, and with the kind of overhead a circus would have, I was sure he had barely been scraping out a living.

Little Drake was fascinated with the glass elevator, which took us up to the twelfth floor, where Mr. Steine's office was located. The lobby of the law firm was very plush, with two secretaries behind big desks answering phones and typing. There were three law clerks rushing about, giving the secretaries papers to type or gathering up documents. The first secretary on the right was also the receptionist. She asked us to sit on the leather couch while she announced our arrival to Mr. Steine. I had just found a magazine for Drake when J. Arthur Steine came out himself to greet us.

He was a tall, distinguished-looking man with graying temples. His black-framed glasses magnified his hazel eyes. As soon as I saw him, I couldn't help but feel there was something familiar about him. Of course, with his three-piece gray silk suit, the gold chain of his pocket watch dangling out of the vest pocket, he looked like one of a number of Tony's business associates.

"My condolences," he said, reaching out to shake my hand and then Logan's. He slipped his glasses down the bridge of his nose and peered over the rims to look down at Drake, who stared up at him with an almost angry curiosity. He was definitely not a timid little boy, I thought. "This must be Drake."

"Yes. Say hello, Drake," I coached. Drake looked at me and then at J. Arthur Steine with an arrogance I thought quite beyond his years.

"I wanna go home," he stated.

"Of course you do," Mr. Steine said and then turned to the secretary. "Don't we have a delicious red lollipop for this young man, Colleen?"

"I think we might," she said, smiling at Drake. He eyed her cautiously, the promise of a lollipop softening his resistance.

"Well, why don't you find him one so he can sit out here and enjoy that while I speak to Mr. and Mrs. Stonewall," Mr. Steine said.

His secretary reached into a bottom drawer to produce a lollipop. Drake took it eagerly and started to turn away.

"You must say thank you when people give you things, Drake," I said softly. He looked at me, considered what I said, and then turned around slowly.

"Thank you," he said and rushed back to the couch to work the wrapper off his lollipop. He didn't seem to mind being left alone.

"We'll be right out, Drake. Just stay here," I said. He looked up at me without responding and went back to his lollipop.

"Right this way," Mr. Steine said and led us through a carpeted corridor, past a beautiful conference room, a large law library, two other law offices, to his own, which was at the end of the corridor. Its windows looked over the city, which that day, because of the soft, nearly cloudless blue sky, provided a magnificent clear view. "Please, have a seat," he said, indicating the gray, soft leather chairs in front of his desk. "You two probably don't remember me," he said, "but I was at your wedding reception at Farthinggale Manor. What a party that was."

"I thought I had seen you someplace before," I mused. "But I'm afraid I don't quite understand . . . you were Luke Casteel's attorney?"

"Well, actually, I represented Mr. Tatterton."

"Mr. Tatterton?" I looked to Logan, but he only shrugged.

"Yes. You didn't know that?" Mr. Steine asked.

"No. You'll have to explain."

"Oh, I'm sorry. I just assumed . . ." He sat forward. "Well, some time back I negotiated the purchase of a circus owned by a . . . a Mr. Windenbarron for Mr. Tatterton." He looked at the papers on his desk. "Yes, Windenbarron."

"Tony bought the circus from Windenbarron? But . . . I thought Luke owned the circus." Again I looked at Logan and again he shook his head to indicate he knew nothing.

"Oh, yes, he did," Mr. Steine assured me.

"I don't understand."

"Well, after Mr. Tatterton bought the circus, he then had me work up an arrangement with Luke Casteel, turning the circus over to him, for a rather small sum." He smiled. "One dollar, to be exact."

"What?"

"You'd have to call it a gift. Anyway, with his and Mrs. Casteel's death, the ownership reverts back to Mr. Tatterton. Last night when we spoke, he asked me to put the circus up for sale and place the proceeds into a trust fund for Drake. He also asked me to look into Mr. Casteel's estate, expedite the sale of their home, and place any and all proceeds and legacies into the same trust. I hope that meets with your approval, Mrs. Stonewall," he said.

I was dumbfounded.

"Actually," Mr. Steine went on, "the matter ordinarily wouldn't be of sufficient size for our firm, but we handle many of Mr. Tatterton's affairs in the South and when he called . . . of course, we'll take care of everything."

I sat back, stunned. Why had Tony done all this? Why had he kept it a secret?

"All the necessary documents are here," he continued. "There really isn't anything you have to sign. . . . It will be a while before we settle matters, but if there is anything you would like to look over . . ."

"He gave Luke the circus?" I said. I imagined I looked rather silly with my mouth open and my baffled expression.

"Yes, Mrs. Stonewall." He paused for a moment and then sat forward. "Now, as to the funeral. The bodies are presently at the Eddington Funeral Home. The service will be at eleven tomorrow morning."

"Tony did all this with a phone call?" I asked. I didn't sound sarcastic so much as I sounded amazed. Tony had completely taken Luke, and my farewell to him, out of my hands. He had truly stolen Luke from me. J. Arthur Steine smiled the smile of pride.

"As I said, Mrs. Stonewall, Mr. Tatterton is an important client of ours. We are happy to do what we can to make things easier for all of you."

"That's Tony for you," Logan said. I looked at him. He didn't realize what this meant. He still didn't know that Tony was my real father, that it was jealousy and possessiveness that he acted from, not pure kindness. I thought, but this was something between Tony and me and Luke and me, something Logan never needed to know.

"But maybe Luke should be buried back in the Willies," I said. I thought about my mother's grave and that slim little tombstone that simply read,

ANGEL
BELOVED WIFE OF
THOMAS LUKE CASTEEL

"Oh, I don't know," Logan said. "Atlanta and the surrounding area did become Luke's home. Do you really think he would want to be taken back to the Willies?"

The way Logan pronounced "taken back" made it sound as if I would be returning him to a lower, uglier time of his life, something he had escaped by coming here to live and by becoming the owner of a circus.

"Maybe not," I said.

"And you've got to think of Stacie," Logan reminded me.

"What about Drake?" I asked, turning back to Mr. Steine.

"Well, as far as we can tell, there are no relatives on Mrs. Casteel's side who would be interested in taking care of the boy. Mr. Casteel had some brothers?"

"They weren't willing even to take care of themselves," I said. "All five of them ended up in prison."

"Well," he said, sitting back, "you're his half sister. What do you want to do about the child? I'm sure you've discussed this with Mr. Tatterton, and he's told me to follow your instructions. If you want, I'm sure you'll have no problem arranging for custody of the boy. You can certainly provide him with a wonderful home."

"Well, of course I want custody," I insisted. "However, since I will be taking custody of Drake, all matters pertaining to him should be directed to me from now on, and not Mr. Tatterton." He heard the ice in my words and straightened up in his seat.

"Fine. Same address, correct?"

"We have an address in Winnerow, too," I said. "We'll give that to you. That's where I want everything sent." He just stared for a moment and then nodded. There was no doubt in my mind that he would be on the phone with Tony the moment we left his office. I wrote out the address of the Hasbrouck House and gave it to him.

"Do you know," I asked, "if we will be able to view Luke's body?"

"From what I understand, Mrs. Stonewall, it's not a pleasant sight. It's a closed casket, better left that way."

I closed my eyes and took a deep breath.

"Heaven?" Logan asked. He put his hand on my arm.

"It's all right," I said. I stood up. "Thank you, Mr. Steine," I said. He came around his desk.

"I'm sorry that the second time we meet it has to be under these circumstances. Good luck to you and especially to the little boy. I'll be in touch concerning all the other matters."

I thanked him again and we left. I was trembling as we walked down that plush corridor to the lobby. Drake had red streaks from the lollipop all over his mouth, his chin, and his cheeks. He looked up anxiously.

"When he eats a lollipop, he really eats it," Logan marveled.

"Is there a rest room nearby?" I asked the secretary.

"Of course. Right to your left, first door."

I picked up Drake and took him into the rest room to wash off his face. He stared at me, stared deeply into my eyes and face. I hoped he saw the love I had for him.

"Are we going home now?" he asked.

"Oh, yes, Drake honey. Home and then to a new home where nothing bad will ever touch you again."

He just continued to stare. Then he lifted his right hand, his forefinger extended, and touched the single tear that had escaped my right eye and zigzagged its way to the middle of my cheek. Suddenly, although he wouldn't accept it, he seemed to understand all that had happened.

As soon as we returned to Luke's house and I opened the car door, Drake lunged out and ran to the front door. Before we had left for J. Arthur Steine's law office, Mrs. Cotton had given me the keys to the house because she would be gone by the time we returned. Drake was surprised to find the door locked when he turned the knob. He looked back at us, a frantic desperation in his little face.

"Where's Mommy?" he asked. "Where's Daddy?"

I put the key into the lock without responding. My throat had become so tight I couldn't speak anyway. When I opened the door, he rushed into the house, calling.

"Mommy! Mommy! Mommy!"

His little feet pattered on the floor as he rushed from room to room.

"Daddy! Mommy!"

His plaintive voice made my heart ache and filled my eyes with tears.

"Maybe it's not such a good idea to stay here tonight, Heaven," Logan said, coming up beside me in the doorway and putting his arm around my shoulders. "Maybe we should just go back to Atlanta and check into a hotel. We'll look around and pack whatever you want to take from this place."

"Maybe you're right," I said, my voice trembling now. "But I'm afraid of wrenching him away from all that is familiar so quickly. But maybe we can make it into a fun, exciting adventure for him." I took a deep breath to get hold of myself. Things had to be done; there just wasn't time to be mournful, and I had little Drake to think about now. I had to be strong for him. "You see if you can find any suitcases, and I'll start going through his things, taking only what's necessary. I want to buy him an entirely new wardrobe."

Logan went looking and I followed Drake back to the bedrooms. Once again he was standing in his parents' doorway, staring at the empty bed. When I lifted him into my arms, there wasn't the slightest resistance. He laid his head against my shoulder, his thumb in his mouth, and stared with glassy eyes.

"What we're going to do, Drake," I said, "is go to your room and pick out whatever you want to take with you. Then Logan and I will pack it into a suitcase, and we'll all go to a nice hotel in Atlanta. Were you ever in a hotel?"

He shook his head softly.

"Oh, you're going to like it. And we'll go to a nice restaurant. Tomorrow, we'll be going on an airplane," I said, and that perked him up. He lifted his head from my shoulder and looked at me with new interest. "You were never on an airplane?" He shook his head more vigorously this time. "Well," I said, carrying him to his room, "we're going to take an airplane ride and then get into a big car and go to the biggest house you ever saw."

"Will Mommy be there?"

"No, honey."

"Will Daddy?" His hopeful voice nearly broke my heart.

"No, Drake. Don't you remember what I told you about God calling them to Heaven?" He nodded. "That's where they are, but they'll be looking down at you and smiling because you'll be so well taken care of, okay?"

I put him down and began searching through the drawers in his dresser. Logan found some suitcases, but I picked out only enough clothing to fill one. I told Drake to choose his favorite toy to take. A few minutes later he stood in front of me holding a familiar toy fire engine. It was a Tatterton Toy, a replica of one of the first fire engines ever made, and it was constructed out of a heavy metal. The pump was actually functional. It had real little rubber tires and a steering wheel that actually turned the front wheels. It was the kind of quality toy just not sold in regular stores anymore. The little firemen, their faces rendered in actual detail, some wearing intense expressions, some smiling, were all intact. The toy had been well cared for these past years. It was the toy I had sent to him after I had first visited.

"Oh, that's a beautiful toy, Drake. Do you know where you got that toy?" He shook his head. "I sent it to you years ago. I'm glad you took good care of it and that's the toy you want to take with you. But do you know what?" I said, pulling him to me and brushing his hair off his forehead. "You're going to have a lot of toys like this, good toys, real toys." His eyes widened with interest. "You know why?" He shook his head. "Because Logan and I own a toy factory," I said. He looked amazed as I smiled to reassure him. "That's right, a toy factory. Okay," I said. "You carry that out to Logan and tell him you want to take it along." I looked around the room and then went back to Luke and Stacie's bedroom.

I decided I wanted the picture of them together in the front of the house. I wanted it for Drake, but I wanted it for myself almost as much.

"I'm making a cup of tea. Want any?" Logan called from the kitchen.

"No, thanks. See if Drake will eat anything, though, okay?"

"Sure. Hey, Drake," I heard Logan say. "Let's see what's for lunch, huh?"

While they were out in the kitchen, I began to search through the dresser drawers, primarily to see if there was anything of value I should take for Drake. I found all of Stacie's jewelry, which was mostly costume jewelry, a watch that looked valuable, and some more pictures of her and Luke. In his dresser under his socks in the top drawer, I found one of Grandpa's whittled rabbits. It brought tears to my eyes as I stood there remembering him sitting in his rocker, working and talking to his imaginary Annie.

Then I found something that amazed me—a *Boston Globe,* newspaper clipping announcing my marriage to Logan. I saw where Luke had underlined the part about my being a schoolteacher in Winnerow. I sat on the bed, holding the clipping in my lap. So he had been interested in me and proud of me all the while, I thought. But why couldn't he have come to my wedding, and why didn't he ever contact me or write to me since? Now he was gone, Stacie was gone, Mrs. Cotton was gone; and anyway, she wasn't the kind of person who could want to answer any questions, and the lawyer was too professional and indifferent to know anything more than legal matters.

But Tony would know, I thought. I felt sure of that now. For some reason he knew and was involved with so many things concerning Luke and his life. I couldn't wait to get back to find out why he had kept it all a secret. Did he think he was protecting me somehow? I was no longer a child; he had no right to hide anything from me.

I put the clipping with the pictures and the rabbit and some other things I wanted to take and started to look through the closets when I heard the front door bell. I paused to listen as Logan went to see who it was. A moment later I heard a familiar voice. Fanny's! But there was a second voice, also very familiar to me. She had come with Randall Wilcox. By the time I came out, she and Randall were already in the kitchen.

"Drake, honey," Fanny drawled, "I'm yer sista Fanny, the one yer Pa loved the most." Before Drake could respond, she scooped him off his chair and into her arms, covering his face with kisses and leaving lipstick streaked over his cheeks and forehead.

"Yer the spittin' image of him, jus' as handsome as he was."

"Hello, Fanny," I said softly. She had come dressed in a sleeveless, black lace dress with a frilly bottom and a low-necked bodice. It fit her a size too tightly around the hips and bosom, but I could see little evidence of her pregnancy—perhaps only a slight thickening around the middle. She wore a wide-brimmed black straw hat and had her hair pinned up behind her head. As usual, her makeup was too thick —the blue eye shadow, the rouge, and the bright red lipstick.

"Well, hello yerself. Say hello ta Randall," she demanded, turning toward him. With his hat in his hands he had been standing in the kitchen doorway looking in. He was dressed in a plain, dark brown suit and looked much older than I remembered. Life with Fanny must be aging him quickly, I thought. He smiled shyly and nodded.

"Hello, Heaven," he said. He looked toward Logan. "Logan."

Logan simply nodded.

"Ya'll could be more cordial," Fanny said quickly. "Randall was

kind enuf ta escort me on this sad journey," she added, threading her
right arm through his while she held on to Drake with her left, "especially with me bein' in a delicate condition," she added, looking slyly
pleased!

"That is very kind of him." I didn't respond to her insinuation. I
wanted to rescue Drake from Fanny's clutches. "Logan, weren't you
giving Drake something to eat?"

"Yeah, sure. His sandwich is ready." Logan suddenly regained the
composure he had lost at the sight of Fanny and put the dish down on
the table. "I made him some chocolate milk, too. That's what you
wanted, right, Drake?" Drake nodded and Fanny reluctantly brought
him back to his seat.

"So," she said, looking around, "ya skinned this place ta the bone
yit?"

"There's nothing to skin, Fanny," I said coldly. "There's little of
value here. Everything that belonged to Luke and Stacie is going to be
placed into a trust for Drake. The lawyer is working on it."

"I'll bet," she sneered. "Told ya she'd have it all wrapped up 'fore
we got here," she said to Randall.

"I didn't have to wrap anything up, Fanny. As a matter of fact, it
was all set in motion before I arrived. Instructions were left," I said,
leaving out that Tony had left them. I still didn't understand his role
in this myself.

"What 'bout the funeral and such?"

"The funeral's tomorrow at eleven at the Kingsington Cathedral in
Atlanta, burial at the church cemetery."

"You payin' for that?"

"It's all been taken care of, Fanny," I reiterated.

"Ya stayin' here tonight?" she asked and looked at Logan. He refused to meet her eyes and busied himself putting away the milk and
peanut butter.

"No, we're going to stay in Atlanta at a hotel tonight," I said. I
wanted to make sure Fanny dealt with me, not Logan. "But you can
stay here and search the house to see if there's anything you might
want."

"Well, he was ma pa. He loved me the most. I gotta right," she
declared stubbornly.

"I suppose you do," I said softly. "Here are the keys to the house.
Just bring them with you tomorrow and we'll give them to the attorney in charge of the property." I dropped the keys into her palm and
she looked up at me with surprise.

"What about Drake?" she said, turning to him. "You wanna stay here with Randall and me, Drake, honey? Then you kin go ta the funeral with us tommorrah."

For a long moment Drake just stared up at her. Then he looked at me and then again at her.

"I'm goin' to a hotel," he said, "and then on an airplane. And then to a toy factory!"

"Oh, ya are?" She looked at me. "Ya takin' him back ta that castle?"

"He's coming back with us, yes. We'll make a home for him."

She stared at me a moment, the strangest blankness in her eyes. It was a blankness devoid of all feeling which I hadn't seen in her before. Then she turned back to Drake. "Well, honey, wouldn't ya rather be in yer own bed tanight?"

"You're confusing him, Fanny," I interrupted. "He's confused enough. It's better his mind is occupied." She turned to me with more characteristic Fanny fury in her eyes.

"I ain't confusin' him."

"She's right," Randall said softly. He looked almost surprised that he had spoken up, but what he saw made him do it. Almost immediately, though, he realized he had brought Fanny's wrath down upon himself.

"Oh, sure, ya'll say she's right," Fanny snapped. "Ya'll probably always take her side 'gainst me, won't ya?"

"Come on," he said, in a pleading tone, "let's go have something to eat at a restaurant. We'll come back later."

She stared at me hatefully and then her face softened and she put on one of her brilliant smiles.

"Randall's right. I've been so upset about Pa, I couldn't think about food. And I'm eatin' fer two now, ain't I, Heaven," she said as she looked straight at Logan. "We didn't eat a thing since we left Winnerow, did we, Randall?"

"No," Randall agreed, obviously confused by the tension between Logan and Fanny.

"Ya wanna go to a restaurant, Drake, honey?" she asked.

"Fanny, can't you see he's in the middle of eating a sandwich?"

"Sandwich." She put her hand on his head and stroked his hair. "Ya'd rather go ta a restaurant, wouldn't ya, Drake baby?"

"I'm not a baby," he said, pulling back.

"Well, I didn't mean yer a baby, honey."

"Fanny, let's go eat," Randall pleaded. "We'll come back."

"All right," she snapped. Then she put on her smile again. "We'll see ya all later on." She knelt down beside Drake and kissed him on the cheek. "Jus' as handsome as yer daddy was," she said. He stared at her as she joined Randall.

"We'll see you at the church tomorrow," I said coldly.

"Oh, God, I forgot," Fanny said. "Poor Luke." She threaded her arm through Randall's. "I jest hate thinkin' 'bout it. Lemme borrow that handkerchief again, Randall, honey," she said and dabbed her eyes gently. She lowered her head.

"So long," Randall said.

The moment he and Fanny left the house, I took a deep breath and tried to calm the coiling rage Fanny had aroused in me. I looked at Logan, who wore a guilty, sad expression.

"I'll take Drake's things out to the car," he said, "so we can leave as soon as he's finished."

I nodded and then sat at the table and began wiping Fanny's lipstick off Drake's face.

Early the next morning, with Drake between us, one of his small sweet hands in each of ours, we entered the church, like a family. Luke's circus employees crowded the pews and spilled over into the aisles of the small church. There were giants and midgets; a bearded lady in a long, black dress; animal trainers with their hair so long they looked like body-building rock singers; acrobatic groups who were so in tune with one another's movements, they looked attached; some glamorous-looking women who assisted magicians and the ringmaster; some management types in business suits; and men who played clowns, their faces so ridden with real grief, it was as if they wore their sad makeup clown faces.

All of them knew Drake, and at the sight of him it seemed as if the entire collection sighed and burst into tears at once. We walked down the aisle to the front pew and sat facing Drake's parents' caskets.

"Are Mommy and Daddy coming here?" Drake asked, his big brown eyes looking around anxiously.

I felt my heart almost break in two.

"This is a special place to say good-bye to your mommy and daddy," I said, holding him tightly.

He looked up at the stained-glass window, at the candles, at the two caskets sitting side by side. The bearded lady had just walked over to Luke's casket and, weeping profusely, leaned over it and placed a single rose atop it.

"He was so kind to me," she whispered aloud to herself.

"Why is Auntie Martha talking to that box?" Drake asked. "Who's in there? Did Melin the Magician put someone inside there?"

"No, honey," I said. I tenderly kissed his forehead.

"I want to look inside! I don't believe you! I don't believe you! I know my daddy's in there!" he shouted, trying to wrench himself free. "Let me go! I want my daddy!"

He ran up to the coffin. But then he suddenly stopped. He put his tiny little ear against the wood and knocked. "Are you in there, Daddy?"

I tried to run up to him and hold him and protect him, but the bearded lady gently took my elbow. "Please," she said kindly, "I think I can handle him. Drake and I have always been very good friends."

Drake hugged the bearded lady. "Auntie Martha, Auntie Martha! Is my daddy in there?"

"My precious, darling Drake. Your daddy is in Heaven; it is only his shell in there. But don't worry, darling, Heaven is just like a wonderful circus. The biggest circus your daddy and mommy ever saw. They will be very happy there. But most important, they want you to be happy here on earth. They want you to go to school, and do well, and stay healthy, and when you grow up, you can be a ringmaster just like your daddy was." She began to cry.

"I want to be a ringmaster," Drake said. "And a lion tamer, too."

"Now I want you to go back and sit down with your sister. She loves you very, very much."

Then the bearded lady swept little Drake into her arms and kissed him good-bye.

"I'm going to be a lion tamer," Drake told me proudly.

"Of course you are, darling, you're going to be everything you want to be, and I'm going to help you," I assured him. "Now, Drake," I said, as I led him away from the casket, "let's sit down and listen to the service, okay?"

He nodded bravely, clutching my hand so hard he seemed to be afraid I, too, would disappear. As we walked back to the pew, I saw that Drake was comforted by the sight of all the familiar faces. As I scanned the congregation, I was surprised Fanny and Randall hadn't yet arrived. But my mind didn't linger on her. We sat down and Logan put his arm around me. I couldn't help but stare at the casket and think about Luke.

The organ music began. Then I heard a commotion at the door and turned around to look. Fanny and Randall were hurrying up the aisle. Fanny was wearing the same black cocktail dress she had worn yesterday and her face was just as heavily made up. As she slid into the pew beside us, she suddenly caught sight of the casket. She grabbed my hand as the tears began to spill down her cheeks, her heavy eye makeup turning her tears into muddy black and blue streams. At that moment I almost felt close to this sister of mine who seemed always to want to hurt me.

The minister appeared. He delivered a fine eulogy for someone who hadn't really known Luke and Stacie. Obviously, Mr. Steine had provided him with some biographical material. The minister talked about Luke's desire to provide entertainment and pleasure for people. He said that some people believed life, itself, was like a circus, and that God was like the ringmaster. He said that Luke had a finer performance awaiting him in Heaven, that God had called him to a greater responsibility. I was glad he had used the expression "God had called him." Little Drake, who stared at the closed coffins before him, looked up with widened eyes when the minister said those words. He remembered what I had told him.

Then the minister talked about Stacie, who had been a good mother and a good wife, and how Luke's and her love for each other must have been so strong, God decided to take them at the same time so they could be together.

Fanny began really sobbing, wailing loud enough so everyone in the church could hear. Randall comforted her, hoping to get her to lower her voice, I thought. For one moment, before the minister finished, Fanny and I looked at each other, and I saw my own sincere pain and sorrow reflected in her eyes. Luke had often shown her affection when she was younger, and Fanny hadn't seen very much of real affection in her life. She was suffering a real loss in Luke's death.

The caskets were carried out of the church and brought to their plots in the cemetery. A monument stone had already been cut and engraved. *Casteel* was written on top and their Christian names below with their birth dates and the date of their death. Under that it simply read, "Rest in Peace." After the final words were said and the caskets lowered, the mourners began to depart.

Out in front of the church Fanny scooped Drake into her arms again, tears streaming down her face.

"Oh, Drake, honey, yer like an orphan now, yer like us." She showered his face with kisses. He didn't resist; he was numbed and overwhelmed by the service and the sight of the coffins. I thought she was overdoing it, however, and pulled him out of her arms.

"He's not an orphan," I said, my face aflame with anger. "He's going to have a home and a family."

Fanny stepped back, stung by the cold tone in my voice. She wiped the tears from her cheeks with Randall's handkerchief and glared at me

"He should be in the Willies," she said. "With his daddy's kind."

"That will never be," I stated, something proud and strong as steel springing into my spine. "Luke left the Willies to make himself a better life, and he would want the same for his son."

"Come, Fanny," Randall said softly. Some of the mourners from the circus had stopped to watch us. "This isn't the place to hold such a discussion."

Fanny looked around for a moment and then smiled.

"Yer right," she said. "Good-bye fer now, Heaven Leigh. Bye, Drake, honey." She threw him a kiss and then pivoted on her heels and sauntered off with Randall.

We drove directly to the airport. Drake was like a rag doll in my lap all the way, sitting limply, quietly, his head against my breast. When we arrived at the airport, however, the excitement surrounding the airplanes and the business of travel revived him. He had some lunch and we boarded our plane. I placed him at the window and he became very animated. "Are we up above the birds?" he asked. "Will we land on the moon?" Logan explained to Drake all about how airplanes flew, how the clouds prevented us from seeing the ground when we flew above them, why the plane didn't disappear in the clouds. Drake was so excited with this new adventure, his face so animated, I felt sure we were going to be able to make him happy in his new family. Logan was going to make a wonderful father. Already he had accepted Drake as his own.

Soon both Logan and Drake fell asleep, Drake's sweet dark head resting on Logan's lap. How peaceful they seemed. I wished I could feel so peaceful, but my mind was abuzz with anxiety. I wanted to know why Tony had given the circus to Luke, why Luke had that clipping of my wedding from the newspaper in his drawer. I wanted to start my new life with Drake and Logan and our new baby clear from the sticky webs of the past, and I was determined to force Tony to clear away every one of them.

Tony was not at Farthy when we arrived. Curtis said he had been called away on business and wouldn't be back until late the following afternoon.

There were all sorts of phone messages waiting for Logan, and he went right to work calling people after we got settled in.

Drake and I took a brief tour of the house. He was enchanted by the murals in the drawing room, and even more impressed by the size of the house. "Is this a castle, Heaven?" he asked. "Am I going to be a prince now?" His eyes were wide with wonder

"Yes, darling," I said, hugging him close to me. "You will be the prince of the castle and have everything your heart desires."

I had the room right next to our suite prepared for him and Logan brought him some of the sample toys that were in the house. Drake was exhausted from the day and the travel, and he fell asleep right after he had some dinner.

After I tucked him into his bed, I stood and stared down at him. He was so sweet, so beautiful and innocent. I promised myself to be a real mother to him, never to make him feel foreign or unwanted. Yes, I could try to undo the past. I could prove with my love that anger and bitterness and resentment could be put to rest once and for all. I would love him enough to undo all the pain and misery I had suffered by hating Luke.

Fanny was right—we were all orphans of a sort, but I would make us a family. The baby growing in me would be as much a brother or sister to him as any baby Stacie would have had. And I would love Drake in a way Luke had never been able to love me.

I tucked the blanket under his chin, knelt down and kissed his soft cheek, and left him. Logan was just hanging up the phone in the bedroom when I arrived.

"Heaven," he said, his face a picture of frustration, "I hate to do this to you so quickly, but I've got to get back to Winnerow tomorrow. The roofers walked off the job over a dispute with my foreman. Everything's at a standstill there. As soon as I settle it—"

"Don't worry, Logan. You go in the morning. I'll be busy getting to know Drake and letting him get to know me and Farthy. And I want to be here when Tony gets back. We have some things to discuss," I said. Logan heard the determined tone running under my words.

"I'm sure that he has good explanations and that everything he did and has done he did for good reasons, Heaven. Tony cares for you. He wouldn't do anything to upset you, especially now that you're pregnant."

"I hope not," I said, but of course, there was much Logan didn't know about my past at Farthinggale. His optimism was understandable.

Logan slept the sleep of the innocent that night, while I tossed and turned, turned and tossed, my mind assailed by secrets and shadows. I lay there wondering and thinking. How odd life was. How like my own life Drake's would become. And how like mine would my own child's be, a child who might never know who his or her real father was? My mind churned on, trying to unravel the cat's cradle that was my life. So many of the knots were centered around Tony—Tony, who had raped my mother, who had caused Jillian to go mad, who had made my love with Troy impossible, and now, it appeared, had tried to run Luke's life as he tried to run mine. Why? As far as I knew, the only time Luke had any contact with Tony was when he called him to tell him he had bought me plane tickets to go to Boston to see him and Jillian and learn about my mother. Tony rarely mentioned Luke after that. Why would he? They came from worlds so far part they might as well have been on different planets.

Yet the telegram announcing Luke and Stacie's death came to Tony, and it was Tony who had made all these arrangements. Why did Tony buy Luke the circus and never tell me he had done so?

It was no use; I would never sleep tonight, I thought. I looked over at Logan. He was dead to the world, tired himself from the travel and the ordeal. His breathing was deep and regular. I got out of bed and slipped into my robe and slippers, moving quietly into the dimly lit corridor. First I checked on Drake and found him in a deep sleep. I fixed his blanket, which he had pushed away during some tossing and turning, and then I left him. But instead of returning to my bedroom, I went downstairs.

How quiet the house was. How still were the shadows in the corners. My own shadow, ten times my size, followed me along the walls like a dark hovering angel as I descended the stairs and paused to reconsider what I was about to do. I had never had the interest or the curiosity before, but tonight . . . tonight I needed answers.

I went directly to Tony's office and turned on the light. The big desk was cluttered with papers. I knew how much Tony hated anyone to go through his things. He even hated the maids cleaning. The office always had a dusty, unkempt appearance, but Tony valued his privacy and his own system of recording and finding things so much, he hated any interference.

My gaze fell on the file cabinets. I was glad that he kept things alphabetized. At first I searched and found nothing. I was looking under the C's for Casteel. Confused and frustrated, I stood there thinking. Then I pulled out the files under the H's, looking for one labeled HEAVEN. My heart sent an electric shock through my veins instead of blood when I found it.

I sat down at his desk and looked through it. At first all I found were papers concerning my schooling. But then I found a simple document, a document that made me colder than the most icy wind shaking through the cracks in the cabin floor and walls in the Willies.

It was a letter of agreement between Anthony Townsend Tatterton and Luke Casteel, turning the Windenbarron circus over to Luke for the simple consideration of one dollar plus the following stipulation:

". . . that he never again make contact in any way, form, or manner with Heaven Leigh Casteel." The agreement being that he would forfeit his ownership of the circus, should he do so.

I sat back, too stunned to rage or cry or scream. Too stunned to know how to react. I understood only one thing.

Once again Luke had sold me.

❧ THIRTEEN ❧
The Sins of My Father

SOON AFTER DAWN'S FIRST LIGHT I WAS AWAKENED BY THE PIT-
ter-pat of small feet. I opened my eyes and spotted Drake in the
doorway, tousle-haired from sleep, shyly staring at me. I had left the
door open so I could hear him should he awaken during the night and
cry out for his mother or father. I smiled and sat up. Logan woke up
immediately, too.

"Good morning, Drake," I said. "Hungry for breakfast?"

He continued to stare at me, his eyes blinking rapidly.

"Morning, Drake," Logan said, getting out of bed quickly. "I'm
hungry. I know that."

"I wanna go home," Drake said. He didn't whine; he just made a
demand.

I got out of bed and went to him, kneeling down before him and
taking his hands into mine. He stood there firmly, his beautiful bright
brown eyes intense, his lips pursed.

"You are home now, Drake. Wherever Logan and I are will be your
home from now on. Don't you remember yesterday and all the things
we said and saw?"

He nodded slowly. I brought him to me, embracing him and kissing
him on the cheek.

"Okay, then," I said in my most cheerful voice. "We'll all get
washed and dressed and have some breakfast, and then you and I will
explore Farthy. That's what we call this house and the grounds,
Farthy, short for Farthinggale Manor. You'll see a pool and a gazebo
and gardens and tennis courts."

"Can I go swimming?" Drake's eyes lit up.

"Of course, darling, but it's too cold now. But we can explore the
maze, although you won't be able to ever go in it all by yourself.

because you could get lost forever and ever. After we take our walk, you can come back up here and play with some of the toys Logan found for you last night. Then, after lunch, we'll have Miles drive us into Boston in the limo, and I will take you shopping and buy you all sorts of clothes. How does all that sound?"

He looked from me toward Logan, who was already shaving.

"You should start with a nice warm bath," I said, standing and taking his hand to lead him to the bathroom in his room.

"I don't wanna."

"Sure you do," I said, looking around quickly. I saw the replica of the *Queen Mary* on a chair by his light walnut dresser, and I remembered that it could actually float. "You'll take your toy ship in the water with you and you'll see that the little lifeboats float."

That caught his interest and from then on it was easy. He even let me wash his hair. Afterward, I dried him down and dressed him in one of his outfits. I put a sweater on him because the early days of fall were here and the wind was already reminding us that winter was not that far behind.

He played quietly in his room until I got washed and dressed, and then we joined Logan for breakfast. He was reading through *The Wall Street Journal,* just as Tony always did at breakfast. I looked at his studious frown, tempted to tell him the truth I had learned last night, and all the other truths I had kept from him for so long. Suddenly he looked up at me. "A penny for your thoughts, honey." He smiled.

Oh, did my thoughts show so easily on my face? I covered my shame with a smile.

"You owe me a penny," Logan continued before I had a chance to say a word. "I know what you're thinking." My heart skipped a beat. He laid down his paper and gave me a big grin. "The baby, you're thinking about the new baby, aren't you?"

I could only smile back at him. "I'm thinking about all my new children, especially this special young man," I said, tousling Drake's hair.

The servants made an extra effort to make Drake feel at home. Rye Whiskey even created a fruit plate that looked like an elephant and brought it out himself. It brought the first real smile to Drake's face. I saw that he had inherited Luke's smile, a smile that began around his eyes and rippled through his cheeks, bringing the corners of his mouth out gently.

Logan had to rush out right after breakfast to make his plane. He kissed me good-bye and then kissed Drake, who looked up with such surprise, I had to wonder if Luke had ever kissed him hello or good-bye. Perhaps Luke had brought with him that resistance to any show of emotion most men from the Willies had. Sentiment was a woman's way.

After breakfast Drake and I went for that walking tour of Farthinggale Manor I had promised him. The trees on the grounds and in the surrounding woods were beginning to wear their bright autumn colors. It was as if God had come along with a great paintbrush and stroked in ribbons of yellow and orange, red and salmon. Because the trees were still full, the sight was breathtaking. The morning air, although a bit cool, was invigorating. Nature filled us with such a strong feeling for life just before she retreated into hibernation before the winter when days could be cold and dark and gloomy, making us long for the first rays of the spring sun. I remembered how welcome were the sounds of the spring waters in the Willies freeing themselves from the grip of ice.

The gardeners were working on the grounds and some men were winterizing the pool. I could see that little Drake was fascinated with all the activity. His eyes went everywhere, hungrily gobbling up the sight of men trimming trees and bushes, men painting the sides of the pool and repairing cracks in the patios.

When we reached one of the entrances to the maze, I explained what it was to him and why it was dangerous for him to go in himself.

"After you go in and make a turn here and then make a turn there, you can forget how to get back because all the turns and all the paths look the same."

"Why did someone make that?" he asked, his eyes narrowing. He was a thoughtful boy, a curious boy. After having taught for a year, I could recognize that love for learning in a young child's eyes. I knew that once he became more comfortable around me and in these surroundings, he would ask many questions. I wondered if Luke and Stacie had been patient with him and had fed his appetite for knowledge. I made up my mind we would get him a good tutor and give him preschool instruction.

"It's supposed to be fun," I said. "A puzzle, but only a puzzle for older people, you understand?"

He nodded.

"Promise me you'll never go in by yourself."

"I promise," he said and I hugged him to me. He looked into my eyes, a warmth appearing for the first time.

"Is my daddy looking down now and smiling?" he asked.

"Oh, I think so, Drake. I really do." I stood up. "Come on, we'll go see what the men are doing to the pool," I said and led him away from the maze.

Right after lunch I had Miles bring up the limo and take us into Boston for the shopping spree. I reminded myself of the time Tony took me into Boston to buy my wardrobe for the Winterhaven School. He said, "I despise the way girls dress today, ruining the best part of their lives with shoddy, common clothes. . . . You will dress as the girls dressed when I went to Yale." Then he took me to the small shops where clothes and shoes cost small fortunes. Not once did he ask the prices of sweaters, skirts, dresses, coats, boots . . . anything. Only Tony had been wrong about the clothes. Not one girl at Winterhaven wore a skirt. They dressed like any other teenager: blue jeans and sloppy tops, too-large shirts or ill-fitting sweaters.

I was determined not to make the same mistake with Drake. I would buy him nice things, but not stuffy clothes that would single him out and isolate him from other children his age. I wasn't about to make him over into something he was not, something Tony had attempted to do with me. I looked to see what Drake liked, what caught his fancy, too. I bought him some dress clothes, but a lot of clothes to play in—jeans, flannel shirts, sneakers.

Miles followed along in the limo and took the packages from my hands as I emerged from store after store. Finally both Drake and I were exhausted from our shopping. We got into the limo and headed back to Farthy. The servants helped bring our packages up to Drake's room, but I dismissed the maids and put things away myself. I wanted Drake to feel my strong bond with him and everything that involved him. He sat on the rug playing with his cars and trucks as I organized his wardrobe. Every once in a while I caught him looking up and staring at me.

I could see he wasn't quite sure yet how to take me, or what to consider me. Was I a stepmother, a half sister, a nanny? He had grown more comfortable with me, but he was still holding back, rationing his words, his laughter, even his tears. I knew it would take time and it was simply a matter of trust, and I, as well as anyone, knew what it was like to start over with a new family and a new home.

He talked a lot more at dinner, telling me about the times he had gone with Luke to the circus, telling me about the animals and the acrobats. "Heaven, there was this woman who knew how to hang by her hair and spin around and around, and sometimes Daddy let me feed the elephants. My favorite, my always favorite was when Daddy let me wear my own clown suit and special clown nose and hair and I got to ride on the top hump of the camel. His name was Ishtar, isn't that a funny name, Heaven?"

He wondered when he would be able to go back to the circus, and I told him that some day soon, I would take him to a circus, maybe even a bigger circus. Talking about the circus reminded him of Luke, though, and of Stacie, and very soon he became melancholy. Rye Whiskey rescued the moment once again when he appeared with a three-layer chocolate cake with a clown face made out of strawberries on top.

"Wow, what's that!" Drake asked, excitement enlivening his features.

"This cake is called a Drake cake." Rye Whiskey smiled. "Tell me if you like it." With that he set the cake before Drake. "Can I have the piece with the nose?" Drake asked.

"Of course, young man," Rye Whiskey said, pretending to steal Drake's nose, putting his thumb between his fingers as he chuckled. "Since I've got yours, you can have the cake's."

Shortly afterward I took Drake up to his room and washed and dressed him for bed. He had had another big day. I let him play a while longer, until he grew groggy. Then I tucked him in under his soft blanket, kissed him on the cheek, and left him to sleep his second night at Farthy.

I went down to the living room, planning to lie in wait for Tony and confront him the moment he returned. The world outside the Farthinggale world seemed to anticipate my anger and accusations. The sky was dismally dark and overcast, with flashes of furious lightning flaming through the sky. No stars dared show themselves on this night. Then the rains came, heavy and hard, sounding cold, like tears of ice.

Suddenly I heard the sound of tires whooshing through puddles, a door slammed outside, then the front door opened. I heard Curtis bid Tony good evening. Then I heard him giving Tony all his messages and recounting all that had happened while he was gone. Tony wandered into the living room, as he always did, and smiled when he saw me.

"I'm sorry I wasn't here when you and Logan returned," he said, coming to me. "Was it a very trying time?"

"Yes," I said sharply. "For more reasons than one. There was surprise as well as sadness, mystery, and confusion."

"Where's Logan?" he asked, as if looking for an ally at this moment.

"He was called back to Winnerow over a labor crisis at the factory. Perhaps we should go into your office and talk, Tony," I said quickly.

He stared at me a moment, his blue eyes narrowing now with suspicion and some understanding.

"I was just heading there," he said. He gestured for me to lead the way and I did so, snapping on the light and going right to his desk. I sat down quickly in the leather chair in front of it and waited for him to go around his desk. He dropped some papers on it and then sat down. "So you met with J. Arthur Steine," he said, as if that conclusion explained it all.

"Yes. And now I want to hear it from you, Tony. Why did you buy the circus and then give it to Luke for only one dollar?"

He shrugged and sat back, lacing the tips of his fingers together to form a cathedral and then pressing his palms together. He brought his fingers to his lips before speaking. It looked as if he were offering up some prayer.

"I was searching for ways to get you to come back to us at Farthy," he began. "I couldn't believe you were going to continue to give all this up for a teaching position in that small town, where the people didn't even appreciate you."

"I wasn't there for the people, I was there for the children," I corrected him.

He nodded. "I know. Anyway, I was at a loss for ways to win your love and your loyalty, and it occurred to me that if I did something for Luke, you might appreciate the things I could do for everyone you . . . you cared for . . . and you would come back."

"But you never even told me what you had done," I said, practically jumping on his words. "Explain what kind of logic there was in that? And you're usually a very logical man, Tony."

"I realize that," he admitted. "But right after I bought the circus and gave it to Luke, I got cold feet. I thought you would think I was trying to buy your love and loyalty, and in the end I would do more damage by telling you this. So I just forgot about it. It was no big expense for me. It didn't matter, and then . . . then the telegram came and the rest you know. So," he said, eager to leave the topic, "how's the little one? I'm sure that—"

"I want to know all of it, Tony. I want to hear the whole story from your lips and I want to know why you did it," I repeated, my eyes fixed coldly on him. I knew that when I wanted to, I could affect his sharp, penetrating gaze. I hadn't only inherited some of his looks; I had inherited the steel in his backbone. We were facing each other down, Tatterton to Tatterton. For what seemed to be an eternity, he sat there, his blue eyes calm and unreadable.

"What do you mean?" he finally said. "I told you why I did it."

"You didn't tell me the truth, Tony." I wondered if in his own mind, he thought that he had. For so long now the inhabitants of Farthinggale Manor had been living with illusions. Perhaps it was no longer possible for him to remember what was true and what wasn't. Sometimes, I thought, you could dream so hard, you no longer know whether it was a fantasy or a real memory.

"What is not true?" he asked.

"The reason you bought the circus and gave it to Luke."

"What I told you is the truth," he insisted. "I did it for you."

"I don't mean that, Tony. In some distorted way I think you did think you were doing what you did in order to win me back here. But I want to hear the whole story. What was Luke's reaction when you gave him the circus?"

"What would his reaction be? He was grateful," Tony said, shrugging. "At first he thought you had everything to do with it. I had to explain that you knew nothing of it, and I had to require that he not ask or tell you about it. He was confused, but he accepted that. And then, as I said, I forgot all about it. So . . ."

"What else did you ask of him?" I demanded. It was as if I had shot him through the heart with my sharp words. His face whitened.

"How do you know I asked anything else of him? Did J. Arthur Steine tell you something else?"

"No, Tony. Mr. Steine is your man right down to the soles of his shoes. But after I heard what you had done and how much you were involved in Luke's affairs, I couldn't stop wondering about it. When Logan and I returned, I had hoped to find out from you why you had done what you had done, but you weren't here. I couldn't sleep last night thinking about it, so I came down here to your office and searched for the answers myself."

"You did what?" Alarm claimed his face. I saw his eyes dart to the file cabinet and back to me.

"Yes, Tony, I looked through your files and I found the agreement you drew up between yourself and Luke, and what I want to know, what I demand to know, is why you did such a terrible thing?" I said. My body was trembling now with my effort to remain strong and determined. I felt my heart thumping and felt tears welling in my eyes.

Stunned for a moment, Tony couldn't speak. He stared at me and then sat back in his chair. He looked down, unable to face me, to meet my piercing gaze, my eyes of blue ice.

"It was a terrible thing to do," he confessed, speaking slowly, like a man lost in his own desires. "I lived with it all this time, promising myself that I would end it soon, and then, when that telegram came, and I realized it was too late, that I could never right the wrong . . ." He looked up. "I didn't have to go away on business. I simply ran away for a couple of days. I wanted to avoid you when you first came back from the funeral and from speaking to J. Arthur Steine. I hoped that somehow you wouldn't be wondering about all this, but of course, that was a silly hope. For you always seek to know everything, every bit of truth even if that truth will bring you to misery.

"Some of the things you once said to me about the way I treated Jillian were true—I did permit myself to live in illusions, and I was trying to do the same with you. I should have realized there was too much Tatterton in you, early Tatterton, for you not to see it."

"Why did you do it?" I pursued. "Why did you insist Luke not have anything to do with me?"

He looked away for a moment, obviously gathering the courage to say what he had to say to me.

"You don't know what it was like when you left after Troy's death. You don't know how much I missed you. I never told you how much you meant to me, how important it was for me to have you here, to be able to see you and talk to you . . . That night I took you to the theater was one of the happiest nights of my life . . . I . . . I had already lost Jillian, in a sense, and it looked like I had lost you, too.

"Suddenly there was some hope you might come back, hope that I could arrange things in such a way that you would spend a great amount of your time here, and then . . . when I heard you had invited Luke to your wedding . . ."

"How did you hear that, Tony? You weren't attending the wedding in Winnerow. You weren't involved in the expense. I paid for that myself," I said, my pride as strong and as straight as a flag in the wind.

"Logan told me," he said.

"Logan?" I sat back. "Logan?" He nodded. "But you barely knew Logan then. I don't understand."

"I called him as soon as I heard you were getting engaged and we spoke. I spoke to him a few times. I begged him not to tell you I was calling him and asking him questions about you. I didn't want you to think I was trying to interfere. He understood. I thought he was an intelligent, sensitive young man."

"And you asked him about my relationship with Luke?"

"Yes."

"So you learned I had invited him to my wedding," I said, eager for him to go on.

"Precisely. I was afraid," he said quickly. "Afraid you would make up with Luke and the two of you would grow so close to each other, that you would want to remain in his world and I would be cut out of your life."

"And then you bought the circus and gave it to him right before my wedding so he couldn't attend. You did that!" I exclaimed, realizing the significance of what he had done. "You actually planned it that way! Kept him from my wedding and then kept him from me!"

"Yes."

"You sit there so calmly and tell me you went ahead and used your great wealth to try to buy my love, not only buy my love for you, but buy my love away from Luke."

"Yes," he said again. "I confess to it all, but you must understand my motives. You must—"

"I must not!"

I stood up. All my rage and fury burst from me like a long-dammed mountain stream, and I yelled, really yelled at him. "All my life I have been passed from one set of arms to another, bought and sold, it seems, no better than a slave before the Civil War. My love has been treated as though it were a commodity, a product, one of your precious Tatterton Toys, something to possess and hoard and manipulate and throw away, and you want me to understand?"

"Heaven—"

"Why must I understand your feelings? When do any of you men understand mine? When do you think of me, and not of yourselves? You and Luke . . . you were two of a kind. It's the same thing to buy or to sell a person's love . . . either one is just as terrible a thing to do.

"Yes, Luke was just as horrible and as guilty for agreeing to your contract, but he wanted his precious circus so much, he was willing to sell any love he might have possessed for me. He wasn't my real father and he knew it.

"But you," I said pointing my finger at him. "To make such an offer, to appeal to his greed, to his passions . . . you're like . . . you're like the Devil."

"No, Heaven. Please." He started to reach out toward me, looking like a desperate man.

"Yes," I said, backing away. "You are like the Devil. You played upon his lusts, his passion for that circus, and like the Devil, you made him sell a part of his soul."

"But only because of my love for you!" he protested.

"I don't want that kind of love. That's not love, true and pure; that's parasitical love, love that feeds off others. You've lived a life of lies, Tony. And you're still living it and it's made you a very selfish man."

"That's not so," he insisted. "Everything I have now, everything I've done, is all for you."

"Is it? What was the one thing you knew that I wanted in my life? What was the one thing that made my life complete, that gave me hope and happiness? The one thing that you kept from me?"

He stared at me in confusion.

"I don't understand. What did I deny you? What did you ever ask for that I turned down?"

"You let me live under one cloud after another, just so you could play the sun and give me rays of hope and happiness whenever it pleased you. You were afraid that if I wasn't sad, that if I didn't live under a dark and gloomy sky, you could never be something bright and alive to me.

"So you let me think that Luke didn't care for me, when in fact you had trapped him within his own prison of greed."

"But . . ." He started forward, hoping to embrace me. I continued to back away from his desk.

"And you let me believe that Troy was dead," I said. The words fell like thunder, echoing in the room. He whitened so, he looked like he had been turned into a statue of salt. I didn't want to give away the secret that Troy and I had held between us. It had been all that was left that was precious and special. But I suddenly realized that if Tony were honest and if he really wanted me to return to Farthy, he would have told me about Troy not being dead and brought me back to help him regain a normal life.

But he didn't want me to return to Troy; he wanted me to return to him and to him only.

"You know?" he whispered.

"Yes. I found him out just before he left."

"It was his wish that you not know, not mine," Tony pleaded quickly. That moment Anthony Townsend Tatterton looked as cheap and as small as a petty thief to me, a petty thief who had tried to lie his way out of his guilt, and when one lie didn't work, he tried another and finally even betrayed those closest to him, all to save himself.

"But you knew that he said those things because he was despondent, because he believed we could never be anything to each other. You could have done more. If you would have told me and I could have seen him . . . by the time I did discover him, it was too late.

"And so he's gone," I said softly, "and a love that was truly unselfish has been lost."

I looked up at him, the tears now streaming down my face.

"For all I know, you drove Jillian into her madness," I said. "And you helped drive Tony into oblivion. Now," I concluded, standing straight, "you've driven me away."

"*Heaven!*" he screamed as I turned and rushed out of his office. I didn't look back. I ran up the stairs to my suite and began to pack. In the morning I would take Drake and leave Farthy. This time I would leave forever.

I looked in on Drake and found that he had brought his blanket up and nearly over his head as if to shut out the world around him. It was the way I felt, too, but I knew that hide as you would, you couldn't escape from the truth. Truth had its way of finding the cracks and the openings in whatever walls of make-believe you set up around yourself, even if you were rich. I felt as though everything around me here was made up of crepe paper and cellophane. It was pretty and bright and colorful, but one strong wind could blow it all away and leave you standing naked, shivering under bruised and angry clouds.

I brought his blanket down around his neck, brushed away some strands of hair from his eyes, and kissed him softly on the cheek. Tomorrow I would take him to Winnerow. As suddenly as he had been brought into this richly elegant and luxurious world, he would be taken from it. I knew it would confuse him, but I also now knew that this was no place for him to grow up. My bloodline might have started here at Farthy, but my heartline was tied to Winnerow, tied to that simpler world where I could look out of the windows of the Hasbrouck House and see the Willies.

It was better that Drake grow up in that sunlight, surrounded by those sounds, than here in the long, empty halls of Farthinggale, surrounded by the moaning ghosts who haunted the Tattertons.

I did some packing for both of us until I grew too tired and then prepared myself for bed. Even though I was both physically and emotionally exhausted, I lay there staring into the darkness, my eyes wide open. I wondered about Logan and about the life we would make for ourselves in Winnerow now. I hoped I could make him understand why I wanted no more to do with Farthinggale Manor and little to do with Tony. Of course, I wouldn't tell him about Troy, but he would know what Tony had done to keep Luke away from me, and I hoped he would be just as upset about it as I was. Mostly, I hoped he would hold me near to him, and in time we could recapture that wonderfully exciting feeling we once shared for each other when we were high school students.

I couldn't help thinking about Troy as well. I wondered where he was and how much he would know of my life, how much he would know of what had happened and would happen. Would he be watching nearby as he had watched my wedding reception? Or had he truly cut himself off from everything concerning me and Farthy?

Every passing day now he became more and more of an illusion, the personification of truly ideal love, the unattainable perfect love, the love dreams are made of, the love you destroy simply by touching it, just as you destroy a beautiful, perfect soap bubble the moment the tips of your fingers graze its thin, fragile surface. Like the soap bubble, such love was something to watch or to hope for, but something never to hold.

I knew that now. I knew that the love I had for Logan was a love whose roots were in reality and I must cultivate that love, nourish it, and help it grow into a sturdy oak, unshakable by any wind and storm life would bring it. With Logan I would build a life, a family, a future. I had lost so much, but I still had much for which I could be grateful, much I could cherish.

Thinking about all this brought tears to my eyes, but I did not cry myself to sleep. I simply closed my eyes and felt myself sink back into the pillow, falling, drifting, slipping away, until the sound of my suite door opening roughly jerked me back into consciousness. I sat up quickly and saw a man's dark silhouette in the doorway. For a moment I thought it was Troy. My heart jumped and then plunged when I heard the voice.

"Leigh," he said, "are you awake?"

It was Tony. Even from this distance I could smell the alcohol on his breath.

"What is it you want, Tony?" I asked, making my voice as cold and as hard as I could. He responded with a slight little laugh at first, and then he found the light switch on the wall and snapped it on. The room exploded with brightness. I covered my eyes and when I took my hands from them, I saw him approaching, wearing only a shirt and slacks, his shirt unbuttoned to his navel. In his arms he carried one of Jillian's sheer nightgowns.

"I brought this for you," he said. His eyes were glassy; his hair was disheveled, looking like he had been running his fingers through it. "I love how it looks on you. Won't you wear it for me again? Please."

"I never wore that for you, Tony. You're drunk. Please, leave my room."

"But you did wear it for me. And look," he said, bringing his hand out from under the nightgown, "I've brought you some of Jillian's perfume. I know how much you like it. You're always trying to get her to give you some. Let me dab some on you," he said, sitting on my bed. I pulled myself farther back against the headboard, but he reached over, pressing the bottle to his fingers and then stroking the side of my neck with them. The heavy scent of jasmine filled my nostrils. I started to pull away when he brought his fingers down to the valley between my breasts.

"No, Tony, stop. I don't want to wear any of Jillian's perfume now. I said stop. You're drunk. Get out of here," I demanded. He looked at me and smiled as if he couldn't hear my words. Then, remembering the nightgown in his arms, he stood up and spread it out on the bed beside me, stroking it with affection as he did so.

"Go on, put it on," he said, "and then I'll lie down beside you as I did when you wore it before."

"Leave my room at once, Tony! I'm going to call the servants if you don't."

"Leigh," he whispered.

"I'm not Leigh!" I shouted. "I'm Heaven! Tony, get out of here! You're frightening me!"

Ignoring me again, he lifted the blanket and slipped under it to get beside me. I tried to escape, but he reached out and seized me around the waist, pulling me toward him.

"Leigh, don't leave me. Please. Don't listen to anything Jillian says. She's mad, jealous of you, jealous of every other woman. She's even jealous of our maids because one has nice hands or one has a nice chin." He brought his lips to my shoulder, pushing my nightgown down my arm with his cheek so he could press his mouth to my skin.

"Tony, stop!" I screamed.

I brought my hand to his temple and pushed him as hard as I could to keep him away from me. When his hand touched my breast, I screamed and clawed his face with my nails.

"Get out! Get out! Don't you know who I am? Don't you remember that I'm your own daughter and I'm pregnant!"

I slapped him across the face.

He stared at me a moment, blinking rapidly. I could see reality pushing the memories away, bringing him out of the past and back into the present. The realization of where he was and what he was doing came to him with a jolt. He swallowed hard and looked around.

"My God," he said. "I thought . . ."

"You thought? You're drunk and disgusting! I want you to get out of here. Get out!" I screamed, getting out of the bed. He stared up at me.

"Oh, Heaven, forgive me. I just . . ." He looked at the nightgown he had brought and then up at me, his hand on his reddened cheek. "I just got confused. I . . ."

"Confused?" The troubled thoughts that always crowded into the darkest corners of my brain came rushing out. I remembered other times when he touched me and kissed me, and suddenly every one of them seemed ugly, lustful, incestuous. Every fear, every sick and sorrowful memory announced itself. I could barely think; my mind was an echo chamber of screams and shouts. I pressed my hands against my ears. "You're no better than any of my backwoods relatives, my hillbilly siblings, as you used to call them!" I shouted so loud my voice broke. "Your money hasn't made a single bit of difference. You're no better than the ignorant Winnerow hillbillies who rape their daughters!"

"Heaven, no . . ."

"Get out! Get out!" I shouted again.

He lifted himself from the bed, scooping up Jillian's sheer nightgown as he did so, and began to back away toward the door, shaking his head.

"Please, please forgive me. I was drunk . . . I didn't know what I was doing. Please," he said, holding his hand out toward me.

I shook my head, the tears rushing down my cheeks, my body shaking.

"Get out," I hissed, my voice a raspy whisper.

"I . . . I'm sorry," he repeated and rushed out the door.

The moment he was gone, I collapsed on my bed and wailed. I cried hysterically, unable to stop the rage of anger and sorrow from possessing me. Every sad thing that had happened restated itself and demanded to be mourned with equal intensity. I was crying for the mother I had never seen or known; crying for Tom; crying for Troy; crying because of Logan's infidelity with Fanny; crying for Luke and for Stacie; and I was crying for Heaven, poor lost little Heaven Leigh Casteel.

The feel of a cool, soft little hand on my shoulder finally stopped my outburst of tears. I took a deep breath and turned my head. Little Drake was standing there looking down at me, his face filled with confusion, but his eyes also showing compassion.

"Don't cry," he said. "I won't go away."

"Oh, Drake. Drake!" I cried and pulled him to me, holding his small body as closely and as tightly as I could. "I won't let you go away. We need each other. Like two orphans." I kissed his forehead. "I'll always be here for you. Always."

He looked up at me, his face still a mirror of my own sorrow.

"I'll stop crying," I said. "Now, I'll stop crying."

I lifted him onto my bed and we fell asleep curled up beside each other like two kittens who had lost their mother.

I awoke with Drake in my arms, his little head nestled softly against my bosom. Quietly, so as not to wake him, I slipped out of bed and got washed and dressed. It was still early and the house was quiet. The servants hadn't yet opened the curtains. Lights left on throughout the night were still on. I went down the marble stairway, moving quickly but softly, and found Curtis getting ready to start his day.

"Up early, Mrs. Stonewall," he said.

"I have a lot to do today, Curtis, and quickly. First call the airlines and make reservations for myself and Drake. We'll be going back to Winnerow this morning. Inform Miles. Send the maids up to Drake's room. I have some clothing I've packed and some I want them to pack. There are some suitcases in my room already packed. Have Miles take them down to the car. Please ask Rye to prepare a small, quick breakfast for Drake and myself. In a day or two I shall send for some other things to be packed and delivered to my home in Winnerow."

"You're leaving Farthinggale?" Curtis asked. I didn't respond. He took one look at the sternness in my face and started to carry out my commands immediately. When I went back upstairs, I found Drake was beginning to wake up. I got him out of bed, washed and dressed him quickly. He was impressed with my intensity and hardly said a word. The maids arrived and I gave them their orders. Drake watched as they began packing his things, but he asked nothing, even when Miles began taking some of it to the limo.

"We're going for a trip to Winnerow and my own home." I told him as I took his hand to lead him down to breakfast.

"Isn't this your home?" he asked me, his small voice filled with surprise and disappointment.

"No, it's Mr. Tatterton's," I said. I couldn't bring myself to say "my father's." "But don't worry. You'll have your own room again, and you know what? Logan is building a toy factory there. You'll see it."

That filled him with excitement and curiosity.

I saw that Curtis had reported my mood to the other servants. Everyone worked quickly, efficiently, quietly, communicated to one another with gestures and looks rather than words. I was expecting Tony to come downstairs any moment, dressed for work, and I was expecting him to try to talk me out of going. However, Drake and I finished our breakfast before he arrived. Even Curtis was surprised.

"Mr. Tatterton is late this morning," he said as if he had to make excuses for him. I didn't say anything. I took Drake back upstairs to my suite and placed a phone call to Logan.

"We're coming home," I told him as soon as he answered.

"Coming home?"

"Drake and I. I'll explain it all when I get there," I said.

I gave him the details concerning our flight and he said he would be at the airport. After I hung up the phone, I looked around the suite, checking for anything else I wanted to bring with me. Curtis came to the doorway to tell me that Miles had everything packed in the limo.

"That's fine, Curtis. Come along, Drake." I took his hand and we started out.

"Mrs. Stonewall," Curtis said when we were out in the corridor, "if I could trouble you for just one moment."

"What is it, Curtis?"

"Well, when Mr. Tatterton didn't come down, I thought I had better come up to check on him. I knocked on his door to see if he wanted anything brought up, but he didn't respond. And then . . ."

"Yes?" I saw that Curtis looked about as uncomfortable as I had ever seen him look. His face was flushed and he kept tugging on the collar of his shirt as though it were a size too small.

"I noticed the door to Mrs. Tatterton's suite was opened and I looked in to see if anything was wrong. Oh, dear," he said, shaking his head.

I was getting impatient with him. "What is it, Curtis? You know yourself I have to be on my way quickly."

"I know, but . . . but I wish you would have a look for yourself. I hope Mr. Tatterton's all right."

I stared at him a moment. I thought Tony was suffering a hangover this morning, a well-deserved one.

"Drake, go down with Curtis. I'll be right along," I said.

"Thank you, Mrs. Stonewall," Curtis said. He took Drake's hand and they went downstairs. I continued down the corridor to what had been Jillian's suite and peered in, just as Curtis had done.

There lay Tony sprawled on Jillian's bed, still unconscious from his drunken stupor. Only that wasn't what had frightened Curtis. It even frightened me. Tony had put on that nightgown he had brought to me and the room reeked of jasmine. Who knew what delusions he had gone through, I thought, or how much more he drank to get this way. But I felt no pity for him; I felt only disgust.

I left him snoring there and closed the door behind me.

"He'll be all right," I told Curtis. "Just leave him alone."

"Very good, Mrs. Stonewall," he said. "Thank you."

I stopped just outside the front door and looked out over the grounds of Farthinggale Manor. The autumn winds were growing stronger and cooler. They shook the trees and tore the colorful leaves from their branches. The downpour of red, yellow, and brown leaves scattered in a frenzy across the long driveway and over the green lawns. It was as if Nature were bringing down a curtain of colors. Branches already stripped of their finery hung naked against clouds as silver as coins. It brought a chill to me and I embraced myself. Then I hurried on to the limo.

Drake sat waiting, his toy fire engine in his lap. Even after we gave him new toys, that was the one he still clung to. He looked so small and lost in the big car, like a baby bird left in its nest. I put my arm around him and pulled him to me as Miles started away.

And I never looked back.

❧ FOURTEEN ❧
There's No Place Like Home

HOME. HOME. THE WORD REPEATED IN MY HEAD AS I BOARDED the plane for Atlanta, little Drake's hand pressed in mine, his eyes wide and staring at the bustle of the airport. "Tell me again where we're going, Heaven," he asked as we arranged ourselves in the seats of the big jet.

"We're going home, Drake. Home to Winnerow. Where I grew up. Where your daddy grew up. And now you'll grow up there, too," I said, putting a cheerful tone in my voice and excitement in my eyes. "And you'll be happy there, so happy!"

"But Heaven, I thought I was going to live in that castle! I liked it there." His voice was disappointed.

"I promise you'll like it even better in Winnerow, Drake. Why, we can go visit the house your daddy lived in. And there's lots of hills and forests to play in called the Willies, and there's fiddlers and a wonderful school and playgrounds and lots of children to play with. Oh, Drake, it's a wonderful place for a boy to grow up. I promise."

Soon we were again in the clouds and Drake was immediately asleep, giving my agitated mind time to play and replay what had happened the night before, and with it the circle of betrayals that was like a noose, growing tighter and tighter around my life until it seemed it would choke me. But I was determined to free myself from Tony's hold once and for all. For now it was completely, irrevocably clear to me. It was at Tony's door that all my troubles could be laid, from the very beginning of my life.

Logan's bright cheerful face greeted us at the airport gate. He picked up the sleepy Drake and kissed his cheeks, then looked at me with a million questions in his eyes. "When we get home, Logan, I'll tell you everything. Not now. Okay?"

He nodded his assent, and the long trip to Winnerow was made in silence. I could almost hear the gears and wheels turning in Logan's mind, like the complicated mechanics of an intricate Tatterton toy.

Although Drake was a little tired from our fast and furious journey, he sat up alertly and took in the scenery as we entered Winnerow. On the telephone lines starlings sat like miniature dark soldiers, puffy, sleeping birds, eyes closed, anticipating the coming cold and waiting for the warming sun. Some of them opened their eyes and peered down at us as we drove down Main Street.

"I remember this street," Drake cried, pressing his face to the window, "Pa's circus was here!"

"You're a bright little boy, Drake," I said, hugging him to me. "You couldn't have been more than four years old."

"I was just a baby then. But Tom said—" Drake suddenly climbed out of my arms and stared wildly through the window. "Is Tom going to be here? Is he? Is he?"

"My poor darling boy," I said, tears filling my eyes, "Tom's with your ma and pa in Heaven, Drake."

Then I quickly pointed out some of the sights of Winnerow. I wanted Drake to start looking into the future, which I hoped beyond hope would only be bright and cheerful for him, rather than his dark and tragic past. Winnerow had only one main street, and all the others branched off that. In the middle of the town was the school, backed up by the blue, smoky mountains.

"That's going to be your school," I said, pointing to the playground. "I used to be a teacher there."

"Are you going to be my teacher? I've never gone to school," Drake whispered, his eyes wide with excitement and fear.

"No, honey, but you'll have a wonderful teacher. I think you're going to like it very much," I said. "And see that big mountain?"

Drake nodded.

"Your daddy came from there, Drake," I said, pointing to our mountain. "You can see it clearly from the front of our new house," I told him. He stared at it, his eyes intense as though he had been waiting to see that mountain all his short life.

"Did Daddy go to my school?"

"Daddy went there, and Logan and I did, too, honey."

"We might be able to get him in this year, even though he's not quite of age," Logan said. It was the first thing he had said for a long while. "Sometimes they make allowances when you know somebody or when a kid is bright," he added. He looked at me, but I didn't respond. A deep furrow ran across his forehead, a sign lately that

Logan was in deep thought. I knew he desperately wanted to find out why I had fled Farthinggale. I hadn't been able to tell him anything about what had happened between Tony and me, because Drake was alert and listening to every word I said. I indicated that I didn't want to speak in front of my little stepbrother.

"Little rabbits have big ears, too," I said. It was something Granny used to say.

Logan, obviously frustrated and impatient to hear all my news, was valiantly trying to make both Drake and me feel comfortable by giving us all the news of Winnerow and the Hasbrouck House. I knew he could tell how upset I was. How sweet and touching he was, trying so hard to raise my spirits.

"I'm afraid I haven't even hired all our servants yet," he warned.

"I think I can get along for a few days without an army of servants, Logan," I said.

"I know that. But it's a big house. It needs looking after, especially now that we already have a child living there."

"We'll do just fine," I said. "Tomorrow we'll start looking for a maid."

"And a cook. I think we'll need a cook," he said. "Not that you can't cook. It's just that—"

"You think we should have one. I know," I said, lowering my voice with exaggeration. "All factory owners have their own cooks." Even he had to laugh at himself.

"I hired a gardener, the gardener Anthony Hasbrouck had," he said quickly. "Just kept him on. There was a butler, but he's long gone. If you want, I'll have the maid that Anthony Hasbrouck had stop by and you can interview her."

"Good. I'm sure if Anthony Hasbrouck was satisfied, I'll be," I said. He nodded and then smiled.

"I have a surprise for you. I wanted to keep it a secret a few more days, but since things have taken a strange turn," he said, "for reasons I'll soon discover, I'll tell you now."

"What?" I sat forward. We were almost to the Hasbrouck House. Even though we now owned it, it would always remain the "Hasbrouck House" in my mind.

"The factory will be ready for the opening ceremonies in a month."

"Really? That's wonderful, Logan. I can't wait to see the production of toys from the Willies."

"I'm planning a gala affair. I had discussed it with Tony—" My heart leapt into my throat at the mere mention of his name. "Some of the arrangements are already under way. Anyone who's anyone within a hundred miles of this place will be there."

"I see," I said. Although I wanted to be happy for Logan, there was only one thing I really wanted to know. "Is Tony coming down for the party?" I asked, trying to keep the quaver from my voice.

"I know he was planning to. Do you think that will change now, Heaven?" I couldn't help but hear the concern in his voice.

"We'll discuss that at home, Logan," I said. Then I cuddled Drake in my arms, and for his benefit I added, "I'm just too tired to talk about it now."

"Of course, darling," Logan said, stealing a glance at me when we stopped for a streetlight. "But I hope you aren't too tired to hear all my plans for the party. It'll be a black tie affair, even though we're holding it outside. I've hired a twelve-piece orchestra to play, and the best caterer in Atlanta. Oh, it will be as elegant as anything ever given at Farthy, Heaven, I'm going to do you proud!"

Even the name Farthy made me shudder. "Logan, if you want to do me proud, let's have a real Willies party. A hoedown to beat all hoedowns. A party where the artisans who'll be making the toys will feel comfortable. This is not Farthy, and we are not Tattertons. I don't even want that name to be on our factory. I want this to be pure Willies, the Willies Toy Factory."

"But Heaven . . ." Logan looked like he'd just been hit in the stomach. "We can't make these unilateral decisions. Whatever problems you had with Tony, we're still partners with him and it's his money that's paying for all this."

My voice was hard as stone, cold as ice, "Believe me, Logan, Tony will go along with whatever I want."

Logan drove on silently. I sat and hardened my resolve. The mood was so thick in the car, I felt suffocated, longing to be home, longing to have all this over with once and for all.

Soon the Hasbrouck House loomed at the end of the block. "There she is," Logan said, turning to Drake, putting false cheer in his voice. "Your new home, Drake." We pulled in and up the long driveway that led to the great colonial house. The branches of tall and full weeping willow trees hung over the driveway, creating a tunnel of green.

"It's not as big as Farthy," Drake said when we came to a stop.

Logan frowned. "No, Drake. Hardly anything is, but this is still big. You'll see."

When we drove up, Mr. Appleberry, the gardener Logan had kept on, came out front to greet us and help with the luggage. He was a small but stocky man whose gray hair grew in small patches over a partially bald head that was covered with the same freckles he had scattered over his forehead and temples. He had a warm face with smiling eyes. Santa Claus eyes, I thought. If he had a beard and a full head of hair, he could play Santa. As long as the red suit was stuffed, of course.

Drake took to him and he took to Drake almost instantly.

"I'll help with all that, Mrs. Stonewall," he said. "That is, me and the young gentleman here. My name's Appleberry," he said, extending his long-fingered hand, the hand of a man who worked with plants and trees and flowers. "And you are?"

Drake nearly laughed, something he hadn't done much of since I had taken him from Atlanta.

"I'm Drake," he said. Appleberry took hold of his hand and shook it vigorously.

"Pleased to meet you, Mr. Drake. You want to take this one?" He handed Drake a small cloth bag and Drake seized it, holding it up against his body with both hands and looking up at me with pride in his eyes.

"Fine. Strong young man," Appleberry said, winking at me.

"Thank you, Mr. Appleberry," I said and we all headed into the house, Logan and Appleberry carting most of our luggage in. I took Drake and one of his suitcases directly to his bedroom.

"Tomorrow you'll start to explore this house, Drake," I said. "It's already getting late and you're tired from our trip. Okay?"

"Very wise move, Mr. Drake," Appleberry said, bringing in the rest of Drake's things. "A good rest makes for a good day. I'll bid you good night, but I'll be around after you've had your breakfast. We've got some leaves to rake, if you are up to it."

Drake looked at me and then at Appleberry. I could see by the look on his face that he was wondering if I would go along with his actually doing real labor. I smiled. Then he nodded quickly.

"Fine, then," Appleberry said and left. I led Drake into the bathroom and washed and dressed him for bed. I heard Logan out in the hall bringing up my luggage and some of his things I had packed and taken from Farthy.

Drake's bed was a wide double with a light oak headboard. The mattress felt hard and new and the quilts were minty fresh and crisp. From what I could see from my quick pass through the house, it had been left in immaculate condition.

After I knelt down and kissed Drake good night, I felt sorry for him, ripped out of one family and home, taken to another, and then spirited away from that one. Once again he was put to bed in strange surroundings, the toy fire engine beside him, his only tie with his immediate past.

"This is the end of your confused journey, dear, dear Drake," I whispered. "I promise you, this will be your home. It's only right that you be close to the land of your father's roots, even if you will be living a far, far better life than he or any of his relations ever did."

It occurred to me that I could take him into the Willies one day and show him his grandmother's and grandfather's graves. He would see the cabin, even if it was now a modern hunting lodge, and play on the grounds Tom and Keith had played on. Luke probably would never have brought him back here, I thought. For all I knew, he would have made up stories about his past to hide it from his son.

I left his room and went directly to the master bedroom to tell Logan all. My heart was pounding, for there was so much I had kept from him that I would now have to explain. Shame upon shame that even he hadn't known. How I hated Tony Tatterton for putting me through this.

Logan was nervously pacing the room, and he stopped when I entered. "Well," he said, "let's hear it. All of it."

I took a deep breath and began by describing what Tony had done to keep Luke away from me, the agreement I discovered in his file cabinet and what he had said when I had confronted him with the information. Logan sat on the chair by the vanity table listening as I paced about and talked. His face was filled with concern, but he said nothing until I paused and sat on the bed.

"Well," he said, "it was wrong, a terrible thing to do. I can understand your anger, but I believe what Tony told you was the truth. I believe he was lonely and afraid of losing you. I can understand his fears."

I couldn't believe that Logan's first reaction was to feel sympathy and pity for Tony. Here I was expecting him to rise quickly from his chair and embrace me, to hold me close to him, and to comfort me for the pain I must have suffered when I learned Tony had bought off the man whose fatherly love I had so longed for. I wanted him to kiss me and stroke my hair and express his anger at Tony for what he had done to me. I craved for Logan to love me the way he had loved me when I was a nobody, a nothing living in a shack in the Willies. I looked for him to do something that would bring back the flood of memories of how sweet our youth had been because we had had each other.

Instead, he sat there trying to be calm and cool and understanding of another man's cruel and selfish behavior. Oh, I was so angry. My face flushed so red that even Logan looked frightened.

Of course, I understood that he had formed a relationship with Tony that bordered on idolizing him. Tony had made him feel important and rich and powerful. He thought the world of Tony and his business sense, and it was hard for him to suddenly see Tony as a weak, selfish little man. I knew, too, I hadn't told Logan the whole truth, the whole frightening and shameful truth.

"I haven't told you all of it," I said. "And when I do, we'll see if you are as understanding."

"There's more?"

"Yes, there's more . . ." I took a deep breath. "More reason for me to have left Farthy. Last night, after Tony and I had our argument and I told him I would leave, he came to our suite. He was drunk and half undressed."

"What did he want?" He nearly cringed in anticipation.

"What he wanted," I said slowly, deliberately, "was to make love to me. I had to fight him off and slap him across the face to bring him to his senses."

For a long moment Logan said nothing. It was as if he hadn't heard what I had just said. Then he sat back like a tired, defeated man, his chin nearly touching his chest, and he shook his head slowly.

"Oh, my God, oh, my God," he whispered. "I . . . I should have . . . have suspected as much."

"Suspected? What do you mean? You knew something but said nothing to me?"

"It wasn't something I knew; it was something I thought I sensed. What was I going to say? Beware of your grandfather—"

"Logan," I said, tears rolling down my cheeks, "Tony is my . . . my father."

"He's *what?!*"

"My father, Logan. I found out a few years ago, and I never told you because I was so ashamed." The words came pouring out of me. There was so much to tell him, I was heedless to whether or not he would understand. "He raped my mother. That's why she ran away. Oh, don't you see? He's evil, Logan, Tony is evil. He tried to do the same thing to me." Then the sobs came and muffled my voice.

"Oh, Heaven, poor Heaven," Logan said, rising and coming to me to embrace me. "How you have suffered." He held me closely to him and kissed my forehead over and over again. "Oh, Heaven, I am so sorry. Now, I'm sorry." He shook his head and looked down again.

"Is that all you can say about it? You're sorry?"

He looked up sharply. "No. It sickens me. I want to get right on a plane and go back to Farthy. I want to have it out with Tony and make him understand what he is and what he's done. Even if it means wringing his neck," he added, his eyes flashing. This was more of the reaction I had expected and wanted, even if I didn't want him to carry out his threats. At least I felt certain that Logan cared more for me than he did for his new business ventures and newly found wealth and power.

"No," I said. "I don't want you to do that. It's not necessary now. I left him a broken, sick man, surrounded by his guilt and his sad memories. We'll cut him off from our lives. He will be exactly what he is . . . a business partner and nothing more. Never again will I think of him as my father, nor should you think of him as your father-in-law. I'm turning away from that part of my life, closing the curtain on that drama."

Logan kept holding me tight, stroking my hair, and gazing tenderly in my eyes. "Logan, we can build our lives here, far away from Farthy and the past. Forget about the factory, forget everything that has anything to do with Tony Tatterton. We can build Stonewall pharmacies into a wonderful empire, all by ourselves. We'll have our baby soon and Drake will be just like your son."

"Heaven," Logan said, letting go of me and sitting up, "I despise Tony more than you can imagine for what he tried to do but—but it's crucial that my personal feelings be laid aside for a time."

"Logan, I don't understand. We can't have that man in our lives anymore!"

"We may not want Tony in our lives, but what about the people of Winnerow, what about the people in the Willies? Without the factory, Heaven, all their hopes will die. And," he said, rising to his feet and nervously pacing back and forth, "and without Tony the factory will die."

"What are you saying, Logan?"

"I'm saying, Heaven, without Tony's capital all our dreams are over. Everybody's dreams are over."

"Logan, I thought you would protect me—"

"I'll handle everything, Heaven. Tony isn't the only one who can play at manipulation." He sat down again, and put his hands gently on my shoulders.

"I know," he said, "that I haven't been what you had hoped I would be. I know I have let you down in many ways, not the least being not paying enough attention to you and our marriage. But that's all going to change now. I swear it. I'll work hard, but the work will always be second to our love and marriage and our family." He patted me gently on the stomach. "Our growing family," he added, smiling. "We'll be together all the time. No more separations, Heaven. I'll make you happy forever, darling. I promise."

"And you must always love and be kind to Drake," I added, fearful that Logan hadn't mentioned him. "He must not be made to suffer for the sins of his father and the sins of other adults."

"He'll be like my own son. I promise." He held up his hand as if to take an oath.

"Oh, Logan." I held him tightly, pressing my cheek against his shoulder. He kissed me again and again and stroked my hair softly. My tears felt like warm raindrops. He scooped me up and brought me to our bed, where he kissed me and comforted me until we both grew tired enough to sleep. I fell asleep nestled in his arms, feeling as secure and as protected as a bear cub, and I was no longer afraid of the morning and the new life to come.

The days that followed were truly days of beginning a new life. I was busy almost every moment, relieved that time passed so quickly, that every hour was filled with something important to do and not something trivial merely to fill the time. Two days after we arrived, I brought Drake to the school. Technically, he was a week and a half shy of the cutoff date for starting the first grade, but Mr. Meeks was more than eager to make an exception. How different he was from the principal I had known as a student and as a first-year teacher. It was almost as if he had never met me before.

Within ten minutes Drake was enrolled in the first grade.

"No problem. No problem at all, Mrs. Stonewall," Mr. Meeks repeated when I told him why I was here. "Whenever a child is precocious, we make exception; and, from looking at Drake, I can tell immediately that he is a precocious young man. I'll see to it."

I couldn't help feeling amused at the change in Mr. Meeks. It was true that exceptions were made, but they were made on the basis of testing, and not on the principal's opinion based only upon his visual observation. Mr. Meeks called in his secretary and had her begin the procedures. Afterward, he escorted me around the school so I could say hello to some of my old colleagues. He then walked me out to the parking lot and opened my car door.

"And tell Mr. Stonewall," he said, "that Mrs. Meeks and myself will be more than happy to attend the opening festivities at the factory."

"Thank you," I said, marveling to myself all the way home. Logan had become quite a manipulator.

I returned to the Hasbrouck House to greet Mrs. Avery, the fifty-year-old woman who had been Anthony Hasbrouck's maid for over twenty years. I thought she had a kind, soft face and saw no reason not to keep her on. Logan had an employment agency send over a candidate to be our butler, Gerald Wilson. He was a tall, graying man in his late fifties, a little stiff and formal, reminding me of Curtis, but I saw no reason not to hire him. The next day our cook arrived. I couldn't help but think that Logan was modeling all his employees after Tony's employees, for the cook was a black man, who I was sure was much older than he claimed to be. His name was Roland Star and he had teeth as white as piano keys and a laugh that was musical.

After our house was staffed, I went to an interior decorator and began planning some changes for the dining room, the sitting room, the guest room, and our bedroom. The nursery was nearly completed and there was nothing I wanted to change in the kitchen. All the things I had bought in Boston had arrived, and within two weeks my new home, my first real home, was complete.

As I walked from room to room that day, surveying all I had created, all I felt I had earned by my suffering, I realized there was still one remnant of the past lingering to be changed. After I dropped Drake off at school that day, I proceeded directly to the local beauty parlor, run by none other than Maisie Setterton. She looked shocked to see me there, but soon enough she had rearranged her attitude to one of fawning attention.

"Why, Heaven," she drawled. "I'm so flattered you'd come to my beauty parlor, what with all your newfound wealth. You'd really let a country girl like me do your hair?"

"I want to go back to my natural color, Maisie," I said, cutting her off. "And this is the only beauty parlor in town." That silenced her, and she didn't speak again while she set about mixing and brushing and coloring my hair. I left two hours later—looking very much like the old Heaven Leigh Casteel, now Heaven Leigh Stonewall. Yes, when the people of Winnerow saw me now, they would have to remember that poor scum-of-the-hills girl they had looked down upon, and realize that it was she who was revitalizing their town. I no longer wanted to look like a Tatterton. Like Luke's Angel. Like Tony's Leigh. The wrong man had seen her in me. For it wasn't Pa's love I had won by dying my hair to look like her, but Tony's lust. Now that, too, I would put behind me. I would be just who I was, and I would never be ashamed of that again. Pride straightened my spine as I ran my errands in Winnerow and noticed the eyes that followed my passage.

I went to the factory site that day to see the finishing touches that were being made. Logan was shocked when he beheld me.

"Heaven," he breathed. "You dyed your hair back."

"Yes, Logan." I smiled. "Now all traces of Tatterton are gone and I am pure one hundred percent Stonewall forever more."

"And more beautiful than ever." He kissed me passionately on the lips. "This is the woman I've always loved. Thank you, Heaven."

He took me on a tour of the factory, explaining and showing me the smallest details. He made me feel like a queen visiting one of her colonies. As we walked down the hallways and in and out of rooms, the various laborers stopped what they were doing to greet me. Logan led me about, even showing me the men's room. His enthusiasm was contagious, for I found myself growing very excited about all of it. The only part that brought some sadness to my heart was when he introduced me to the ten artisans he had hired to begin making the Willies toys. Two of them were at least as old as Grandpa was when he died.

Toward the end of the month, documents and information concerning Luke's estate and Drake's trust fund began arriving from J. Arthur Steine. Apparently he had conferred with Tony, and Tony had told him to go ahead and do whatever I wanted done. The circus and the house were sold rather quickly, which J. Arthur Steine didn't hesitate to brag about.

The first night Roland Star was at the Hasbrouck House to cook a meal, Logan invited his parents. I was amused by the changes in Loretta Stonewall, especially in the way she now treated me. She had prepared for this evening as though she were attending a dinner at the governor's mansion. She had her gray hair permed, her nails done, and had bought an expensive dress. She wore her fur coat and her most expensive diamond necklace and earrings. Logan's father looked troubled and embarrassed by his wife's extravagance. I could almost hear their argument about it—after all, they were only going to their son's home for dinner. Yes, but what a home and what a dinner!

I was quite underdressed in comparison, but Logan's mother didn't seem to notice or care. She was too intimidated even to mention the change in my hair color, but she was extravagant with her compliments of everything I had changed in the house. Suddenly, almost overnight, she had become my mother-in-law in more than mere name.

"You must never be afraid to call me, ever for the slightest thing, as your pregnancy develops, Heaven. Why, when I was four months along, I was big as a house. But you look slender and beautiful as ever, Heaven. How do you do it? Are you tired? You know, I'd be more than happy to do all that I can to help with little Drake. What a darling little boy." She reached out to pat him on the head, but Drake would have none of that. He shifted his body out of reach. "Anyway, I insist you all come to my house for dinner the night after the factory affair. I know you will all be so tired."

"Thank you, Loretta," I said.

"Oh, please, please, Heaven, honey," she said, reaching across the table to place her hand softly over mine, "call me Mother."

I stared at her for a moment. How many women had I called Mother in my life? One I never knew, one who had been an overworked drudge, one who had resented me, and now one who was so infatuated with her new standing in the community she wanted me the way someone would want an expensive and impressive jewel. She wanted to wear me about her to impress her friends. But I was too tired to resent her for it. I could even understand her excitement, and if money and power had finally made me welcome in her home and in her life, why hate her for it? My husband was happy; my children would be loved, and I would at last have a real family.

The dinner went well, but after they left, I was once again besieged by memories of my own family. My mind played and replayed the scene with Tony. I still didn't know whether or not Tony would show up at the factory celebration, and I felt like a bird trapped in a cage with a cat lurking outside the window.

I decided to calm my nerves by throwing myself into the preparations for the affair, to be so busy that I didn't have time to dwell on unpleasant memories. I helped put together a real Willies shindig. The menu would be fried chicken, collards, corn bread, and black-eyed peas. I hired Willies women, famous around the hills for their recipes passed on for six or seven generations. I bought cherry and rhubarb pies, apple and sweet potato, baked in backwoods ovens. I hired the Longchamps, the fiddlin' band that had played at our wedding, and some of the local high school boys and girls to act as waiters and waitresses. The only professionals I hired were bartenders from the local taverns; they'd promised to mix me a moonshine punch that would, as one old-timer promised me, "start even the wooden toys to dancin'." We were holding the party on the wide lawn in front of the factory. I called the florist and told her we wanted only local wildflower arrangements. Every night Logan and I chatted on into the late hours, talking about the factory, the employees, and the arrangements for the party. Every once in a while I'd jump up from bed and writ down another thing we had forgotten to do. We were like two children planning our first party.

We had a wonderful fall day for it. There wasn't a cloud in the sky and there was barely a breeze. I had ordered from one of the local seamstresses a traditional Willies gingham dress, complete with lace and rickrack. She had to make it special to accommodate my growing belly. I wore my black hair in braids tied up in ribbons, just the way I had when I was a child of the Willies. This was the day the Willies would be celebrated. This was the day the hill people would be the important people in town. My pregnancy was beginning to show; when I looked at myself in the mirror, I thought even my face looked fuller. I remembered how bloated Sara, Pa's second wife, looked when she was pregnant. Every day her body, and especially her face, seemed to inflate a little more. I even had the funny idea that the baby within her was blowing air and she was filling up like a bicycle tire. I remember how Tom had laughed when I told him.

I brushed on a little rouge and put on some lipstick.

"How do I look?" I asked Logan. Logan chose to wear a conservative business suit, but he tied a country bow tie around his neck. He stopped tying his tie and smiled.

"You look more beautiful than ever. The baby inside you is making you bloom like some brilliant rose."

"Oh, Logan. You're becoming a super salesman," I said to kid him.

He looked hurt. "I'm not being false to you, Heaven. Never will I ever be false to you. You do look beautiful." He came across the room to kiss me. He held me tightly and it felt good to be securely in his arms. "Oh, Heaven," he said, "do you remember when Tony presented us with the Rolls at the wedding party and I said I thought I was the happiest I could ever be? Well, I'm happier now.

"We don't have Farthy; we don't have a castle and an army of servants and we're not mingling with the bluebloods, but we've got this wonderful home and the chance to build upon our own energies and imaginations, and I think that makes us richer than ever.

"Especially," he said, holding me out at arm's length, "because we have each other and the blessing of a child to come. Let's put all the unhappiness behind us. Nothing but good things lay ahead."

"Oh, Logan. I hope you're right," I said, nearly brought to tears by his expression of happiness and contentment. We kissed again, interrupted by Drake's entry.

"I'm ready," he said. I had left him in his bathroom to brush his own hair. He stood in the doorway and looked in at us. He was dressed in a pair of light gray slacks, a dark gray shirt with a dark blue bow tie and a dark blue sports jacket. I never thought a little boy his age could be so proud of his clothing and how he looked.

Drake had his hair brushed neatly back and had worked a little wave up front.

"And so you are," Logan said. "Who is this handsome gentleman, Heaven?"

"I don't know," I said. "There was a schoolboy here a while ago, who had dirtied himself in the playground. I think he had sand in his hair and small patches of grass growing in his ears. Could this be the same boy?" I smiled, but Drake, so serious and deep-thinking a child, made his eyes smaller.

"I'm Drake," he said. I could see the anger brighten in the corners of his mouth.

"Of course you are, honey," I said. "Logan and I were just fooling with you. Come, we'll all go downstairs. We don't want to be late."

Logan held out his arm to me. "Ready for your day, Heaven." His smile beckoned like a glittering diamond. Little Drake came running.

Drake had helped us plan special activities for the kids—three-legged races, a bean-bag pitch, and apple bobbing. He could barely contain his excitement as we drove to the factory grounds.

We had two bars set up at either end of the lawn and an enormous tent between them in the rear with tables and chairs. When Drake first saw it, he thought Pa's circus had arrived in Winnerow. The bandstand was draped in red, white, and blue streamers.

Over the entrance to the factory, we had a large gold banner welcoming people to the opening of the WILLIES TOY FACTORY. It was my idea to leave off the Tatterton name.

Folks were already dancing and drinking, laughing and talking. Suddenly, out of the hubbub of old trucks and station wagons pulling into the parking lot, a sleek black limousine with dark smoked windows glided up. My breath caught in my chest. There was only one person this could be. The door opened, and a shiny patent-leather shoe emerged, followed by an elegant, tuxedo-clad Tony Tatterton. I desperately looked around for Logan, but he was nowhere to be found. I took a deep breath to steal myself for what was to come, held my head high, and stepped forward to greet Tony Tatterton.

"Mr. Tatterton," I said stiffly as I walked toward him. "We didn't think you would be able to attend."

His eyes drank me in.

"Heaven," he gasped, "your hair!"

"Do you like it? I braided it myself. It's the height of fashion in the Willies "

"The color," he stammered.

"It's my real color, as you know, Mr. Tatterton."

For a moment he couldn't take his eyes off of my hair, as though he were staring not into a black head of hair but into a black abyss of lost memories. I could tell he was reading the symbolism of my gesture. I no longer wanted to be associated with the Tattertons. Everything he saw in me now was pure Winnerow Casteel. Then he slowly gathered himself together and glanced disapprovingly around. "It's quite a little shindig you and your country boy husband have put together." For a brief moment the insecure little girl in me was chastened by the judgment and scorn I read in his eyes. But I quickly chased her away, and stiffened my spine with pride and glared back at him, smiling as though I owned the world.

"I noticed you've renamed the factory," he said after an uncomfortable silence that seemed to stretch between us for hours.

"Logan and I decided that the name Tatterton was inappropriate for this particular factory. May I get you something to drink, Mr. Tatterton?"

"No, I don't think I'll be staying very long. I don't exactly fit in," he said, running his hand over his silk tie, "do I? Unless of course your husband has a pair of overalls I can borrow." He smiled, and I could tell he was trying to make a joke, but I kept my heart hardened against him.

"Please don't, Tony. Despite everything that has happened between us, Logan once loved and admired you very much. Show him a little respect."

Tony looked down, shaking his head sadly from time to time. Then he looked once again into my eyes, his own filled with tears.

"Please, Heaven, can't we be alone for a few minutes? I need to talk to you so badly."

"I shall never, ever be alone with you again," I said coldly.

"You don't understand, Heaven. I was drunk. I was out of my mind with grief over Jillian's death. I was—"

"Your bereavement took on a strange form of grieving."

"Heaven, come back to Farthy. Logan and you and I can start over again," he said, suddenly pleading like a little boy. "I just know it could work! I just know it!"

A tinge of pity for him enveloped me. He suddenly looked so old and gray and helpless.

"I know we would all be happy there again," he continued. "Besides, Heaven, I think you exaggerated my behavior that night. I was only trying to embrace. I only wanted to love you like a father!"

"Get out of here now," I said quietly but with ice in my voice. "Leave here this very minute."

Tony looked completely defeated. "I suppose you've told Logan everything."

"He's my husband. Of course I told him everything," I replied coldly. He nodded and his blue eyes swung to fix on the banner above the party site.

"I'm not going to ask you to forgive me. That's something you will do on your own or you won't. I only ask that you consider my motives," he said. "In any case," he went on before I could reply, "I won't be coming back here for some time. I have a great deal to do now in Boston, so you will have sufficient time to consider everything in its proper perspective. And" —he looked at me with his blue eyes softening for the first time since he had arrived— "time is magical. It heals all our wounds."

"But leaves scars," I said. He nodded with obvious disappointment.

"Good-bye, Heaven. I'm sure you and Logan will do very well here," he said and pivoted quickly to walk to his limo, where Miles stood like a sentinel. I watched him get into the rear of the car. Miles closed the door, looked my way for a split second, and then got in and drove the vehicle off. I waited to watch it disappear down the road, drifting away like a memory made smaller and smaller with the passage of time until it was completely forgotten, driven out by the tick-tock of a hundred thousand clocks.

I turned and the lively sounds of fiddling, the chatter of voices, and the sounds of laughter enveloped me.

I decided the only thing to do was to immerse myself in the party. Logan and his foreman ran tours of the factory. Samples of Willies Toys had been put out on display, puppets and carved animals we were planning to manufacture. But their wooden faces began whirling around me, the whittled animals appeared to come to life. I felt so dizzy and strange, standing among those toys, toys that I had grown up with, in gingham and braids, after all I had been through. I leaned against one of the display cases.

Logan's mother approached me, insisting on taking me about to be introduced to the wives of influential businessmen and professionals who lived in Winnerow or its surroundings. I could barely recognize their faces, they all looked like the puppets to me.

"Mother," I said, "I'm feeling a little dizzy."

"You do look pale," she said. "Perhaps you should lie down for a while. I know Logan had a cot in his office. You lie down there."

"What about Drake? Where is he?" I asked, feeling my legs almost give way beneath me, "I promised to take him to the apple-bobbing contest, I promised—"

"Heaven, just take a look for yourself," she said, pointing out to the lawn.

I saw that Drake had already made friends with some of the children his age and was well occupied.

"There are loads of children here, and you know the hill people. They all look after one another. Now, you run along and lie down. Drake's not your only child, remember?"

When I awoke, darkness was falling. I was stunned that I had slept through the whole party. I wandered back outside. The crowd had thinned considerably. Only Logan, his parents, and a few die-hard drinkers were left.

"Well, look who's come back to the world," Logan called out, smiling.

"I didn't realize I'd slept so long," I said as he put a protective arm around me.

"Pregnant women need lots of rest," Loretta Stonewall interjected.

"Well, did everything go well?" I asked as I surveyed the remnants of the party. The food tables were empty, the band was beginning to pack up their instruments. All the cars, save ours and the Stonewalls, were gone. Suddenly I realized Drake wasn't there. "Where's Drake?" I asked, the cold finger of fear beginning to travel down my spine.

"Drake? I thought he was resting with you." Logan looked alarmed.

"He told me he was going to find you about an hour ago," Loretta said worriedly. "I just assumed he was with you."

"Drake!" I shouted.

"Don't worry, Heaven," Logan said, but I could hear alarm fill his voice. "He's probably playing with some of the sample toys. He's probably lost in his own world."

"Where?" I asked. "We've got to find him!"

"We will, don't worry," Logan said.

We split up and began wandering all over the factory and grounds, calling Drake's name.

"Drake! Drake!" I shouted.

The yellow light above the factory gate was lit, casting an eerie glow over the parking lot. On a small patch of lawn we'd set up a swing set for some of the children. I ran toward it. Drake was nowhere in sight, but one of the swings was still going back and forth, back and forth, as if a ghost sat on it. I looked into the darkness for a moment.

Behind the factory there were acres and acres of undeveloped forest. *"Drake!"* I called loudly. "Drake, where are you?"

The only sound was the distant metallic cry of a train threading its way through the darkness in the distance. I waited a moment and then called again.

Intense panic began to set in, rattling my bones. My legs felt as though they were ready to crack with fear.

"Drake!"

There was something about the silence and the darkness that told me he hadn't just wandered off exploring, as boys his age were wont to do. My screams finally brought Logan to my side.

"You haven't found him? *You haven't found him?"* I cried.

"No, no," he said. "My parents are still out searching. I'm going to call the police. But it's only a precaution. I'm sure, Heaven. I'm sure he'll turn up any minute."

I knew, by the tone of Logan's voice, he was as frightened as I was.

"Call them," I said. "I'll keep looking."

"Drake!" I screamed again.

"Please, you'll get a cold out here. I'll get some of the men to look. Come back to my office and we'll wait for the police."

"I'm staying right here, Logan Stonewall. I'm going to look for Drake."

"Heaven, it's too dark. You can't see anything. Please."

"I'll stand under the gate light so that Drake can find me. Just hurry and call the police," I said.

Logan ran back to the office. I stared out into the night, the black line of trees, the tiny sliver of a moon. Somewhere in the distance an owl hooted. And then, as if the hand of fate had tapped me on the shoulder, I knew where my Drake was as well as I knew my own heritage. There was only one place he could be. There was only one person who would know where he was. And I was certain of it as I was certain of my own name. Fanny!

❧ *FIFTEEN* ❧
Love Held Hostage

MY HEART WAS ENVELOPED IN A HEAVY CLOUD OF DESPAIR. I waited silently with Logan while the Winnerow Police patrol car made a quick sweep of the factory neighborhood. We had asked his parents to go wait at Hasbrouck House in case Drake turned up there, or in case anyone who found him called.

"Maybe he went into someone's house," Jimmy Otis, one of the officers, said when he stopped the police car in front of the factory.

I looked at Logan, who nodded thoughtfully.

"You might be right, Jimmy," he said. "The boy's not afraid of people and very curious about things."

"I'll keep cruisin' around here," Jimmy said. "Just call the station if he returns and they'll radio me."

"Thanks, Jimmy," Logan said.

"If he's not found in another hour or so, I'll have Mary Lou call the chief at home. We'll want to get the guest list from the party so we can see if anyone saw him go anywhere."

"Okay," Logan said. As soon as the police drove off for another search, I told Logan what I feared.

"Fanny could have done something like this," I said. "We didn't invite her to the party."

Neither Logan nor I had mentioned Fanny when we were making the guest list. His reasons were obvious, and I simply didn't want another confrontation with her.

"Do you really think so?" he asked skeptically.

"All she had to do was drive by and see him. She would stop to talk to him and talk him into getting into her car, telling him she would bring him right back. I know he's smart for his age, but he's just a little boy, Logan, and he knows Fanny is his sister."

"I suppose she could have done that," Logan said thoughtfully. I looked up at the half moon half hidden by dark clouds, an omen of something terrible, I thought.

"I'm going up to her house," I said and started quickly toward the car.

"Shouldn't I go along?" he asked softly.

"No. You had better remain here just in case Jimmy Otis is right and Drake wandered into someone's home. I'll be right back," I said. Logan stayed on at the factory and I got into the car and drove to Fanny's.

As soon as I pulled up, those mangy watchdogs of hers came charging out, circling the car and barking as madly as hound dogs that had a fox trapped in a hole. Fanny's house was brightly lit and I could see she had a visitor. There was another car there. My anger and my concern for Drake overwhelmed my fear of the dogs.

I slammed my car door shut and stood straight as the dogs came around to snap at me, but I didn't retreat an inch and they kept their distance, barking a little more hysterically as I made my way to the front door of Fanny's home. When I pressed the buzzer, the dogs barked louder, but remained a few feet behind me. I had to press the buzzer again before Fanny opened the door. She stood there with her arms crossed under her breasts like Granny, her face screwed tightly, her lips pressed together in a tight line, and her blue eyes flashing.

"What'dya want, yer highness?" she asked without backing up a step to let me in. The dogs continued their yapping.

Even though Fanny was putting on this face of wrath, I could see through her mask and I knew I had been right.

"Let me in, Fanny," I said. "I'm not going to stand out here with those dogs barking and talk to you."

"Oh, so ma home's good enuf fer yer, but I'm not good enuf fer you to invite to your shindig, huh?"

"Let me in, Fanny," I repeated sternly. She stared a moment and then backed up so I could enter and close the door on the dogs behind me. As soon as I did so, I turned to the left and saw Randall standing in the living room doorway. He looked as troubled as a man haunted by an unrelenting conscience. His eyebrows dipped. His head was bowed and his shoulders sagged.

"What'dya want?" Fanny snapped. I could see by the way she looked quickly at Randall that she was putting on a show for him.

"Fanny, Drake's missing," I said in as controlled a voice as I could. I knew how important it was not to show any weakness. She would pounce on it with the speed of a cat pouncing on a helpless mouse. "Do you have him here?"

Fanny didn't respond right away. She smiled brilliantly, her white teeth flashing. It was a wicked, hateful smile, but a smile that built assurance, confidence. There was also something in Randall's expression that told me she had convinced him to help her. She had known I would show up here and she had told him so.

"What if I have? He's ma brotha, too. I got a right ta have him in ma home. He belongs here more n' he belongs with you and Goody Two-shoes."

"Fanny, did you take him?" I demanded, my voice now throwing off the ropes of restraint and sounding a note of hysteria.

"He's where he belongs," she said, admitting it.

I started toward her, my anger, fear, and hate twisted and rolled together like a ball of barbed wire. Her eyes widened in surprise as I rushed forward and seized the collar of her flimsy, cotton blouse, pulling her roughly toward me.

"Where is he? How could you do this? Damn you!"

Fanny gathered her courage and clutched a handful of my hair, her nails digging into my scalp. We struggled only for a moment before Randall rushed in between us, pulling us apart.

"Hold it! Stop! Hold it!" he cried. "Heaven, please. Fanny. Stop!"

Separated, we glared at each other, both of us breathing hard and fast.

"Ya keep yer hands off me, Heaven. We ain't in the cabin in the Willies and ya can't boss me around," she said, straightening her blouse.

I caught my breath and turned to Randall.

"Where's Drake?" I demanded.

"He ain't gonna do anythin' ya tell him nuther. He knows what ya are, too."

"Randall!"

"You'll have to work it out between the both of you," he said in a tired and defeated voice. "She has just as much right as you do," he added, turning his back on me and walking back to the living room doorway.

"That's right, Heaven. I do. I have more right. Pa loved me more n' he loved ya and he'd a wanted me ta be a motha ta Drake, not you. Ya hated him and Drake knows that now."

"What?"

"I told him all about it," she said, her hands on her hips. "All 'bout how ya went ta the circus that day, dressed as yer motha, just so yer could punish him and how yer caused that accident that killed poor Tom and nearly killed Luke. Drake knows what ya are. He knows it." She smiled again. "He thinks ya made his motha and father go ta Heaven."

"Where is he?" I demanded again, more panic in my voice. "You can't keep me from him!" I started into the house, but Fanny blocked my way.

"This is ma home, Heaven Leigh, and I don't want ya here, understand?"

"You can't keep Drake from me," I said. "I've called the police and I'll have them up here in moments. You can't stop me from getting him."

"No? Well, I been ta a lawya, Wendell Burton, and he says I have just as much right ta be a motha ta poor Drake as ya do. Especially," she added, turning toward Randall, "since Randall and I are gettin' married and we kin give Drake a home."

"What?" This time when I looked at Randall, he returned my gaze, and I understood that he was so infatuated with Fanny, he would do anything she wanted him to do. Fanny looked very sure about him.

"She's right, Heaven. You had no right to just assume you could take Drake into your home. Fanny has rights, too. She's family, too."

I stared at him a moment and then looked at Fanny, who had gathered herself together again and was looking more confident and satisfied than a wildcat with a fish between its paws.

"You can't just do this . . . kidnap Drake and fill his head with stories to turn him against me. You can't."

"I kin too. I got rights. Ya heard Randall and we spoke ta a lawya," she repeated, making it sound more like a chant.

"Fanny, you don't want to do this," I said, trying to take on a softer, more reasonable tone. "You don't want to take this into a court where everything about us will be exposed like naked mannequins in a storefront for all to see and laugh at. How would you like that?"

"How would you? Yer the one who hasta look high and mighty here. How would yer new family of Stonewalls like it? Think Logan's ma would like it?" she said, turning her shoulder at me. "Think Logan will like stuff brought out in public?"

"You're trying to blackmail me into giving you Drake," I said. I looked at Randall, but his expression was unchanged. "Well, I won't let you. I'll fight you and you'll be the sorry one. I swear it."

She simply smiled.

"Damn you," I said. Her smile faded quickly and was replaced with a face filled with flames. Her eyes burned at me.

"Get outta ma house," she ordered. "Drake doesn't even wanna see ya since I told him the truth."

"My God, what have you done to him?"

"I just brought him home ta his own people," she said proudly. "And that's where he'll stay."

I looked at Randall again. My body was trembling now. Fanny would have never been able   stand so firm and tall against me if Randall hadn't been there,   ought. She was performing for him as much as she was for me n   t had become a matter of her ego and pride, and when ego and priae are at stake, cowards and beggars could become heroes and kings.

"I'm terribly disappointed in you, Randall," I said softly, hoping to appeal to his kind and better nature. "You seemed to me to be a sensitive and intelligent young man. You don't know what you're getting involved in here."

"Oh, yes, he does. He's a college student, ya know. Ya ain't the only one with brains, Heaven."

I felt my throat tighten, my eyes water, but I knew I must not show any signs of weakness here. I bit down on my lower lip and glared at Randall. Then I turned to Fanny and, drawing deeply from the well of my Tatterton ancestry to bring up the grit and strength that turned them into ruthless and successful businessmen, I spat my words at her in the most threatening, frightening voice I could muster.

"I'll come after you now," I said. "With all the power and fury my money can buy, and when this is over, you will truly understand the meaning of vengeance."

She couldn't hold my gaze; she had to turn away. I glared once more at Randall and then I opened the door and stepped out of the house, slamming the door behind me and starting up those annoying watchdogs. This time I practically didn't hear their barking as I walked back to my car.

I don't remember driving away from the house. I don't remember making turns and stopping for traffic lights. I don't remember how I brought myself back to the factory, but suddenly I was there.

Logan, who heard me pull up, came out of the factory quickly.

"Well?" he asked. I just sat there behind the steering wheel staring ahead. "Heaven?"

"She has him," I whispered, like one in a trance. "And she wants to keep him."

"What? You're kidding?"

"No," I said, turning to him. "We've got to go to court to win custody of him."

"Well, that's not going to be hard. We'll just—"

"It's going to be terrible, Logan," I said quickly. "Everything will come out. Everything," I added, to drive home the point. He understood and instinctively turned around to look at his new empire.

"I see," he said.

"But I don't care," I added firmly. He nodded, but I sensed his fears and reluctance. "Nothing matters more to me than getting Drake back, Logan. Do you understand?" My voice reached a hysterical pitch.

"Yes, yes, of course. Let's go home and tell the police we've found Drake, and tell Mom and Dad what's happened, and then we'll think out our next step."

As we drove to Hasbrouck House, the past few weeks played in my mind—how I had been slowly winning Drake's love and trust. Because of his sorrow and all that had happened to him, he had formed a hard shell about him, just the way Luke had formed a hard shell about himself right after my mother, Leigh, died giving birth to me. But I had been slowly chipping away at that shell around Drake and I felt I was making good progress. Now Fanny was destroying it. I pictured how handsome Drake had looked in his little suit at the party, and just before we turned into the driveway of the Hasbrouck House, the dam broke and a flood of tears rushed out.

Was I destined to travel through life with Despair and Sorrow at my side, twin sisters who were comfortable in my home? Or maybe happiness, the happiness I kept thinking I finally had within my grasp, was like a beautiful bird. If you held on to it too tightly, you broke its wings and crushed it to die; and if you held onto it too lightly, it would fly away.

Had it flown away?

I was all right until I entered the house, went upstairs, and stopped by Drake's room. Then I burst into tears again and ran into my bedroom to flop on the bed and cry. A short while later Logan came up and closed the door softly behind him. I couldn't hold back the tears or stop my sobs. I felt his hand on my shoulder and turned over to look up at him.

"Now, now," he said. "There's no point in getting so upset over it. You know how Fanny is."

"What do you mean, Logan?" I wiped the tears away with the palms of my hands.

"She likes to do spiteful things and then, after she's satisfied, or thinks she's satisfied, she stops. How long do you think she's going to want to have a little boy as a responsibility?" He laughed. "Fanny? I can't imagine it."

"Randall Wilcox is going to marry her, Logan."

"Randall Wilcox? I can't believe it. His father will disown him. It's just a story she concocted to make things seem worse to you."

"No, it's true. He was there at the house. She has him under her thumb. She even has him disliking me. But the important thing is Fanny will have a husband and will be able to claim she has a fit home for Drake."

"I still don't believe she'll want to care for—"

"Logan! What do you expect me to do, sit around here and wait for her to get bored with Drake? She's already filled his head with terrible stories about me, turning him against me. Every passing day will add to the disaster."

He nodded thoughtfully.

"Well, I'll get one of my attorneys to do the paperwork and frighten her with a court action. She won't know the first thing about what to do and—"

"She already has a lawyer," I said quickly. "Wendell Burton."

"Wendell Burton?"

I nodded. "He's already given her some legal advice."

"Wendell Burton. He's an ambulance chaser of the worst sort, a parasitic, wormy type. Whenever someone dies in an accident, he's at the funeral parlor handing out his card, hoping they'll hire him to sue someone."

"It doesn't matter what kind of a lawyer he is or how good he is. The point is she has gone that far. It's not as simple as you think. We're going to have to go to court." He stared at me for a moment.

"I can't believe this . . . just when we get the factory started and we're making a mark for ourselves in this community, we have to have a family squabble aired in public."

"It's more than a family squabble, Logan. Far more. A little boy's life is at stake."

"I know that; I know that," he said. He stood up to pace about. "Maybe we can still work something out behind closed doors."

"We can't. You might as well face it."

"Well, jeez, Heaven, can't I at least try for an easier way out of this? I'll make some calls, see what can be done."

I shook my head and sat up.

"You're just like Tony. You think you can solve everything with a phone call or lawyers meeting behind closed doors."

"I'll just try," he repeated, holding his arms out.

"Try," I said. "But I'm not going to let more than a day pass."

"They won't abuse him," he said, trying to make it sound less severe.

"Logan." I narrowed my gaze on him. "You promised me you would think of Drake the way you would think of your own child."

"I know and I will," he protested.

"Well, would you let someone do this to your own child? Take him away and fill his head with terrible things about you?" He didn't respond. "Would you?"

"Of course not."

"So then . . . I'm calling J. Arthur Steine tomorrow and getting his advice and the name of an attorney in Virginia. I'm going to have the best possible legal help and put all the money I have to into this."

"Sure, I understand," he said softly.

"And if it means hanging out our torn and filthy laundry for all to see, I'll still do it to get Drake back. I don't care what these people think of us."

"Well, you said the magic word there, Heaven," Logan said. "Us. We have other people to think about . . . my parents, for instance." There was such heat in my chest, I thought my heart had caught fire. The glow moved up my throat and neck and into my face. I felt my cheeks burning.

"You didn't think about them when you made love to Fanny in the cabin, did you, Logan?" I asked quickly. He blanched. "Well?"

"I told you how that happened. Do I spend my whole life paying for it?" he whined.

"I don't know," I said. I wiped the remaining tears from my face. "Maybe it's time we all owned up to our pasts and our actions. Maybe this had all happened so we can cleanse ourselves," I said. "Whatever the reason . . . I'm determined to do what is right and necessary with or without your support."

Logan stared a moment and then nodded.

"I'm sorry. I didn't mean to sound selfish. Of course you have my support, and of course I'll be right at your side. I love you too much to ever let you suffer anything alone," he said. "I'll do what I can in the morning to stop this, and if I can't, I'll go anywhere, do anything you want to bring Drake back where he belongs."

"Thank you, Logan." My eyes filled with tears again.

"Don't thank me for loving you as much as I do, Heaven. It's what makes my life worthwhile."

He reached out and we embraced.

"It will be all right," he whispered and kissed my forehead. "You'll see."

"I hope so," I said.

In the morning, right after breakfast, Logan went off to see his lawyers and make his phone calls. I didn't go down to breakfast. Mrs. Avery brought me a tray with coffee and a piece of toast, all I could manage to eat. She didn't say anything, but I could tell that she knew something bad had happened. She must have inquired after Drake and Logan must have told her something. She was too discreet to ask any questions, but for a moment I longed for someone her age to talk with, a real mother in whom I could confide my fears and problems. How lucky were those girls who had mothers and sisters they loved and could trust, I thought.

After I had my coffee, I got a firm hold on myself and did what I told Logan I would do—I phoned J. Arthur Steine. He came to the phone immediately, interrupting a meeting he was having with his associates. He listened sympathetically.

"Can she do what she has done?" I asked quickly after I summarized all that had happened.

"Well, from what you tell me, she is a mature woman, a sibling, too. It never occurred to me at the time of our meeting in my office to ask about any of your brothers or sisters. You seemed to be taking charge of things."

"But Fanny doesn't have the background, the stability, the sense of responsibility," I pleaded and related some of her life to him.

"I see," he said. "And you say she's getting married now?"

"Yes."

"Well, I think there will have to be a custody hearing, Mrs. Stonewall, and these things will have to be brought out for the judge to view. But with the kind of home you can make for him and your own background, I think the decision will be in your favor."

"I want to be sure," I said. "Please recommend an attorney in Virginia who is an expert in these things. I have a high regard and confidence in your opinion," I added.

"Thank you. Yes, I know someone. His name is Camden Lakewood. You just sit tight and I'll have him phone you as soon as possible."

"Thank you, Mr. Steine," I said.

"It's no problem, Mrs. Stonewall. Please don't ever hesitate to call me if I can be of any assistance to you. Once again, I'm sorry for your troubles, and I will have Camden call you immediately. My regards to Mr. Tatterton," he said.

I thanked him again. A short while later Logan called to deliver the same legal opinion—Fanny did have rights and there would have to be a custody hearing. He wanted me to use his lawyer.

"It's all been taken care of, Logan," I said. "I spoke with Mr. Steine and he's having an attorney who specializes in these matters call me very soon."

"Oh. Well, if that's what you think we should do . . ."

"I'll speak to you right after I speak with him," I said. I knew that Logan wanted to take control of things, that he probably saw it as the manly thing to do, but the only way I could keep myself from sitting around all day and crying was to keep myself involved in what had to be done to get Drake back.

It wasn't long before Camden Lakewood phoned. I didn't waste any time with him on the phone.

"Mr. Steine recommends you highly, Mr. Lakewood," I said. "Cost is not a concern. How soon can you be at my house?"

"Mrs. Stonewall," he said in what I thought was a distinctly Harvard accent, "I just got off the phone with Arthur Steine and he has filled me in on your family and the problem. I'll be there in less than two hours," he replied.

For really the first time since I had gone to Farthy and reclaimed my mother's family with their wealth and power, I appreciated what it all could do. It boosted my confidence and strengthened my determination. The words I had spat at Fanny would come true, I thought. Nothing she had done when we were children, all the selfish things she had said included, and nothing she had said or done since, including her seduction of Logan, turned me as vehemently against her as her kidnapping of Drake and her poisoning him against me. Somehow she had always managed to get my anger at her to cool and my sympathy for her to grow, but this would not happen now. For the first time I wanted to hurt her back. I wanted vengeance, Willies vengeance.

I wanted it so much it made my blood boil. I looked at myself in the mirror and saw how red my cheeks had become. Anger and pain, hatred and despair were all the ingredients I mixed together in my mind like some witch's brew. I could practically taste the concoction on my lips.

I swallowed to prepare myself for the ordeal to come.

Just as Logan predicted, news of the custody hearing spread quickly through Winnerow and its surroundings. Because of the factory and the splash we had made with our opening, everything we did and everything that concerned us was headline news here. I remained sequestered in the Hasbrouck House, coming to life only whenever

Camden Lakewood visited to prepare for the hearing. He brought a secretary along to take notes. We sat in Logan's office and I described and listed all the things I thought would work against Fanny. A list of witnesses was drawn up and Camden sent an investigator about to gather evidence.

Just like J. Arthur Steine, Camden Lakewood was a man who looked successful. He was a tall man in his fifties, lean and fit with sharp, clear blue eyes that fixed themselves so intently on the person to whom he was talking, you could almost see his mind at work—scrutinizing, weighing facts and data, making conclusions.

He had what advertising executives would call a distinguished appearance, the man to be seen in a magazine ad promoting the sale of an expensive car or clothing. There was a firmness to his posture and an air of authority about him. I felt very confident that he was pleading my case.

Although some of the things I told him were ugly and unpleasant, he never expressed any disgust. It was as if he had heard it all before. His attitude helped me to relax, and before long I was able to tell him the hardest thing.

"Fanny's pregnant," I said. "And it appears virtually certain that my husband is the father of her child." My throat closed quickly after I uttered the words and tears came to my eyes. I had to look away to catch my breath. Mr. Lakewood's secretary looked up from her note pad and then looked down quickly. Camden got up and went out to fetch Mrs. Avery and ordered her to bring me a glass of water, which she did instantly.

"How damaging will this be?" I asked.

"When you say 'virtually certain,' how do you mean that?" he asked, making me more aware of the words I chose.

"Logan has admitted to sleeping with her." I described the incident just the way Logan had described it to me. Mr. Lakewood didn't change expression.

"In the worst scenario," he began, "it's a trade-off. She came to him in the cabin, and from what we have learned, to put it mildly, Fanny sleeps around. First, stop all payments to her. We no longer agree that Logan is responsible for the pregnancy. We'll insist on blood tests when the baby is born. From what you're telling me, you're not going to make out much worse financially even if the blood tests prove Logan responsible.

"Since she's marrying Randall Wilcox now, and since it's common knowledge she has been with him for some time, be it on and off, we will develop the possibility that the child is his. In any case we'll depict Fanny as a very loose woman and that should work against her.

"Logan's indiscretion isn't helpful, by any means, but men stray. The judge, Bryon McKensie, is a man and will not rule against us simply on the basis of Logan's one night with Fanny. Unfortunately, adultery is a great deal more common today, or at least, revealed more.

"That incident aside, it would seem clear to me that your household has a much more moral atmosphere. However, Mrs. Stonewall, I'd be negligent not to tell you this is not going to be a pleasant affair. I've had some research done on this other attorney, Wendell Burton, and his methods and style appear to be . . . shall I say of questionable taste? You'll be on the stand and he'll have an opportunity to question you. I'll be there to raise objections, of course, but you must be prepared for the worst kind of courtroom antics and treatment."

"I'll be prepared," I said.

"And your husband?" he asked, his eyes narrowing for the first time. He had met Logan and had already sensed his fears.

"He'll be prepared, too," I said with added determination.

I know that I was only hoping that would be so, for as the hearing date approached, Logan became more and more nervous, and although I had had only a few short phone conversations with his mother about the situation since Fanny took Drake, I knew that Logan and his mother had been discussing it a great deal. The afternoon before the hearing was to begin, Loretta Stonewall came to the Hasbrouck House. I was reviewing my recollection of the events I had told Camden Lakewood so my testimony would be consistent.

Mrs. Avery came to the office door to announce Loretta's arrival.

"Show her in, please, Mrs. Avery, and please make us some tea."

It was a rather cold day. Temperatures had dropped dramatically the night before, making it one of those days Granny used to say were "too cold even fer snow." Loretta was wearing the long silver fox fur coat Logan had bought her for her birthday. She came sweeping into the room, looking flushed and excited, as if she had run the entire distance between her home and the Hasbrouck House.

"Oh, it's so cold," she said. "How are you, my dear? How are you holding up?" She dropped herself into the large, cushioned chair in front of the desk and caught her breath, pressing her hand against her throat like someone feeling for a pulse.

"I'm fine," I said. "Mrs. Avery will bring us some tea shortly."

"How thoughtful. You are so thoughtful and clever. That was one of the first things I said to Logan when he told me how fond of you he was. She's a very clever girl, I said, to have pulled herself up so high so fast."

"Thank you, Mother Stonewall."

"Oh, please, just call me Mother. Mother Stonewall makes me sound like someone's great-grandmother," she added and followed it with a short, thin laugh.

Ordinarily, I might have laughed at what she had said, but it reminded me of Jillian the first time I had met her and she asked me not to call her Grandmother because she had done so well hiding her true age from her friends. Would I be as vain when I reached their ages? I wondered. I hoped not. Vanity was a heavy burden, chaining us to a world constructed of falsity where people exchange a currency of lies.

I sat back without replying.

"This thing begins tomorrow, then?" she asked.

"Yes. I was just preparing for it."

"Oh, dear, dear, what a terrible situation for you and for Logan. Is there no way then to avoid it?" she asked, leaning forward.

"Only if Fanny would return Drake and relinquish any claims to him," I said. "But if she hasn't done it up to now, you can be sure she's prepared to go ahead. She thinks she has less to lose and it's her way at getting back at me. There's nothing more I can do but proceed."

Loretta waited until Mrs. Avery served us the tea before continuing.

"This is all anyone's talking about here," she said as soon as Mrs. Avery left.

"I know."

"Heaven," she said after a long pause. "Logan has told me everything. He was preparing me since it would only come out at the trial. I know what he did was wrong, terribly wrong, and I think it's wonderful of you to be so forgiving, but to let this out in the community, especially this community, would be a terrible mistake. Winnerow is almost the buckle of the Bible Belt. It will be so difficult for both of you here afterward, no matter how successful the factory might be. People will snicker and talk and—"

"I don't care," I said quickly. "Drake is more important than worrying about the gossip of some religious hypocrites."

"But, my dear, you have your own child to think about, too. He or she will go to school here and have to socialize with the other children, whose parents will fill them with tales. It will be so hard."

"What are you suggesting, Mother?" I asked, tired of the whine in her voice.

"Can't you find some way to settle this discreetly? What if you permitted Fanny to have the boy for part of the year and you have him the remaining part?" she asked, smiling as if she had come up with a wonderful solution.

"For one thing, she wouldn't go along with such an arrangement. She is determined to hurt me in some way and she is using this as a method. I told you . . . she's always been jealous of me. For another thing, I couldn't live with myself knowing Drake was under her influence for six months out of every year. It would take me the next six months to undo all the damage she had done. She's already poisoned him against me."

"But as Logan says, she'll probably grow tired of taking care of him, especially since she has her own child on the way. And if there is no promise of big money . . ."

"It's out of the question, Loretta," I said. I didn't want to call anyone "Mother" who made such a suggestion. The smile left her face as if I had slapped it.

"You're not thinking of your own family, of Logan and your own child," she said sternly.

"Drake is my own family," I said.

"But my dear," she said, leaning back, "you and I know he's not."

I stared at her. Apparently, there wasn't anything Logan hadn't told her. I wondered if he had told her what had happened between Tony and me.

"Drake is, too, my family," I said slowly, my eyes narrowed, my gaze pointed and sharp as steel knives. "I resent your saying otherwise."

"I'm only trying to be helpful," she said. "I'm only thinking of your welfare."

"Thank you, Mother," I said, smiling, my face dripping with the same false cordiality. "It was so nice of you to come over here in this bitter cold."

The false softness quickly left her eyes. Her hand shook and she nearly dropped the teacup.

"Well, I think you're making a terrible mistake going through with this, but if you're determined to do it, there's nothing more I can say." She put the teacup down so sharply, it nearly shattered. "Please," she said, standing. "Don't tell Logan I came over here to advise you. He asked me not to do it."

"Then why did you?" I asked quickly.

"Sometimes a mother knows what's better for her child . . . instinctively," she said.

"That's exactly how I feel, Mother," I said. "Although I am not

Drake's mother, I know instinctively what's better for him, and like his mother, doing what his mother would surely want, I intend to win him back. I hope you'll be there to support us during this trying time."

"Oh, of course, I will," she said quickly. "Poor dears. Of course." She came around the desk to kiss me. Her lips felt cold against my cheek. "Just call me, anytime. And we'll be there right beside you," she said.

She shook her head and sighed and then she left.

I sat back and looked out the window. It must have warmed some, I thought, for it had started to snow, but my heart still felt as if it were caught in the grip of a cold hand. Of course I was frightened about tomorrow. Of course I was concerned about the future of my own child, but I couldn't stand the thought of Drake growing up and someday looking at me with Luke's eyes, filled with a similar resentment. I wanted so much to win his love and have him cherish me as his sister. Fanny sensed just how much I wanted it, and so she set to take it away.

I was tired of losing the people I loved.

"No, Loretta," I whispered, "there is no other way. This journey filled with pain and suffering has come to an end where it all began . . . in the Willies. And that's as it should be. Surely, that's as it should be."

I turned back to the papers on the desk, determined I would be ready.

❧ SIXTEEN ❧
The Trial

THE COURTHOUSE WAS STUFFED LIKE A THANKSGIVING TURKEY, with so many people crowded in, it was full to bursting. Nearly in tears Logan's mother told me some people in Winnerow had actually planned to close their shops and leave their jobs to attend the hearing.

This early November day brought us our first true winter weather. It had been snowing heavily all morning; a sharp, brisk wind churned the flakes into wild dervishes. In such bitter, brutal weather I didn't think many people would venture out, but it seemed most of the town had come to witness the spectacle. When Logan and I entered with Camden Lakewood, people stared and whispered, their voices like dry leaves blown before winter's first wind. Everything about us was fodder for their grinding jaws—the clothes we wore, the expression on our faces, and the way we carried ourselves as we walked down the aisle to our seats before the judge's table.

It was Camden Lakewood's idea that we should create a distinct contrast between ourselves and Fanny and Randall immediately, so Logan wore one of his expensive dark blue suits and his lamb's-wool topcoat. I wore a dark blue wool dress, my matching diamond bracelet, necklace, and earrings and my silver fox coat. I had my hair brushed down, but pinned up on the sides.

Logan's parents sat right behind us, his mother looking as though she were holding her breath. Her face was already flushed and she wore the most agitated expression. His father smiled warmly and nodded with encouragement.

The crowd's murmur rose in volume the moment Fanny, Randall, and their attorney, Wendell Burton, entered. They had been married two days ago in a quick civil ceremony. Fanny swept in a few steps in front of them. She had her rich black hair pinned into a bun and wore long, silver earrings that dangled from her lobes like icicles. I was surprised at how smart she looked in her heavy dark green wool jacket. It had a detachable cape that she unfastened the moment she came through the door. Beneath her coat she wore a high-collar black wool dress with three-quarter sleeves. She wore no jewelry other than her earrings.

Randall wore a light overcoat. His hair was shiny and wet from the snow, and although he looked frightened and tense, he did appear neat and distinguished in his dark brown suit. Fanny looked directly at people in the audience and smiled. She waved to some people, people I recognized from the Willies. A few smiled and waved back, but most just stared in awe. Randall pulled out Fanny's chair for her. They sat on the opposite side of the courtroom. I felt Fanny's eyes on me, but I didn't look her way. I wanted to wish her away, wish her right out of existence. Was this going to be her way to finally bring me down to her level, to air all our shame before the entire town? Oh, Fanny was so jealous of me, still and forever jealous and spiteful and now she had her day to be heard, and I knew she would show me no mercy. And I had done nothing to her! Nothing! She didn't want Drake to be her child; she wanted only to humiliate me.

When the judge, the Honorable Bryon MacKensie, entered the courtroom, everyone stood up and hushed, the Willies men holding their hats in their hands. The judge spread his black robes as he sat down, very elegantly, and scrutinized his large audience. He appeared slightly taken aback by the size of the crowd. He was a highly respected judge in these parts, presiding over many of the society cases and keeping company with senators and statesmen. He was a tall, lanky man with dark brown hair and dark brown eyes.

He shuffled through some papers on his desk for a moment and then picked up his gavel and rapped it loudly. "This court is now in session," he intoned.

A few people coughed nervously, but other than that, it was as silent as a funeral parlor.

"I expect this hearing to be conducted in an orderly manner," he began. "The audience will not, I repeat, will not voice comment, clap hands, or in any way disturb the factual presentations and examination of witnesses. Anyone who does so will be forcibly removed and in jeopardy of being held in contempt of court."

He glanced at his papers once again.

"This is a hearing to determine custody of one Drake Casteel. Mr. and Mrs. Logan Stonewall have moved to have the court assign them full guardianship of Drake Casteel, who, we understand, is presently under the care and supervision of Mr. and Mrs. Randall Wilcox.

"Mr. Lakewood, since your clients have moved for this proceeding, I would ask you to begin."

"Thank you, Your Honor," Camden said, rising from his seat. "It is our contention, Your Honor, that my clients Mr. and Mrs. Stonewall are not only in the best position to provide a proper home environment for Drake Casteel, but that in the case of Mr. and Mrs. Randall Wilcox, the opposite is true. We will prove through our arguments that the environment of the Randall household is unwholesome morally speaking, and that the motivation for Mrs. Wilcox's guardianship of the child in question is not in his best interests.

"For this purpose, Your Honor, I would like to present certain witnesses who can not only qualify our arguments but prove to this court the superiority of my client's intentions and home environment."

"Very well, Mr. Lakewood," the judge said mechanically, "please call your first witness."

"We call Mr. Peter Meeks, principal of the Winnerow Schools."

Like trained seals, all the heads of the good folk of Winnerow turned toward Mr. Meeks, who rose quickly from his seat and walked to the witness stand, where he was sworn in. In his arms he carried a folder. Camden Lakewood leaned one elbow on the stand as Mr. Meeks took his seat.

"Please state your name and position for the record."

"My name is Peter Meeks. I am the principal of the Winnerow Schools."

"And for how long have you held this position, Mr. Meeks?"

"Nearly twenty-eight years," he said with obvious pride.

"So you were principal of Winnerow Schools when Fanny and Heaven Casteel were students there?"

"I was."

"I will ask you, Mr. Meeks, to direct your memory to those years, and give the court your evaluation of these two schoolgirls."

"Well," Mr. Meeks began, settling himself more comfortably in the hard wooden seat, "I do remember them vividly because their family was one of the poorer mountain families, and, unfortunately," he said lowering his voice as if whispering a loud secret to the judge, like a schoolboy who wants his secret heard by all, "these families and their children give us most of our discipline problems. They come to school undernourished, poorly dressed, and are not very motivated when it comes to learning."

"Please get to the point, Mr. Lakewood," the judge said.

"Yes, Your Honor. Mr. Meeks, how would you characterize Fanny Casteel in relation to the kind of student you just described?"

"Oh, typical. A constant discipline problem. Poor grades."

"You say 'typical,' but were her discipline problems that typical?" Camden asked quickly.

"Well, actually, no. She was what we call a promiscuous young lady."

"Go on, please."

"She was . . . often reprimanded for conduct unbecoming to a young lady, especially one only twelve, thirteen, or fourteen."

"Mr. Meeks, would you give the court an example of this conduct."

"Your Honor," Wendell Burton said, rising to his feet. "Ah object to this line of questionin'. What Mrs. Wilcox was like as a young girl should have no bearin' on this hearin'. Jist about everyone in this courtroom did some hell-raisin' in one way or t'other when he or she was younger. But we all grow up; we change and mature, and we're here today ta talk about the mature Mrs. Wilcox and the mature Mrs. Stonewall."

"Mr. Lakewood?"

"Your Honor, it is our contention that Fanny Wilcox did not grow up, did not mature, as Mr. Burton describes, that in fact she has a continuous history of promiscuity."

"I will let the witness go on," the judge said, "but I advise you, Mr. Lakewood, I am concerned that we develop a factual history here, not simply innuendo."

"I understand, Your Honor. Mr. Meeks, an example?"

"Well . . ." He opened his folder. "On one particular day in March of her second year in junior high school, Fanny Casteel was discovered in the boys' locker room with two young men. She was only half dressed. She was reprimanded and sent home early. On another occasion toward the end of that same month, she was found with an older male student in the crawl space under the stage. The teacher who found them wrote in her report that they were embraced in a licentious manner. Again, she was sent home."

"How old was she at the time?"

"Thirteen."

"I see. Do you have other examples?"

"At least half a dozen."

"Your Honor, I don't wish to be redundant and waste the court's time with the recitation of more examples, but I would move for

Fanny Casteel's school record to be entered as evidence for you to consider when making your determination."

"So moved."

"I have no further questions for Mr. Meeks."

"Mr. Burton?" the judge said. Wendell Burton smiled. He had a syrupy face with large blue eyes and lips that moved like two strips of red licorice. There was a prominent mole just over his right eyebrow. His hair was slicked back, the top flat and parted just two inches off center. He stood about five feet ten and was a little stoop-shouldered. I noticed that he had a habit of rubbing his hands together before he spoke.

"Mr. Meeks," he said, without leaving his table, "ah assume ya brought Heaven Casteel's records as well today?"

"No."

"Oh, and why was that?"

"I was only asked to bring along Fanny Casteel's records."

"Ah see. But knowin' what this hearing was all about, ah assume ya took a look at Heaven Casteel's records."

Mr. Meeks squirmed in his seat, looked my way, and then back at Wendell Burton.

"I did take a quick look just in case I would be asked any questions pertaining to those records."

"Oh. Good, good," Burton said, starting toward him. "Now, would ya tell the court what ya discovered when ya looked at Heaven Casteel's attendance records."

"I don't understand," Meeks said, looking toward the judge.

"Especially durin' her last year at Winnerow. What was her attendance like, for example?"

"Well?"

"Was she not in fact absent a great deal?"

"Absent?"

"Mr. Meeks," the judge said. "Please answer the question."

"Yes, I suppose you could say that."

"Oh, ya could say that?" Wendell smiled widely at the audience and then looked at Mr. Meeks. "Is that the behavior of a good student?"

"No, but—"

"Isn't poor attendance a serious discipline problem?"

"Of course."

"Despite her immature behavior in school, Fanny Casteel at least attended school more often that year, if we check those records, did she not, Mr. Meeks?"

"On the surface, I suppose you could say that."

"Mr. Meeks," Wendell said, suddenly looking sympathetic. "I understand how ya feel. Ta judge whether one adult woman is goin' ta be a better mother than another adult woman on the basis of junior high school is about as valid as lookin' into a fortune-teller's crystal ball, isn't it?"

"Objection, Your Honor," Camden said. "He's asking the witness to pass judgment on the value of his own testimony."

"But Y'Honor, Mr. Lakewood's been askin' the court ta place validity on Mr. Meeks' judgment all along here."

"I don't see it that way, Mr. Burton," the judge said. "Mr. Lakewood has brought out factual data. Rest assured, I will be the one to pass judgment on the validity of the information. Objection sustained. Do you have any further questions for this witness, Mr. Burton?"

"None, Your Honor. Oh, yes . . . one more," he said, turning suddenly. "Mr. Meeks, recently Mrs. Stonewall brought Drake Casteel ta your school ta enter him as a student, did she not?"

"Yes." Mr. Meeks sat back, pressing his hands together as if in prayer.

"And ya entered the boy even though he is not quite of age, did ya not?"

"Yes, but—"

"In other words, ya made an exception ta please Mr. and Mrs. Stonewall?"

"No, not just to please them. We can make exceptions when a potential student shows exceptional promise."

"Ah see. Then Mr. and Mrs. Stonewall's position and influence in this community had nothing ta do with yer decision?"

"Objection, Your Honor!"

"Or yer testimony here today?" Wendell Burton added quickly.

"Your Honor?" Camden pursued. I was glad to see he could be just as aggressive as Wendell Burton.

"Y'Honor, ah'm tryin' ta show that this witness is a prejudiced witness," Burton said.

"Mr. Burton, I've already told you, I am concerning myself only with the factual data Mr. Meeks has brought to this courtroom, not with his subjective evaluation. Therefore, it is unnecessary to try to prove his prejudice in the matter. Now, do you have any further questions?"

"No, Y'Honor."

"I have one more question, Your Honor," Camden said.

"Proceed."

"Mr. Meeks, recently Mrs. Stonewall returned to the Winnerow

Schools and worked as a teacher there. Based upon your objective evaluation as her principal, how did you rate her work?"

"She did very well. The students took to her, she knew her subject matter, and the staff accepted her."

"Then she related well to children?"

"Oh, yes. They missed her when she left and I was disappointed when she decided not to return," Mr. Meeks said. It brought tears to my eyes to hear him say that, and it reminded me of how sad I had felt when I turned away from teaching to live at Farthy. Logan sensed my feelings and reached under the table to take my hand.

"Thank you. No further questions, Your Honor."

"You may step down, Mr. Meeks."

"Your Honor," Camden said, "we would like to call the Reverend Wayland Wise to the stand."

This time there was a soft sound from the audience as if they had all sucked in their breath together. Reverend Wise, who was standing way in the rear of the courtroom, began his slow but deliberate progress toward the witness chair. Never did he look more fierce and distinguished. People in the aisle seats leaned away as though he were parting the air before him as he walked, just like Moses parted the Red Sea. Even the judge looked impressed. The reverend's voice was loud and firm as he was sworn in. He didn't just rest his hand on the Bible. He clutched it. His face was serious, his eyes as intent as they were in church when he seemed to be looking directly into the face of the Devil and defying him with his biblical words.

Anticipating his testimony, my heart began to beat madly, but when I gazed over at Fanny's table, she looked relaxed and comfortable. She whispered into her attorney's ear and he smiled and nodded and patted her on the hand. Randall stared ahead, little or no expression on his face until he turned my way. He looked like a man caught in a trap, no longer as sure about what he was doing or even why he was sitting there. He looked as if he wanted to apologize to me. But Fanny nudged him and he turned away quickly.

"Reverend Wise, would you tell the court under what circumstances you took Fanny Casteel into your home and treated her as you would your own daughter?"

"The Lord enables us to help one another in many ways if it is in our hearts to do so," Reverend Wise began. "I learned about the poor plight of the Casteel family, children without a mother, and for a good deal of the time, without a father, living in a shack in the Willies, hungry, cold, uncared for. My wife and I discussed the situation and decided we should take at least one of these poor children into our own home and provide for her as the Lord has provided for us," he said. Some of his parishioners nodded and smiled self-righteously.

"And so you brought Fanny Casteel to your home to be your daughter. You even gave her your name and replaced her Christian name, is that not so?"

"We did, happily."

"Please describe what Fanny was like when you first brought her to your home."

"She was grateful, happy to be there. Naturally, I began to instruct her in the ways of righteousness. I knew the circumstances under which she had lived and how that would affect her moral upbringing."

"Did you make satisfactory progress with Fanny?" Camden asked. Reverend Wise's beady black eyes fastened on Fanny and then darted across at the audience.

"She was a difficult child, often promiscuous as described. I felt the Devil had indeed taken hold of her."

"I see. So the conduct Mr. Meeks described continued even though she was in a warm home, loved and cared for? Is that not correct?"

"The Devil is indeed a clever foe."

"Please, Reverend, just answer the question yes or no."

"Yes."

"And at this point Fanny was maturing into womanhood," Camden said. He took a dramatic pause. You could hear a pin drop, so eagerly were ears bent to listen to the scandalous truth. For a moment Camden scrutinized his audience, then suddenly reeled around to face the reverend. "Reverend Wise, did Fanny Casteel become pregnant while she was residing at your residence?"

For a long moment the reverend did not speak. He bent his head as if in silent prayer. Then, very slowly, he raised his eyes, drilling them into Camden Lakewood.

"She did."

"And what did you offer to do?"

"My wife and I, who were childless at the time, decided we would take the baby as we had taken Fanny and raise her as our own. We decided the Lord had given us another opportunity and we have indeed felt blessed because of it." There was some murmuring in the audience, but when the judge slammed down his gavel, it ended abruptly. Nobody wanted to be thrown out and have to miss the drama. "We did pretend the child was my wife's child, but it was a deception of good intentions, designed to make life easier for the innocent baby. We wanted her to be accepted in the community. It was how the Lord intended it."

"I'm not here to question your motives, Reverend, but did you not offer Fanny Casteel ten thousand dollars if she would sign away all rights to her own child?"

"I did, but it was not my intention to buy her child. My wife and I felt she needed the money to provide for herself once she left our residence and went out in the world to make her way."

"But the papers stated that the child, and the sworn secret of the child's parentage, be forever kept silent for the sum of ten thousand dollars, isn't that correct?"

"Yes."

"And did Fanny Casteel willingly sell her own child to you?"

The reverend only nodded.

"The record will show the witness's answer as affirmative," Camden instructed. "No further questions, Your Honor."

Camden told me his strategy would be to avoid embarrassing the reverend in hopes that his damaging testimony would imply that Fanny slept around, became pregnant, and sold her child. He hoped Fanny and her lawyer wouldn't want the real circumstances bandied about while her morality was in question. But they were willing to take the risks.

"Reverend Wise," Wendell Burton began, this time shooting up out of his seat like a cannonball, "was yer only motivation fer givin' Fanny Casteel ten thousand dollars fer her child yer interest in her welfare?"

"I'm not quite sure, I—"

"Were ya not and are ya not indeed the father of Fanny Casteel's first child?"

The stillness in the room felt so complete it was as if all the air had been drawn out to create a vacuum. No one even dared cough.

"I was and I am," he confessed, his voice not faltering. There was a common gasp from the audience, but this time the judge didn't need to rap his gavel. No one uttered another sound. They all just strained forward to catch every word.

"Ya impregnated a teenage girl in yer own home, an unsophisticated, trustin' child, who had been given over ta yer for moral safekeepin'?" Burton continued, leaning toward the reverend.

"Mr. Burton, I never claimed to be anything more than an ordinary man whom the Lord hath chosen to carry His word to other ordinary men. I did my best to reform Fanny Casteel, but it wasn't to be in my providence to do so."

"So ya seduced a fourteen-year-old girl?" Burton snapped.

"Believe me, no man would have ever needed to go to the trouble of seducing that promiscuous young girl. That wicked, sinful girl," he said, pointing at Fanny, his arm extended like the arm of a prophet about to pronounce God's very words, "did steal into my bed and with her lewd, naked body pressed against me, did seduce me, for as I have told you, I am only a man, made of flesh and blood." He lowered his arm and then his head, shaking it slowly. "Pitifully, shamefully human."

"But the fact remains, ya were the adult and ya did not turn her out?" Burton pursued.

"No, I did not," the reverend said, looking up sharply again. "But I have never once doubted that the Devil was in her and through her, had found a way to pierce the armor of my Faith, for my Faith was wounding the Devil fatally in Winnerow, as my people will testify. I was glad to get her out of my house," he said. "And I understand why the Lord instructed me to buy her baby. He did not want this child brought up in the home of such a woman, a woman firmly held in the Devil's grip."

"So ya tempted a young girl with ten thousand dollars ta sell her child. What could she do anyway? She was only fourteen," Burton said.

"Objection, Your Honor. Counsel is asking and answering his own question."

"Objection sustained. Mr. Burton, are you asking Reverend Wise the question?"

"No," Burton said quickly. "No further questions."

"Reverend Wise, let me ask you the question," Camden said before another beat went by. "Did Fanny Casteel have any other choice but to sell her child to you?"

"Of course. She could have kept it. There's welfare; there's charity." He looked out at the audience. "She could have insisted I support her and the child."

"The fact is she didn't want her child, is that not so?"

"No. She only wanted the pleasure, the sinful pleasure, and not the responsibilities."

"No further questions, Your Honor," Camden said.

The reverend stepped down. As he moved back up the aisle, he kept his head high, his gaze just as intense as it had been when he approached the witness chair, but I thought I saw relief in his face, the outline of a slight smile. He had done what he must have wanted to do all these years, confessed his sin and confessed it in such a way that his congregation would have no hesitation in forgiving him. I was sure that his next sermon would be built on the statement "I have seen the

Devil and I know his evil power, but I have seen the Lord's forgiveness and I know He is mightier."

When I turned toward Fanny, I saw that she wasn't smiling the way
she had when the reverend first took the stand. Her lawyer was leaning over and whispering in her ear again, but what he was telling her
wasn't making her happy. Randall had his head lowered and was
doodling with a pencil. Despite myself, I couldn't help but feel sorry
for the two of them. Little did they know, but we had only just begun.
Fanny should have never doubted the power of money and influence, I
thought.

"Your Honor," Camden said, "we would like to now call Mrs.
Peggy Sue Martin to the stand."

Fanny looked up sharply and her lawyer looked confused. I saw the
expression on Fanny's face turn to one of deeper worry. Both Randall
and Wendell Burton were asking her who Peggy Sue Martin was, just
as most people in the audience were asking one another. The judge
rapped his gavel and the audience quieted down as Peggy Sue Martin,
a woman in her late fifties, early sixties took the stand.

She wore a cheap, imitation fox wrap and her face was heavily made
up, almost as heavily made up as Jillian had been in her madness . . .
rouge patted over her cheeks, her lipstick too thick and wide, her
eyelashes almost weighted down with light blue liner. Her hair, dyed a
bright yellow, looked as though it had turned to straw. Although she
brushed it forward and curled it, you could see where she was losing
it. Her thin, lavender dress clung to her heavy hips and the skirt
reached just short of midway between her knees and ankles. We had
paid her two thousand dollars plus her expenses to bring her here
from Nashville.

She was sworn in quickly and sat back, crossing her legs and smiling at Camden as he approached her.

"Mrs. Martin," he began, "please tell the court where you live and
what you do."

"I live in Nashville where I own and operate a half dozen houses as
a landlord."

"Mrs. Martin, do you know Fanny Casteel?"

"Yes, I do. Fanny came to one of my houses a few years back. She
had come to Nashville to try to be a singer, just like hundreds of other
girls." She smiled at the judge, but he remained expressionless.

"When you say come to one of your houses, you mean to rent a
room?"

"That's correct."

"She had money for rent then?"

"In the beginning she did. Then she started bein' short from time to time. I ain't heartless, but there's just so much time I can keep someone. I need to make income. I got my upkeep."

"Wasn't Fanny Casteel earning anything as a singer?" Camden asked.

"Oh, goodness no." She started to laugh. "She could no more sing than I could."

"So then you evicted her?"

"I did not."

"Well, then," Camden asked, turning slowly toward Fanny and then back to Peggy Sue Martin, "what did she do to get the money she needed for the rent?"

Peggy Sue Martin shifted herself in her seat and pulled down on her imitation fur wrap a bit.

"Well, I don't condone what goes on in my houses. It ain't my business as long as the tenants don't break anything and pay their rent on time."

"Yes?"

"Well, some women entertain men from time to time."

"And get paid for it?" Camden said.

"Yes. I don't encourage it," she said quickly, looking at the judge, but he continued to sit there like a cigar store Indian.

"Mrs. Martin, aren't we talking about prostitution?"

"Yes," she said softly.

"Mrs. Martin, could you please speak up," the judge said.

"Yes," she repeated much louder.

"And you know for a fact that Fanny Casteel occasionally earned her rent this way?"

"I do," Peggy Sue Martin said.

I recalled the trip I had made to that rundown house with its peeling paint and sagging blinds in Nashville. How naive I had been not to know what sort of things went on there. I should have realized when I saw that pretty blond girl in shorts and a halter top, a cigarette dangling from her lips, that such things were going on.

Fanny had been only sixteen and all alone with barely enough change to buy herself something to eat. I was so worried about Jillian and Tony and the way they would react should Fanny ever show up at Farthy that I didn't see the terrible state she was in. I took her out to eat and promised to send her money, but I didn't realize what had been happening to her up to then.

Well, now it was all coming out, spread over a table like the secret contents of a private drawer displayed for all to view, and it was her own fault. I warned her, I thought, hardening myself against her once again. She shouldn't have taken Drake.

"No further questions, Your Honor," Camden said. I looked at Fanny. She wore a hateful expression, staring daggers at me. I turned away.

"Mr. Burton?" the judge said. Wendell Burton spoke with Fanny for a moment and then turned to the judge.

"No questions for this witness, Y'Honor."

"I'd say round one is over," Camden Lakewood said, taking his seat beside me, "and it's almost a knockout."

"This court is now in recess," the judge declared, and slammed the gavel three times.

⊱ *SEVENTEEN* ⊰
Evil at the Bottom of the Hill

THE MOST SENSITIVE INFORMATION—LOGAN'S IMPREGNATING Fanny—was still to come, and it was Camden Lakewood's feeling that when he called Fanny to the stand, he shouldn't bring it up, once again hoping that she and her attorney had decided it was not to their advantage to offer this information to the court.

I was surprised at how refreshed Fanny looked when we all returned. Despite what could only have been a degrading and unpleasant time for her, she looked as relaxed and confident as a cat sprawled before a mouse hole. Randall still looked quiet and uncomfortable, but Fanny was visiting with people, laughing loudly, shaking hands and waving. Of course, I understood she was putting on a show for Logan and me, turning our way every once in a while to see if we were watching her. How like a child she still was, I thought. She simply didn't realize what she had gotten herself into when she took Drake.

Logan's mother looked happier. Her friends had gathered around her during the recess, clucking like hens. All the information brought out so far had made Fanny look bad and our position look good. Loretta, too, was hopeful now that Fanny wouldn't want her incident with Logan revealed. With things going so badly for her, why would she want to reveal more unpleasantness?

And then, of course, there was Randall to think about. My lawyer pointed out that if she had gotten him to marry her by making him think she was having his child, she would risk losing him by stating it was Logan's. What I feared in my heart, though, was that Randall wasn't as important to her as hurting me and getting Drake.

During the recess, parents of many of my former students and many members of the Winnerow business community came over to us to wish us good luck. As I expected, most people thought the Reverend

Wise had been a courageous man to confess to his own sins in a public forum. He had challenged the Devil face to face and the Devil had taken one step back. During the recess he had stood off in a corner, his devoted parishioners gathered around him, listening to him recite passages from the Bible that he thought fit the situation.

As we all streamed back in, I caught him gazing at me. He was wearing an expression of self-satisfaction. When I had come to him years ago to argue for the return of Fanny's child, I had threatened to expose him in his own church. He'd warned me then that his followers would never turn against him.

After the hearing resumed, Camden Lakewood entered certain financial documents into evidence, papers stating that Logan and I had been made executors of Drake's estate. Then he called Fanny to the stand.

She rose from her chair and patted her hair gently on the sides, smiled at Randall, and sauntered across the courtroom to the witness chair as if she were making an entrance on stage. She held a smile so tightly on her face, it looked like she was wearing a mask. Then she deliberately paused just in front of our table and stared down at me.

"I suppose yer satisfied now, Heaven," she said. "But ya ain't goin' ta be long."

I shook my head and looked away.

When she was asked if she would tell the whole truth and nothing but the truth, she replied, "A course, I will." There was some snickering in the audience.

"Mrs. Wilcox," Camden began, "I understand you just recently became Mrs. Wilcox. How recently was that?"

"Randall and I got hitched two days ago. We went ta Hadleyville and got married by a preacher all right and proper."

"I see. How long have you known Mr. Wilcox?"

"I knowed him a while," she said, smiling at me.

"Now, Mrs. Wilcox, this wasn't just a marriage of convenience, was it?" Camden asked.

"Huh?"

"You didn't get married just so you could make a good case for becoming Drake's guardian, did you?"

"Objection, Y'Honor," Wendell said. "Ah resent that implication. There is no evidence—"

"That's what we're here to determine, Your Honor," Camden said softly. The judge thought a moment and then nodded.

"Overruled. I think the question is in order and I would like to hear Mrs. Wilcox's response. Mrs. Wilcox?"

"Yes, Y'Honor?"

"You can answer the question."

"What question?"

"I'll repeat my question," Camden said. "Did you marry Randall Wilcox only so you would appear to have a proper home for Drake?"

"Well . . ." She looked at Wendell, who shook his head quickly. Camden Lakewood caught the glance and the motion and positioned himself between Fanny and Wendell so her lawyer was blocked from her view. "Yer askin' me if'n this is a phony marriage just so I kin git the judge ta give me Drake," she said, obviously recalling what Wendell Burton told her she might be asked. "Well, it ain't. Randall loves me and I love him, so we both figured it was time ta tie the knot. And we do have a proper home. You kin have a proper home without bein' rich as Heaven, kin't ya?"

Some of the audience silently nodded their agreement.

"You were married before, were you not, Mrs. Wilcox?" Camden asked, coolly ignoring her outburst.

"Uh-huh. I married Ole Mallory."

"Old Mallory. I take it your first husband was considerably older than you were?"

"Oh, yeah, 'bout forty years."

"Forty years older than you were?"

"Uh-huh."

"Were you in love with him, too?"

"He loved me and wanted ta take care a me, so I married him. I wasn't as old as I am now and I wasn't as wise, and I didn't have a whole lot of experts tellin' me what ta do and what not, like some people," she added, looking my way.

"Why did you divorce him?"

Once again she looked toward her lawyer, but Camden remained in his way.

"We couldn't get along nohow," she said.

"Isn't it true that you divorced him because he wanted to have children and you didn't?" Camden asked quickly. She flinched.

"No," she said.

"Didn't you tell people that, people we will call to the stand today, if need be?"

She looked down and then up, her eyes blazing at me. I didn't change expression. I had told her I would throw everything at her I could.

"I didn't want ta have any kids with him 'cause he was too old. I mean, what happens after he dies, huh?" she asked, turning in the seat so she could face the judge. "I'm left with children and no husband and then who wants ta marry me 'cause I got children. So I told him no and we had a fight. Then we got divorced and then he did die and he didn't leave me nothin'. So I was right."

"But you have a history of not wanting children, Mrs. Wilcox. Isn't that so?"

"No, it's not," she said. "Look, ain't I havin' ma own now?" she said, jabbing her right thumb toward her stomach.

"And you were married only two days ago?" Camden asked softly and looked toward the judge.

"I already told you that," Fanny said. "Don'cha 'member?" she asked, and the audience laughed. The judge pounded his gavel.

"Now, Mrs. Wilcox, can you tell the court how you've come to have Drake Casteel in your home?"

"What'dya mean, come to have him? I picked him up and took him there."

"Picked him up? Picked him up from where?"

"From outside the Willies factory at the party. I seen him left alone while Heaven and Logan was off partyin', showin' off their new factory. So I drove up and told him he should come with me. He got in ma car and I took him home where he belongs."

"Just picked him up off the street without telling anyone?"

"Didn't hafta. He's ma brotha."

"But didn't you think anyone, Mr. and Mrs. Stonewall especially, would be concerned about the boy's disappearance?"

"Well, they weren't concerned 'bout what I thought." She turned toward Logan and me again, her black eyes blazing. "They neva asked my permission or nothin', just took him to that castle near Boston and then ta their big home here in Winnerow. Well, Pa woulda wanted me ta be his motha, not Heaven. He didn't like Heaven as much as he liked me and she knows it. She knows he'd want Drake with me. You know I'm tellin' the truth 'bout that, Heaven," she said, glaring at me.

I always believed he loved her more, I thought, but somehow I always knew he had more faith in me. He knew that I had a sense of responsibility and he knew that Fanny was spoiled and selfish. No, I thought, if Luke could be here, brought back from the grave to testify, I think he would say he wanted Drake living with me. After all, he made me executor of his estate. I felt confident that it was I he would have wanted to have custody of Drake.

"But you at least knew where he was, Mrs. Wilcox. Wasn't what you did very irresponsible? Take a child without telling anyone? They had the police searching. And once you had the boy in your home, why didn't you call them then to tell them?"

"I told ya," she said. "They neva called me to tell me nothin'. They didn't even call ta tell me they was here in Winnerow."

"Still, Mrs. Wilcox—"

"It was the right thing ta do," she still insisted, nodding. "Heaven thinks she can do whatever she wants 'cause she's so rich. Well, I don't care how rich she is. Drake belongs to me."

Fanny's resentment of me was clear enough for everyone to see. I was embarrassed and hurt by it.

"No further questions, Your Honor," Camden said.

Wendell Burton stood up, but this time, when he approached the witness stand, he held his hands behind his back. He stopped about midway between Fanny and our table and turned so he could look at both of us. Then he rocked once on his heels and I knew what was coming. My heart thumped to a stop and then started to pound.

"Mrs. Wilcox, this baby you're carryin'. Whose baby is it?"

"It's his," she said, pointing toward Logan. "He made me pregnant!"

I heard Logan's mother gasp. The crowd broke out into an uproar. I looked quickly at Randall and saw the look of astonishment on his face. What I had suspected was true. He started to get up, but Wendell Burton, who had quickly returned to the table, seized him by the arm and said something to him that made him sit down again. Perhaps he had told him that Fanny was lying, just so she could get Drake. The judge pounded his gavel again and again, his face reddening with fury.

"I warned everyone," he said. "If another outburst like this occurs, I will clear the courtroom. Proceed, Mr. Burton," he said. Wendell said something else to Randall and then returned to Fanny.

"Mrs. Wilcox, ya pointed to Mr. Stonewall, your sista's husband?"

"Yes, I did. And you kin't deny it, Logan Stonewall!" she exclaimed. "Yer been paying me to take care of it and yer last payment's overdue."

Logan looked at me, but I didn't change expression even though I was crying inside. I felt as if Fanny had jabbed her finger into my heart when she pointed at Logan. I didn't turn around or look down. I knew that everyone in the courtroom was staring at me, watching for my reaction. All of them must have thought this was the first time I had heard the information. Apparently, as Camden Lakewood had feared, Wendell Burton felt Fanny's moral credibility had been damaged so badly, he had to do something to damage us.

"Mrs. Wilcox, the point was made that you got married only two days ago. Did your husband, Randall Wilcox, know that Logan Stonewall made ya pregnant and was sendin' ya money ta help pay costs? Did Randall know this before he married ya?"

"Yes, he did. Randall's a real gentleman. He loves me and he's tired of me bein' abused by rich and powerful people," she said, reciting it so mechanically, it was clear to me that her lawyer had made her memorize the line. She looked as proud as a schoolgirl in a school play.

But it was also clear that they had left the innocent and naive Randall Wilcox out of their game plan. He looked totally bewildered.

"And so he wanted yer baby to have a father and ya all to have a proper home?" Wendell asked, making it sound more like a conclusion.

"Uh-huh."

Camden Lakewood leaned over to us. "I'll have to call Logan to the stand now," he whispered, "and have him give his side."

"I understand," Logan said. "I'm sorry, Heaven. I really am."

"I know. Let's just do what has to be done and get it over with," I said quickly.

"Now, Mrs. Wilcox," Wendell Burton continued, his syrupy smile growing wider, "ya've heard some mighty nasty accusations made about yer moral character here t'day. Ah think it's only fair and proper ya get yer side told. How did ya come to live with Reverend Wise?"

"Ma pa sold us, five hundred dollars a piece. Reverend Wise bought me."

"Like a slave or somethin', the reverend bought ya for five hundred dollars?" Wendell Burton asked, widening his eyes and looking out at the audience. "The man who accused ya of bein' a pawn of the Devil?"

"Yes, sir, he did."

"And would you tell the court briefly what it was like livin' in the reverend's house."

"It was nice in the beginnin'. They bought me things and the reverend talked about the Bible and stuff, but then he started gettin' funny."

"Gettin' funny? How do you mean, Mrs. Wilcox?"

"He'd come inta my room after his wife was asleep ta sit on ma bed and talk ta me and stroke ma hair, and then he began strokin' other things."

"Ah see. And how old were you then?"

" 'Bout fourteen."

" 'Bout fourteen. And then, without gettin' into the grizzly details, ya became pregnant with his child, is that so?"

"Yes, sir. But I didn't go inta his room like he says and crawl naked beside him. He came inta ma room. I didn't wanna have a child. I was too young and I was scared, but I had no family, no one ta help me. No one to talk to. So when he told me he wanted to give me ten thousand dollars to keep the baby, I agreed. But then I wanted my baby back."

"Oh? You say ya wanted yer child back? Tell us about that," Wendell Burton said, once again rocking on his heels and turning toward the audience.

"My rich sista came to see me in Nashville and I begged her to buy my baby back, ta give the reverend twice as much money. It wouldn't a meant nothin' ta her ta offa him the money. Ya shoulda seen how much she carried in her pocketbook."

"Did she do it?"

"No, she didn't do it. She didn't want me bein' a motha and havin' a child. She wouldn't have nothin' ta do with me. She sent me money sometimes, but I couldn't come see her 'cause her rich relatives would get sick at the sight of someone as poor and as backward as me," Fanny said and took a handkerchief out of her sleeve to dab her eyes.

"Ah see. Then you married Mr. Mallory, who did want to look after ya, but ya could see no future in that marriage?"

"No, sir, he was too old, as I said."

"So ya got divorced and came ta live here where ya have set up home and gotten married?"

"Yes, I have."

"Thank you, Mrs. Wilcox. That's a lot different from the version we heard before. No further questions, Y'Honor."

"You may step down, Mrs. Wilcox," the judge said when Fanny didn't move.

She looked up, tears streaming down her face, looking like the victim. For a moment even I thought that maybe she was. Like all of us Casteel children, she had to undergo the indignity of being sold. Fanny acted as though she were happy about it at the time, but that was probably because she expected to be loved and cherished the way she always hoped she would be. Then the reverend raped her. I was never in doubt about that. She did have a hard life afterward. I could understand why she did the things she had done in Nashville and why she had married Mallory and later divorced him. Perhaps I had been too selfish, I thought. Perhaps I should have gotten her child back from the reverend. Maybe having the responsibility of a child would have changed her.

But she had struck back at me in the most painful way she could. She seduced my husband and now was trying to take Drake away, not because she wanted him—but to punish me. I had to put aside my guilt feelings and once again harden myself against her. Drake's future depended upon it.

"I would like to call Logan Stonewall to the stand," Camden said. Logan stood up. There was a loud rustling in the audience, but Judge McKensie's eyes were enough to keep any chatter down. Logan's mother sobbed once behind us, but we both ignored her. I squeezed his hand for a moment and then he went to the stand.

Logan looked as nervous as a little boy. I saw his hand shake when he placed it on the Bible, and his voice cracked when he said, "I do so swear." He looked toward me again as he took the seat and I smiled to encourage and support him.

"Mr. Stonewall," Camden Lakewood began, "you've just heard the testimony of Mrs. Wilcox in which she has accused you of fathering the child she now carries. Are you indeed the father of this child?"

"I don't know. Maybe," Logan said.

"Then you admit to having had intimate relations with Mrs. Wilcox?"

"Yes," Logan said.

Once again the audience broke into an uproar, but the judge's quick gavel ended it.

"Can you describe the circumstances under which this occurred?"

"Yes, I can." Logan straightened up in the seat, assuming a take-charge position. His voice deepened and he spoke louder and with more authority. "My sister-in-law often hung around the factory site in Winnerow. She seemed to have nothing else to do and no one else to talk to. Whenever she was there, she brought me things to eat or talked to me about how hard her life was living alone, with no family nearby. I was staying in our cabin in the Willies, and I did start to feel sorry for her. One night she appeared with wine and food. She made me dinner. We drank a great deal of wine and she cried a great deal. Before I knew it, she was undressing herself and clinging to me. We . . . ended up in bed together. I was drunk and I regretted it immediately."

"Have you seen her intimately since?"

"No, never again."

"Just that one time?"

"Yes "

"And then you and your wife were told she was pregnant with your child?"

"Yes. And I explained everything to my wife," Logan said, looking my way. "She understood and forgave me, and I love her more than ever because of it," he added. Tears sprang to my eyes, but I didn't raise my hand to wipe them away. I would give no one in the courtroom the satisfaction of seeing me brought to tears by Fanny's actions. I sat up even straighter.

Fanny was staring at me. The slight smile on her face faded and an expression of surprise and awe replaced it. How much she wanted to see me broken, I thought. This whole proceeding, everything she had done, was simply to see that happen. Jealousy lived inside her like a parasite all these years, feeding off her and growing bigger and uglier and stronger until it filled her completely. Would Fanny wake up one day and regret the things she had done? I wondered.

"So, Mr. Stonewall, you never questioned that you were the father of Fanny's child," Camden continued, "even though you knew she had other boyfriends?"

"Objection, Y'Honor. Mr. Lakewood is makin' an obvious insinuation here 'bout Mrs. Wilcox's character."

"I think I will sustain that objection, Mr. Lakewood. It hasn't been established that Mrs. Wilcox had other boyfriends with whom she was intimate at the time."

"Very well, Your Honor. I'll phrase my question in another way. Mr. Stonewall, did you know for a fact that Mrs. Wilcox was seeing other men at the time she visited you at the factory site?"

"I knew she had been seeing Mr. Wilcox often."

"I see. Knowing this, you still began sending her money to cover her doctor bills and provide for the birth of the child?"

"Yes, we did."

"And without even being certain as to your responsibility, you did what was best for Fanny Wilcox and the child to be born?"

"Yes."

"No further questions, Your Honor."

"Mr. Burton?"

"Mr. Stonewall," he began, even before he rose from his seat. "Ya said ya knew for a fact Mrs. Wilcox had been seeing Mr. Wilcox at the time ya made love to her in yer cabin?"

"Yes."

"Do ya know for a fact whether or not Mrs. Wilcox slept with Mr. Wilcox at that time?"

"For a fact."

"Well, ya didn't go spyin' on Mrs. Wilcox. Or did ya?"

There was some laughter in the audience. Logan's face turned almost as red as a ripe apple.

"Of course not."

"Did Mrs. Wilcox tell ya she slept with Mr. Wilcox?"

"No."

"Did Mr. Wilcox tell ya he slept with Mrs. Wilcox at that time?"

"No."

"So, ya have no factual information not ta assume the child Mrs. Wilcox is now carryin' is yer child, isn't that correct?"

"I suppose not," Logan said.

"And so ya not sendin' Mrs. Wilcox money for the baby out a pure charity or a civic sense of responsibility only, then, are ya, Mr. Stonewall?"

"Objection, Your Honor," Camden said. "Mr. Stonewall has already testified as to why he and Mrs. Stonewall have sent Mrs. Wilcox money."

"Ah don't think the full sense of fault was established, Y'Honor," Wendell said.

"I think we get the point, Mr. Burton," the judge said. "Let's move on with the questioning. Objection sustained."

"No further questions necessary, Y'Honor," Burton said, smiling widely.

Logan looked around like someone who had been struck sharply in the head. Then he focused on me and I smiled and nodded. He rose from the seat and walked back to me. I reached up for him and he kissed me on the cheek. I didn't look at Fanny, but I knew she must be burning inside.

"Your Honor, we would like to call Randall Wilcox to the stand," Camden said quickly.

Randall looked up sharply, turned toward me, and then rose slowly. Fanny said something to him, but he didn't seem to hear her. He looked troubled and could barely be heard swearing in.

"Mr. Wilcox," Camden began after he was sworn in, "when did you learn that your wife was pregnant?"

"A few months ago," Randall said softly. The judge asked him to repeat it and he spoke up.

"Is that when you asked her to marry you?" Randall did not respond. He looked at Fanny and then he looked down. "Mr. Wilcox?"

"Please answer the question," the judge commanded.

"Yes."

"Not until you were told she was pregnant," Camden emphasized.

Randall nodded. "Did you want to marry her then because you believed she was having your child?" Randall looked up sharply. "You felt you had to do the right thing by her, isn't that right, Mr. Wilcox?" Camden demanded, sounding as if he had just then realized it himself.

"I—"

"You were lied to, weren't you?" Camden pursued. "And you wouldn't have married her otherwise, isn't that correct? Isn't it?"

"No. Fanny's been through a great deal of hardship in her life." He looked at her. I could tell by the expression on his face that he meant what he said, that he really did feel sorry for her. "A great deal of what she has done is understandable."

"But she did tell you you were the father of her child, did she not?"

"Yes."

"And now she's saying it's Mr. Stonewall who is the father. Is she lying now or did she lie to you?"

Randall didn't reply.

"I know you can't answer that, Mr. Wilcox. Mr. Wilcox, why didn't you marry her before she told you she was pregnant?"

"I wasn't ready to get married."

"And two days ago you were?"

"Yes."

"But how have your circumstances changed, Mr. Wilcox?"

"I dropped out of college and got a job in Winnerow."

"Working as a short-order cook?"

"Yes."

"Your parents are upset, are they not?"

"Objection, Y'Honor. Mr. Wilcox is not on trial here. His family relationships are—"

"Your Honor, I am trying to establish the climate of the Wilcox household, a climate Drake Casteel might be living in."

"Objection overruled."

"You left an expensive college education with a promising career on the horizon to get married, isn't that so, Mr. Wilcox?"

Randall's eyes began to tear. He looked out at the audience in the direction of his parents.

"Yes."

"Mr. Wilcox, I ask you, isn't it possible that Fanny Casteel used you, lied to you about her pregnancy, just so she could get you to marry her and come to this hearing a married woman?" Randall simply stared ahead. "Please answer the question, Mr. Wilcox." He shook his head. "Mr. Wilcox?"

"Maybe," he said and the audience broke out into loud chatter again. The judge rapped his gavel.

"No further questions, Your Honor," Camden said, and walked toward our table smiling widely.

"Mr. Burton?" the judge said. Wendell Burton smirked.

"No questions, Y'Honor," he said.

Randall got off the stand and started toward Fanny's table and then turned and walked out of the courtroom.

"We will adjourn this hearing for today," Judge McKensie said, "and resume at nine-thirty tomorrow morning." He rapped his gavel and stood up. The moment he did so, the crowd broke into an uproar. The town gossips had so much news to chatter over telephone lines and at one another's houses. They couldn't believe their good luck.

"By this time tomorrow Drake will be back in your home," Camden Lakewood said. I looked across the room to see Fanny and Wendell Burton hurry out a side door. When I looked at the crowd, I saw many people smiling our way. Even Loretta Stonewall seemed to have gotten over her crisis and was happily accepting the sympathy of friends.

"I'll call you later this afternoon and we'll decide on a time to go over the testimony you will give tomorrow," Camden said. "That should really lock it up," he added.

"You did a wonderful job," Logan told him and they shook hands before we started out.

The heavy snowfall had lightened considerably while we were in the hearing. Sunlight even peeped through some thin clouds, making the world look dazzling because of the way it reflected off the snow. Logan put his arm around me as we headed for our car.

"Well," he said, "the worst is over."

"I hope so," I said. "For Drake's sake more than my own."

"Looks like you were right to get Mr. Lakewood. Quality and experience shows." We got into the car and started off. As we pulled away, I looked back and saw Fanny talking to Randall. She was gesturing wildly, small puffs of her breath popping out of her mouth like the smoke from the chimney of Old Smokey, our Willies cabin coal stove.

"Once something evil starts to rollin', it's hard to slow it down," Granny used to say. Evil is like a boulder rolling down a hill, picking up speed and power with every turn. If you don't stop it at the start, you can only stand back and wait until it's run out of steam. Had the evil that tossed the Casteel children all about this world run out of

steam? I could only hope that the actions we had taken in the courtroom today would help slow it down.

That night, when Logan and I went to bed, he took me in his arms
and kissed me.

"I was so worried about you today," he said.

He stroked my hair softly and kissed me again. "We're going to
come through this stronger than ever. You'll see. Nervous about tomorrow?"

"I'd be a liar if I said I wasn't."

"I'll be right beside you every minute just the way you were for me.
Just look my way if you get upset."

"Oh, Logan, you do love me just the way you used to love me when
we were young in Winnerow, don't you?" The smile left his face and
he looked as serious as ever.

"More, because I've learned just how precious and important you
are to me. Then it was just a schoolboy's infatuation. Now it's a man's
mature love. I need you, Heaven; I'm no one without you."

"Oh, Logan," I said. He kissed my first tear the moment it appeared
on my cheek and then he hugged and kissed me more passionately
until we both wanted each other. Because I was pregnant, our lovemaking was gentle, but nevertheless full of fire. Our sexual ecstasy
took us far away from the pain and the torment of the moment. We
traveled to a world without tears where we could love each other
purely and wholly without fear of the darkness or of the light. His lips
on my breasts, his mouth against mine, his body pressed to my body
drove away the memories of unhappiness. I rushed to him eagerly, like
a desert wanderer longing for an oasis.

"Heaven, my Heaven," he whispered. "There will be many moments like this. I'll always be here for you, always."

My tears were now tears of happiness and hope. We were like two
schoolchildren discovering each other and discovering just how wonderful love between a man and a woman could become. Afterward, we
fell asleep in each other's arms, quietly drifting in the warmth that
followed.

When the phone rang, it jarred me out of sleep. Even so, I was
reluctant to awaken as it rang again and again. Finally Logan awoke,
too. He reached over for the receiver and brought it to his ear.

"Hello," he said, his voice cracking with the effort. For a long while
he only listened. Then he said, "I understand. Come right over," he
added and hung up.

"What is it? Who was that?" I asked quickly. I saw from the expression on his face that he had heard bad news.

"It was Mr. Lakewood," he said. "He's coming right over to speak to us. He said he has some information that will—" He swallowed as if the words had choked in his throat.

"That will what? What, Logan?"

He turned to me slowly, his face a mask of shock and despair.

"Will most definitely give Fanny complete custody of Drake," he said.

❧ EIGHTEEN ❧
What Money Can Buy

OUR BUTLER GERALD ANNOUNCED CAMDEN LAKEWOOD. LOGAN and I had gone to the large living room to await his arrival. Even though the three crystal chandeliers were lit like diamonds dangling in the noonday sun, I felt a gloomy darkness overtake me. The windows on this room opened to the north side, so the room didn't get as much light during the daytime as I would have liked. When I redecorated, I introduced as many light colors as I could. Now I sat wrapped in my private darkness, surrounded by the bright hues I hoped would fill our days, waiting for the news that would tear Drake out of my life and leave a void even a rainbow could not fill.

Mr. Lakewood hovered in the doorway a moment, holding his briefcase. Logan, who had been making himself a gin and tonic at the wet bar, came around to greet him. I remained sitting on the couch, too tense and too frightened to move. "Mr. Lakewood," Logan said, "please come in. Would you like a drink?"

"No, thank you," Camden said and sat on the settee across from me. "Sorry to demand such an immediate meeting after a trying day, but—"

"Please, Mr. Lakewood." I was unable to contain myself much longer. "Just tell us what you have learned that has caused you to become so pessimistic about the outcome of the custody hearing." I couldn't believe how overwrought my voice sounded.

Logan came up beside me. I reached up to take his hand and he pressed his fingers around mine reassuringly.

"Well, this has all been something of a shock to me, Mrs. Stonewall. I must say, this story gets more and more intricate by the day," Camden Lakewood began.

"Go on, please," I beseeched.

"I received a phone call from Wendell Burton soon after we left the courtroom today and then, on the basis of the information he gave me, proceeded to make phone calls and do some investigating. As you know, Anthony Tatterton's lawyer, J. Arthur Steine, has some interest in this case and it was he who—"

"Just tell us what it is, Mr. Lakewood," I interrupted, unable to contain my impatience.

"Yes, Mrs. Stonewall. I'll get right to it." He took a deep breath and sat back. "It seems Mr. Burton had a meeting with Mrs. Wilcox right after the hearing, mainly to explain to her why he thought she would lose custody of Drake. During the course of this discussion, Mrs. Wilcox revealed, in a manner that illustrated that she didn't understand the significance of the information, that Luke Casteel was not, in fact, your father. She told him your real father was Anthony Tatterton," Camden Lakewood concluded and shook his head.

I loosened my grip around Logan's fingers and sat back. Logan sat down on the arm of the couch. I felt the blood rise up my neck and fill my cheeks with heat.

"What does this mean?" I asked in a voice barely more than a whisper.

"What this means, Mrs. Stonewall, is you have no blood relationship to Drake Casteel, whereas Mrs. Wilcox does. Obviously, that changes the picture."

"We can fight this," Logan bellowed. "It's Fanny's word against—"

"I'm afraid not, Mr. Stonewall. You see, Mr. Burton has already moved to subpoena Anthony Tatterton. I spoke with Mr. Steine, who immediately spoke to Mr. Tatterton. Needless to say, this creates a great deal of complication," he said, shaking his head. He was already sweating and had to wipe his forehead with his handkerchief. I understood from the look on his face that Mr. Steine had placed certain pressures on him.

"Then Tony admitted . . ." Logan muttered.

"Yes, he admitted it to Mr. Steine and the implication was clear that if he were put on the stand under oath . . . well, from the way Mr. Steine was speaking, it would appear that Mr. Tatterton is under some emotional strain these days and—"

"He would admit to it?" Logan said incredulously.

"It's just his way of getting back at me," I said softly, shaking my head. "But what I don't understand," I realized, looking up quickly, "is how Fanny found out. I never told her anything about my relationship with Tony and—"

Camden Lakewood carefully cleared his throat.

"She claims to have a letter, written to her by her brother, Tom—"

"Tom?" I repeated, stunned.

"Evidently. Luke Casteel had told Tom the truth about your parentage and, in despair at your not being related by blood to him, he confided his sadness to Fanny." His eyes looked at me sadly. "I'm very sorry, Mrs. Stonewall."

Oh, oh, oh. Tom. My Tom had known the truth. And he had told Fanny. Oh, he must have been so upset! My strong steadfast supporter Tom now had lost me Drake. Tom, who would never do anything to hurt me. Tom, who was the only one to help me believe in myself. How hurt he must have been. That explained why he had given up on his dreams, why he had followed Pa's way, never believing himself smart or talented enough to go to college and work toward his dream of being President of the United States. Oh, how we had helped each other with our impossible ideals. How we had hurt each other! Oh Tom, Tom, why does life have to be so cruel?

"Can such a letter be used as evidence?" Logan asked Camden.

"I'm afraid it can be," he replied. Then he turned to me. "And you know now that Anthony Tatterton will corroborate what's stated in the letter," he warned.

"But . . ." Logan stammered, "but surely after all that was brought out today, the judge . . ."

"Fanny Wilcox is a blood relation. The boy's her half-brother, and we assumed he was Mrs. Stonewall's half-brother. We made important points, but only if Mrs. Stonewall and Mrs. Wilcox are on an equal footing, if you know what I mean. Her past aside, Mr. Stonewall, why should the court award the custody of the boy to Mrs. Stonewall, who is not a blood relation, instead of awarding him to Mrs. Wilcox, who is? She's not a criminal. In fact, she's never been arrested for anything."

"But Randall Wilcox said—" Logan muttered.

"None of that is important any longer."

Mr. Lakewood leaned forward and lowered his voice as though he were about to tell us confidential information.

"Burton already let me in on what his line of attack's going to be after he establishes Luke Casteel was not Mrs. Stonewall's real father. In his words we have a situation in which someone with a great deal of money is trying to use her power to deny Fanny Wilcox her familial rights.

"I have to tell you, it doesn't look good, and on that basis Mr. Steine has asked me, as a professional courtesy, to do everything I can to prevent Mr. Tatterton's being subpoenaed. My advice at this point is for you to simply drop the motion."

"Like hell we will!" Logan shouted. "If Tony is crazy enough to permit himself to be questioned by that sleazy lawyer in front of everyone here and make such a confession—"

"The point is he will, Mr. Stonewall." Camden Lakewood remained coolly realistic. "The point is that Anthony Tatterton has volunteered to testify. Obviously, his lawyers are urging him not to."

"I still can't see why any judge . . ."

I could not have Tony testify. All of it would only hurt Drake in the end. "Logan," I said numbly.

"Well, I can't, and we were willing—"

"Logan!" I stood up. He stared at me a moment and then looked away. "Thank you for what you have done up until now, Mr. Lakewood," I said firmly, my intentions clear.

"I'm sorry, Mrs. Stonewall. If I had known all the facts before we started . . ."

"I understand. Please, excuse me," I added and ran from the room. I rushed up the stairs and when I entered my bedroom, I stopped and took deep breaths.

It wasn't that Fanny was beating me or that the echo of Logan's infidelity lingered on and on, or even that Tony was willing to reveal his sexual involvement with my mother that tore away the walls of my heart. It was that I was losing Drake, and through that loss I was losing Luke again.

Suddenly all those times when in my secret and put-away heart I wanted Luke to let me touch his cheek or wrap my arms around him or have him touch my hair lovingly returned. I remembered how it was when I would see him looking lonely and lost, staring off into space, looking as if life had cheated him. There was always such a deep need in me to love him and be loved by him. All the time we lived in the Willies, that aching need was there, waiting to ignite and burst into a bonfire of love and affection, if only he would have acted as if he saw me or encouraged me to believe he did love me, even a little.

But he never did and fate cheated me of any hope of it ever happening when that drunk driver smashed him and Stacie into oblivion. I had hoped that through Drake I would find him and find the love I had lost. I had planned on a lifetime of giving Drake love and receiving his love. I had even dreamt of him growing into a strong young man, the spitting image of Luke, and as such a handsome young man, looking at me with love and affection.

It wasn't so accidental or ironic that Tony, through his terrible admission, could deny me Luke's love a second time. Who knew what was going on in his broken and twisted mind since I had fled Farthy and refused ever to see him alone again at the party. In a strange and horribly distorted way he probably was now envious of my loving Drake or Drake loving me.

I felt overwhelmed, defeated, drenched in a downpour of envy and hate, caught in the winds of a twisted hurricane of emotions. There was Fanny on one side and Tony on another, both pulling and pushing, jabbing me with pins and needles. Two people who should have loved me and I should have loved were making me more miserable than I was when I lived in the Willies.

Right now I almost wished I were back there living in that poverty, but at least having people around me who loved me. I wished Tom and I were off somewhere in the Willies talking about our dreams, believing we were of the same blood, brother and sister forever.

I sat on my bed, too tired and too defeated to cry. A few moments later Logan appeared in the doorway. Neither of us spoke for a while.

"I should have flown to Farthy that very night and wrung Tony Tatterton's neck," Logan began. "I should have believed you when you warned me about it, I should have put an end to his controlling our lives. What kind of husband am I, Heaven, to have failed you so?"

"You're a good husband. The only husband I want," I consoled him. "Now, please don't talk any more about revenge and hating. I can't bear it anymore." A plan was brewing in the back of my mind, a plan I would have to put into practice all by myself. I was tired of hating people, tired even of hating Fanny. "I'm going to go talk to Fanny," I said.

"You're not going to go beg her. I couldn't stand the thought of that. Let me go, if that is what you want. I should take some of the responsibility."

"No, that's not what Fanny wants. She would see you coming up there like one of my servants to do my bidding." He saw I was right about that.

"But what will you say to her? What will you do?"

"I'm not sure," I responded, even though what I was going to do was taking shape in my mind. I just didn't want to reveal it at this moment. Logan seemed to understand that. He nodded.

"Whatever you do, I'll support you."

"Thank you, Logan." We stared at each other for a long moment and then he rushed to kneel at my feet, burying his head in my lap, and began to sob. I stroked his hair lovingly

"Oh, Heaven, Heaven, how I'm paying for not being stronger, for being blinded by Tony. I'm so sorry and I love you so much. Please forgive me."

"I have nothing to forgive you for, Logan. Please," I whispered, lifting his head so that we looked into each other's eyes. "I was as dazzled by all he offered as you were. I'm not perfect, either."

"Oh, yes, you are. You are perfect. It's no accident your name is Heaven. You are a piece of heaven on earth and I bless the day we knew we loved each other."

I kissed him softly and we held each other tightly. Then I rose from the bed and took off my robe. Logan watched me dress and fix my hair and my makeup. I wasn't going to look defeated when I faced Fanny.

"I'm going now, Logan," I said when I was ready.

"Shouldn't I go with you?"

"No. This is something between Fanny and myself. It's more than just Drake and you."

"But I feel so helpless here," he pleaded. "Maybe I'll just ride along and wait outside in the car."

"It's not necessary and I wouldn't want her to look out her window and see you."

"Heaven," he called as I started out. I turned in the hallway. "I love you!" he cried.

"I love you, too," I mouthed and went down the stairs and out of the house, closing the door softly behind me. I looked up toward the Willies. The sky had cleared and the stars were sharp and bright like tiny jewels pressed against the velvet night. Appleberry, who was shoveling one of our walkways, paused as I started for the car.

"Going somewhere, are you, Mrs. Stonewall?"

"Yes, Appleberry."

"Well, it's a cold night, but the air's as fresh and clean as a new blade of grass. Makes your skin tingle in a nice way, though."

"Yes, it does." I smiled.

I paused at the car just after I opened the door and looked up at the Willies again. The hills and the mountains loomed quietly before me, waiting triumphantly, just as I always knew in my heart that they would.

Fanny's house was so dark I was afraid she wasn't at home. It looked to me that there were lights on only in the living room. For once she had her dogs penned up. They barked madly when I drove up and got out of the car. Then I saw another lamp go on in the living room. My heart was pounding like a tiny metal hammer beneath my breast. I took a deep breath and headed for the front door. She opened it before I arrived.

"What'dya want, Heaven?" she asked standing in the doorway, her arms folded tightly under her breasts. She had her hair brushed down loosely around her face and she looked to me as if she had been crying. Her eyes were bloodshot, her mascara was smudged, and I saw what I knew to be tear streaks across her cheeks.

"I want to talk to you, Fanny."

"My lawya don't want me talkin' ta ya without him bein' present."

"Fanny, I think you and I can talk to each other without lawyers. I didn't bring my lawyer. I didn't even bring Logan." I gestured behind me.

She looked past me at my car, but she didn't move.

"It's cold out here, Fanny."

"Awright, then, you kin come in, but I ain't sayin' nothin' you kin use against me in court tomorra. You kin count on that."

"We're not going to be in court tomorrow, Fanny. There's no point to it."

She smiled widely and stepped back.

"Oh, well, then, ya kin come in, Heaven Leigh."

"Where's Drake?" I asked after I entered.

"He's in his room. He has his own room here, too, ya know." Her eyes flashed as if pride flowed through her body like electricity to light them. Even though there was no blood relationship between us, I still felt that was one way in which we were very alike.

"Is he all right?"

"Jist tired," she replied, but I thought she was lying.

"Is Randall here?" I asked, looking about and wondering why she was keeping the house so dark.

"Oh, so that's it. Ya come to ask him to help ya some more, didja?" She nodded quickly, thinking she had discovered my reason for the visit.

"No, Fanny, I didn't."

"Well, it don't matter. He ain't here. He's gone."

"Gone?"

"Ta think things ova. I told him ta make up his mind if he loves me or not and not ta come back here if he don't."

"I see." I realized that she must have just had this fight with him and maybe little Drake had witnessed the turmoil.

"But don't go thinkin' that might help ya with the judge. My lawya says whether I'm married or not don't matter anymore, since ya ain't really Drake's sista."

"He's probably right about that, Fanny."

She looked at me with surprise at my reasonable tone of voice. But that only confused her and she tightened up in expectation.

"What'cha want now, Heaven? Ya got somethin' on ya mind or ya wouldn't a come up here. So spit it out."

"Can't we sit down?"

"Go on, sit down if ya want. I'm standin'." She pulled her shoulders back in emphasis.

I walked into the living room and sat in a chair by the corner table. Fanny followed, keeping her arms folded and eyeing me like a nervous squirrel.

"So, Fanny," I began, "you're going to win the custody of Drake, which means you'll have two children to care for."

"So what?" Her black eyes flashed again. "Ya don't think I kin care for them properly?"

"I didn't say that, but if Randall does leave you, it will make things hard. What about your financial situation? It can't be too good."

"My lawya says ya still got to send me money to support the baby that's comin'. He says no matter what fancy lawya ya hire, ya can't get outta it."

"Maybe. Still, we're not talking about a whole lot of money for you anyway, are we, Fanny?" She didn't reply; she simply glared at me, her black eyes narrowing.

"What did ya come here to tell me, Heaven? It wasn't that. What is it?"

"I came to make you an offer, Fanny."

"What kinda offa?"

"I'm going to offer you one million dollars if you will agree to give me custody of Drake."

I could see that it took a moment for the meaning of what I was saying to register in Fanny's mind. She blinked and then edged herself toward the couch. Then she smiled, but I saw immediately that this was a different smile from any other of Fanny's smiles. It was a calculating smile that sent a chill through me. She sat down, never taking her eyes off me for a moment.

"Well, I'll be. Fancy this. Ya come here ta buy Drake jist the way the reverend came ta buy me. Jist the way Cal and Kitty came ta buy you. Ya want me ta do jist what Pa did: sell a child. But yer really no betta than all them people who came ta buy us Casteels, and that was somethin' ya said ya hated. Ya hated Pa fer doin' it and made him feel guilty till the day he died, didn't ya? Didn't ya!" she shouted.

I looked down. I couldn't keep the tears from streaming down my face.

"So there's finally somethin' ya want so much ya'd even do somethin' ya thought was so terrible ya went ta get revenge fer it and caused Tom's death."

"Fanny . . ." My heart was beating so hard and so fast, I couldn't breathe.

"Don't say nothin'," she said, turning away. And then suddenly she started to cry, to cry what I was sure were real tears. She spoke without looking at me. "Sure I want a million dollars so I kin live high and mighty like you do." She turned to me, her eyes full of anger and pain. "But don'cha think I want somethin' else you always had and somethin' ya have now? Don'cha think I want love?" She shook her head. "I'd neva had it like ya did, neva, Heaven. You were the one who had the nice boyfriend when we was jist kids."

"But Fanny, you were so loose, no nice boy wanted to be with you," I protested.

"I was jist tryin' ta get one ta love me and care 'bout me. I thought that was how I could get one ta do it. And then I went ta live with the reverend and I thought now I got someone who wants ta love me, so I didn't complain when he started ta come inta my room and touch me. I even thought he would love me becuz I was havin' his child, but all he wanted ta do was pay me off and get me outta his house.

"Then I went ta Nashville, but it was always the same. Men didn't want ta love me, not like they love you, Heaven. My brothas and sistas never wanted nothin' to do with me. Ya didn't. Don't say ya did jist because ya came ta see me once and sent me some money. I even called Luke a couple times, but ya know what?" she said, her tears flowing freely now. "He only asked 'bout you. Yes, jist 'bout you. I was hopin' he'd a wanted me ta come live with him and his new wife, but he neva said nothin' like that.

"So I married Ole Mallory, but he was too old ta love me like a man should love a woman. Afterward, there were a lotta men around all the time, but I neva had a steady beaux I liked until I found sweet Randall. Now he's somewhere thinkin' 'bout it jus' 'cause I lied to him. No one loves me like men love you.

"Even Drake, even now, likes ya more than he likes me, no matter what things I tell him. I kin see it."

She turned away again and we were both silent, except for the sound of our sobbing.

"You can't force people to love you, Fanny," I said through my tears. "You try too hard; you demand it before they have a chance to give it. You've got to have more trust and let it happen naturally."

She shook her head.

"You have a child coming, just like I do," I said, swallowing the tightness out of my throat. "And no one's going to take this one away from you. You'll have a chance to love your baby and your baby will love you. You'll learn from that, Fanny. You'll see that love develops slowly, and that the love that does develop slowly is a stronger love.

"But keeping Drake and trying to force him to love you just so you'll have someone love you more than he loves me is not going to make you happy. You'll see. I'm sorry," I added almost under my breath. "I'm sorry for a lot of things. I'm sorry I didn't fight harder for Darcy; I'm sorry I left you in Nashville and ignored you so long, and I'm sorry for what it has all done to you and for what you have become."

I stood up, but she didn't look at me.

"Good-bye, Fanny," I cried and started for the front door.

"Heaven."

I turned slowly, wiping my tears away with a small handkerchief.

"I'll take the million and you can have Drake," she said.

Drake was sitting on his bed in Fanny's house, his little hands folded in his lap. He looked up when I came to the doorway, and I saw that although his face was filled with confusion, he was happy to see me. There was a warmth in his eyes that betrayed his inner feelings.

"Hi, Drake. Can I take you home with me again?" I smiled through my tears. He didn't answer right away; he leaned over to see if Fanny was standing right behind me. "I know that you've gone through a confusing time here, but it's all over now. You'll come back to Hasbrouck House and your room and your toys. Logan's waiting for us," I added, when he didn't move. "And all the new friends you've made and Mr. Appleberry . . ."

"Fanny said you hated my daddy," he said, his face tightening with hesitation.

"I didn't hate him, Drake. I loved him, only I never thought he loved me. We had a very hard life when we were your age." I knelt down beside him and took his hands into mine. "Sometimes, it's not easy to love someone even though you want to very much."

"Why?" He looked skeptical, but his curiosity beyond his years made me smile. I thought about Luke and I thought about Troy and I thought about Tony, and how their love for me and my love for them had gotten twisted and lost.

"Because they don't let you love them. They're afraid of it or they're afraid of their own feelings. I hope it will be easy for you to love, Drake. I know it's going to be easy for me to love you."

He studied me for a long moment. I could almost hear his little mind working.

"Why is it so hard?" he asked, shrugging his little shoulders. I laughed and hugged him.

"Oh, it shouldn't be hard. You're right, honey. It should be easy to love and hard to hate. Let's make it that way forever and ever between us, okay?"

He nodded and I stood up, still holding his hand.

"Are we going now?" he asked.

"Yes, honey."

We walked out to the living room, where Fanny sat curled up on her couch. Drake stared at her in anticipation.

"Yer goin' ta go live with Heaven after all, Drake, honey. She's got a bigger house and servants and kin take better care a ya, but I'll still see ya from time ta time. Jus' be a good boy and don't fergit yer sista Fanny," she added and held out her arms. Drake looked up at me before going to her and I nodded. Fanny embraced him and then quickly kissed him and released him.

"So long, Fanny." She stared at me and then she turned away to gaze out her window. Once again she was to be alone. Perhaps Randall would return, I thought, especially when he found out how much money Fanny was going to have. Only that didn't make me feel better for her. "Don't let your lawyer take advantage of you, Fanny," I advised. She nodded without turning my way. "Okay, Drake," I said and we started out.

I looked back after I got Drake into the car and saw her face pressed against the window, framed in the frost, a portrait of loneliness. She would be rich, rich enough to feel she had caught up with me, but she would be so poor.

Drake was silent in the car as we rode back to the Hasbrouck House, but when we pulled into the driveway, I saw his face light up like a Christmas tree.

"My fire engine still there?" he asked.

"Of course it is, honey. All of your toys are still here."

He opened his door and ran around the car. I followed him to the door. As soon as we entered the house, Logan came out of the study and his face brightened instantly.

"Hey, champ," he said, "welcome back."

I nearly cried again when Logan rushed forward and took Drake into his arms, covering his cheek with kisses.

"He hasn't had any supper yet, Logan."

"Oh, no? Good, because Roland's made a roast. A big beautiful roast. How do you like that, champ?"

Drake smiled and then thought.

"I love roast beef, it's my favorite meal. That's what I always got on my birthday. Is today my birthday?"

Both Logan and I laughed hard. It felt so good, I didn't want to stop. Our outburst puzzled Drake, who finally smiled and then laughed himself.

He was really home, and in that moment I saw that we already were a real family.

❧ NINETEEN ❧
The Music Box

THANKSGIVING WAS TRULY A FEAST OF THANKS THAT YEAR, WITH Logan and Drake and Logan's parents, and my baby growing inside me. By Christmas I began to feel its little kicks, as if life both inside and outside of me were dancing in celebration. Drake loved to put his warm little hands on my burgeoning belly and feel the baby moving inside me. For the first time in my life, I had my own home, my own family, my own happiness.

Logan never asked me what I had offered Fanny to have her give up custody of Drake. I never told him that I had telephoned Steine to contract Tony and ask that he transfer one million dollars to Fanny. I knew Tony would do it; I knew he still hoped he could buy my affection again. But I had neither thanked him nor even acknowledged his compliance. That would come another time, when old wounds were better healed.

One night before bed Logan smiled and said, "Drake's a wonderful little boy. I'm glad we've got him back."

"Oh, Logan. Thank you." I hugged him.

"Thank me? For what?"

"For loving us as much as you do," I sobbed. It made him laugh.

"Couldn't stop that if I tried." He kissed me softly on the forehead.

A few days later Logan returned from the factory to tell me he had heard Randall had left Fanny and gone back to college, but Fanny wasn't very upset about it.

"Some of my employees were jabbering about her during lunch. Seems Randall told some people how she treated him. She said," Logan continued, imitating Fanny, "now that I'm rich as Heaven, I don't want ya ta come back. Well, I got more money than I kin spend and lots a handsome young men will be knockin' on ma door. So don't

come back here later on with yer tail between yer legs and 'spect me ta
go runnin' inta yer arms." He paused and looked at me expectantly.
"Where did Fanny get the money, Heaven?"

I told him the truth and he listened without a word of judgment. He
didn't tell me that I had done the same thing to Fanny that Tony had
done to Luke, he didn't chastise me. He only smiled and said, "Well,
I'll just have to work that much harder to make the Willies factory a
huge success and pay all that money back to Tony, so we'll never owe
him anything again."

I embraced him and gave him a hundred kisses for being the best
husband in the world.

We went about our lives, hearing stories about Fanny from time to
time, the things she bought, the people she associated with. Occasionally, she came around to see Drake. He was always very polite to her,
but I could see he was afraid she would try to take him away again.
Every time she came and left, I reassured him that wouldn't happen.

The winter flew by, and one day spring burst forth in all its glory. It
was as if God had unwrapped a gift of flowers and green grass and
warm blue-sky days. The whispering in the leaves, the songs of the
wind in the grass, the wild flowers that scented the air with sweet
perfume filled us with hope and made the days of sadness retreat with
the chill of winter. Sunlight was everywhere.

Appleberry pruned and planted and our home blossomed like a
great flower itself. Drake's melancholy moods thinned until they were
hardly ever there, although once in a while he would become pensive
and thoughtful and wonder about his mother and father.

The factory got off to a wonderful start. Logan surprised me with
his insight into marketing. He traveled all over the country, setting up
outlets, finding markets. It wasn't long before he was expanding the
work force at the factory, and people in Winnerow were even prouder
of the enterprise.

One morning, just after breakfast, the phone rang and I answered it.
"Ya'll betta get ya husband right ova here," Fanny crooned. "Ma
water done broke."

"Who is it?" Logan asked.

"It's Fanny," I said. "You'd better warm up the car. Her water just
broke and she needs someone to take her to the hospital."

"Heaven, I can't leave you now. You're expecting any minute, too,"
he said. He tried to take the phone out of my hand, but I covered the
receiver with my palm.

"Darling, despite all Fanny has done, she is my sister and she has no
one else."

"All right," Logan finally agreed, "but you're coming with me. I don't want you left alone with only the servants to rush you to the hospital. Besides," he said, grinning, "all those hours in that Lamaze class would be wasted. I'll get your suitcase. You tell Mr. Appleberry to watch Drake. He always thinks it's a party when Mr. Appleberry plays with him."

"We'll be right over," I told Fanny.

"Well, ya better be, 'cause I'm about to pop any minute now. An I ain't gonna have ma baby en route. Ya tell Logan ta get here quick, ya hear?"

Fanny was waiting for us on her front porch with two gigantic suitcases.

"Ya put them in the trunk, Logan," Fanny said, spying me through the window. "Hey, Heaven, ya come to see how it's done?"

Logan was struggling with the suitcase. "Fanny, what on earth do you have in here?"

"All ma clothes and new slippers and . . . Ya'll expect me to dress common now that I got me all this money?" Fanny said. Then she winced and grabbed hold of Logan's arm. "We betta hurry," she stammered.

Logan sped to the hospital and pulled into the lane where the ambulances normally pull in. Fanny was yelling and carrying on in the backseat.

"I'm gonna die from the pain!" she screamed. *"I'm gonna die! Get me some of those knock-out drugs quick! I wanna be put ta sleep!"*

A couple of orderlies brought a gurney out and laid Fanny on top of it, covering her with a white sheet. She was still screaming when the automatic doors burst open and they rushed her down the corridor.

"Give me somethin' to put me ta sleep!"

Logan turned to me, putting his arm around me. "How are you doing, darling?"

"I don't think my coming along with you and Fanny was a wasted trip," I said, smiling.

"What?!" Logan stammered.

"The baby's on its way," I said.

"Oh, my God, I'll run and get a stretcher. I'll—"

"I don't think that will be necessary," I said, laughing. "I can walk just fine."

Logan paced back and forth, back and forth, as we waited for a labor room. The contractions had begun, but the pain wasn't bad, not bad at all. Sometime many hours later, with my sweet Logan at my side, counting my breathing and the minutes between my now painful contractions, the nurse came in to tell us that Fanny had given birth to a little boy. Early in the evening my own baby came into the world, screaming with two healthy lungs.

"It's a girl!" the doctor said.

A nurse quickly cleaned her and wrapped her up and laid her carefully on my chest. I folded down the blanket. She had my cornflower blue eyes, but dark brown hair, Troy's hair, hair that even curled at the back like his did. I gently counted her toes and fingers, and saw that her tiny fingers were shaped like Troy's, Tatterton fingers, fingers that might one day craft miniature people and houses. Logan didn't seem to notice any of that. He was so thrilled and taken with our child.

"Would you like to hold her, Logan?" I asked.

"I'm afraid I might break her, she's so small," he said.

"Darling, you're the gentlest man I know. Here's your daughter," I said, lifting her to him.

He carefully cradled the baby's head and drew the bundle to his chest. "Heaven," he said, staring enchanted into the infant's face, "all my life I thought you were the most beautiful girl on earth, but now I know our love has created a child even more beautiful."

"Logan, I'd like to call her Annie, after my Granny."

"Annie," Logan whispered to his daughter. She burst into furious screams.

We both started to laugh. "I guess she knows her name," Logan said, handing me my beautiful baby.

Soon the nurse came to insist that Logan go home to get some rest and let me rest. She took the baby into the nursery and I slept for a few hours. I dreamed of my baby, of Logan and of Troy, and awoke with Annie's name on my lips. Oh, I was certain, I just knew she was Troy's baby, and I vowed Logan would never know—her love for him, and my love for him, would make it all up to him.

I painfully scooted myself out of bed and slowly walked down the hall to the glassed-in nursery. A raucous voice greeted me from the end of the hall. "Well, looky who's finally up and about."

Fanny was sitting in a wheelchair being pushed by a private nurse.

"Which one's your little boy?" I asked.

"Luke? I named him after Pa. Luke's there, the handsomest one in the row," she said. I could see her filled with genuine love and pride.

"He is a beautiful baby," I agreed.

"I knew ya would think so, Heaven. Ya married his fatha and he looks just like 'im. Where's yer little girl?"

I pointed out Annie. She was howling.

"Are ya sure, Heaven? Why, she don't look like no one around here."

That sent a chill through me. Fanny could never know, never suspect the truth. I pasted a smile on my face. "Why, Fanny," I teased her, "with her wailing like that, she looks a little like you did last night."

Even Fanny had to laugh.

"I'll be seein' ya, sista," she said. Then she had her nurse push her back to her room. "An' don't go too fast! I wanna peek inta all the rooms," Fanny instructed her. "It's just like General Hospital in here."

Ten days after we brought Annie home, I was upstairs in my bed nursing her when Logan arrived from the factory. He was so excited about our child that he would often leave the factory to make what he called "baby visits." He would rush in, hold the baby in his arms or watch her sleep for a while, and then go back to the factory.

This particular afternoon when he came upstairs, he carried a box in his arms. It was marked FRAGILE.

"What is it?" I asked, shifting the baby in my arm so I could sit up straighter.

"I don't know," Logan said. "It was just delivered."

He opened it and carefully lifted out its contents, placing it at my side on the bed.

It was a perfectly rendered miniature of Troy's cottage. Everything was there, even the maze behind it.

"Well, I'll be darned," Logan said. "Look at this. The roof lifts off."

He removed it and tinkling chimes played Troy's favorite Chopin prelude. Within the cottage a man who looked just like Troy rested on the floor, his hands behind his head. At his side sat a girl who looked very much like me when I had first come to Farthy. Everything was just as it had been: the tiny furniture, tiny dishes, even tiny tools to make toys.

Only Troy could have made this. Only Troy. He knew. He knew she was his. And he wanted me to know he knew. This was his way of telling me, his way of claiming his daughter. Oh, Troy, how I wished things could have been different. And she was perfect! So perfect!

"I don't see a card," Logan broke into my reverie. "Isn't that silly? One of our craftsmen made you this amazing present and forgot to put in a card. How can we thank him? I'll have to have some of my men see if they can find out who made this. It's spectacular, isn't it,

Heaven? Such attention to detail. I'll bet," Logan said suddenly, "that Tony had someone do this. Maybe it's his way of apologizing, huh?"

"Yes," I whispered. I could barely talk, so overwhelmed was I by this token of Troy's forever abiding love. Logan thought it was because I was so taken with the beauty of the gift. "Could you put Annie back in her crib?" I whispered hoarsely.

"Sure," he said.

He took the baby from my arms and placed her gently in her crib. "I'll take this downstairs," he said, reaching for the tiny cottage.

"No, that's all right, Logan. Leave it. I want to look at it for a while."

"Sure. Well, I've got to get back to the factory. I'll talk to you later, okay?"

"Okay."

He kissed me on the cheek and rushed out.

Again I opened the roof and the magical tinkling music filled the room. A cloud that had been blocking the sun moved off and the warm light came streaming through the window to caress the tiny cottage.

The door to one of the closets of my memory opened and once again I heard the soft piano notes. The melody grew louder and then seemed to get caught up in the breeze that made the curtains on my bedroom window dance lightly against the glass. I looked out at the blue sky as if I could see the music find its way home, and then I put the roof back on the cottage.

I would put the toy on a shelf in Annie's room until one day, many years from now, I would tell her what this cottage meant. I was sure that when I did, she would understand why I had to do as I've done. Because I would always tell her the truth, the truth that was me. And the truth always heals.